Champagne

Books by Janet Hubbard

Champagne: The Farewell

Champagne:
The Farewell

A Vengeance in the Vineyard Mystery

Janet Hubbard

Poisoned Pen Press

Copyright © 2012 by Janet Hubbard

First Edition 2012

10 9 8 7 6 5 4 3 2 1

Library of Congress Catalog Card Number: 2012936467

ISBN: 9781464200779   Hardcover
        9781464200793   Trade Paperback

Poisoned Pen Press
6962 E. First Ave., Ste. 103
Scottsdale, AZ 85251
www.poisonedpenpress.com
info@poisonedpenpress.com

Printed in the United States of America

For
Astrid Latapie, my partner in crime
and
for my children,
Luke and Ramsey Brown

Acknowledgments

Chin-chin to my superhuman editor and fellow Francophile, Barbara Peters, who proved to be a genius at transforming an unwieldy manuscript into the novel I had intended to create.

Cheers to publisher Jessica Tribble, and all the staff at Poisoned Pen, for their exceptional work on my behalf.

I raise a glass to my agent, Kimberly Cameron, my very own 'writer whisperer,' whose enthusiasm, warmth, and tenaciousness turned my dream into reality. Sipping wine with her in a café in Paris was like being inside a champagne bubble.

Santé to my niece, Kate Vieh Redden, who remained on call throughout the revision—editing, asking all the right questions, and making great suggestions. My BFF (Best Friend Forever), Valerie Andrews, set it all in motion.

Chin-chin to University of Warwick (UK) law professor Jacqueline Hodgson, author of the book *French Criminal Justice: A Comparative Account of the Investigation and Prosecution of Crime in France,* an extraordinary source book and great read for the layperson.

I propose a toast to my beloved teachers Jean-Jacques Guyot and Eleanore Newbauer, whose encouragement and love keeps my glass half-full. Author Craig Johnson and his wife Judy took me under their wing at a crucial time in my career. Thank you to author Lisa Brackmann for her generosity in reading my manuscript and offering a tutorial in marketing, and deepest gratitude to two authors whose mysteries inspired me to write: Julia Spencer-Fleming and Martin Walker.

Chin-chin to the experts: former *jiu-jitsu* queen in Vermont, Regina Darmoni, pilots Fabio Schulthess and Peter Boynton, wine writer Barbara Ensrud, and my French community—Astrid Latapie, Colette Buret, and Valou and David Calder, and Benoit Tarlant.

Cheers to my readers, whose reviews counted the most: Mary Moffroid, Pierre Moffroid, Dana Jinkins, Jill Bobrow, and Kay Meyer. And to the nurturers: Lisa Doherty and Wayne Ensrud.

Santé to my mother, Lily Hubbard, and to my sister, Harriet Hubbard Gaillard, for making sure I stayed at the keyboard.

"A perfect champagne has one taste in the mouth and leaves another at the back of the throat after it has been swallowed; the latter, known as the farewell, is often more of a glow than a definite taste."

—Nicholas Faith

Chapter One

"u r full of shit," Max Maguire texted from her phone, as she watched her mother carefully fold the suit she had bought for her to wear to the wedding, and gently place it on top of the clothes in the suitcase.

"Your hat will be the most beautiful one there," her mother said, filling the cavity of the millinery wonder with tissue paper, and putting it gently into a hat box.

"Wouldn't a mother say *you*, not your hat, will be the most beautiful one at the ball?"

"In America, yes. In France, no."

Max laughed, for *la petite* Juliette de Laval Maguire should know, having grown up in the French bourgeoisie. Max thought she might ditch the hat once she was out of her mother's sight. It was enough to have to wear the mauve silk suit and stilettos that she had watched Juliette pack.

Hank Maguire stuck his head in the door, tapping his wristwatch. "Time to get moving if you plan to catch your flight. We're going in the cruiser." Max rolled her eyes. That meant he would be blasting the siren all the way out to JFK. He waited for her to close the suitcase and in a few strides had picked it up and was on the way down the stairs of her apartment building. She picked up the small hat box and found it so light that it flew out of her hand. "Damn."

"Give it to me, *chérie*," Juliette said. "And hurry. *Dépêche-toi*!" She paused, "You are wearing cowboy boots to France?"

"I'll be the envy of every woman there. I'm right behind you." Max locked the door behind her and ran across the hall to say good-bye once more to her dog. An elderly woman looking like a munchkin opened the door and Max swept the toy poodle up in her arms. "Woof, you be a good boy for Irene." She handed him back, planted a quick kiss on her neighbor's cheek, and ran down the two flights of stairs.

"I wish you were coming, *Maman*," Max said when she caught up with Juliette. "Thank you for making this happen."

"*Pas de quoi.* Think nothing about it. Next time I will go, but for now the money is too tight."

"If you hadn't spent the price of a plane ticket buying clothes and perfume for me, you could have come."

"I was there a year ago, and now it's your turn. Perhaps you will meet Mr. Right."

"I couldn't bear having a Frenchman correcting my French the rest of my life."

Hank was waiting outside the cruiser, looking impatient. Ignoring her daughter's remark, Juliette said, "Watch your tenses. You did okay with your French last week except for the tenses…"

Max leaned down and kissed her mother on each cheek, then put her long arms around her tiny frame and squeezed her in a bear hug. "Max Maryse!" Her mother laughed.

"*Je t'aime.*" Max lowered herself into the passenger seat. Once the door was closed, she said to her father, "You'd think I was going to China. For two years."

Hank simply sped off, not saying anything. Max's phone rang and she picked up. Lowering her voice she said, "I told you that you were full of shit because I don't believe you didn't sleep with her. I'll call you once I have my boarding pass." She hung up and cast a surreptitious glance in Hank's direction, who was scrutinizing her while waiting for the light to turn green.

When it did, and he had the cruiser moving again, he said, "If you think he slept with her, he did. You know I try to stay out of your personal business, but the rumor around the precinct is that you and Joe Laino are more than official partners. You'll never make Level One that way."

"Hank, I can handle it." Max wanted to add that she was almost thirty and that it wasn't easy dealing with helicopter parents, although she understood the hovering bit. Her brother Frédéric had been hit by a car and killed on his way home from school when he was twelve and she was eighteen. Sometimes she wondered if she had become a detective to deliberately tempt fate. Maybe, she thought, the money I'm investing in *jiu-jitsu* should go to therapy instead. Hank's comment about Joe was on the mark, and it was hard to rally a defense when she also wondered how she had gotten herself into a relationship that was based solely on pheromones. She had used the excuse for a while that it hadn't been easy coming into the precinct as the daughter of Captain Hank Maguire, NYPD legend. She had finished college before entering the police academy, which made her older than most of her fellow neophytes at the Eighty-Second Street Precinct. Joe—tall, lean, and hard—had been relentless in his pursuit of her, and she often wondered if it had to do with her easy access to Hank.

If Frédéric had been able to grow up he would have become the detective, she thought. The old guilt and sadness were creeping in when Hank suddenly pulled up behind a truck that was being pulled over by a cruiser with lights flashing. Hank was out of the car with no explanation, telling Max to stay put. She watched him, gun drawn, pursuing the two men who had jumped out of the back of the truck and run into the shadows of a subway bridge. Though she had barely been paying attention, she knew they were on the Van Wyck Expressway. She heard a gun report, and rolled out of the car into the ditch. No one in sight. Glancing back at the truck, she saw that the officer had his gun on a third man. She crouched and moved stealthily into the shadows where Hank had disappeared. Another sharp report and this time she ran toward the sound. An instant assessment told her that Hank's bullet had grazed the arm of one of the men, who was swearing under his breath. The other man was nowhere in sight.

"Where's the other one?" she asked.

"I'll get him. Hold the gun on this one." Too late. A short, panting guy was running at her with a pen knife. Max instinctively turned her body sideways to allow the expected jab to pass her on her left side while grabbing the wrist of his knife hand as it moved into the plane of her body. Max then lifted his wrist to her shoulder, and violently pulled and dropped his extended arm atop the hard bone found there, instantly breaking his arm at the elbow. He dropped the knife. She let go of him with her left hand to apply a hard elbow strike to his now exposed rib cage, which gave him something else to think about. She stepped forward and quickly pivoted to face him, still gripping his broken arm at the wrist. She formed a "C" with her right hand, and dealt him a hard, cupping strike to the throat, using it to drive him downward toward the ground as she easily and simultaneously swept his right leg out from under him with her own.

The officer ran up yelling, "Ma'am! What the hell are you doing?" He looked to be about her age.

"I'm Hank Maguire," Hank said out of the side of his mouth. "That's Detective Max Maguire. Where's your partner?"

"A fourth guy ran from the truck, sir, and he chased him." Max could see that the cop couldn't believe how the scene was playing—legend, daughter, and all.

Hank stood while the officer handcuffed the two guys and said, "Where's the one you caught?"

"Handcuffed to the steering wheel, sir. I've called for back-up."

"Take these two."

Hank turned and starting walking toward the car, Max walking fast alongside. Back in the cruiser, he pulled out on the highway and blasted the siren. "I thought I told you to stay put. You're a mess." Looking down, Max saw that the front of her crisp white blouse was smudged with dirt. She was glad she had chosen black jeans.

This time she was prepared to argue. "I wasn't going to let you go out there with no back-up."

"You weren't, huh?" Suddenly, Hank laughed. "That was some move you did back there."

He was praising her, and it felt good. "I wish you'd come take a class with me. Get in shape."

"I'm retiring next year. I've made it this far." He veered off to the airport. "See, Max, you were behaving like a partner. I might be wrong about Joe Laino, but my hunch is he won't have your back when you need it."

She was relieved to see the Air France sign directly in front of them. "See you next week, Dad." She gave him a quick kiss and hopped out of the car, slamming the door. She hadn't gone ten steps when she heard a shrill whistle. She turned and saw Hank holding the hatbox up in the air. She paused, then shouted at him over the noise of the flight announcements. "I left it intentionally."

"Do it for your ma." He walked toward her.

She snatched the box away from him and walked inside.

◇◇◇

Once in her seat, Max exchanged her usual allotment of five seconds of pleasantries with the woman in the seat next to her, and checked her cellphone before turning it off. A text from Joe read, "we r over."

So he did sleep with her, thought Max.

If she hadn't been on her way to France, it might have hurt more, but for the moment she was relieved. She removed her laptop from her big shoulder bag and began scrolling through her inbox to find her friend Chloé Marceau's most recent email, which she hadn't had time to open. As soon as the plane was airborne, she ordered a glass of Cabernet Sauvignon from the flight attendant and breathed a sigh of relief. A week in the lap of luxury in Champagne, France, she thought. What could be better? No drug arrests, no one threatening her life, no murderers to pursue around France. She began reading the email: *I can't believe we'll be seeing each other again in a few days.*

Max had spent a semester of her junior year at the Sorbonne, where she and Chloé had become close friends. Sending her to Paris had been her mother's last-ditch effort to unearth the French side of her and it had failed. Max felt ashamed of the way she had partied the semester away and returned with only a slight knowledge of French—and the decision to follow in her father's footsteps. Chloé had remained loyal throughout, making several trips to New York over the past five years, once with her parents. *And,* Max continued reading, *you'll be meeting Marc. To be honest, my parents are a little put off by his mother, but that has nothing to do with Marc and me.* Max thought Chloé's parents, Marie-Christine and Jacques, would only be happy if their beloved daughter married a prince. *Your friend Ted and my aunt Léa de Saint-Pern are an item here. Since Marc started working for Léa, he refers to her as the tyran.* Tyrant, Max translated.

Though Max had never met Léa, her life had taken on mythological proportions when she and Chloé were at university together. Léa had married the owner of de Saint-Pern Champagne Company, Charles de Saint-Pern, and the two were always being mentioned in the society pages. When Charles was killed while flying a small plane, Léa had inherited the company. She had taken the helm, and to everyone's surprise displayed a remarkable business acumen, turning their champagne, *L'Etoile,* into one of the top ten most recognized labels.

Max returned to the email: *Marc's upset because the rumor mill is that Léa is thinking about selling her company. It was to be Marc's future. Or, I should say, our future. Oh, it's all ridiculously complicated. As for me? I'd love nothing more than to leave Champagne and move to Paris, or maybe New York (?) and live in a tiny flat. I'm sure that I could get some journalism work. We shall see.*

Max lowered her window shade. It did sound complicated, but what did she know about the trappings of vast wealth? With Marc's degree in business, she wondered why he didn't just find a job and forget about trying to be in the de Saint-Pern firm. What she had found most intriguing in the email was that her old college friend Ted and Léa were together. She wondered why he hadn't mentioned it to her, though they only emailed intermittently. He had taken a couple of French immersion classes five years ago, then using a small inheritance from an aunt, moved to Paris into a small apartment near Place de la République and started his website for tourists. She had periodically checked out the enterprise and thought his blog fun. She didn't know if he had made a success of it or not. But how had he met Léa? All the answers were waiting.

Max shut off the computer, put it under the seat, and pulled down her tray. Dinner arrived and she ravenously ate the chicken and rice, and ordered another glass of wine. The tone of Chloé's email bothered her. Chloé would never complain outright, but Max could tell that something was amiss, and that it would take a couple of glasses of champagne to pry it out of her. She reached up and shut off the light above her, then placed her head against the pillow she pressed against the window, trying to keep her long legs from sidling off into her neighbor's space.

Chapter Two

The Vallée de la Marne in the central part of Champagne was as familiar to Olivier Chaumont as his own bed. He had driven out from Paris the day before to his parents' village, Avenay-Val D'or, an apt name meaning golden valley. Olivier felt sometimes that living there was like being in a dream, with the wide river and the canal that ran alongside, where you could see boats drifting by. The atmosphere seemed blurred at times, a remarkable light distinctive to this area that Pierre Auguste Renoir had so successfully captured when he was spending summers in Essoyes, one of the hundreds of villages in the commune, some with populations under one hundred.

June was Olivier's favorite time of the year, when the vineyards started to look lush as the grapes were starting to ripen, and everything was potential. The wine growers planted right up to the rims of the villages, and Sourières was no exception. Jacques Marceau and his family lived in the family house where he had been raised. Most would describe it as a château but for the house to be called a castle the owner had to be descended from royalty, which the Marceaus were not. Though Jacques was a decade older, the two men had become good friends. Olivier admired the man who presented as formal and perhaps a little austere, but who was warm once he knew you. Jacques, like his father and grandfather before him, was a premier winemaker, and now in his fifties, a highly-respected man in the community.

The wedding of Jacques' daughter Chloé was to be Olivier's first foray back into social life in the region since his divorce eight months before. As he entered the village he began to question why he chose to put himself through the stress of attending the same function with his ex-wife Diane and the horse trainer who had stolen her heart while Olivier was building his career in Paris. He and Diane Villiers both hailed from old *Champenoises* families, and since their teens it had been expected that they would marry. Yet he and Diane waited until their late twenties, and though he wasn't in love with her, as with all aspects of his life, he honored his commitment. Only after they were married did he learn that Diane didn't want to have children, and a year after that she bought horses, which had always been a stronger passion for her. She began commuting the hour and a half to Champagne on a regular basis, and he delved into his career with ferocity.

"*Putain!*" he yelled out his window at the man in the SUV who was passing him on the narrow road, and realized it was the third time he had shouted an epithet at a carload of tourists on their way to Epernay to enter the ornate and gilded entry gates to the hallowed Champagne companies that could be misconstrued as port of call to the Elysian Fields. He took a sharp left into the *porte cochère*, an access for cars that was cut into the high stone wall that surrounded the Marceau property, shielding it from the gaze of passersby. He parked his Porsche Cayman off to the side of the grand house and maneuvered himself out of the car. He waved to the Marceau maid Mimi, who was setting a table for luncheon on the terrace. Such civility, he thought, relaxing into the vision of the emerald stillness below.

Chloé Marceau came running toward him. "Olivier, Papa will be so happy to see you. He seems lost in a sea of women." They exchanged *baisers*, the kiss on each cheek.

"Are you having wedding jitters?"

"Of course!"

A handsome man of athletic build and charming smile raced up and held out his hand. "Olivier, you remember Marc," Chloé said. They shook hands.

"Of course I do," Olivier said, though his response was slightly exaggerated, as they had met a couple of times at family gatherings but had never engaged in a one-on-one conversation. "You're a lucky man," Olivier said. "Have you two decided where you will start your new life?"

Chloé said, "*Tante* Léa is training him to be…"

"I'll continue working at de Saint-Pern," Marc interrupted, "and there is a possibility we'll live on Léa's estate. The small house that Bernard and Caroline are in." Olivier smiled at the reference to the property, for Léa's château was on a par with the great neo-Renaissance Château de Boursault, built in the early 1800s by the son-in-law of the famous young widow, Nicole-Barbe Ponsardin of *Veuve Clicquot* fame.

"What will Bernard and Caroline do?" Bernard, Olivier knew, was a cousin of Léa's late husband, and an officer in the company. If Olivier remembered correctly, the couple had lived there for years rent-free, and served as quasi-caretakers.

"I can't imagine those two turning over their little house to us," Chloé said. "Léa suggested it, but knowing my aunt, she's already forgotten."

Olivier watched Chloé out of the corner of his eye. Always unassuming, even shy, which he attributed to the typical parental protection of an only child, she looked, he thought, slightly chagrined by her fiancé's attitude of entitlement. He recalled the last time they spoke that she was excited about moving with her new husband to Paris, or perhaps somewhere farther afield. The couple would have to be strong, he knew, to live alongside Léa de Saint-Pern, who was a force in their beautiful valley.

"How is your *Tante* Léa?"

"She's on her way here. She and I had lunch in Paris two days ago with her new American boyfriend that she's been afraid to tell my parents about."

"Oh?" Olivier smiled at the notion of Léa being afraid of anything. A year older than he, she was, at thirty-nine, considered one of the most beautiful women in France. Olivier thought her wealth and beauty were detrimental, in that they had put her in the realm of the unattainable. It was no surprise, then, to learn from Chloé that Léa would go to the extreme of latching onto an American, which may have been precipitated by the news of her niece's wedding.

He had to admit that the notion of Léa being with an American gave him pause. He had overheard in private conversations too often the catch phrase, *Ils sont cons, ces américains.* The Americans are stupid. Paradoxically, someone would come up with, "If they're so stupid, why have we adopted their music, their films, their clothing, and incorporated their language into ours? "Beneath the expected criticism hovered a thin layer of admiration.

Jacques, seeing his friend, rushed over and shook hands. "Come have a glass." Oliver nodded, picking up the flute Jacques had just poured and handing it to Chloé. "*Non, merci.* I'm off to pick up my friend from New York at the train station." Halfway to the parking area, she called back, "Olivier! My friend is single!"

Olivier chuckled as he turned back to Jacques. "So I'm being matched with someone for the wedding? An American at that?" He thought it prudent not to mention what Chloé had just said about Léa having an American boyfriend.

"Chloé met Max when they were at the Sorbonne eight or nine years ago. I happen to like her influence on Chloé, but Marie-Christine worries that Max is a bit too assertive and confident."

"American, in other words."

"Is there a hint of prejudice in your comment?"

Oliver knew he was teasing. "I wouldn't be French if I didn't have some prejudice, *n'est-ce pas?*" They sat in chairs on the terrace, which gave Olivier the chance to appraise the stately Marceau home that could be described as a French manor house. Constructed in the 1700s of *pierre de taille*, the same stone used on buildings in Paris, it was three stories high, with an abundance of mullion windows on the lower two floors, and with the traditional wooden shutters that opened and closed like the pages of a book. Large dormer windows projected from a rolled tile roof. A formal and graceful structure, with no hint of grandiosity.

He shifted his attention to the array of flowers blooming in orderly fashion, and stood up to inspect the new varieties of peonies Jacques' wife Marie-Christine had added. Glancing toward the house, he saw her approaching with a tray holding four glasses and a bottle of champagne and rushed over to take the tray from her.

A black Aston Martin DB7 pulled in, and they turned to see Léa de Saint-Pern wave from the convertible. In a moment she had joined them, and the obligatory kisses were exchanged. "I offered Chloé my finest champagne for her wedding, but she may end up showing her devotion to her papa," Léa said to Olivier. "We need an arbiter."

Olivier recognized the scent of *Hermès Perfume 24 Faubourg*, and closed his eyes for a second to allow the jasmine, vanilla, and orange blossoms to waft over him. Léa's tawny hair was pulled loosely from her face, and when she removed her sunglasses, her eyes went from periwinkle blue to violet. She wore a simple black linen shift, and light fishnet stockings. An orange cashmere cardigan was draped casually around her shoulders. Olivier found the contrast between the two sisters almost startling. Marie-Christine appeared to be far older than the nine years that separated them. He thought it had to do with her irritable disposition, for when she let down her defenses she was quite attractive. She had taken on the responsibility of her fifteen-year-old sibling when their mother died of cancer, and Léa had proved to be a challenge.

"I'm going to check on lunch," Marie-Christine said after greeting her sister.

Jacques removed the cork with no drama, and poured the golden nectar into glasses. He smiled at his sister-in-law. "You look ravishing. A new lover, perhaps?"

"I look tired and old, you silly man, and don't think that a lover is the only thing that can make a woman look ravishing."

Jacques said quickly, "What else does? Tell me."

"A warm bath with lots of salts and fragrance, or, for a little contrast, a business deal where I come out on top can do it."

Both men chuckled. Marie-Christine rejoined them, the maid Mimi behind her with another tray. Jacques said, "We were talking about what makes a woman appear ravishing."

Marie-Christine's lips puckered, and her expression announced that she didn't have time for such foolishness.

"There's another thing that can make a woman glow," Léa said. "I'm pregnant. Three months."

Her three listeners stopped and stared. Léa had dropped a bomb. When no one said anything, Léa said, "The father is the American blogger, Ted Clay. The one I asked you to invite to dinner and to the wedding. I know this is a shock, but if not now, when?"

"But who *is* he, and what is a blogger?" Marie-Christine asked.

"I don't know how to describe him. Tall, gangly, funny, charming."

"This says nothing at all," Marie-Christine sniffed. "And blogger?"

"Bloggers keep a running internet commentary about a myriad of things, usually focusing on a particular subject or two of their choosing. Somewhat like a columnist on the internet instead of in a newspaper. Ted writes about Paris and wine and being an ex-pat. It's fun." When no one responded, she said, "He and Max went to university together."

"*Mon Dieu!* He's young!"

"I was right, then," Jacques said, a smug look on his face.

All Olivier could think was that Léa was sounding more American than French and that it had to be the influence of her new American lover. "Congratulations." He lifted his glass. Marie-Christine and Jacques refused to raise their glasses. In the spirit of compromise, they took a quiet sip.

"Oh, dear, the soufflé has dropped," Marie-Christine said. Mimi had left a salad and a plate of various cheeses. Olivier assured his hostess that it would be fine. The repast was, in fact, delicious, though he noticed that he was the only one eating with relish. "The kids will be back shortly, and there will be no conversation after that. Léa, I must speak to you about what I read in the paper about Baptiste Dupuis buying up shares as fast as he can in your company."

"I suspect someone in my company is telling him who's vulnerable. He's being predatory, but he doesn't have a chance unless I die." She smiled at her sister's contorted face. "Or sell."

"Sell? Why now?"

Too late. They heard a car drive in, and from the parking area came peals of laughter, enough to cause Marie-Christine to focus her disapproval onto someone else. "Chloé changes around her American friend. She becomes *l'idiote.*" Jacques and Olivier exchanged a smile.

"She's too serious," Léa said. "And so is Marc. Let her be."

Marie-Christine, putting her hand over her sister's, said, "It's hard to imagine what our mother would be thinking if she were here today, Léa."

Léa looked impatient. "The question is, what do you think?"

"Change frightens me. You know that."

"And the baby?"

Olivier saw the vulnerability in Léa's eyes. She would need her sister this time. Marie-Christine said, "It's the biggest change of all, but I will try to adapt. You are approaching forty and I can't blame you for wanting a child. I only wish the father was French."

Chloé and Marc were upon them, followed by a tall woman with short, platinum blond hair and a wide grin that lit up her face. "Hi," she said enthusiastically, going over to exchange kisses with Marie-Christine, and giving her a strong embrace that made the older woman flinch slightly. Jacques was next, and he stood, and, obviously amused, bestowed kisses on the foreigner.

Then, fixing her gaze on Olivier and Léa, she said, "Max Maguire," and stuck out her hand.

Olivier stood. "Olivier Chaumont," he said, extending his hand, noticing her ample lips. He also noticed a stain on her white shirt, which she didn't bother to hide.

"Oh," Marie-Christine said, "Your shirt."

Max laughed. "My dad and I stopped and chased three guys on the way to the airport. They're sitting in jail now."

Léa smiled up at her. "That makes you a heroine. Or with a name like Max, a hero. Is it a nickname?"

"My parents couldn't agree on a name. My mother claimed she was reading the poems of Maxine Kunin at the time, but I think my father thought I was being named after his uncle."

Olivier was intrigued by how Max appeared to be in perpetual motion, even when standing still. Léa glanced over at him, and then back at the American. He could tell she was amused by her. Marc picked up Max's suitcase. "Which room?"

"I'll show you," Chloé said, and they ran off.

Max sat in the chair next to Léa, who slid her flute of champagne in front of her, then focused her attention on Olivier, "Will you please come with me to the airport to pick up a gentleman who is coming in from Germany?"

"Who?" Marie-Christine demanded.

"It's my last wild card of the day. I'm going to use him to rebuff any further offers from Baptiste Dupuis."

Marie-Christine eyed her sister suspiciously. "I can't imagine this business deal taking precedence over our wedding weekend." Léa pouted. "And he is not invited to the wedding. The seating arrangements are done."

"He's flying in and out in his own plane, and is due to arrive shortly. Thank you, *chérie*." Marie-Christine didn't respond, except to get up and march indoors. Léa gave Olivier a beseeching look, and he stood, a little reluctantly. It seemed rude to leave the newly-arrived detective, who had sat quietly listening.

He turned to her and raised his glass slightly. "*A votre santé.* You must speak French if you studied in Paris?"

"*Un peu,*" she said. "I'm afraid I was more interested in partying than learning. But I can read *Le Petit Prince* in French."

Léa glanced at her watch impatiently. "*On y va, Olivier*. I'm late."

"My apologies," he said to Max, and realized he was lingering. Max smiled, and fluttered her fingers at him.

Once they were out of earshot, Léa teased, "Do I notice a flirtation, or am I imagining things?"

"Since when did a simple question turn into flirtation?" He liked bantering with Léa.

"Did Chloé tell you Max is a detective?"

"I assumed something of the sort after her story of chasing criminals."

They both lowered themselves into the little car. "I think she's just the dalliance you need. Someone who strikes me as uninhibited, and she's obviously in good shape. Much better shape than you're in, I have to say. I can recommend a gym."

"That helps my recovering ego."

Léa laughed and blew the horn spontaneously, motioning for Max to join them. Max leaped up and jogged over to where Léa and Olivier sat in the little convertible.

"Jump in."

Before Olivier could open his door, Max had lifted a long leg over the side of the car and hoisted herself into the back seat. Léa peeled out the driveway. Was there a female conspiracy afoot, Olivier wondered.

Chapter Three

Max had to lean forward to hear what Olivier and Léa were saying. She was curious to see if she could follow their French before joining in. Occasionally a worker in the vineyards would wave, and she would stick up her hand. The car slowed as Léa followed the directions on her GPS, then she spoke to Olivier in French, "Hans Keller is coming with the determination to purchase de Saint-Pern. I might consider his offer and move to California with Ted."

"That counts as two wild cards. I hate to sound like your sister, but aren't you going a little too fast?"

Léa laughed, "Are you referring to my car or my life?" She grew more serious, "Maybe being on the verge of forty has something to do with it. Now that you've cut the strings from Diane, don't you have a desire to be a little wild?"

Max's ears pricked up.

"Wild? Bordeaux will be a change."

"Oh, Olivier, I'm not talking about a move like that. You need somebody to loosen you up. The way Ted is teaching me to be more casual. To have fun."

"I never realized that was a problem for you." She turned a hard stare on him, but her face softened when she saw that he meant no harm. She wheeled into the area designated for private planes and stopped. "That has to be him," she said, looking at the tall, slender man speaking to an airport employee. He turned and put up his hand.

Léa said to the backseat in English, "Sorry for all the French. We'll be switching to English." Max knew they had assumed from her *Petit Prince* remark that she was completely ignorant of French, but being the nosey woman that she prided herself on being, she thought she might carry this on a little longer. Hank had emphasized the importance of using the senses, the way an actor would. Eavesdropping on strangers' conversations had become a hobby. Olivier and Léa would never have spoken so freely had they known she understood what they were saying.

Hans was upon them, blue eyes, blond hair drifting around his face. She would describe him later in her journal as cocky. They maneuvered themselves out of the car and Léa shook hands with her visitor who dwarfed her. He swung around and greeted Olivier, and then shook hands with Max, holding her hand a second too long.

He pointed out the Beechcraft Bonanza that he had flown himself, and seeing Olivier's eyes light up, said, "It has three-hundred hp, and retractable gear. It costs around four-hundred-thousand Euros. I can take you for a spin if you like." He paused, "I'm better at English than French. Anyone have a problem with that?"

Olivier shook his head, but Max detected a flash of annoyance, and wondered if it had to do with being forced to speak English or more with Hans Keller controlling the situation. Léa walked ahead with Hans to the plane, laughing at something he said. When she stopped to wait for them, Olivier asked her in French if she really wanted to go. "It's time," Léa said. "Doesn't this fit in with our new risk-taking stance on life?" Max thought the exchange was in reference to her husband having died in a plane crash.

Once they were at the plane, Olivier became enthusiastic, mentioning that he had taken lessons years ago, but never completed them. "I find it the most exhilarating experience imaginable," he said. Max couldn't wait to be aloft.

Hans lowered the steps that were attached hydraulically, and opened the door to the plane. The interior was luxurious, with six dove-gray leather seats. Léa sat behind the pilot's seat and Olivier took the seat beside her.

"I need a co-pilot," Hans said to Max, and she readily took the seat in front. "Everyone has headphones above their seats. Make sure they're on appropriately." He leaned over to help Max, and whispered flirtatiously, "Can you hear me now? Can you hear me now?" She laughed at him mocking the U.S. commercial.

Hans got into the pilot's seat, and prepared for take-off. Within moments he had received the okay from the tower and they were sailing skyward, and shortly afterward he announced they were at one-thousand feet. "Look below at *Notre-Dame de Reims*," he said, and banked slightly. A cross that had been carved out of stone covered a large portion of the roof of the thirteenth century Gothic cathedral. It was an act of pure devotion, Max thought, perhaps put there for God to see. There surely was never a thought in those medieval artisans that humans would be viewing their cross from a flying machine. She wished that her devout mother could be with her.

"This is a great introduction to Reims," Olivier said. "The city was destroyed and then rebuilt after the First World War. Thus the bright colors of the buildings."

Léa added, "And during the Second World War the Nazi troops camped in the city for four years. My husband Charles' grandparents never forgave them."

"It's also where the Germans surrendered," Hans retorted, and then, putting his hands up, added, "And I surrender now. Again. No war talk!" Max was surprised that the subject was still tender. "Where is your *château* exactly, Léa?"

Soon they were gazing down at the patchwork of fields with orderly rows of vineyards planted up to the periphery of the gardens that were interrupted by a few narrow roads carved out for easy access for farm machinery. "Your château looks fabulous from here," Hans said. "I want a tour."

Max peered down and saw the fairytale castle rising up from the landscape, with formal gardens planted behind the house that were breathtaking. As impressive as it was, she thought how stifling it must be at times to always be among the people you grew up with, never feeling anonymous. She believed this to be one of the great freedoms rarely mentioned.

Olivier pointed out the distant vineyards of Avize, Cramant, Epernay, and Chouilly, and Max thought that she, too, would like to take up flying. She was surprised by how contained she felt in the plane. Flying this way, she decided, felt like a meditation, where thoughts and words seemed unnecessary in the vastness of sky. Her reverie was interrupted by Hans asking her to trade places with Léa so they could speak about business and she obliged.

Olivier was obviously enjoying himself. "This is the Jaguar of small planes," he said, "and now that I'm aloft again, I'm determined to take lessons in Bordeaux. It's been a dream of mine since I was ten to own a plane." He pointed out the white, chalky soil that reflected the sunlight back to the vines, causing them to thrive in a cooler climate, and offered to take her on a tour of the *caves* below ground where millions of bottles of champagne were stored. "They occupy hundreds of kilometers that date back to Roman times."

Léa's voice raised in annoyance boomed through the headphones. "I never said that I would sign a contract this weekend, Hans. You insisted that this was the only time you could come." Max noticed that she was holding what appeared to be a contract in her lap.

Hans' voice was steely, "I have a tape recording of our conversation, my dear, and will be happy to play it when we land."

Without warning, he banked the plane and Léa shrieked.

"It's only a twenty-five-degree turn." Max leaned up to watch him return the yoke to neural, holding back pressure on it until the turn was completed.

Was he trying to be amusing, or was it a warning? Max glanced over at Olivier and saw that he was no longer smiling. The plane banked again, this time to the other side, and Olivier stood up and moved toward the front of the plane. "It's time to land."

Max experienced the first sensation of nausea since they had boarded. Hans ignored the command and said to Léa, "A week ago you seemed quite desperate to sell your company, and I raised the money, practically overnight. Returning without a contract will be difficult for me to explain to my father."

"My family is also upset. Any more pressure from you and I will cancel everything. You're not alone in wanting ownership of my company. An American company is bidding, and if I have to, I'll reverse and sell to Dupuis."

Hans banked for the third time, and Léa grabbed a barf bag and threw up in it. Olivier, who had toppled sideways, but caught himself, said to Hans, "If you do that again, I will have the police waiting when we land."

"I've done nothing to be arrested for, monsieur. Please sit or I will force you to."

Olivier whipped his ID out of his pocket and shoved it in front of Hans' face. Hans' lips became a thin line as he maneuvered the plane back toward Reims. Within fifteen minutes they were on the ground, and Léa was out of her seat. As soon as Hans opened the door, she clomped down the stairs and marched across the tarmac.

Hans turned to Olivier and laughed, as though he were speaking man to man. "She won't get away with using her womanly wiles to squeeze out of this deal. I was making my point, you understand."

"As was I," Olivier said. "Detective?" He stood back to let her pass. Max exited the plane, feeling slightly short-changed by the ruckus over bidding and buying. Hans followed, unfazed by the animosity he had caused. "You're an American detective?" He burst out laughing. "You carry guns and shoot people?"

"If I need to."

"If I had known Madame de Saint-Pern had her police force with her, I would have brought my bodyguard." Olivier walked past them on his way to the car. "I have to close up. Be there in a minute," Hans shouted after him. Max didn't know whether to run to catch up with Oliver, or be casual and amble over with Hans. She decided to do the latter. He pulled out a leather suitcase and a smaller bag, which he handed to her, cautioning, "Don't let that out of your sight. There's a small fortune in it."

"Isn't there a limit to the amount of cash you can carry across a border?"

"Now you're acting like a detective. I suppose there is, but who's checking?"

She walked alongside him to the car, and hoisted herself over the back seat before anyone had a chance to open the door. Olivier climbed into the back seat next to her, still too irked to be polite, and Hans took the passenger seat.

"I see that you fly, too," Hans said to Léa as she accelerated away from the airport. He pulled his mobile from his jacket pocket and held it to his ear. He tapped in a number when no one responded, and spoke in rapid German. How obnoxious, Max thought. Léa glanced in her rearview mirror at Olivier, as if to ask what he was talking about. When Hans placed the phone back into his pocket, Olivier, from his tone, ripped into Hans in his own language.

Léa was pleased. She drove too fast around a curve and her passengers hung on. Max decided she and Hans were in a pissing contest, and it wasn't all that serious. When Léa turned up the radio Max recognized the French band, AaRON, that had taken France by storm over the past year. What the hell, she thought. She sang the English lyrics "something's coming up, my friend." Léa knew the song, and joined in. When Max glanced over at Olivier, he was smiling, and even Hans' jaw had relaxed.

Léa pulled into the small parking lot of the Oiseau Inn down the street from the Marceau house. "I was having some fun," Hans said. "That's all. It would be unfortunate if you refused to make a deal because of that."

"I am a businesswoman, and I rarely make decisions based on emotions, nor am I known for making mistakes. I will be here at seven to discuss your offer, and you will be out of here first thing tomorrow, *d'accord*?"

Hans got out, slammed the door and sauntered to the office. Olivier extricated himself from the cramped back seat, and ensconced himself in the passenger seat. "I would hate to imagine him owning de Saint-Pern."

"He's a *connard*," Léa said. Asshole, Max translated. "I should go in now and tell him any deal is off. But I might need him. That's the way of the business world and part of the reason I want out."

Olivier said, "He assured someone during his phone conversation that he wasn't leaving until he had a deal, and that he had brought something that would let you know he was serious."

"What, a gun?" Léa laughed at her joke.

Max thought about the small bag that he had taken back from her and placed at his feet in the car.

They were entering the Marceau driveway. "My sister will hate him. But why should I care that she is freaking out over selling my company?"

"Because you were brought up to care," Olivier said. "Take your time, and don't sign anything until I've seen the papers."

Léa's eyes welled with tears. "Ignore me. It must be the pregnancy. I was thinking for the first time when we were in the airplane that I have to do what's right for this baby."

"You've managed alone for five years. But now Marc has joined the company, and you will have an heir when your baby comes. These are positive changes, no?"

"I hope that's the case with Marc. He's overtly ambitious, which is unlike people around here, but I can forgive him that. The problem is, and this is confidential, I was nice to him and he started to behave as though he were smitten with me."

Like everyone else, Max thought.

"I decided that introducing him to Chloé would be the perfect distraction. And look what happened. I think my niece was feeling a bit desperate. French girls after age twenty-six or twenty-seven begin to panic about marriage. I worry that Chloé will be hurt."

Max had also questioned Chloé deciding to marry so soon after meeting Marc, and the email she had read on the plane made her wonder if something was amiss. Chloé had mentioned friction between Marc's mother, Geneviève Durand, and her parents. Max knew that Ted had had a fling with a woman named Geneviève when he first arrived in Paris. Could this be the same woman? It was odd, now that she thought about it, that Ted hadn't let her know about him meeting and falling in love with Léa de Saint-Pern, especially because he was aware of Max's friendship with the Marceau family.

When Max turned her attention back to the French conversation Léa was saying that Jacques was paying someone to do a background check on Marc's family. Max thought about her own mother, who had been banished from her French family because she insisted on marrying Hank. That knowledge made Max want to take up for Marc, no matter what. She decided she would go out of her way to get in a game of tennis with him in order to get to know him better. She could see why Chloé was attracted to him. He had a brooding look that she had seen on many Frenchmen, which women often found sexy. She only hoped that the brooding didn't equate with depression.

Léa said, "I don't know much about Ted either, but sometimes we have to trust. My friends think he's after my money."

Max wanted to butt in and say she could vouch for him on that issue, but decided to wait for Olivier's response.

"Is he doing well with his…blog?"

"It's catching on. I've lent him the money to make it fly."

Olivier shrugged. "You're right. At some point you must follow your instinct and trust. A good lawyer can organize it so that he can't take what isn't rightfully his."

"*Merci,* Olivier."

Once they were in the parking area, Max stood up. "Max!" Léa said, "You were so quiet I forgot about you. We were having a conversation about the past. Nothing interesting." To Olivier she added in French, "Thank god she wasn't able to understand our gossip."

I should really clear up this language misunderstanding soon, Max thought, though their overheard confidences had whetted her appetite for more. They gave her an insight into Olivier, who was starting to fascinate her.

Léa waved and drove off, which left Olivier and Max in the parking area in a suspended moment of shyness. Gardeners and caterers were milling about below, where the reception was to be held. "Care to take a walk?" Olivier asked, leading them to a footpath that seemed to course through the forest. "I never tire of observing wild flowers. Have you noticed the poppies scattered throughout the vineyards?"

"The red flowers?" Max shrugged. "I only see flowers in parks."

Olivier led them to apricot-colored roses growing in the branches of a linden tree. "We have five-hundred varieties of roses," he said. "This one, a French rose, was introduced by a man named Turbat in 1916. One of my favorites."

"I saw the rose bushes planted at the ends of the rows of vineyards. Is that an old tradition?"

"They are the canary of the wine world. When they exhibit signs of the fungus *oidium*, or mildew, the wine growers immediately spray the grapes to stave off infestation."

She didn't know when her brain switched from rose talk to the almond shape of Olivier's brown eyes that bordered on black, beneath beautiful naturally-sculpted eyebrows. His lips turned up puckishly when amused. He brushed his hair back with his hand. Their eyes interlocked for a second, and he quickly asked if she liked working for the NYPD. She nodded, "I've just spent twenty months in street narcotics, which earned me a gold shield. That's the goal, to acquire that as fast as you can, though it often doesn't work as quickly as you'd like. I'd be lying if I didn't say my father is a big influence. He's a legend on the force."

"And there are many women like you?"

"No. I joined up later than most after getting a degree from university, which meant I had to work harder to be accepted by the other women in my precinct. Women make up eighteen percent of the force." What she didn't feel like going into was how deep down she felt she would never have become a detective had fate not decreed it.

They were at the Marne River, where they stood and watched a barge move slowly through a lock. The river was wide, bluish-green in color, and mesmerizing. "This is as opposite to my life as can be imagined," Max said. "I've read that your childhood landscape forms you, which makes me some kind of kinectic object hurling through space—especially next to your phlegmatic constitution."

Olivier smiled. "The Champenois, actually, are a paradox, for often they are assumed to have the personalities associated with the beverages they produce, when in fact they are indeed more like the landscape and climate here, which can be harsh and unforgiving. Far more reserved than the Burgundians."

Max recalled the comment she'd heard Léa make to Olivier about finding someone who would loosen him up. Now that she'd been dumped by Joe, it seemed like a fun challenge to take on. Ambling along in the late afternoon, their conversation segued to the wedding. When Olivier asked her if she had ever been married, Max volunteered the information that the guy she was seeing in New York had texted her on the flight over that they were done. "That's another story," she said.

"I have the awful challenge of being at the wedding with my ex-wife and the man she left me for."

Max smiled. "I will face the same situation at work when I return."

Olivier glanced at his watch, and she could tell he was uncomfortable with the intimate discussion. "I'm stealing you from the Marceau family."

"I like being stolen." He looked at her curiously with a slight smile playing at the corner of his lips. She was surprised both at her boldness and at the tingling sensation in the pit of her stomach that his smile had caused.

The moment passed as he turned to examine large, lavender flowers that he explained were in the hibiscus family. Chloé was waiting when they arrived at the parking area. "I've been looking for you," she said to Max, her face a blend of curiosity and irritation. "My mother's stressed out about the dinner, and the fact that Monsieur Keller was invited. And I have to put up with this when I'm getting married tomorrow."

Max experienced a moment of guilt over abandoning Chloé, who had earlier mentioned going for a walk. "Give me five minutes," Max said, and mouthed "later" to Olivier as she took long strides to the wing of the house where she was staying.

Chapter Four

Chloé looked at Olivier with beseeching eyes. "Papa sent me to find out if you're still here. He insists that you come to dinner."

"I accept, then."

"I think meeting Max changed your mind. Didn't I tell you you'd like her?"

"You did and I do. And I hope to get to know your husband better. I'll have a dinner for you when I'm back in Paris. You're keeping your apartment there?"

"For the time being. I hope you don't mind that I invited Diane's *amour* to the wedding. It felt like the right thing to do, as they are living together."

Olivier felt his breath catch, but assured Chloé that she did the right thing. "Would you please excuse me for a few moments," he said. "I need to make a couple of phone calls."

"Of course. *A tout!*"

It felt like the American detective, while not in the least aggressive, was coming on to him, and he was tempted to pursue the attraction. Léa had been right about his circumscribed life, and his lack of risk-taking, though he wondered how she would construe his fling with the model Véronique? And God knew that the road to becoming an examining magistrate had its own set of risks that people didn't know about, and furthermore weren't interested in. But Léa was referring to something else. He had never allowed himself to fall completely for anyone. He knew there was something different—and perhaps terrifying—about this most unusual cop with the longest legs in Champagne. A woman who set herself up to be shot at on a daily basis.

He strolled down to the area of the lawn where the reception would be held the following day, and noticed the orderly way the tables were arranged. He glanced up the hill and saw the detective—a sign of his confusion was he didn't know whether to think of her as "the detective" or as Max—taking long strides toward the house. She had changed into a short black skirt and cowboy boots, which would raise eyebrows among the more stolid people at the dinner. On the other hand, his friend Jacques seemed genuinely fond of her, and he couldn't think of anyone he respected more than Jacques. Max carried an air of wild abandonment about her that was natural, unlike Véronique, whose magazine photos taken in the Serengeti were supposed to imply the same, but to him screamed false. He wandered back toward the house and into the salon, where his eyes interlocked instantly with the detective's, who smiled widely when she saw him. He found her openness disconcerting.

Marie-Christine came and placed her hand delicately on his sleeve. "Join them," she whispered and he nodded, walking to the little group clustered around Max, Hans Keller among them. He recalled that she had been sent to entertain the German.

She was telling a story about how the room they were in reminded her of roped-off rooms in American museums that her mother used to take her to. It made him curious about her provenance. He tried to see the room they were in from her eyes—the parquet floor covered in Persian rugs, and oil paintings, mostly portraits of Marceau ancestors in gilded frames, taking up most of the wall space. To him it wasn't exceptional. He had always admired the ancient tapestry that covered the far wall depicting a melancholic landscape, a theme in vogue during the Renaissance.

"My brother and I grew up in a two-bedroom apartment in the Chelsea area of Manhattan," Max said, "before it became chic."

Hans asked the question that had arisen in Olivier's mind. "Why don't you have a New York accent like we hear in the movies?"

Max laughed. "There were too many accents around me for me to pick just one."

"Your brother is a police officer, too?" Olivier asked.

For a beat, he noticed her flinch, and then she said, a little too nonchalantly, "That's another story and not worth going into. Marc, you're the mystery man here. Tell us about you."

"I'm in the moment," he said, "the prince who arrives from another kingdom, on a quest to meet his fairy princess." He leaned down and planted a kiss on Chloé's face. Olivier thought both he and the detective had been clever at deflecting any answers that were revealing.

Hans said, "I've told Marc that if Léa and I close the deal, I'm inviting him to stay on at de Saint-Pern."

The announcement was jarring, as Olivier thought it was intended to be. Chloé, trained in discretion since she was old enough to speak, was obviously shocked, but said calmly, "No business deals taking precedence over my wedding day, please. And, Marc, you know not to broach this subject with my father."

"I'm sorry if I spoke out of turn," Hans said. But it was a calculated remark, Olivier thought, and it had stirred emotions, exactly as he planned it.

Jacques entered the little group and refilled their glasses with champagne. "This is quite good," Hans said. "It compares favorably to de Saint-Pern's *L'Etoile.*" Olivier sipped his and thought he could taste hazelnuts and another scent from childhood, perhaps the lilies that his father grew.

Jacques' brow furrowed, "It really doesn't compare. The *Hortense* has a much more robust style, monsieur, whereas the *L'Etoile* is more similar to the lighter wines produced by Taittinger and Perrier-Jouët."

Marie-Christine called, "*A table!*" and they all turned to her. Hans immediately took Max's arm. "Sit with me and I'll translate for you."

She gently removed his hand and said, "I'll never learn French that way, Hans."

"My mother has a seating order," Chloé said. "Let's go in." Olivier noticed Jacques' brother Antoine standing in the hall, and went to say hello. Marie-Christine seemed flustered. "Monsieur Clay and Madame Durand are due any moment," she said. "They told us to go ahead. Please take your seats."

"Madame Durand is Marc's mother, right?" Max whispered to Chloé, who nodded and rolled her eyes skyward.

"Drama queen," she whispered back.

◇◇◇

The oblong table had been elegantly set with a hand-sewn linen tablecloth and Limoges porcelain. A cluster of crystal glasses was arranged around each plate, and a ravishing mound of peonies formed the centerpiece. Jacques, now standing at the head of the table, indicated that Max should sit to his right. "Your American friend can sit beside you," Jacques said. "Though you should be encouraged to speak French after this."

When Antoine plopped down on the other side of Jacques, Marie-Christine dashed over to him and discreetly said that the seat was reserved for Chloé. Antoine's eyes roved around the room and landed on Chloé. "I need to talk to my brother. Okay with you?" She nodded. Jacques shot his wife a look that implored her to acquiesce, and she did. Léa made an entrance, looking stunning in simple black dress and diamond earrings. She said to Marc, "I can't imagine what is taking your mother and Ted so long."

"Neither of them is known for being prompt."

"Go and call them again."

The peremptory command from Léa went unheeded. Marc turned to speak to Chloé as though he hadn't heard Léa. Her obvious pique was eclipsed by Jacques, who offered a standing welcome to their guests before ceremoniously opening another bottle of champagne.

Hans said, "The sound of a perfectly opened bottle should be as gentle as a sigh."

Antoine would have none of it. "That saying has been copy-righted, you know. Wasn't it Dom Perignon who said it first? And oh yes, what's the cliché about drinking the stars? That was attributed to the old monk, too."

Jacques stood. "Here's a toast to Herr Keller, who, according to him, is the hopeful new owner of de Saint-Pern. I thought it appropriate to open a special bottle to celebrate." Marie-Christine gasped and stared at her sister, as if demanding the truth. Jacques calmly poured the champagne into the flutes, but Olivier knew that he was angry that Léa hadn't confided in him about the German bidder, and no doubt hated having him here at his table. "I wish him well in his battle against our neighbor, Baptiste Dupuis."

Mimi brought out a large tureen of soup, *lait ardennais* made with leek, potato, escarole, and milk, a favorite of Olivier's. Suddenly the double doors to the dining room swung open and all eyes shifted to the couple entering the room. Geneviève Durand was appallingly thin, her cheekbones, chin, shoulders, and elbows reminding Olivier of a Cubist painting. She cut a commanding figure in the doorway, her back slightly arched, her black eyes looking around the room, dark red lips upturned, as though she had just won an award. "I'm so sorry," she said, "I'm happy to see that you have started."

Ted, wearing a charcoal grey suit, his pale hair splashed across his forehead, cut a dashing figure. Spotting Max, he took great strides across the room American-style and gave her a hug when she stood up. "It's so great that you're here," he said. "Have you had a chance to get to know Léa?" He turned to his fiancée, who not very discreetly turned her head when he leaned down to kiss her.

Marie-Christine came and formally shook hands with him, and motioned him to sit, then brought a bowl of soup and placed it in front of him. Marc had rushed over to his mother and escorted her to the chair next to him. The room was alive with several conversations taking place at once. Olivier, acutely aware of Max's presence, watched her interact with her friend Ted. He said something that made her burst into laughter. She seemed comfortable, not at all out of her element, which he thought puzzling for someone who claimed to have grown up in a modest apartment in New York.

Antoine, now saturated with wine and who knew what else, said, "Léa, *chérie*, the mystery is killing me. Are you, or are you not, selling de Saint-Pern?"

Léa stood. "It is unfortunate timing," she said, "for this to be happening on Chloé's wedding weekend. And so, I will answer all questions the day after the wedding."

Olivier thought it a fine response.

Just as the guests were starting to relax back into their individual conversations, Geneviève said, "To sell de Saint-Pern would be like selling the soul of Champagne itself. I don't think the region would ever be the same."

Who does she think she is, coming from Paris, and who knew where before that, to make such a pronouncement? Olivier thought.

"What do you know of Champagne, Madame?" Léa retorted. "Actually, we are a global community, and you are speaking as a traditionalist. I don't see how a Parisian seamstress can feel so passionately about the sale of a champagne company."

Olivier winced inside.

"She seems to care more than you do," Antoine said. "Because I think she's right. You are being callous about the people who work for you. Selling out…"

"De Saint-Pern is mine to do with as I please," Léa shouted at Antoine. "Look at you! What do you do for the people of Champagne, except leech everything you can from your brother. I don't have to answer to you. Ever!"

"I'm going to speak to Baptiste Dupuis about purchasing my de Saint-Pern shares."

Hans said, matter-of-factly. "I want them. We'll talk later."

"This has gone too far," Léa said, getting up and leaving the room. Ted followed her out.

Marie-Christine, her lips pinched, blurted, "Antoine, you're drunk. Please leave my table." The silence that followed was heart-pounding. "We have a wedding tomorrow and look at Chloé."

Antoine's head jerked up and he gazed at Marie-Christine with pure scorn. "You married into this family. You had nothing before that. So don't tell me what to do."

Jacques stood and grabbed Antoine's arm, but he jerked away and staggered across the room to the double doors. Geneviève stood and lit a cigarette, walking dramatically across the room. "For a wedding party there appears to be a lot of angst," she said. Marc asked his mother to sit down.

Just then, Mimi bustled in with the main course, *un filet detruite au vin de champagne*, trout cooked in white wine, chives, cloves, and special Burgundy truffle that the region was known for. Jacques had brought out two bottles of the estate chardonnay and was opening one.

Olivier saw that Max was frozen in her seat and thought it must be strange for her, to watch this live soap opera that she couldn't understand. Those who remained attempted to lighten the conversation, but unfortunately a pall had settled over the room. The conversation was desultory after that. Eventually they were herded into the salon for coffee and Jacques brought out a 1911 Armagnac. Max huddled with Chloé, and in a few moments they excused themselves for the evening.

Jacques came to Olivier when he announced that he was leaving, and asked, "Did you know about this Hans Keller fellow?" Olivier shook his head. "There is more to this than meets the eye," Jacques continued. "Something Léa's not revealing. Though she has always been impulsive, this business of selling the company rather than deal with Baptiste is uncharacteristic of her. At least Baptiste is French."

"She hates the way Baptiste destroys the artisanal quality of everything he touches. You know, Léa's desire to sell may be nothing more than her wanting change. Her company is doing well. Her champagne is huge in the Asian market now. Champagne sales are at an all-time high. Land is at a premium."

"Which reminds me, your boss, the Minister of Justice, asked me recently if there was anyone on the periphery of Champagne who might want to sell land. Some of those farmers are sitting on potential goldmines, but it's all speculative."

Olivier's ears perked up. "Philippe Douvier?"

"We were in school together."

Olivier had also attended one of the French elite schools, and knew how friendships there carried over into politics and business to the point that it bred corruption. Olivier was well aware of the acreage Jacques was referring to. Global demand for champagne was on the rise, but as the grapes for champagne could only be grown on land approved by the *Appellation d'Origine Controlée,* there was a need for more land to be officially designated for growing grapes.

He knew that a group of so-called government experts had drawn up a secret list of forty communities for possible approval. The larger champagne companies were in favor of expanding the current designation, which Olivier assumed meant that politics and business were again in bed together. He thought a select few would be informed about which of the communes would receive first approval, giving them a leg-up on where to purchase hectares.

Jacques said, "I hope if he knows something he'll let me in on the big secret."

"You don't want to get involved with him. I need to go." The two friends shook hands. Once in his car, Olivier slid in Beethoven's First Piano Concerto and drove to his parents' house. He answered immediately when his mobile phone rang. "What a night. I don't think anyone will be speaking to me tomorrow."

It was Léa.

"I will be. We can discuss Arthur Rimbaud or some other poet." She laughed and he thought it a lovely sound.

Chapter Five

The church where the wedding was taking place dated back to the twelfth century and was a blend of Roman and Gothic architecture. Built of grey stone, it was typical of churches of that era. Its austerity reminded parishioners to shed the superfluous, while its loftiness caused the spirit to soar upon entering. The stone floor was slightly uneven, so that heels tapping against the stone created an echo in the hollow space. Great shoots of white lilies mixed with arum extended from crystal vases that had been placed on the altar, perfuming the air with their sweetness. Ushers welcomed the guests as they entered the side doors, and showed them to their seats. Family was seated in the Gothic chancel. Guests took seats on the oak pews in the central nave beneath the typical Roman wooden ceiling.

Max took the arm of the usher, who walked her down the wide aisle to the third oak pew in the central nave. An older couple watched her and issued polite smiles when she sat down. She had been given the opportunity to sit in the chancel with the family but declared her desire to be where she could see everything that was going on. Her heels were a bit high, she thought, and she felt self-conscious about the hat with large pale pink flowers adorning it that added another four inches to her height.

The man beside her leaned over and said, "*Quel chapeau! Ma femme est jalouse.*" How perfectly charming, Max thought, translating, *What a hat! My wife is jealous.* She grinned at him, and in the same moment noticed Olivier on the other side of the woman, looking straight ahead.

"Merci," she whispered to the man she presumed to be his father; she turned her attention to the other side of the church, avoiding eye contact with Olivier. She overheard the woman she assumed to be Olivier's mother whisper to her husband, "She's an American detective. Olivier just told me."

"Do you think she wears the hat when chasing a criminal?" the man beside her whispered back to his wife.

Max was amused. The organist had begun and the beautiful strains of Mozart floated up to the ceiling. Max watched the guests arrive and be seated: a sartorially elegant man and his blond wife whose identity she learned when a guest behind hissed his name; a woman in bright pink and auburn curls who sat gabbing with the man at her side while he stared ahead, ignoring her; and Hans the Manipulator, whom she now hoped would fail in his bid for de Saint-Pern. A dark-haired, athletic woman who sported a tan entered and sat in the pew across the aisle from Max. A ruggedly handsome man put his hand over hers the moment he sat down beside her.

She couldn't avoid hearing Olivier's mother say to her husband, "Diane came after all. I'm disappointed that she would show up with Olivier here. These are our friends, not hers." Her husband gently shushed her.

Max cast what she hoped was a surreptitious glance in Olivier's direction, but he was looking directly at her. She tried to give a casual smile. He said something to his parents, then stood and crossed in front of them in order to sit beside her. "I like your hat."

"I use it when chasing criminals." He looked perplexed, and she didn't explain. They were distracted by Geneviève, who was coming down the aisle in an upswept hat that had a huge bow on the front. Max was sure she had had a facelift. She wore a creation of off-white that was cut to enhance her reed-thin figure. Her dark rimmed eyes, sleek hair pulled back off her face, and the elaborate hat made her look like an exotic bird.

Marc had walked out into the chancel, wearing the traditional gray tailcoat over a vest and light-striped trousers. She thought her mother would deem the top hat and gloves a bit much. She also recalled Chloé's exasperation about a shoe mix-up and assumed that it had been resolved. Chloé, she had learned, had been clear with her parents that if they tried to prevent her from marrying Marc she would elope with him. There had been so much confusion that Max had forgotten to ask if Marc's mother had revealed the identity of his father. How odd that she would only agree to tell him the eve of his wedding. Max wondered what would prevent her from making up a name?

The organist began playing "Solemn Procession" from *Denes Agay*, and heads swiveled to observe the bride slowly walk down the long aisle with her father. Chloé looked straight ahead, smiling at the man who was waiting for her. The ceremony was lovely, and after the couple had signed the church register Chloé turned to her new husband for a kiss. Max glanced to her left and saw Olivier's ex-wife staring at her, obviously curious. Felix Mendelssohn's "Nuptial March" played loudly, and the couple rushed up the aisle and waited on the stairs to greet their guests who poured out behind them. After the requisite photography session in front of the church, they ran down the stairs where they were pelted with rice and rose petals. They climbed into a Peugeot 210, circa 1932, for the short trip to the Marceau home.

"Come ride with me," Olivier said, and Max agreed. Just then his parents walked up and Olivier introduced them. The day had a surreal quality to it, far removed from Max's life in New York that had her dealing on a daily basis with the seediest people imaginable.

"I'm your translator today," Olivier said.

All the more reason to continue the language subterfuge, Max thought. "Thanks. I have a feeling that Ted will be spending all of his time by Léa's side. I thought she looked jealous of Geneviève last night, though I can't imagine why a successful and beautiful woman would care about her." Just when it hovered on the tip of her tongue to reveal that Ted had had a fling with Geneviève, Max decided not to say anything. She didn't want Olivier to think her gossipy.

"Madame Durand is rumored to be the mistress of a top politician. I have no idea who that might be," Olivier said.

They had arrived at the Marceau estate where the elegant reception was already in progress. Olivier pointed down below the terrace where the guests, the women in their splendid hats and men in dark suits, mingled. "*Voilà!* It's time to celebrate."

The waiters seemed to have walked out of a Champagne poster in their classic *casquettes*, or caps, and aprons. They moved with grace through the crowd, dipping their trays for guests to take a glass of champagne. Women in crisp black and white uniforms carried trays of appetizers. The weather on this late Saturday afternoon was perfect, calm and sunny but not too warm. Olivier took Max's elbow and led her down the path. Ted, holding Léa's hand, waved and she waved back. Max whispered that she was surprised to see Hans Keller moving among the guests. "Herr Keller is doing exactly as he said he would to his caller yesterday, which is to attend the wedding if he had to in order to seal the deal," Olivier said.

"What did you say to him that made his face turn blood red?"

"That I wasn't going to repeat his words to Madame de Saint-Pern, but that they were recorded in my brain in case there were any threats or coercion."

"I think you'd like my dad."

Olivier's parents joined them and in a few moments each of them held a tall, slender flute of champagne. Max removed her jacket and placed it on a chair. "What is the painting on your arm?" Olivier's father asked curiously.

"It's a tattoo. A drawing of a woman in a martial arts pose. I take *jiu-jitsu* lessons."

"And the words, 'kick ass'?" He read it slowly.

"Hmm. I'll think of the right word in French and get back to you," she said, moving quickly ahead and entering the tent.

◇◇◇

White freesias and roses encircled with green foliage stood in the center of each table. Max noticed that the women who had entered the tent had removed their hats and she excused herself to go to her room to freshen up. Her hair stuck up like an artichoke, but she finally managed to tame it by dabbing water on it. She could barely admit to herself that the prospect of the evening ahead with Olivier made her feel more vibrant than she had in years. She heard music in the distance and realized that she would be expected to dance. She went to her window and peered out, admiring once again the slopes of the vineyards that rose to the tree line. She hadn't danced since her brother died. She hadn't made a conscious decision to stop, but the inclination hadn't been there. She thought that deep down she had simply stopped all activities that made her joyful. She scribbled in her journal, "Dance. Talk to future therapist."

As she arrived at the stairs, she heard voices below and hesitated. "I don't want this German fellow outbidding me," a man with a cultured voice said.

"I knew nothing about Hans Keller making a bid. Léa went behind my back." Max tried to lean over to see who had responded, but only had a view of the top of his head, which was covered with a few strands of hair.

"I'm paying you a lot to keep me in the know," the first man said.

Max heard a loud sigh. "There's another problem. Marc is starting to side with Hans Keller."

"Ambitious, huh? " There was a pause. "Who is he anyhow, this Marc Durand, other than the husband of Chloé Marceau? Who is his family?"

"No one seems to know. Or care. He wants my place in the company."

"Get me the formula for the *L'Etoile* and find out tonight what Keller is offering. It's imperative that I know before morning so that I can top it. You will get that vacation house."

"*D'accord.*" Max sensed a hint of defeat in the answer. When she shifted her weight from one foot to the next in order to lean down again and look over the bannister, the wooden step creaked. For a second all was silence, then she heard a door open and close. She casually walked down. At the bottom of the stairs she found herself face to face with the tall, slender man she had noticed at the wedding who had striking blue eyes and gray hair. He had stayed behind to slay the dragon. "*Bonsoir,*" he said. "*Je m'appelle Baptiste Dupuis.*"

"*Enchantée.*" Then, switching to English, "I'm a friend of Chloé Marceau's. Max Maguire."

"My wife was admiring your hat. Where do you come from?" he asked in heavily accented English.

"New York." He's worried that I understood his conversation in French, Max thought. Let's see how he gets the information he needs.

"I came in to find a washroom," he said. "My wife is waiting for me."

"I'm staying here at the house. It was time to get rid of that flower garden on top of my head." They began walking together back toward the reception.

"How do you manage with the language barrier? Or perhaps you speak French?"

They were almost at the tent. I was right, she thought. He suspects I overheard his conversation, and he's worried. "I'm hopeless with French," she said. His relief was palpable.

When they entered the tent, Marie-Christine, looking regal in blue, walked over, and shook hands with Dupuis, who was joined by his wife, Jacqueline. Wispy thin and chemically blond, Max estimated her to be a decade younger than her husband. She gave Max an appraising look to ascertain how snobby she wanted to be with her. "*Vous êtes une grande femme,*" she said, looking up with not a trace of admiration. "*Et très forte, aussi, je vois.*" She hesitated, "Oh, pardon, I speak in English now. You are very big, and appear to be quite strong."

Max hated being called big because she was tall and had muscles. "And you are *très, très petite*, in English very small, like a ladybug," she said, smiling.

Max maneuvered her way to the center table where Jacques and Olivier sat in conversation. The first course had arrived, a *gazpacho et sa glace à la moutarde de Meaux*, which Olivier described as mustard ice cream in gazpacho. Max was introduced to Bernard and Caroline Martin. When Bernard spoke, Max recognized his voice as the one she had heard speaking to Baptiste Dupuis at the foot of the stairs. Later she would stand and see if his balding pate was a match, just to make sure. Caroline's suit was too pink and her hair too red. Yeasty white breasts protruded from the tight bustline of her jacket. Her face was extremely pale. She giggled often, and loudly. Her husband told Max he was a cousin of Charles de Saint-Pern, and an officer of the de Saint-Pern Company. And a back stabber, she thought.

When the time was right, she would definitely repeat the conversation she had heard to Léa.

Bernard switched to French with Jacques. "Things are changing too rapidly. I might be forced out of my home if Léa caters to your new son-in-law. I realize that Léa owns it, but still, I've been there for twenty years."

"It's Léa who wants the couple to live next to her. You may not have to worry if Léa sells. But if she says anything again about kicking you out of your house, I'll step in. I'm adamantly opposed to Chloé living there."

If Léa was trying to get him out, Max thought, she might be suspicious about his dealings with Dupuis. Marie-Christine came and sat next to her husband, followed by Léa and Ted. Geneviève arrived next, looking uncharacteristically upset. Ted leaned over and asked her if she was okay, and Max overheard her say that she and Marc had had a spat, but it was nothing. She picked up her glass of champagne and took a sip. It occurred to Max that there wasn't a Durand table; in fact, she wondered who in the room represented the groom's side of the family.

The second course arrived, a *salade de homard bleu en vinaigrette acidulée*. Blue lobster in an acid vinegar salad. Olivier explained that the lobster came from Brittany, and that when caught they were blue, but changed color after they were cooked. Olivier freely poured the red wine that was being served with the *gigot d'agneau juteux* and *haricots verts du jardin*. Geneviève barely ate anything. Olivier engaged her in polite conversation, and Max noticed how she placed her hand on his arm when she spoke. "And you," Geneviève said to Olivier, "I read recently where the *juges d'instruction* are about to be eliminated from the system."

"There are only sixty-four of us, so it does feel as if we could become an extinct species. Sarkozy wants to return to the seventies when the ministry could block politically sensitive investigations. It always boils down to the personal."

"Judging from the investigations you are known for, Olivier, I agree. On a different note, I find it incongruous that an examining magistrate bar-hops around Paris with Véronique Verize. *The* Véronique. I'm impressed."

Quelle bitch, Max thought as she watched her place a hand on his arm. Olivier cast a glance her way that indicated his helplessness.

At midnight Chloé danced with her father, and Marc approached their table to invite his mother to dance. Max thought if she had any advice for Chloé for the future it would be to move far from Geneviève. But I'm not one to talk about getting away from parents, she reminded herself.

Before she could offer up any resistance, Olivier swept her out to the dance floor. "What appears in a gossip column, as you surely know, is rarely the truth," he said, referring, she knew, to the comment about Véronique. Ted grabbed her hand before she had time to respond, and they danced with abandon to "YMCA," stopping to throw up their arms with the other dancers. The groomsmen picked Marc up high in the hair and twirled in a dervish-style dance in great circles. Strobe lights with their laser effect added to the intensity of the music, and it all felt overwhelming to Max, as though everyone was slightly out of control. Marc, she noticed, had become more disheveled with each passing hour. Chloé had told her that all the young crowd were planning to stay awake all night and that she should change into jeans later on and return for the "real" party.

When Max went back to the table, she didn't feel steady on her feet. She had taken her shoes off when the dancing began. She noticed that guests were starting to leave. A slow dance was playing and the DJ announced the last dance. Olivier stumbled slightly as he led her to the floor. "*Tu es envoûtante.*"

She laughed. "*Bon. D'accord.*"

He laughed and pulled her close, then leaned back, "What does this 'kickass' on your arm really mean. In English?"

He was just enough taller to cause her to look up, and she felt herself drowning in his charm. Though tipsy, she felt completely in the moment.

"It means…if you don't kiss me I'm going to kick your ass." She burst out laughing at his surprised expression.

"It's against French law to threaten a magistrate," he said.

"Then arrest me." He took her by the hand and they exited the tent.

Chapter Six

Olivier felt as if something foreign had inhabited his mind and taken over all decision-making. Perhaps it had to do with seeing his ex-wife making out on the dance floor with her lover, combined with more alcohol than he was accustomed to.

"*Où?*" he asked. "Where?"

"*Ma chambre?*"

"*Chambre*," he corrected her pronunciation. They made their way up the back stairs of the wing where Max's room was. It occurred to Olivier that he was in his friend's house, and at any moment Jacques or Marie-Christine could come around the corner. No matter, there was just something about this woman that he could not resist—so sexy in a simple sheath dress that revealed the tattoo of a woman warrior. He reached for her and cupped the back of her head as he brought his lips to hers. She opened the door to her room without even breaking their embrace. As soon as the door closed behind them, his hands found the back of her dress and he slowly began to pull the zipper down. The dress fell to the floor, and she stood there in matching lace bra and thong. She was as voluptuous as he had imagined. This woman is such a dichotomy, he thought, as the image of the tough detective chasing down criminals vanished. His hands travelled sensuously up her arms until they touched her face gently, and he leaned in to bring his lips to hers. Her hands blindly found the front of his shirt and began undoing the buttons when suddenly the bedroom door flew open and Ted stood there with a stricken look on his face.

Max grabbed her silk robe. "Ted! What are you doing?" Music from the tent floated in as the party continued on the terrace below.

"It's Léa! She's on the ground. She might be dead." Olivier's first thought was she was having a miscarriage. Until Ted stammered out, "Her face is bashed in."

After a stunned silence, they all moved at once. Max grabbed a flashlight from her bedside table as Ted walked alongside Olivier, babbling in French, saying that he was to meet Léa half an hour ago, that this was all his fault, and who would hit a woman for God's sake. Olivier, assuming Ted was in shock, turned and gently asked him to stop talking. Olivier instinctively glanced to the parking area, noting an American-made SUV, which he thought belonged to Baptiste Dupuis, who had presumably left an hour ago. To his right, across the terrace and on the other end of the house, he saw lights on in the tent and heard rowdy laughter.

Ted led the way through the grass, down toward the lower part of the yard where the afternoon reception was held, stopping a few yards from the reception tables that hadn't been taken down. Silver ice buckets were lined up on the serving table, their metal glinting in the moonlight, with up-ended champagne bottles protruding from the tops.

A few feet from a stone bench, Léa lay curled on her left side in a fetal position, her hair draped over her face. Olivier scanned her body, noticing the pistachio colored skirt pulled up slightly, one shoe on, the other off. A half-opened red rose was clutched in her left hand. He knelt to feel her pulse, while Max dropped on her knees and gently rolled Léa over onto her back. When Max gasped, Olivier followed her gaze to Léa's face. The left side of her forehead was a reddish-black pulp. Her cheekbone was smashed and the swelling had forced her right eye closed. A cloud crossed in front of the moon and they were pitched into darkness for a few seconds.

Max swore when her flashlight didn't work. "Ted, go find a flashlight," she commanded, and he ran back toward the house. The moon emerged from behind the cloud, and Olivier moved his hand up to Léa's neck to check for a pulse. When he shook his head slightly, indicating that he had not found one, Max began CPR, pressing twice on Léa's chest, releasing, and pressing again. Time seemed to stand still for Olivier. Max continued her desperate attempt to revive his friend. "Still no pulse," he said, finally, fumbling in his pocket for his phone. When Max didn't stop, he said gently, "*Arrête.*" His hand reached for her shoulder. "Stop, please. *Elle est morte.*" He reached down and closed Léa's other eyelid. Then in English, "She's gone." He touched his watch and a light flashed on. Two-twenty.

Max gingerly moved her hands to feel the back of Léa's head. "My guess is her assailant hit her from behind and she turned to face him and he slammed her hard on the cheekbone and… he must have been in a rage to have attacked her face in that manner. Chances are he knew her. The other thing I noticed is that her pearl necklace is missing. Maybe she took it off…"

Olivier wondered if he sounded that objective when he confronted families who had lost someone close to them and if they felt as infuriated as he did now. "You are in France," he said sternly. "Not New York City. Or on American TV." She took a step back. He saw the slight rise of her eyebrow and her eyes turn steely, yet he didn't care. She had already labeled Léa's death a murder, which it so obviously was, but he wasn't ready to hear it. He had never experienced a loss of this magnitude, so shocking in its violence that it threatened to overcome him. And underneath he already knew he held himself responsible. He had been on the premises and should have been able to make sure this crime didn't happen.

He had to alert the police. Without answering Max about the necklace, which he had not noticed, he dialed the young man he had mentored, and one of the few he trusted, Abdel Zeroual, and was relieved to hear his voice. "I'm at the Marceau home in

Sourières," Olivier said. "You know where it is. There is a death. Inform the commissaire."

"Okay."

Abdel's family referred to the young police officer as an "Olivier rescue." He was the grandson of Zohra, the woman that Olivier's mother had hired to be the *jeune fille* for her two sons. Zohra had fled Algeria during the French-Algerian War in the 1950s, leaving her husband and an abusive relationship behind. She had a friend in the Champagne region and moved there with her son and grandson. Her son had died tragically in a car accident, and she had raised her grandson, Abdel. When Abdel had gotten into trouble as a young man, Olivier had persuaded the authorities to give him another chance. He had enrolled in the National Police and now, at thirty-two, was a detective, and in Olivier's mind, a great role model for his friends. He would be coming from Epernay and should be there within fifteen minutes.

Olivier tried to recall the name of the police chief in the village, but could not. Jacques would know. He glanced over and saw that Max was bent slightly, looking down at the ground, spiraling out from Léa's body with the flashlight in hand, no doubt searching for evidence. Obviously unfazed by his sarcastic outburst. Her short silk robe rose up the back of her legs as she bent over, but they had both gone far beyond the realm of flirtation and seduction, having instantly transformed into crime solvers.

Olivier next called the chief prosecutor in Epernay, Claude Reynard, and when he answered explained what had happened. Reynard said that he would call the gendarmerie and would see him soon. The gendarmes were under the umbrella of the Ministry of Defense, but the National Police were connected to the Ministry of the Interior. In Paris the police would step in, but in a rural area like this the gendarmes were called first. It would be up to Reynard to formally open the investigation, which was called the instruction, when suspects and witnesses would be targeted. The danger was that Reynard would want to shape the investigation before he had to hand it over to an examining magistrate he chose within twenty-four hours, which could be extended to forty-eight.

Because Olivier was friendly with the Marceau family, he had the challenge of convincing Reynard that there was no conflict of interest, and to do that he would need to stretch the truth a bit. He walked over to the bench where Ted and Max sat. "The police are on their way, Monsieur Clay, and will want to interrogate you immediately, so please go to the salon and wait." Ted looked shocked.

Max stood up. "I'm going to change and find Chloé. Ted, why don't you come with me to the house?"

"I'd prefer that the guests not be told what has happened yet, but family is okay," Olivier said.

Max nodded and started walking up the gradient with Ted, then turned back to Olivier. "I've investigated a lot of murder cases. I want to help."

"I think the family needs you more than the police."

He saw car lights flash across the lawn and knew it was Abdel. He watched the two detectives pass each other, and wished he had been a little less hostile to Max, who was only trying to help. He thought her friendship with Ted Clay would demand a lot of her over the next few days. Just then, Marc and a friend appeared from around the side of the tent, laughing and unaware of the scene they had stumbled upon. Unaware was the operative word, for when Olivier approached Marc to steer him away from the scene, he appeared to be stoned, or drunk.

"What's going on?" Marc asked.

"There's been an accident. We are taking Léa to the hospital," Olivier said. He motioned to Abdel, who jogged over and took Marc by the arm, explaining that everyone was to meet in the salon. Marc jerked his arm away, and said, "I'm a member of the family. I'd like to know what happened."

Your membership in this family is a few hours old, Olivier wanted to say, and won't be affirmed until you've proven yourself. Instead he addressed him as monsieur, and used the formal version of you, *vous* instead of *tu*, which Marc and his friends would know was a subtle reprimand, unless they were too drunk to care, which Olivier thought was the case. "Your wife needs you now. You should find her and take her to the salon." Marc looked befuddled, then, sensing the seriousness of Olivier's manner, reluctantly turned away and moved back toward the house.

As Olivier glanced up toward the parking lot, a Renault Clio arrived, delivering several gendarmes, including their superior, Captain Pascal Canon. Olivier saw a short, compact man who had a soldier's bearing walk in front of the headlights, barking orders to the young men around him. With him was Chief Prosecutor Claude Reynard, who, seeing Olivier, moved briskly to shake hands. "Where is Monsieur Marceau?" he asked.

"Someone has just gone to inform him."

The officials moved en masse down the slope to the body, and when they arrived at the murder scene, halted as though someone had issued a command, and stood in silence.

"Get the lights. The tape! You know what to do!" Canon called out. The area was quickly transformed into an official crime scene, with workers swarming around, taking photographs, collecting potential evidence, and setting up the lights. Canon joined them, but Olivier stood back, observing. Abdel, looking impressive in the French summer uniform of short-sleeved white shirt, dark pants, and a hat with a visor, came up to him. "This must be hard for you, monsieur," he said in a low voice. "I know you were friends."

The young man's sympathy was almost more than Olivier could take. "Thank you, Abdel." They glanced up to see Thomas Girard, Commissaire of the *Police Nationale*, appear at the top of the slope, pausing before moving toward the lights. Olivier remembered him from school days in Epernay when Girard was the star of the soccer team. He towered over Canon as he went up and shook hands. Abdel had moved in to assist the gendarmes.

The medical examiner arrived, and after a perfunctory greeting to the group at large, went straight to the body and began his inspection. After what seemed like a long time to Olivier, who had moved closer to observe, the examiner looked up at

Reynard and Olivier. "I think she was hit from behind first. When she turned to face her assailant, he went into a rage and that's when he delivered the blow to the face."

"Do you think it was personal?" Olivier asked.

"It often is when there is so much damage to the face. I'll be able to tell if she was hit first in the back of the head, or in the front." Exactly as Max had stated.

Reynard said, "This will be a front-page story. Léa de Saint-Pern murdered. *Ce n'est-pas possible!*"

"I hope you'll consider appointing me *juge d'instruction*."

"You seem the obvious choice, Olivier, but that's not a promise. Be aware that there could be potential conflict between Canon and Girard."

"I know Thomas Girard and detective Abdel Zeroual would come aboard as my assistant."

"I'm still concerned. We'll talk later."

A burly man in street clothes approached and introduced himself as the local police chief. "I live in the village and heard the baying of the siren a few minutes ago and got up to see what was going on." He surveyed the goings-on with a steady gaze. "Who is it?" Olivier told him. "This is a tragedy. I know Monsieur and Madame Marceau and their daughter went to school with my son. What do you want me to do?"

"You've lived here a long time?"

"I brought my family here came from Pau a decade ago."

"Will you ask around among the neighbors? See if anything interesting turns up."

"*Absolument.* The closest neighbor, of course, is Antoine Marceau, who lives in a little cabin on the river."

"I know who he is. I walked down the path there yesterday and didn't see anything."

"You wouldn't have. You have to exit out of the *porte cochère,* and to the right a narrow hidden driveway leads right to it."

"Could you get there from here without going onto the street?"

"Sure can. There's a footpath veering off from the path you took. You wouldn't notice it if you weren't aware of it."

Thomas Girard walked up and shook hands with Petit and Olivier. Petit reminded him that they had met once at a parade organized by the mayor. Girard asked him to make a list of names of neighbors within a five-kilometer radius, and Petit nodded. Turning to Olivier, Girard said, "You're a *juged'instruction* now, Monsieur Chaumont?"

Olivier nodded, "I'm surprised you remember me."

"There weren't that many of us at the school. You've exposed some of our most corrupt politicians. I don't imagine you're very popular in some realms."

"No, I suppose not."

Petit said he had to go, and that he would be asking around, but wanted to make sure he wasn't stepping on anybody's toes. Olivier thought there were an awful lot of toes to step on. They thanked him and he strolled off.

Girard got right to the point. "Any ideas off the top of your head about suspects?"

Olivier shook his head. "It's going to be tough, with all the wedding guests floating around. It also occurred to me that you should be checking all the boats that have passed by over the past couple of days."

"Good idea. You got the case?"

"Reynard hasn't appointed me yet, but I'm expecting him to. Tread lightly around Canon."

"I can work with him. It's Reynard that's the problem. I think it'll be determined that this is a big enough case that the ministers will want the police in on it. I'll have Zeroual make a list." Girard hesitated, "You were at the wedding?"

"My parents were invited to the wedding. Jacques Marceau is an acquaintance, of course."

"You knew Madame de Saint-Pern?"

"Same as you. From school. I've been in Paris a long time, and have seen very little of her over the years. I hope you don't mind that I called Detective Zeroual first."

"Not at all. He's a good man. I'm just sorry that he's transferring to Bordeaux. Although I know it's a good opportunity for him." Olivier didn't have to state the obvious, that his goal was to help Abdel rise to the position in Bordeaux that Girard occupied here.

"Who found Madame de Saint-Pern?"

"Her fiancé. A man named Ted Clay. American."

"I'll start with him."

Olivier wanted to get to Jacques and Marie-Christine before the chief prosecutor did. He walked toward the terrace and stopped. All the upstairs shutters were closed except for Jacques' room.

Odd.

Chapter Seven

Even as the rational side of her brain was excusing Olivier's polite rejection of her offer to assist, Max felt frustrated. The French criminal system was inquisitional rather than accusatory like it was in the states, which said to her that the various officials would talk themselves to death before the action started.

Ted sat in the chair in her room. "Did you hear Olivier tell me that I'll be questioned first?"

"That's normal. You discovered Léa's body." Max stepped out from behind the screen wearing jeans, white shirt, and cowboy boots. She picked up her journal and started making notes.

"Alright. What do you know about the criminal justice system here?"

"All that's necessary to know is that Reynard is in charge in the beginning, then he appoints the examining magistrate, who takes over from there.

"So these magistrates don't run around the way detectives do in the states?"

"Hardly. Don't get me wrong, though. He's brilliant."

"Catch me up to speed on your personal life. I have a feeling I'm your only advocate. From Chloé I know there are… entanglements. And they will be analyzed. Why were you with Geneviève and not with Léa at two in the morning?" Too late Max realized that an accusation was embedded in the question.

"Marc asked me to walk his mother home. Léa made no bones about being pissed off, but told me to go ahead and she'd meet me at the stone bench. I was torn, but they were waiting for me to decide, so I said okay."

"Was Léa aware that you'd had an affair with Geneviève?"

"No. But that's ancient history."

"It doesn't matter. Every possible link will be uncovered." Ted gave her a dispassionate look. This was the time when suspects, confused and in shock, confessed to something they didn't do.

"I want you to have a lawyer when the police question you. Do you know one?"

"I think a lawyer would be worthless. It's only very recently that a suspect is even allowed a lawyer during the initial questioning. If I came in with a lawyer, the authorities would think me guilty."

Max wanted to scream.

"I'm worried about what Geneviève will say."

"Why?" His eyes blinked a couple of times and she knew it wasn't good. "What happened with Geneviève? Were you later meeting Léa than you said you would be?"

"There's something you don't know, Max. Léa is…was… pregnant." Max, stunned, wondered why the subject was coming up now. "I told Geneviève in the car driving out to Champagne, and she was unreasonably upset about Léa and the baby. It surprised me."

"Why?"

"I'm not sure. I hadn't seen her in ages when she called eight months ago and said that Marc was job-hunting, and would I introduce him to Léa. Léa ended up hiring Marc and was initially enthusiastic about him, but then found him a nuisance because he was flirting with her. But then he met Chloé and they fell in love.

"What happened at the inn?"

"Geneviève tried to seduce me."

"You said no and left?"

"Sort of."

Max could picture Ted trying to appease her, over-explaining, and excusing himself. She had an urge to tell him he deserved whatever crap was coming his way for being weak.

"Let me guess. You stayed and listened to her whine about her loneliness and her sad life."

Ted sat wide-eyed, impressed with her accurate assessment of Geneviève. Poor hapless Ted, she thought, recalling the same behavior when they had been friends in New York.

She wished she had time to give him a lesson in how to conduct himself in front of his inquisitors. She had to get to the family first, though. "The only advice I'm going to give you is to think before you speak."

He nodded, and they went out into the hall. She stopped. "Ted, how did you know to come to my room to find me?"

He gave a brief smile. "I saw you and Olivier going out of the tent, and I had a hunch, shall we say?"

"Oh." How many others had observed them leaving the tent together, she wondered.

They parted ways, and Max knocked lightly at Jacques' door. "*Entrez.*"

"Jacques?" she said, entering. The room was dark except for a shaft of moonlight falling across the floor.

"*Oui?*"

A dim lamp clicked on. He was sitting in a leather club chair, wearing his dress shirt and wedding pants. He reached for his glasses and put them on, then looked at her expectantly. She took a deep breath, and said, "Léa has been found murdered on the lawn. I'm so sorry."

The room felt like a tomb. Without a trace of emotion, he said, "*Merci.* I will go and tell my family. The police are here?"

"Yes. They want everyone to gather in the salon. Did you hear anything between one-thirty and two-thirty?"

"I don't know the time, but I heard an argument and recognized Léa's voice. She shouted something. I thought her American fiancé was catching hell. I've seen her fly off the handle at people."

"I noticed your shutters were open."

"You think I had a ringside seat? I didn't see anything."

"Okay. May I use your office to call my dad?"

"Sure."

She went into the office that formed an oasis of warm paneling, rich carpeting, and soft lights. She picked up the phone and dialed Hank at home. When he answered, she thought she might cry, but collected herself. "Chloé's Aunt Léa was murdered a couple of hours ago. Bludgeoned."

"Nasty. Who did it?"

Hank's belief was that the first instinct was usually the right one. "No idea."

"Murder weapon?"

"Nothing yet."

"You want us to go through Interpol to see if they'll let you work on the case?"

"I'll let you know. There're already lots of fingers in the pie."

"Don't make a big deal out of being on the team. Work quietly, the way we do here. Talk to people. Keep your eyes open."

She told him everything Ted had told her.

"That Geneviève is a woman scorned. Keep your eye on her." He paused, "Any chance Ted could have done it?"

"Doubtful."

"I'm glad you didn't say no."

"I want to solve this case more than I've wanted anything in a long time, Hank."

She thought he had hung up when he replied, "I'm also glad to hear you say that." She put the phone back in the cradle.

So he knew how she had been feeling the past few years. Though she was considered a competent detective, and had managed to acquire her gold shield, she couldn't remember the last time she had felt any passion for her profession. Or anything else for that matter. The relationship with Joe happened because they were together a lot. It seemed easier hooking up with him than going out of her way to meet someone.

Her life since her brother's death felt as though it was happening by default, as though she hadn't made any conscious choices. Sometimes she thought it was because she felt overshadowed by Hank. He was always there, checking behind her, making sure she was safe. Perhaps the determination to help solve Léa's murder had to do with her being away from that protection. She had actually never solved a crime without Hank or Joe or her boss, Captain Walt O'Shaughnessy, enabling her in some way. She had for years felt herself holding back ever so slightly, carrying the knowledge that if anything happened to her, her parents would have a hard time surviving. But, she thought, how long can I continue like this? Maybe another question to put on the future list for the therapist.

Jacques, transformed back to master of the house, paused in the doorway, and they went together to the kitchen, where they found Mimi holding Marie-Christine, who was sobbing uncontrollably.

Jacques did not go to his wife, but stood awkwardly. "So you know. How?"

"Mimi. I sent her home but she returned after a few minutes and told me."

"The police were there then?"

"*Non, monsieur,*" Mimi said. "I had my little flashlight. I almost fell over Madame."

"She was taking food to Antoine before going home," Marie-Christine interjected.

"You two have never stopped spoiling the hell out of him," Jacques said angrily. "I'd like to know his whereabouts when your sister was killed."

"Stop, Jacques. He didn't kill her. We have to go tell our daughter."

Jacques walked in front of her to the door, and Max felt a chasm widen between them. She could hear voices coming from the salon. Peering down the hall from the kitchen doorway, she saw the cop she believed to be Olivier's assistant ushering guests in. Hans Keller entered, protesting that he couldn't be held against his will. Chloé's and Marc's friends Delphine and Yves, who was disheveled, and others she didn't know, filed in. It would take at least two hours for the police to sort through the guests and send those who had concrete alibis home.

Max took a flashlight off the wall in the pantry and set off for Antoine's. She couldn't be accused of nosing around, because she had told Olivier that she was going to tell family, and Antoine was family, she reasoned. She walked across the sloping yard, shielded by shadows and a row of plane trees. The voices of the forensics crew yelling back and forth pierced the night. Arriving at the tables that had been stripped of tablecloths after the earlier reception, she absentmindedly brushed her hand along the dozens of metal ice buckets that were lined up, the empty bases of the champagne bottles protruding from them. She couldn't believe how many there were. She came to a halt when her hand touched a bucket that was still cold. She wondered if Léa had brought a bottle of champagne down for Ted and her. Or had someone else been planning a rendezvous? Should she take the renegade bottle up to the crime scene, she wondered. Showing up and proffering an ice bucket might have her accused of tampering with evidence. She would check on her way back.

She followed the path that she and Olivier had taken, and halfway down noticed lights through the trees. She jogged toward the house, calling out to Antoine.

"*Qui est là?*"

"It's me, Max." She approached the porch and looked closely at him to see if she could perceive any signs of someone who had just committed a murder. Ella Fitzgerald was singing in the background, her mother's favorite vocalist.

"I can only think it's ominous that an American detective is staring me in the face at this hour of the night—or morning."

"It's Léa."

"Of course it is. Is she dead, and I'm being blamed?"

"No blame yet." Max thought the two brothers' responses as peculiar as any she had ever heard.

"Come in. I'll get you a drink. Do you want a glass of champagne?"

She did, but thought she'd better not. The tiny kitchen was a mess, with bottles and cans all over the place. "I wasn't expecting guests," he said. "I know from Chloé that you're some kind of detective. I can confess, and say you dragged it out of me, but that would only delay finding the real culprit."

She smiled. "A French detective will be coming here shortly if you don't return with me to the main house."

"We don't have murders in Champagne. We're much too civilized." He lit another cigarette. "Who would want Léa dead? She was a pain in the ass, but we loved her. I wish we hadn't argued." He stood. "Who did it, Max?"

For an instant she thought Hank had spoken. "I don't know."

"How did she die?"

Horribly, Max wanted to say. Face to face with her killer. Carrying a baby.

"She was bludgeoned."

"*Merde.* Listen, Max, I'll tell you something but you can't use it."

"Don't worry. I'm not officially a part of the investigation."

"Good. I got pretty drunk at the wedding, and snorted some cocaine. I shared it with some other guests but those names will go unmentioned." Max couldn't imagine why he was telling her this. She followed him into the rustic living room that had an ancient stone fireplace, and books falling out of shelves that went from floor to ceiling. "This house was supposed to be a temporary abode," he said. *War and Peace* was open on the table in front of the sofa. "The kids were dancing late, you know that. I don't know what time it was. I decided I had had enough and headed home. But I got turned around, as we drunks are wont to do. Anyhow, I must have passed out on my way home. When I came to and started walking again, something ran into me. Knocked me over."

"A person?"

"It was a person but with the force of an animal when he ran into me. He stood over me, panting, and then he took off.

"Do you know who it was?"

"No. Here's what's really weird, though. I sensed that he was deciding whether to kill me or not while he was standing over me. I made a point of not looking up."

It was a chilling story, and Max believed every word.

"You know how it is when you have a word on the tip of your tongue and it won't come? I feel that the identity of that person is logged somewhere in my brain, but I can't quite reach it. Some form of amnesia."

Max knew that extreme fear sometimes caused forgetfulness.

"*Bonjour*," Antoine said. "The whole world is coming to call."

Max whirled around and saw a tall, olive-complexioned man standing in the doorway. "I'm Abdel Zeroual," he said. "I need you both to come with me."

Antoine looked over at Max. "We're under arrest."

Max went over and shook Abdel's hand. "Max Maguire. Detective with the NYPD."

"Monsieur Chaumont told me about you. Are you doing detective work here in this gentleman's house, *mademoiselle*?"

Addressing her as mademoiselle instead of detective told Max what her status was with the police. Single woman visiting friend for wedding. "Monsieur Chaumont gave me permission to tell the family. Antoine is family."

Antoine went to the kitchen and returned with a bottle of beer. "I'm ready." It was impossible not to notice the look of consternation on Zeroual's face.

It was going to be a long walk if she didn't do something. "Will the interrogation begin immediately?" she asked.

"Once everyone is accounted for, we talk to likely suspects." Max thought he was around her age. "I'm addicted to your crime shows," he said. "They helped me to learn English. You are like Olivia on *Law & Order, SVU,* perhaps?" Max knew he was referring to the character Olivia Benson on *Law and Order,*

Special Victims Unit that she had watched in college. They must have been showing reruns in France.

"I wish I were successful every time with my crime-solving, the way she is."

"I'm a big fan of the United States. Especially New York."

They passed by the tables, and Max decided to take a chance and share with Zeroual her discovery of the cold ice bucket. "You know," she said. "I passed the reception area on my way here, and idly ran my fingers along the row of ice buckets, and was surprised to find one that was still cold. An unopened bottle was in it."

"Show me," Zeroual said. Max told Antoine to continue, and led Zeroual to the table. He pulled out his flashlight and ran the beam over each bucket.

"Not here," Max said. "What the hell." She didn't dare voice her suspicion that one of the gendarmes had found a gift for his wife.

"We should go," Abdel said.

The air was soft as velvet. Max felt deflated. Olivier wasn't going to champion her wish to join the investigative team, which meant she needed to have Abdel on her side. "Somebody came and collected that ice bucket over the past half hour to forty-five minutes," she said to Abdel.

"You can check the kitchen." He clearly had no interest in the missing bottle.

"Who is the *commissaire?*"

"Thomas Girard."

"You get along with him?"

"He's my boss."

"And Olivier Chaumont. What's he like?"

"Like?" There was the look of consternation again.

"Two words that sum him up."

Abdel shrugged, caught off-guard. "Courageous. Compassionate."

"He will ultimately be in charge of this investigatin?"

"With luck."

"I heard at dinner that the examining magistrates' positions are in jeopardy."

"President Sarkozy would like to eliminate the position. The prosecutor is easier to control."

"You think he'll succeed?"

"The judges have been going after politicians since the 1980s. The people need these guys, though, otherwise there would be no monitoring of public officials."

Abdel was smart, Max decided. They had arrived at the house, and stopped to wait for Antoine.

"What two words describe you, detective?" Abdel asked.

Good, she thought. Now I'm a detective. "Curious and consumed. And if pushed, lean and mean."

He had a goofy smile, which surprised her. "Those words go with your tattoo?"

She laughed. "I got it ten years ago in a rebellious moment. It's as outdated as *Law and Order*."

"I watch CSI now."

"I do, too."

Antoine finally caught up. "We're about to enter hell, my dear, so prepare yourself."

Chapter Eight

Olivier looked up from his work at the crime scene to see Jacques, Marie-Christine, and Chloé approaching. He went to meet them halfway, glancing behind him before speaking in a low voice to them, "I must say something quickly, and I apologize. It's imperative that I seem neutral if I am to be appointed the judge for this case."

Captain Canon marched up and spoke directly to the family. "Who are you, and why are you here?"

Olivier would have laughed had the situation not been so grim. "This is the family of the victim," he explained.

Jacques said, "We're here to say farewell to Madame de Saint-Pern."

The gendarmes had lifted Léa's body onto a stretcher and were preparing to put her into the Citroën CX station wagon parked a few feet away. Seeing the grieving family, they gently placed the stretcher on the ground, and Marie-Christine and Chloé rushed to her and knelt down. Marie-Christine said over and over, "*Adieu*, my beloved, *adieu…adieu.*" Olivier thought it the saddest word in the French language.

Their lamenting seemed incongruous in the harshness of the crime scene. It's unsettling enough for those of us who choose to do this for a living, Olivier thought. I can't imagine what it must be like for a loved one of the victim.

Jacques stood back with Olivier, looking stoic. "You will be in charge if I have to go to Douvier personally," he said. Here was the cronyism that Olivier hated, now offered in his behalf. "Our gendarmes aren't called often to murder investigations, but I hear Superintendent Girard is supposed to be quite good. He worked in Lyons before he married."

"I know him."

"I also want Max to help."

Olivier was flummoxed by his friend's wish. And if he were being honest, a little stung by the request. "The language barrier will make it difficult," he said, "and we would have to go through Interpol."

"Let's see what Girard says. It doesn't have to be official, you know. We can break a rule for once, Olivier."

"She'll be a distraction." Olivier knew he was being recalcitrant, and didn't care.

"She needs to prove herself. You'll understand when you know more of her story."

The case, involving friends and family, was going to become deeply personal, Olivier knew but not to this extent. And not when they were only a few hours into it. He rushed over to help Marie-Christine up. Captain Canon was upon them in a flash, "Madame, my men will escort you to the house."

"Monsieur, I am able to walk to my salon without a young man with a gun thinking he is protecting me." She took Chloé's hand and Jacques took his daughter's other hand, and they started toward the house. Olivier watched, feeling profoundly sorry for them.

"Interesting," Canon said after a moment, "How these people think they're above it all. Yet with all their wealth and power, they're are not immune to murder, are they?" The German word, *schadenfreude,* which translated into the satisfaction felt over someone else's misfortune, came to mind but Olivier elected to remain silent. "You're not cozy with these folks, are you?"

"*Non.*"

"She was a beauty. I can tell she was, even with all the damage done to her. And what a figure, eh?"

"Enough, *monsieur*. We're not in a bar, but in the presence of a tragic death. Please have your men place Madame de Saint-Pern in the hearse now."

The captain gave Olivier a hard stare, but obeyed. Olivier walked into the shadows, away from everyone. He was having trouble processing everything that had happened. He sat on the bench, noticing how the full moon cast everything in a mystical light. He could distinguish the peonies, their blossoms closed, their heavy heads bent toward the earth. In the distance rose the shadowy row of plane trees, their tops sculpted to perfection.

Distraught and restless, he started walking toward the river where he and Max had been the day before. His thoughts drifted back to the scene in her bedroom. Was that just hours ago? He wondered if Max had prevailed upon Jacques to use his influence to include her in the investigation. This was to be his case, and he felt as strongly about solving it as Detective Maguire did. She was an interloper, and certain people needed to be reminded of that. He ambled back up the path. The breaking morning light, with the mist rising up from the fields, seemed like a promise of better days to come. He felt calmer, as was always the case when he was in nature.

The salon was full of people in various states of dishevelment when he entered. Chloé had changed into jeans and was sitting quietly beside her father. Marc, also in jeans and shirt, and barefoot, sat with his mother, who was saying something to him that was obviously making him unhappy. What a horrific wedding night, Olivier thought. It will take a lot for this couple to transcend the horror. Madame Durand still had make-up on, which he thought curious, but what did he know about a woman who seemed more mannequin than person. Abdel had fetched her from the inn. He told Olivier that she had been feral in her *résistance*. Olivier wondered why it was taking him so long to reel in Max and Antoine.

Looking around the room again, he thought it fitting that Herr Keller had been caught in his own little web of deceit, and was in fact a strong suspect. He had heard at the reception that Hans' plane was in need of a repair and that a part had to be ordered, and that was why he stayed. Olivier hadn't believed a word of it then, and he didn't now. Marc moved over to where Hans was sitting, and they sat talking.

Olivier was surprised to see Bernard Martin and his wife from the de Saint-Pern Company, and could tell that they were surprised as well to find themselves in this gathering. This would give Madame Martin enough fodder for her gossip mill to last a lifetime. She must have been able to convince her husband to stay for the dancing, Olivier thought, which was why they were here. He continued scanning the room and his eyes fell on a young couple who were holding hands. He recognized them as close friends of Marc and Chloé's, but didn't know their names. Every time he had seen her during the reception she had been acting enamored of Hans. Ted sat in a chair tapping on his iPad, which Olivier found irritating. He would have it confiscated.

Max's voice behind him got his attention. He turned in time to see her enter the room with Girard. He felt his face flush. "Oh, Olivier," she said in a respectful tone, "I'm sorry you had to send Abdel after Antoine and me. Girard knows of my father's reputation. It's such a small world."

There she was, with Girard already on her side, made obvious by his hanging onto her every word. "I understood half of her stories," he said. "My English is not so good."

"But far better than my French."

When Olivier refused to indulge in their inanities, Girard switched to French, explaining that there were approximately thirty guests still at the party, and all but the ones gathered here had been sent home. Olivier's mobile rang, and he saw that it was the Minister of Justice in Paris. He excused himself, puzzled as to why Philippe Douvier would be calling him. They were aware of each other as they had shown up at various social events together, but Douvier would normally be speaking with Reynard about the case, not him.

Douvier got right to the point. "Reynard told me that Hans Keller is among the suspects. He's in France partly doing business for me. Any idea if he and Léa de Saint-Pern signed a contract?" Olivier was stunned by his audacity. Before he could respond to his boss, Douvier said, "Why do you happen to be there? Your parents?"

Olivier made himself sound bored, though he was anything but as he tried to figure out the game they were playing. "*Oui, oui.* They had this wedding to attend, and wanted me to join them. You know how it is."

"No conflict of interest?"

"*Non.*"

"Good." Pause. "Keep me informed about Keller. He's not a murderer."

The language was so veiled that Olivier spent a few minutes interpreting the message between the lines after they hung up, then thought the exchange easy to decipher—it was the old "you scratch my back and I'll scratch yours." Douvier wanted protection for Keller in exchange for making sure Olivier got the case, which would surely bring him international attention. Olivier grew morose after they hung up. Not only am I lying about the conflict of interest, he thought, but I'm also lying to myself by not admitting that there's an additional conflict of interest that's even more personal—my interest in Max Maguire vying with my burning need to solve this case.

Chapter Nine

Antoine caught Max's eye and she went to stand with him. "I told you you were entering hell."

Jacques was at her side before she could respond. "Max, let's go into my study. Excuse us," he said to his brother. Max got up and followed him into the office, and took a chair across from his desk. Before she could speak, he said, "The less discussion with my brother, the better. I don't think I have to explain."

"I find him to be quite honest."

Jacques gave her a strange look. "We have a different word for it. His behavior at dinner was inexcusable and he still owes my wife an apology."

Max thought that some of the problem was that Antoine was treated as a naughty boy, a persona he had created and seemed to enjoy. Antoine had nothing to lose, and she found that often created a blunt honesty that could be refreshing. "I'm going to say what I have to say in English, but I know I don't speak correctly," Jacques said.

The language game was becoming tiresome, yet she reminded herself of the information she had gleaned from overhearing Bernard Martin and Baptise Dupuis. She would share it with Jacques when he was done with his diatribe in English.

He led her into his office from which she could see the mist rising across the fields. She stood for a moment, in awe of the light and the setting. "I'm glad you're here because you can help Chloé through this tragedy. She has never known such heartache."

"I will try."

He smiled at her, "You wield a big influence on her, but you probably know that. She sees you as brave and confident, qualities she wishes to have."

"If I have those qualities they crept up on me. I was paralyzed with fear after my brother died. I felt it threatening to take over again when I saw Léa on the ground."

"Which brings up the investigation. Olivier. He is the best of the examining magistrates in France, but he will have the triple challenge of working with a prosecutor who wants to be in charge, being objective with suspects he knows, and making sure that no one perceives a conflict of interest."

"But there is a conflict of interest, isn't there?"

Jacques scowled. "Everything is relative, Max. I mentioned to him that you were interested in working on the case and he was resistant."

"Maybe I'm too intimidating. My mother tells me this all the time."

"Olivier isn't easily intimidated. You'll have to be accepted on your own merit. I've done my part. My only advice is to stop being your father's son."

Had she misunderstood? Their eyes interlocked and she knew she hadn't.

"Be Max. Not your brother. Or who you think he would have been. And whatever you do, be discreet. The French admire discretion, and the Americans don't know the meaning of the word." He smiled at his own joke.

"I'll ease my way in by asking Olivier if I can listen to the interrogations."

"But your French…"

"I understand a lot more than you know. Don't forget my mother is French."

"Chloé said you resist your French heritage."

"I was angry at my mother's family, but I'm over that."

"You want to keep this information from Olivier?"

She nodded. "It's my only leverage at the moment."

He began to speak in French. Léa's…murder…well…I will never be the same. I was depressed the night of the wedding over all her news. The baby. Selling her company. Going to America."

Max wondered if he was going to confess.

Tears streamed down his cheeks, and Max realized she was barely breathing. "We grew very close after her husband died." He waved his hand in the air. "That was a long time ago."

Five years isn't so long, Max thought. She wondered if Marie-Christine knew. She recalled how hurt she had been when she learned Joe was fooling around. And she hadn't been married to him.

"The thought of her selling her company, though, made me angrier than anything has in a long time. And to a German! I know I am prejudiced against them, but my father was in the *Résistance*, and I hold them responsible for his death. It was awful here during the war years. You can't imagine. When Léa told us about Hans Keller wanting to buy de Saint-Pern, I really hoped that something would happen to prevent it. I prayed for divine intervention. I didn't go to a church and get on my knees, but still, I appealed to all the saints I remembered. And I cursed Léa for selling out."

And for not loving you, Max thought.

"And then she died."

"I told you I heard a woman's shout while sitting at my window. A woman's voice yelled *Arrête!* I know now it was Léa and she was fighting for her life. Instead of rushing to her aid, I poured another brandy."

"Are you certain it was Ted?"

"No. A few minutes earlier I had heard that Kraut trying to persuade Chloé's friend Delphine to go back to the inn with him. It could have been he arguing with Léa."

Max exhaled. "Are you thinking that you could have saved Léa's life?"

He nodded. "I think I might have prevented…what happened. *Oui.*"

Max thought about her brother, and how she still believed fervently that had she picked him up at school on the day he was killed by a car, as was her habit, that he would be a drop-dead handsome and happy twenty-two year old today and her parents would not carry an air of sadness about them that permeated everything in their lives. And in hers.

"But you didn't seem surprised that she was dead when I entered your room."

"I knew when I heard the tap on the door."

"You will tell all of this to Olivier?"

"I don't know. Olivier is a good friend, and I have shared many things with him, but I don't like Reynard, and so I will see when I am called what I want to divulge. No matter what I do, these old secrets have a way of coming to the surface."

The door opened and Marie-Christine stuck her head in the door, then started back, but Jacques called to her. "What is it?"

"Chloé has disappeared. She said she was going to change her clothes, but someone saw her run out of the house."

"I'll find her," Max said, jumping up. She jogged down the hall and stairs and came to a halt when she saw Olivier standing on the stoop in the back. She went up to him. "I'm going to look for Chloé."

He gazed at her with impenetrable eyes. "She's there, down at the gate. I watched her go. Your friend Ted is being questioned now by Girard."

"Ted's way too garrulous."

Olivier's eyes grew large, and she knew they were both back in her room when Ted barged in.

"Which means he'll be indiscreet?"

"Olivier, he'll probably tell the truth. That he walked in on us and saw me undressed. To be honest, I don't care. I have nothing to hide."

"I don't want it in the record that I was there, and I don't understand why you don't care. This information could be leaked and put me in a compromising position."

So that was it. "Is this about you not wanting *la Véronique*, as Madame Durand referred to her with the highest admiration, to hear about this?"

"*Non.* She has nothing to do with anything."

Max had brought the personal into the professional. Damn. "I apologize for bringing her into the discussion. I was about to ask if I could sit in on your interrogations."

"I have Monsieur Zeroual working with me, but I will speak to him and see if he has any objections."

Maybe a touch of light-heartedness would help, she thought. "That's in my favor. He likes Americans."

"He doesn't seem to be alone in that sentiment from what I've observed."

"I hope that includes you."

She bounded off and could sense his eyes following her. The same way she had felt them on her as they stood by the river and she thought he was going to kiss her and then decided she was being ridiculous. And when she saw him watching her from Marceau's garden, the night of the dinner though he had no idea she knew he was there. She recalled the way their eyes interlocked when he entered the salon just before the dinner. She had seen the desire in his eyes only a few hours ago when they were in her room, and a little drunk, and she hoped he didn't hold that against her or think her a slut, though she had to ask herself why she cared, and pretended she didn't.

Chloé was waiting for her at the gate. "Are you okay?"

"No. Not in the least. But my problems are minor compared to everyone else's."

"Neither am I." Max saw that her eyes were swollen from crying.

"We can't go far. All of us will have to go through some initial questioning. We don't want to be missing in action."

They opened and closed the gate behind them, and entered the worn path that led through a small forest. "I can't bear the thought of all these people who are family and friends being questioned," Chloé said. "I wish Olivier and his men would try to find a real criminal. What if someone came from a barge on the river and attacked Léa?"

"It's possible, and that will be checked out for sure." Max had forgotten how innocent people were whose lives didn't revolve around crime. They arrived at the gate on the other side of the forest, and exited. They passed small houses, each with window boxes overflowing with geraniums and tiny vegetable plots in the yard.

"Oh, there's Mimi in the window!" Chloé ran toward the woman who had been a constant presence in her life. Mimi came to the door and invited them in. "She doesn't speak a word of English," Chloé reminded Max.

"Finally, someone who refuses to speak to me in English. Shouldn't she be at your parents' house?"

"She had to come down for her medication. A policeman will come for her."

They entered a small living room that was neat in appearance, and contained a little wood stove, a shabby sofa, and rocking chair. An ancient television sat on a table in the corner, and a crocheted rug occupied the center of the room. A framed photograph of two boys holding up fish and smiling at the photographer caught Max's eye and she walked over to have a closer look.

"That's papa and Antoine," Chloé said, then turned back to her conversation with her *jeune fille*, the French term for nanny. An eight-by-ten photograph of Chloé in a silver frame must have been a gift, Max thought. She was half listening to the conversation between the old woman and Chloé, but came to full attention when she heard Mimi describing seeing Antoine.

"I was making my way down to the reception area with my little flashlight when I saw Monsieur Antoine standing stock-still like a statue, and I put the light on his face, and could tell that he was drunk. I told him that I had some dinner for him, and I asked if he was okay. He mumbled something about running into an animal, it made no sense. I told him to wait, that I would walk with him home. He was frightened of everything when he was a boy. Then I almost fell over Léa. He stood there in horror, and fled."

Could Antoine have killed Léa, Max wondered.

"That was the right thing to do," Chloé reassured her nanny. "I'm so glad you didn't hang around because the killer could have attacked you!"

A knock at the door interrupted them, and a young gendarme said he had come for the *jeune fille*. Max and Chloé followed her out, and said they'd meet them at the house. Max's thoughts were tumbling around like the balls in a lotto machine. From what she had heard so far, people had been passing each other in the night around the hour Léa was murdered. Mimi must have missed Ted by minutes, or maybe seconds. Mimi went to the kitchen to tell Marie-Christine and Ted ran to her room. Jacques had heard Léa shout and done nothing, he said. He also could have killed her and had time to return to his room.

She and Chloé hurried back through the gate, stopping when they heard voices in the distance shrieking and laughing. "Let's get out of here," Chloé said.

"No, wait here. I want to see what's going on."

"You're still *fouine*, Max. What's the word in English?"

"Nosey. Be right back." She ducked to avoid a branch and moved quickly toward the sounds. Four boys no older than twelve were smoking cigarettes and talking loudly, and knocking each other around. They appeared to be drunk. When they saw Max, they took off running. Max wanted to check them out, but hesitated when she heard Chloé call. The boys were none of her business.

Chapter Ten

Olivier watched Max walk at a brisk pace across the lawn to where Chloé was standing and put an arm around her. A thin mist was rising, making the panorama before him seem a little out of focus. He had hoped that Véronique's name wouldn't come up, but Max had made sure that it did. He supposed that Véronique would consider them to be in relationship, but though they spent quite a lot of time together when she was in Paris, he didn't feel committed to her, or to them as a couple. Max had been right, though. He would go to great lengths to prevent Véronique from learning of his attraction to the detective. He had thought that moving to Bordeaux would create the space and time he needed to sort out his feelings. Véronique had already asked if she could use his apartment when she was in Paris, and he had said yes. He decided to go to his parents' house and shower and change clothes, then return for lunch at one. Marie-Christine had announced that Mimi was preparing a dish she was known for, a white pudding tart with *aiguillette sauce vigneronne,* a mushroom and beef gravy, made with a local *pinot noir.*

Abdel emerged from Jacques' office, where Girard had set up an interrogation room, and said as he passed Olivier, "Sir, I must speak with you as soon as possible." Olivier felt a sense of foreboding. He followed Abdel outside.

Abdel was all business. "I'm to get a statement from Baptiste Dupuis, which means I have to go to his office. Someone said he was in the parking lot when the murder occurred."

"I saw his car. What was he doing there at that hour?"

Abdel shrugged.

"Why don't you drop me off at my parents' place on your way and we can talk?"

"Let me clear it with Girard." He loped across the terrace, and disappeared into the house and returned in a few minutes. They got into Abdel's Citroën and as they headed out onto the narrow country road, Abdel said, "It's strange. Most of these people don't have good alibis. They were wandering here or there, or were on their way to the inn or to their room, but they all seem vague, as though they had been sleepwalking."

Olivier thought his description on the mark, especially with the amount of alcohol consumed. "What's bothering you?"

"Monsieur Clay is a blabber-mouth."

"Did he mention that I was in Detective Maguire's room when he came to report finding the body?"

Abdel lit a cigarette, and Olivier thought about complaining about the smoke, but decided not to when Abdel lowered his window. "That's what I wanted to talk to you."

Merde.

"Could you tell Girard's reaction?"

"*Non.* But my boss is getting pressure already from the press and from the top, and I think he'd like to accuse Monsieur Clay."

"Because he's the most obvious? A scapegoat who will appease the prosecutor?"

Abdel nodded.

"Do you agree by any chance?"

"Somewhat. He found the body, and he's very emotional. Maybe too much. It turns out he borrowed a large sum of money from Madame de Saint-Pern. And there is the Madame Durand issue."

"Which is?"

"It seems that the two women were rivals for Monsieur Clay. Before he was due to meet Madame de Saint-Pern in the garden, he helped put Madame Durand to bed, as she claimed she was having a problem with dizziness." It was obvious to

Olivier that the conversation was embarrassing for Abdel, who, he was certain, had been shocked by the social behaviors of the bourgeoisie. "He claimed she tried to seduce him."

"None of this is cause for arrest."

"It could have caused an argument that became lethal when he went back to Madame de Saint-Pern."

Olivier rolled his eyes, and was glad that Abdel hadn't seemed to notice. "What Girard hammered away about was why Monsieur Clay ran to his friend Max's room instead of to the host, Monsieur Marceau, who could have called the ambulance right away. Clay's answers were vague, and he seemed somewhat disoriented when trying to recall the facts. I think Girard felt his emotionalism a little off-putting."

"Did you?"

"Are you referring to the behavior of guilty defendants who tend to weep uncontrollably when asked about the victim?"

"Exactly. What about a murder weapon?"

"Nothing. We've scoured the grounds. It had to be a heavy object to have done that much damage. We found a stone carved rabbit and are having it examined. Perhaps there will be something lodged in Madame's face or skull that will give us a hint."

They had arrived at Olivier's parents' house in Val d'Or. Abdel turned off the ignition. "The American detective wants me to condone her snooping around on her own. It came through Jacques Marceau."

"So are you asking me what I think?"

"I said that I would. I can't rule out that she might be an asset." Abdel lit another cigarette, and they both got out of the car.

"You have to stop smoking, by the way. We'll enroll you in a program in Bordeaux." He led the way to a large perennial garden on the side of the two-story stone house that hosted a wild array of color.

Abdel said, "First impression?"

"I quite liked her. Very clever at getting people to disclose things they normally wouldn't."

"Such as?"

"She asked for two words that describe you."

"And?"

"I said courageous and compassionate."

"That was generous."

"She wanted to understand about the role of the *juge d'instruction,* and I explained. Then I asked her for two words that would describe her."

Olivier couldn't hide his interest. "What did she say?"

He smiled. "Curious and consumed. And on a bad day, lean and mean."

Abdel told Olivier about the ice buckets, and how she had been frustrated that the cold one had disappeared. They continued strolling along the garden path, as though they had all day, stopping to look at the vista behind the house—the bushy vines with the grapes now visible, the red poppies looking saucy between the rows, and the vineyards stretching across the hill that ended at a forest. "I think the *Commissaire* would say yes. He just divorced, you know, and he told me he likes the detective's smile."

"The perfect reason to invite a stranger to join an investigation. Let's go back to Monsieur Clay. How explicit was he with Girard about running to Max's room to seek help?"

"He said he pushed the door open to the detective's room, and that she was near the wash basin wearing panties and bra, and you were standing in the middle of the floor."

"That has nothing to do with the case at all. It casts Detective Maguire in a bad light."

"Somehow I don't think she cares." Olivier knew she didn't. "Here's what I think about her snooping around. If she doesn't get verbal permission, she will do it anyhow."

Olivier's parents were in Australia visiting his brother and the housekeeper, Zohra, was spending time with her family before making the move to Bordeaux. He showered and changed into jeans and a clean shirt. Abdel was back in exactly forty-five minutes, and when Olivier joined him, he said, "Monsieur Dupuis will have his driver bring him to meet with you. He claims that he had dropped his wife off at home after the reception when she realized that she'd forgotten her handbag, so he had his driver take him back to the Marceau property to retrieve it. He's furious that we're making him come in, and has threatened to call Douvier and Sarkozy if he has to."

"No surprises there. I can't imagine a handbag needing to be picked up that late at night. They could have returned the following day."

They had arrived in Sourières and when they saw the chief of police walking, Abdel stopped. "How's the investigation going?" Petit asked.

Abdel said, "Slow. Have you learned anything?"

"I was just heading over to the Marceau house to find you. The owners of the Oiseau Inn said there was quite a bit of coming and going as the night of the wedding wore on. A Kraut—their words, not mine— named Keller had a room there, as did the groom's mother, Geneviève Durand. The groom was there with his mother prior to the wedding and they had a quarrel. The owner heard the mother yell after her son, "You are nothing to them, and trust me, you'll get nothing!"

"I noticed she was upset at the wedding dinner."

"And a tall American male escorted the mother of the groom to the inn. The owner said she was acting faint and clinging to him like he was her last chance. The little village is abuzz," Chief Petit said. "To think that a murder has happened behind that wall is almost more than we can take in."

Their eyes followed his gaze. "You know," he added, "a wall says a lot." The stone wall separating the Marceaus from the rest of the world was at least eight feet high, and all that was visible from the other side was the mansard roof of the Marceau house. "Most people in this village have never been on the other side of that wall. I'd only been there once myself before this happened, when Antoine got into a little trouble."

Olivier didn't know how to respond and remained quiet. "It's a class thing. I know that," Petit said.

"Thank you for your help," Olivier said, and Abdel pulled away slowly. "The police chief, I think, has turned up more information than anyone else."

"Unless the American detective has brought the case to a close since we left."

Olivier burst into laughter.

"You haven't called her by name, you know."

"It's Max."

"I know. If I were you I'd start practicing saying it." Olivier was about to offer a rebuke, but was won over by the Arab's wide-toothed grin.

The table was set on the terrace, and as they approached it, Olivier saw that Girard and Max were deep in discussion, only glancing their way before they went *tête à tête* again. It appeared that Max had taken the time to shower, for she looked fresh. She wore very little make-up. A light tint on the lips was about it. Olivier noticed for the first time that Girard would be quite attractive to women with his large shoulders and raspy voice. He laughed, displaying even teeth, and Olivier felt a twinge of jealousy when Max responded by leaning toward him, and smiling.

After perfunctory greetings were issued, Olivier sat and listened to Marc and Hans planning a tennis tournament, which he found offensive under the circumstances. On the other hand, he thought, it might rid them of some testosterone, then felt like a fuddy-duddy for thinking it. Chloé sat in conversation beside Geneviève, whose make-up looked garish in the natural light. Olivier, seeing her plate empty, decided she didn't eat. It reminded him of Véronique.

"I will take you to the train at four," Jacques announced to Geneviève.

"Bien."

Observing her through the corner of his eye, Olivier decided that tomorrow he wanted to meet with her in Paris on an informal basis. And giving a quick glance across the table again at the newly-divorced Girard conversing with the American, he thought he would ask Max to join him. By nightfall tomorrow, he would know if he was to be in charge of the case. Mimi entered with the white pudding tart, and Jacques began to serve everyone.

The day could be called flawless were there not a murder overshadowing everything. All that was visible from the crime scene now was the orange tape that was extended almost up to the terrace, but Olivier was certain that the appearance of Léa's battered face would not be far from his mind for a long time to come.

A tray of champagne glasses was brought out, and Jacques dutifully poured. The *pièce de résistance*, though, was the native cheese, *cendré*, that Mimi brought out on a tray. Olivier thought the cheese, refined in ashes, and a little like a brie, was one of the great treasures of the area. He put some on bread, and took a bite, and was transported back in time to his childhood when he had spent weekends with his grandparents. He accepted a serving of the grape tart, and noticed that only he and Max were indulging themselves. It spoke volumes about her, and he decided he would like to cook for her.

Thomas Girard said, "I must excuse myself. Monsieur Dupuis is arriving soon."

Geneviève was passing the door, a small suitcase in her hand, which Olivier took from her. "Madame Durand, we didn't have a chance to get to know each other. I have to go into Paris tomorrow and wonder if I might stop by."

They were at Jacques' car. "I don't know," she said, looking flustered. "I have appointments."

"It would be for a short time."

"I don't think so."

"It would be better to meet there than the interrogation room in Epernay, don't you think?"

She stood still, pursing her lips. "In that case, alright."

"Good. I'll see you around two." Jacques came forward and lifted the suitcase into the trunk of the car. She opened the passenger door and once inside, slammed it shut, not bothering to look back.

Chapter Eleven

Max was surprised when Olivier invited her to go into Paris with him to pay a call on Geneviève. He asked her not to reveal the purpose of the trip, which made her think this could be a test run to see if they could work together. She scratched a few reminders in her journal: Practice discretion. Prudence. Patience.

The sky was overcast, and she picked up her short, black trench coat as she left the room. Ted had taken the train into the city the day before, and it might be possible to check in with him. She realized that she was excited to have a day in the city that she loved passionately—and left behind eight years ago. I have a grandmother there, she thought, whom I've never met. One day.

Jacques was in the dining room having coffee, and Max joined him. Marie-Christine entered from the kitchen. She had circles under her eyes. "I've had no sleep," she said. "I barely know what I'm doing."

Jacques reached over and took her hand, which Max could see surprised her. "I received back the report on the Durands," he said. "Especially Madame Durand."

Marie-Christine's eyes popped open. "What did it say?"

"Not as much as I had hoped. Madame Durand moved to Paris in 1980, and studied at the École de la Chambre Syndicale de la Couture, the school that turns out the most skilled seamstresses and tailors in the country. Within five years she had listed herself as designer and had a small shop, where she sewed suits and other items for women. Marc was born six months later in 1981. There is no father listed on the birth certificate."

"Most of this we know. Why wouldn't she have listed the father, I wonder?"

Max understood where Chloé got her naiveté. It made her feel like a seasoned old broad around the mother and daughter. Did wealth create ignorance of evil, she wondered. Hadn't the high stone wall surrounding the Marceau property succeeded for many generations to do just that? Until now. The family had invited a sick mind to move among them. That someone had driven through the portal in the wall and shared meals with them, and listened to their stories. To Max that scenario was more horrifying than the nasty street killers she targeted in New York.

"Maybe the father refused to accept her claim that the child was his," Jacques said. He sipped his coffee, and leaned back, sharing more of the story. "Geneviève was quite fashionable and beautiful in an odd way. Men were drawn to her. In 1990 she became involved with the man who is now Minister of Justice, Philippe Douvier."

Max dropped her spoon and bent down to pick it up, hoping she wasn't showing the shock that she was feeling.

"They were lovers for nine years. He left her last year."

"*Incroyable!*" Marie-Christine said.

"Why so shocked? This isn't unusual. Look at Mitterand, for god's sake."

"Still. To be with someone of that caliber. It must have put her in the center of politics."

"Oh, I get it, you're impressed," Jacques teased. "I thought you were being morally indignant."

"Well, that too." He laughed, and her lips turned up in a smile. Max wondered if he had confessed about Léa, and the relief was so great that they had made up. She hoped so.

Max's mind was racing. Geneviève had slept with her friend Ted, and she had been her uncle's mistress. Max wondered if she being morally indignant, or if it was it all too close to home.

She wanted to talk to her mother. Hélène, the wife of Philippe Douvier, was her sister, after all.

Jacques said to Max, "Don't you have some uncle with an important position in Paris?"

Max tried to appear casual. "By marriage, and I don't know him. My mother and her sister don't speak.

"It's a pity, but more common than we realize. You're off to Paris with Olivier? What's he doing there?"

Marie-Christine perked up. "Paris?"

"He has to get clothes, and see Monsieur Reynard on the way back."

Jacques sat up, interested. "Reynard means fox in French. The man is appropriately named. He wants to announce an arrest as soon as possible. You will find that he and Olivier don't get along well, though they are from the same school. The same club, you might say. Both are *magistrats*, only in different positions. The prosecutors have more power now than they ever have before, and Olivier will chafe under that. Be prepared."

"Thanks for the warning."

He turned to his wife, "Do you think a man would find Max intimidating?"

"What a question. What men find intimidating is power and power and power. And maybe beauty."

Jacques, looking stunned, was about to reply when a light tapping on the door stopped him. Olivier entered and shook hands with Jacques, and kissed Chloé, who had just wandered in before him. "*Ça va?*" he asked.

"I finally slept," she said, taking the chair beside her father, who put his arm around her.

Olivier turned to Max and she stood and slipped her feet into black sandals with low heels. "We'll be back at the end of the day," Olivier said. Max turned to give her finger wave, and felt self-conscious all of a sudden. The trio sat at the table, transfixed. The door hadn't closed behind them when Marie-Christine said, "Was that why you were asking me if I found Max intimidating, Jacques?"

Max felt the blood rush to her face.

They had gone a few steps when Olivier asked, "Should I be intimidated?"

"You didn't hear the first part of the conversation, and I'm not going to tell you." He laughed.

Once in the car, Olivier turned to business. "Madame Durand did a good job of remaining aloof from all the chaos of yesterday, which made me curious. This visit is unofficial."

"But you want to unnerve her, right?"

"I'm waiting to see. It piqued my curiosity that the owner of the inn told the local police chief that she and Marc had had a fight before the wedding."

Max thought that didn't sound unusual, with all the tensions mounting before the big day. So far nothing had come across as blatantly unusual, and yet everything was. Why was Léa sitting on a bench in the moonlight waiting for Ted, instead of waiting inside, or going home on her own? Had someone heard her tell Ted where she would be and followed her? Or had she agreed to meet someone? And why was Jacques in his room with a bottle of brandy and his shirt hanging over his pants. When she knocked and entered, had he just killed Léa? How odd that the maid stumbled over Léa's body. Did she witness Antoine running from the scene? And what about Antoine thinking that someone who almost knocked him over considered killing him? It had seemed true when he told her, but now it sounded like madness. Should she share these thoughts with Olivier? She decided not to. They weren't even close to being partners, the way she and Joe had been. It took a while to trust.

"Girard told me that your explanation for me being in your room was that you were quite ill and that I had walked you to your room."

"Oh. Yeah."

"What changed your mind? I had accepted that you were right and that the truth should prevail."

"My decision to lie was selfish. I didn't want everybody thinking me a slut."

"I see. I thought you did it to protect me."

Their conversation felt like the most subtle flirtation she'd ever engaged in. So subtle that she wasn't sure if it was that at all. Maybe he was just being his pedantic self. She would volley one more comment back at him.

"Why would I do that?"

She hadn't realized until he smiled that he had a dimple.

Geneviève lived at 38 rue des Saint-Pères, in the Sixth Arrondissement on the Left Bank. It was a few blocks from where Max had shared an apartment with Chloé. Jacques had already rented the apartment for Chloé, and insisted that Max's parents only pay tuition. It was a chic area, which Max hadn't appreciated at the time.

Olivier entered the code on the building's main door, which Geneviève had given him when he called to confirm their appointment. Once the door buzzed, they walked into a quiet, inner courtyard. Olivier led the way to the small elevator that took them to the third floor, where Geneviève stood in the doorway, her dark hair encircling her face. Max thought the casual hair made her look younger, not that forty-six was ancient by any means.

The entry room had a high ceiling, and as they followed Geneviève into her salon, the sun shone through lace curtains, creating a beautiful effect the way it highlighted the red and gold colors in the Oriental rug in the center of the room. It struck Max as the home of a cultured woman, albeit a cold one, with the baby grand piano in the corner and the paintings that ran from abstract to traditional landscapes arranged in orderly fashion on the white walls. A vase containing an impressive array of red roses was on the mantle. Max thought about her parents' apartment where they were lucky to afford a new sofa every ten years. Her mother was so elegant and yet never complained about not having enough money. She could easily have spent her life in such a place as this.

"You're fortunate to have a Bonnard drawing," Olivier said in English, walking over to have a closer look.

"It was given to me by a friend years ago," Geneviève said. Max wondered if it came from Philippe Douvier. "It's nice to have someone come in who appreciates art."

"I've attempted a few paintings of my own."

The guy is a Renaissance man, Max thought. And what I find intimidating is an intellectual who flies planes and paints and goes after politicians.

"I saw your parents' Paris apartment featured in *Maison Française*," Geneviève said. "The Renoir on their wall is magnificent. Few know that he spent much of his young adult life in the Champagne region."

"You seem to have a knowledge of, and a love for, our commune," he said. "I admired you for defending it at dinner the other night."

"Oh, that," she said. "I didn't intend to stir up a hornet's nest."

Oh, but you did, thought Max.

"I assumed from your passionate defense of the region that you must have come from there. I was in agreement with everything you said, by the way."

I know this tactic, Olivier Chaumont, Max thought. You have them thinking you're on their side, and build them up until they're saying things they never intended to let slip.

"I was really referring to all of France, all the places where the French are allowing foreigners to buy them out. Really, how many champagne companies are owned by original families anymore? Which reminds me….I'm being a bad hostess."

She walked over to a table upon which sat a crystal ice bucket containing a bottle of champagne. Max felt her mind wandering back to the cold ice bucket she had discovered soon after Léa had been found dead. She made a mental list of who had been in the vicinity—Antoine, Mimi, Ted, Hans, and maybe Jacques.

Geneviève handed Max a glass of champagne. "You prefer the *l'Etoile*?" Olivier asked, referring to the signature champagne of de Saint-Pern.

"To the Marceau's *Hortense*? I read Ted's blog and think he's on the mark. He likes the *Hortense*, which is dominated by the pinot noir grapes. Marc thinks de Saint-Pern should make a more robust champagne than the *l'Etoile*, and so he has already started experimenting."

"Is he working with their *chef de cave*, Monsieur Martin?"

"No, they don't get along very well. Monsieur Martin has been riding on the wave of success created by the *l'Etoile* for a long time, and doesn't want any interference. I'm maybe speaking out of turn, but he should be thoroughly questioned about some of his shady business moves. Marc said that Léa knew he was in bed with Monsieur Dupuis."

"I appreciate the information. It brings up my reason for being here. I know you gave a statement to the police, but I want to be a bit more thorough." She eyed him warily, and told him to continue. "I'm intrigued by your relationship with Monsieur Ted Clay."

"We became lovers when the man I was with and I separated briefly and remained friends. As for my son's wedding night, I was on an anti-anxiety medication at the wedding and after toasting with the champagne, I felt too dizzy to walk home alone. Ted was gracious enough to volunteer to escort me."

"I thought Marc implored him to walk you home."

"Oh, what difference does it make?"

"Do you recall the time?"

"No."

"Ted stayed longer than he intended at the inn because you needed help getting undressed."

She gave Olivier a surprised look. "Is that what he said? Actually, he left so fast he forgot his jacket. I have it here."

Hank was right, Max thought. She's going to get revenge for any rejection she may have experienced.

"Ted told you about the baby on your drive out to Champagne."

She answered in a whisper, and Max recalled how she had placed her hand on Olivier's arm when they conversed at the wedding dinner. "Ted confided in me that he was unhappy about the baby and he was upset that Léa wasn't going to list a father on the birth certificate. If you ask me, she had no intention of marrying him. At the same time, she was insisting that they move to California. They'd been arguing about it for days. He had also run out of the money Léa had lent him."

Lies and more lies! The words screamed inside Max's head. Yet the longer she listened the more she began to wonder if there was a semblance of truth running through Geneviève's story. Guilt took over for allowing a doubt to arise.

Geneviève took the bottle out of the bucket and started to refill Olivier's glass but he declined. Max held her glass up for more, and watched Geneviève pour. She seemed to struggle with the weight of the bottle. Max felt like suggesting that she invest in weights. The bucket of ice and champagne near the murder scene surfaced in her mind, and then disappeared.

"May I please use *les toilettes?*" she asked. Geneviève got up and led the way down the hall and pointed to a door.

"May I ask why you're here?" Geneviève asked. "Marc said you're a detective of some kind?"

"That's my job in New York. But I'm not on this case."

"But you're friends with Ted."

Forget prudence and patience, Max thought. She hissed, "I don't know how you could think he'd kill anyone."

"He tried to strangle me once, Max. He'd had a lot to drink, and he flew into a rage. And it wasn't over anything big. Ask him. Marc was there and can also verify this."

She recalled Ted getting into a brawl once on Ninth Avenue after drinking too much in a bar, but it hadn't left a big impression. His father, she knew, had beaten Ted and his two brothers, but he had only brought it up a couple of times in all the years they had known each other. But there it was: another second of doubt. Geneviève was Ted's only alibi, and now Max sensed Ted's chances of remaining above suspicion dissolving in front of her eyes.

Geneviève's stilettos striking on marble floor echoed until she was out of sight. Max waited until she heard her telling Olivier the same story about Ted attacking her, then dashed down the hall, and opened one of the closed doors and peered in. It had to be Geneviève's bedroom. It was all cool elegance, with a monochrome background. There were a few colorful accents like a red rose in a silver vase, and a red hat perched jauntily on a partition. Max hated it.

She stepped across quickly to look at the framed photographs that were hung in orderly fashion on the wall facing her bed. They were of Geneviève at a party, Geneviève announcing a new line of clothing, Geneviève on holiday holding the hand of a little boy of around seven. She exited Geneviève's room and went quietly to the next room, where the door was open. It was still decorated as Marc must have had it when he was growing up. Six airplane models covered a table pushed against the wall facing her. So another man with a passion for flying, she thought, recalling Olivier's excitement when he was in Hans' plane. Max leaned in closer to see the snapshot of Marc, Léa, and Chloé standing arm in arm in front of the imposing structure of the de Saint-Pern Champagne Company. She moved over to the desk, and aside from the book *The Little Prince* propped against the lamp, nothing was there except a receipt for the clothes Marc had rented for the wedding, with a note attached about the shoe exchanges.

Max re-entered the salon in time to hear Geneviève say to Olivier in a teasing voice, "If you keep this up, I'm going to call my lawyer. The answer is yes, we did have a mother-son argument, and if I yelled 'You'll end up with nothing,' then I'll have to wrack my brain to recall what the subject was. I think I was referring to his future inheritance from me, as I am in a terrible situation financially, and I had asked him to help me."

"He's only just started working. Is he able to do that?"

"He will eventually."

Olivier switched to French, speaking with compassion, "That must be difficult. You don't have…other assets?"

Geneviève's face grew bitter. "I am…was…the mistress to a very important person in Paris. Six months ago he abandoned me for reasons that I won't go into. I'm not ready to reveal his name just yet, but I could ruin him publicly. I gave him nine years, the last of my youth."

I know your dirty little secret, Max thought.

Max had never met her uncle, but he had been awful to her mother, encouraging his wife to never speak to her sister for making the choice she did. Geneviève's face hardened as she spoke and Max thought hers had not been a well-lived life, even with all the symbols of wealth surrounding her.

Chapter Twelve

Max pulled out her journal and wrote: Another question for future therapist: how do I avoid becoming a bitter and hostile woman at fifty?

"What's that?" Olivier asked. They were on their way to his apartment.

"I've always kept a journal. And detectives in New York carry some form of notebook. I brought this one to write about my trip, but it's also my homicide book. I'm just about to write about Geneviève."

"What's your impression about her character?"

"She's a lying bitch, and my hunch is she's not one bit sorry Léa is dead. You didn't believe any of that crap about Ted trying to strangle her, I hope." He thought he might be catching a glimpse of Max in detective mode, and it wasn't attractive in the least.

Max's rant continued, "My father was right. Geneviève is a woman scorned. Ted wouldn't let her seduce him and she's gonna make him pay. *Did* you believe her?"

"I didn't believe or disbelieve. I listen to all the stories and then I start making up my mind. Not until."

"She's not who she says she is. I'd bet my toy poodle on that. It's just a feeling I have about her. Her apartment, her life, none of it seems authentic to me."

"She was a single mother when it was extremely difficult to raise a child and work. You have to admit that there are some things to admire."

"She was a mistress. What's so hard about that? Other than the fact that you owe the man your soul. And your body. Pretty minor."

He felt his face flush. "Judgments aren't as harsh here about those things."

"Publicly they're not. But how do you think his wife feels?"

"When a woman like Geneviève is supported by her lover, the wife is usually aware. These people would prefer to keep the family together than divorce, and so an arrangement is made."

"Which makes me think of Marc. I wonder how he felt about it."

Olivier shrugged. "He seems to be well-adjusted. A little arrogant, perhaps. Children accept more than we give them credit for."

"I hope he doesn't lie like his mother."

"Your strong reaction may mean that she was perhaps a little convincing."

"Maybe. It's an intimate murder. I much prefer street crime."

"I don't know anything about that, but I see your point. Here we are with no murder weapon, no clues, and too many suspects. Probably in New York you would have the case sewn up."

"God, no. We go out of our minds with frustration over wrong turns and false leads. We work as a team though, and it expedites things."

"For example?"

"Jacques."

"Jacques?" He could see her struggling as to whether or not to tell him about his friend.

"This is in strict confidence. I'm sure you know that he and Léa had an affair five years ago after her husband was killed."

Olivier had heard the rumor but had thought it just that.

"When I went to tell him that Léa had been murdered, it was as if he already knew."

"I saw his shutters open and thought it odd."

"He said he had heard her shout *arrête*! and thought she and Ted were arguing, but he was so furious with her about the baby, and her selling out, that he poured another brandy instead of going to her assistance. Again, though he is implicating Ted, when it's quite possible that Jacques could have killed her."

Now Olivier felt reactive. "Motive?"

"The old saw. Unrequited love."

Mon dieu, he thought. She's an impossible romantic. She exudes compassion around Antoine, and practically accuses Jacques. He would have to warn Jacques away from confiding in her. He had barely gotten started with interviews and she was going from person to person and collecting secrets. He wanted to yell at her that she was taking over his job, but knew that wasn't it at all. He hated hearing about Jacques and Léa from her. He would never say it, but he was disappointed in Jacques, who had been a strong role model for him. Unrequited love! It sounded absurd!

He maneuvered his car into a parking space and led Max through narrow streets where she stopped in front of shop windows, exclaiming, unaware that he was quite unhappy.

"You don't agree with me about Jacques?" she asked.

"*Non.*"

"It's all supposition," she said. "This is what I mean about teamwork. We hash it all out, everything on our minds, and sometimes a solution pops up. I don't deep down believe he did it."

The thought of conducting an investigation in this manner was anathema to Olivier. Much too touchy-feely.

The steep climb didn't seem to affect her in the least. They came to a three-story, fourteenth century building, and he tapped a code into a box on a wall outside the wrought iron door. They stepped into a spacious courtyard where vivid flowers spilled over from huge urns. The concierge, one of a rare breed these days, stuck her head out and waved to Olivier, who continued on to a hidden elevator that three people could fit into. Max was wearing that gorgeous fragrance that he was still trying to figure out. She smiled at him, a little uncertain he could tell. But bold, always bold. That had to be her father's training.

Keys in hand, he led the way to an old wooden door and unlocked it. As they entered, he flicked on a light switch. He would miss the place, he thought, as he scanned the metal staircase that looked like a sculpture and the bookcases that went from floor to walkway above. A large white beam formed an arch over the room they stood in. Chairs were placed at odd angles around a small, black fireplace, over which hung a Warhol painting. Walking briskly through the dining room, he noticed Max surveying the metallic ceiling and copper table. She seemed duly impressed.

"Where the hell does all your money come from?"

The question jolted him. The French simply never discussed money. *Jamais.*

"This is a fairly modest place."

"You're probably a trust-fund baby. They abound in the U.S."

"I'm sorry. I have to make a call. Make yourself at home." He led her into the minimalist kitchen, where an eating bar protruded from an alcove.

"I feel like I'm in a *Star Trek* film," she said.

"Enjoy the adventure." He escaped quickly up the stairs to his bedroom, where he threw some clothes into a suitcase. When he returned, she was studying a framed photo of Véronique that was propped up against some books.

"No one should be this thin."

"You're right." He knew what it had taken for Véronique to become perfect for magazine covers. She was anorexic, with no breasts and no hips to speak of, and a recovering drug addict. But he wouldn't break her confidence.

"What's she like?"

"She works hard, actually. And she revels in her job. She went through a grim period when she was on drugs, which is how I know where to send Antoine, and she got through that. And yes, she's quite beautiful."

"Modeling is foreign to me."

"And police work would be for her, trust me. Enough talk about Véronique?" Max nodded, and followed him out.

"You're quite beautiful, too, you know. I forget that you're half French. Where did your mother grow up?"

"In Burgundy, I think."

"Perhaps one day you'll want to explore your French roots." They left the apartment and he announced that it was time for *déjeuner*. They walked to *l'Arpège*, a local restaurant where he was friends with the owner. A handsome, silver-haired man greeted Olivier warmly.

The waiter arrived with a *scampi carpaccio* with *oscietra* caviar and a dash of fine Japanese olive oil, one of Olivier's favorites. The white translucent raw scampi formed a rose, encircled by a thin line of sturgeon eggs that had a hint of gold on the surface. The sweetness of the shellfish versus the vivid salty flavor of the caviar expressed a dualism, which would reunite under the palate to form the most exquisite and perfect equilibrium. He looked over at Max, who seemed to be practically swooning, and smiled. There was nothing like the sensuousness of a great meal to remove all tension. They sipped on vintage champagne from the Joseph Perrier Company, *Joséphine,* a favorite in France."

"I hate to rush you," Olivier said after two hours, "but Monsieur Reynard is waiting. He can be impatient."

"I'll be thinking about that dish on my deathbed," Max said, and Olivier laughed at the exaggeration.

◇◇◇

Olivier had realized on the way back to the Valley that he was squeezing too much into one day, but the situation was urgent. Max hadn't seemed the least bit tired, and in fact appeared to be enthusiastic about everything they were doing. Reynard awaited them in Epernay, and Olivier debated about taking Max in to meet him. Today had been a trial to see if she could cooperate.

He explained about the culture of the *magistrats*, pointing out that the French magistrate was employed by the state and was put in charge of the most difficult criminal investigations, while the *procureurs* were directly under the power of the Ministry of the Interior and were sometimes compromised in their decisions because the Minister was the one who recommended promotions.

"Which sets up competition, right?

"It can." Max was child-like in her enjoyment when entering the Valley of the Marne. He had always secretly thought it like entering a magical kingdom. The light from the chalk fields highlighted the emerald fields that stretched as far as the eye could see.

"It's the chalky soil that gives our area a hazy appearance," Olivier explained. He pointed out the giant statue of Pope Urban II who had his hand up in a blessing or a greeting, and Max said she'd like to go up in it another day. They drove past the champagne companies lining the Avenue de Champagne in the capital. "The Marceau Company is down that way," Olivier said. "They give wonderful tours of the *caves* far below. It's a custom for family members to start out giving tours in their teens. I hope you get to go."

◇◇◇

"Mademoiselle is a detective with the NYPD and is writing an article for a small paper about our investigative system," Olivier said to the chief prosecutor. He was surprised to find himself lying about her role, and realized that he wasn't comfortable thinking of her as part of the team. "I thought of you immediately, with all your expertise on the subject." A quick glance at Max told him that she knew why he was dissembling. Reynard looked pleased from the flattery, and offered them seats in his office."

"It's a pleasure, detective," he said. "I know that your police are not encumbered by judges overseeing an investigation, so this should be quite different." He seemed happy trying out his English, and soon the two were engaged in a conversation about the French judicial system. Olivier had noticed that almost everyone Max talked to immediately started jabbering in English, no matter how few words they knew, barely giving her a chance to speak French.

Max fed back to Reynard exactly what Olivier had just explained to her, and he was won over by her intelligence. Reynard explained to Max that he had to discuss something private with Monsieur Chaumont, and she stepped outside.

"I'm handing this case to you," Reynard said, "but I have some concerns. Your attendance at the wedding could be perceived as a conflict of interest, though Girard assures me that you are only acquainted with Jacques Marceau. As he is a leading figure in the area, it would be difficult to find someone who hadn't made his acquaintance. I spoke at length with Captain Canon, and later with Commissaire Girard about the American Ted Clay, and suggest you focus on him. I think it odd that he went to Detective Maguire's room to report the crime, don't you?"

"I believe they're old friends."

"Still. They could be in collusion and then you'll have a real mess on your hands."

"I'm aware of that."

"I'm not completely convinced that there is no conflict of interest, but Minister Douvier has approved. In my mind this is a case for the égendarmerie, and I'm worried that Captain Canon doesn't hold you in high regard."

"Nor do I respect someone who makes lewd remarks about a dead woman's body. Which I plan to put in a report if I need to."

Already a stand-off, Olivier thought.

"The press is all over this, and I will handle that for now. I want it stressed that there are to be no leaks."

Olivier had high regard for many of his colleagues, but he hated being grouped with the likes of Reynard, one of those people who would stop at nothing to get ahead. Reynard had managed to ace the competitive examination they all had to take to enter the *École nationale de la magistrature* (ENM), where a law graduate is transformed into a *magistrat*. What bothered Olivier most about the man, he realized, was that the education process made people like Reynard the new nobility, replacing the nobility of blood of the *ancien régime*, of which he himself was a member.

Reynard had worked hard, Olivier knew, first as a *substitut du procureur* in a small court, and moving up to *procureur* in the Champagne commune. But what Olivier also knew was that Reynard's climb up involved all kinds of chicanery and subter-fuge, and thus Olivier didn't trust him. For his part he was ready to thwart the unscrupulous climber without a backward glance when the time came, although he would have to be exceedingly careful in doing so.

Olivier knew that Reynard envied him his heritage and was a little in fear of the reputation he had acquired over the years for boldly calling out public figures for their crimes. Olivier had held to an ethical code that had cost him in some ways, but it had also increased the respect people like Girard had for him. He was glad when it was time to leave. Max was standing in front of a retail champagne shop, and waved. She dashed over.

"You don't like him, do you?"

"I don't trust him. He's too ambitious." They were in the car, and heading back to Sourières. "The case is mine, though, and that's what counts."

"I'm glad to know why I'm here. The article I'm writing?"

"Oh, that."

Max's presence felt distracting all of a sudden. She was a keen observer and had gotten people to confide in her, but he could do that, too. He could actually force them if he wanted to.

"Actually, why *are* you here?"

She shot him a surprised look. "Because I'm a damn good investigator. And I'm taking this murder personally, which might make me even better."

"How old are you?"

"Twenty-nine."

"And you started late. How much experience does that entail?"

Her eyes became slits again, as her eyebrows shot up, and she folded her arms across her chest. "I'll have my resumé faxed over."

"Abdel took care of that."

She went quiet, which surprised him, and made him uncomfortable. After ten kilometers, she spoke. "I think I should work solo from now on, Olivier. And no one will even know that I'm snooping. I don't need to be competitive. I'll send you a report of any findings as often as you want, but I'm not returning to the states until this case is solved."

That wasn't what he wanted. Or was it?

"I'm not used to team work, Max. Abdel is the first time I've worked with someone steadily, and it took a long time for us to understand each other. I will give it a try with you." The words had come out in a begrudging tone, he knew.

"I can tell that isn't your first choice. I'll stay solo."

While the atmosphere in the car wasn't tense, Olivier felt on edge. She had grown quiet again. But when she spoke next, he wished she hadn't opened her mouth.

"Oh, I forgot to tell you what Jacques told me this morning. The man who was Geneviève Durand's, shall we say, 'benefactor' for nine years, is the Minister of Justice, Philippe Douvier."

The news came as a thunderbolt out of the sky. *The man who was head of all the magistrates in France had as his mistress a potential suspect in his case?* A sense of fear, doom, Olivier didn't know what to call it, fell over him.

Chapter Thirteen

"And he's my uncle," Max wanted to say, but stopped herself. That information could jeopardize her uneasy status among these magistrates, police, and soldiers, and besides, she didn't even know her uncle. She thought Olivier had been shocked at her announcement about Douvier, but he hadn't said a word. He had become impossible to read, like many other introverts she knew. She also thought it was a little more challenging for him to separate the tender moments they had shared from the work at hand. She was a pro at it because of the time spent with Joe. No matter, she was in a precarious position, where she could end up a scapegoat like Ted. She wasn't playing games when she told Olivier she'd prefer to work solo. He needed space, and so did she.

As if he had read her mind, Olivier said, "I hope you don't mind that I'm not talking."

"I'm grateful."

She leaned her head against the headrest and closed her eyes. She had been on hyper-alert for most of the day, trying to be acutely aware of everything that was going on, the way her father had taught her, while at the same time making sure that she remained in the background.

Her thoughts drifted back to Geneviève's apartment and to the woman who in one sense had to be admired for her survival tendencies. Had she been banished from her family the way

Max's mother had been for being with the wrong man, or for having a child out of wedlock? Perhaps she was from an old, noble Champagne family and had lived autonomously all these years. On the other hand, she didn't hide a strong, vindictive streak.

Max decided she would ask Jacques if she could read the background report on Geneviève. They were getting close to home, and Max yawned. Olivier turned the music down. "I'll drop you at chez Marceau, and as I will be interrogating tomorrow morning early, you can have Jacques bring you to the office in Epernay. Or Commissaire Girard will be passing by and can pick you up."

She was duly annoyed by the reference to Girard, but didn't want him to know it. "I'll figure it out, thanks."

It had started to rain, and she stared out the window and thought about the condensation on the outside of the chilled ice bucket that she had touched. The line-up of champagne buckets popped into her mind. She had a fleeting image of Geneviève bringing out the champagne in a crystal ice bucket. She understood what Antoine had been referring to when an image was right there, and then became elusive before any meaning could be made of it.

Another image of the kids in the forest beyond the fence entered her thoughts. And remained. They had been been drunk. Chloé had been in a hurry to get home and had pulled her away before she could satisfy her curiosity. What were four children doing getting drunk in broad daylight?

"Olivier!"

"*Quoi?*" She had startled him out of his own reverie.

"There was an ice bucket among the many on the table that still had ice in it, and an unopened bottle of champagne. I took Abdel to see it, but someone had taken it away."

"I don't understand anything. You're speaking too fast."

He entered the Marceau property. The green lawn of a couple of days ago looked swampy with the soggy grass and bent-over peonies. Dark clouds hovered overhead.

"Okay, there was an ice bucket on the reception table near the crime scene that I figured someone had brought down for a rendezvous with either Léa or someone else. I have been haunted by it."

He glanced over at her, an impatient look on his face. "And?"

"Yesterday morning, remember, Chloé and I went through the gate to the other side of the forest toward the river. There were some kids behaving strangely. I know now they were drunk." She wanted to switch to French, but that would have become another issue after all of her denial. "I'm going down there because I have a hunch."

She opened the door and started walking through the grass, stopping to step out of her shoes.

"Your raincoat is here. Your clothes…"

"Never mind. I think I know where the murder weapon is."

She saw him pause, and then he was following her. Her heart was pounding, for it was her first "aha!" moment. Her father said he lived for those, the way a writer lived to have the perfect *dénouement*. She stopped at the gate. Locked! Jacques must have started locking it after the murder. She thought she could climb over, but what about Olivier? He was was upon her, "This is ridiculous. I will go to Jacques and get the key."

"I'm going ahead. If you tell them, then they'll all come running, and what if you're right and I'm completely on the wrong track and they'll think I'm crazy?"

"You're worried about *that*?"

She had climbed up the four-foot wall by sticking her toes into crevices the way she did at her gym in New York, and wrapping her hands around the top of the ornate gate and hoisting herself up. Olivier stood staring up at her.

"You'll have to take your shoes off," she said. "You can put your toes in where I put mine."

He stepped out of his loafers and dropped his trench coat, and started climbing up, sliding down twice and yelling "*putain!*" three times before he managed to pull himself up. "I could have the police do this," he said.

Max was crawling under the dense brush, in the ungroomed part of the estate, in the same vicinity where she and Chloé had seen the boys. Olivier yelled something, but a loud clap of thunder drowned him out. She shrieked, and he demanded to know what was wrong.

"I'm terrified of thunderstorms," she admitted. Thunder clapped again and a streak of lightning split dark clouds above their heads. Max could barely see Olivier for the veil of rain pouring in front of her face.

He grabbed her arm. "This is dangerous. I'm going to call in the police."

She stood up, water dripping from her hair into her eyes. "No! I know it's here!"

"Here includes an entire forest!" he yelled. The area they were in was much larger than she had originally thought. She knelt down and moved through the tall grass, moving her hands around on the ground. The boys had been close to the wall, she recalled, and she went in that direction.

Olivier said in a fake calm voice, "Max. Explain."

She told him the story between her startled shouts each time it thundered. "The ice bucket was there. I think whoever killed Léa took the full bottle of champagne from the bucket and clobbered her with it, put it back and ran from the scene. Between the time I went to Antoine's and returned, the murderer had snuck back in, taken the bottle, and run through the gate, which has never been locked until now, tossing the unbroken bottle into the woods. I saw these kids who were drunk in the woods when I walked with Chloé yesterday and they ran when I showed up. What if that's the bottle?"

"Okay," he said, as though he were calming a person who was about to jump off a ledge. "We're going to the house to bring in the police with searchlights. And you can return with them."

Like hell, she thought. "You go."

"But you're afraid. You can't stay here alone." He was growing frustrated again.

She stood her ground for another moment, then started toward the gate, bedraggled and defeated, kicking the underbrush as she went. Olivier was now leading the way, both of them soaked through to the skin. Still barefoot, her toe hit something and she stumbled and almost fell.

"OW!"

Olivier turned back to her, as if to say, what now? She bent down and saw the empty champagne bottle. Affixed to it was the special label Jacques had ordered for the wedding: *Pour le mariage de Chloé Marceau et Marc Durand. Le 21 Juin.* They both stared and then Olivier said, "We don't want any extra fingerprints on it." He took off his shirt and picked up the bottle with it. "Let's go," he said.

Not even a "thank you" or "kiss my ass," Max thought.

Max was undeterred. She knew what it was, and she had been right to pursue her hunch. She felt great. They were at the gate, and Olivier stood back while she climbed over first. She took the bottle, cradled in the shirt, and waited for him to pull himself up and over, which seemed to take an eternity. The rain had let up. Olivier limped slightly, and it struck her that his state of dishevelment made him look sexy. She smiled as he approached, ready to celebrate, but he simply said, "I need to find my shoes."

"Oh, they're over here." She skipped over and picked them up and handed them to him. He had taken the bottle back, still wrapped in his shirt. "You do think this find is significant, don't you?"

"I don't speculate. We'll have it tested for fingerprints for sure."

"I speculate about everything. First, there was the feeling of the cold ice bucket. And it locked into my subconscious. Then the kids who were drunk. That stuck. I watched Geneviève struggle with the weight of the champagne bottle when she took it out of her ice bucket, but even more than that I couldn't get the crystal bucket out of my head. And I thought, wait, those bottles are made out of super thick glass. I've read that they're indestructible. They probably don't break easily, at least not if they're whacked against somebody's face. Even when people pound them against ships, a lot of them don't break. I began to speculate, what if…what if…"

They had arrived at his car, and he opened the door and placed the bottle on the seat, along with his shoes, then turned and looked at her. "I want to get this to the forensics lab right away."

"May I come?"

He stared at her askance. "I don't see any reason, and you'll catch cold if you don't get dried off soon."

I wonder what he's like at Christmas, she thought. She had just found the murder weapon, she had shared most of what she knew with him, and she felt like more of an outsider than when she had started.

"I have a mother," she said, and walked toward the house. Once in her room, she stripped and took a hot shower, then sat down and made notes in her journal. She wrote about her intense frustration at Olivier's condescension, and then his rejection when she wanted to go with him. She wrote down everything she could remember from the hour or so spent at Geneviève's. And she recorded the brief time spent at Claude Reynard's. She wrote about finding the murder weapon, then placed the journal on the bedside table. The family must be gathering in the salon by now. She slipped into skinny black pants and a shirt, and, picking up the journal, scrawled in big letters: To hell with Olivier Chaumont.

Hans Keller and Marc were playing chess in the far corner of the salon, and Chloé was reading a magazine when Max entered. "You're here at last! We were getting worried."

"We thought you'd been swept away by a French cowboy," Hans said.

"I'm surprised to see *you*," Max said.

"I have to be interrogated tomorrow, and what I have to say will cause an explosion I think you say in English."

Her ears perked up.

Marc looked up from the chess board, "My mother said that you and Olivier paid a social call that wasn't a social call?"

"Olivier thought a change of scenery would be nice for me."

"Aha!" Marc's didn't take his eyes off her. "How considerate of him."

Max smiled. "Your mother and Olivier were in conversation and I was having a hard time keeping up, so I nosed around. I went into your room, with all the airplane models and photographs."

"It was a passion for most of my childhood."

"I can teach you to fly," Hans said. "My interest in it came from my father."

"My father's dead, so okay, I'll take you up on your offer."

Max was surprised, as she knew Marc's father's identity was a mystery, but no one had said he was dead.

Marc changed the subject. "Ted called, by the way. Olivier is also interrogating him tomorrow, and he's staying at the Oiseau Inn for the night."

And Ted isn't invited here to dinner, but Hans Keller is? Max thought.

Hans got up, "Marc and I are going to the local bar later. Care to join us? Chloé said she'd come if you came."

Max accepted readily. What she had almost said to Olivier before he could see no reason for her to go with him was that she wanted a drink. Not a little glass of champagne with the family, but a fat glass of red wine, or maybe even a tequila.

"Sure."

◇◇◇

Le Bar was a classic village hangout, where the farmers stopped in mid-morning to have a *Pernod* or a *vin blanc*, and where a few unexceptional dishes were offered up for lunch and dinner. Max, in jeans and cowboy boots, was happy to be away from the pall that hung over the house. She had come to the conclusion over dinner that Marie-Christine and Jacques were simply too weary to say no to Marc's request to have Hans Keller to dinner, though she could tell that Chloé was not happy about what was going on. Max secretly thought there was a good chance that Keller had killed Léa and was a sociopath who could carry on as though nothing were amiss. She hoped that after she and Chloé had imbibed a couple of drinks that they could find a place to talk. She glanced at her watch and was surprised to see that it was ten o'clock.

She climbed in the car with Marc, Chloé, and Hans. They stood in the center of the dimly lit room for a minute and allowed their eyes to adjust. Peering out from a corner was Olivier, who raised his brandy glass when he caught Max's eye.

I wasn't the only one in the mood for a drink, she thought. The second thought was upon her before she could waylay it: the bastard could have invited me.

The others had moved up to the small bar. Marc asked her what she wanted.

"The forensics special," she replied, making sure Olivier could hear her.

Marc looked puzzled.

"What the magistrate is having. A brandy."

Olivier walked over. "I've had a chance to think about our discovery."

Our discovery. Nice.

"And I'm now convinced that we have the murder weapon." She could barely hear him he was speaking so low. Marc came up to them with her drink and handed it to her.

"Oh, you're a fan of brandy?" Olivier asked her, one eyebrow perched higher than the other.

"Sure am."

Which means I've drunk it twice in my life.

"That's impressive." She took a sip and felt the narrowest imaginable streak of heat race laser-like to her belly button.

A loud scuffling from the doorway got their attention. Max ran toward the commotion and saw two people going at it, both tall, both slender, both fair-haired—one German and one American.

Chapter Fourteen

Max grabbed Hans' right arm and brought it up behind him. When he turned with a vengeance on his assailant, ready to hit with his left fist, the shock of seeing Max threw him off guard. He lost his momentum and staggered, falling clumsily onto a chair. For a suspended moment, Olivier, like everyone else in the bar, stood transfixed.

Hans quickly picked himself up. "You bitch!" he yelled, shaking her off and looking around to see who had witnessed him being overpowered by a woman. "You'll pay for this!"

Olivier, feeling slightly out of his element as an enforcer, stepped in and quietly commanded Hans to sit at a nearby table, then switched his attention to Ted, who was doubled over and gasping. Max was standing over him, and obviously knew what she was doing as she checked for injuries. Olivier called Abdel, and told him to come to the bar immediately, then announced to the bar patrons that they should remain for a short time, as the police needed witnesses.

Chloé and Marc were at the bar, where Marc's hand was wrapped in a towel. Olivier went over and asked Marc what had happened. Marc spoke quickly, the adrenaline still pulsing, "It all happened so fast. Monsieur Clay attacked Monsieur Keller, and I jumped in to help Max."

Chloé interjected, "I saw Hans say something to Ted, but didn't hear what it was. Then Ted reacted."

Max joined them. "Ted should go to the hospital," she said. "I think his jaw is broken. He's bleeding from the mouth, and there's a sizeable lump on his jaw. He also seems to be having difficulty breathing properly."

"Does he need an ambulance?"

"I didn't mean to hit him that hard," Marc said.

Max reached for the drink she had left on the bar, took a sip, then said, "According to Ted, Hans Keller accused him of murdering his fiancée, and added that he had no intention of taking the blame."

It occurred to Olivier that it would be convenient for just about everyone if Ted was proven to be the murderer. The Marceaus—Jacques and Marie-Christine, Chloé and Marc—would be far wealthier now than they had ever dreamed of being, and that wealth would more than likely end up coming from Hans Keller. Geneviève Durand would also benefit, with her son ensconced in the company and able to support her, and Antoine could continue on as he had always done. For a fleeting moment, Olivier didn't like any of them, and a second later chastised himself for his cynicism. What brought relief, however, was the realization that a murder case never unfolded exactly as expected and the outcome that seemed completely obvious was rarely correct. In Ted Clay's case, people needed a target, and he was looking like the perfect scapegoat.

"Neither of you should have reacted in the way you did," Olivier said. "Technically, all of you could be arrested for assault."

The door swung open and Abdel entered, followed by the village police chief, Petit. Olivier suspected that a patron had called him. After all, it was a small village where everyone knew everyone. Petit nodded to a couple of the patrons as he surveyed the room. His eyes rested on Ted, holding an ice pack to his face.

"Looks like a hell of a lot more than a minor altercation. Should I call anyone?"

"It's related to the de Saint-Pern case," Olivier said quietly. Petit nodded, then lumbered over to the table where the locals had gathered and took a seat.

"Then you don't need me. But I'll be at the bar if you do."

Olivier instructed Abdel to take a statement from Hans Keller. Olivier had overheard Hans saying that he was going to make sure the American detective paid for the injury she had caused.

"Make sure Monsieur Durand gets a drink on me for saving my life," Hans yelled to the bartender. Olivier looked over and Chloé rolled her eyes. "Can we go?" she mouthed to him, and he nodded. It was obvious that Marc was on the verge of being inebriated. Chloé said something to him, he shook his head, but she whispered in his ear, and he smiled and took Chloé's hand and she led him out. He's lucky to have her, Olivier thought.

Though it was difficult for him to speak, Ted confided in Olivier. "I know they're all thinking I killed her. Even the Marceaus. They didn't invite me to dinner, but they had that sociopath Keller at their table?" Olivier secretly agreed, but said nothing.

"We're going to get you to the hospital," Olivier said. "I'll have a gendarme posted there for security purposes." He made eye contact with Abdel, who indicated that his interview with Hans was over. At midnight, just when Olivier was starting to experience relief that he and Abdel had managed the fracas without the police or gendarmes involved, Commisssaire Girard walked in wearing jeans and a t-shirt, and made a beeline to the local table now also inhabited by Max.

Olivier glanced at Abdel, who shrugged ever so slightly as if to say he hadn't informed his boss that he was here. After greeting those gathered at the table, Girard ambled over and they shook hands. Not until then had Olivier noticed a slight swagger in his walk.

"Pierre there called me," Girard said, pointing to a man at the table with Petit. "Everything under control?"

A burst of laugher from the local table distracted them for a second, and they glanced over to see that Petit was being entertained by Max, who was trying to tell a story in French, gesticulating as she did so. She's incorrigible, Olivier thought. Was this payback for not bringing her with him to the bar? Or was it her crime-solving technique to connect with everyone of importance to the case? So far she had Girard, Petit, and he would even say the chief prosecutor, Reynard, in her corner. He wondered if this method worked as well in her personal life. Certainly not as far as he was concerned.

As though reading his mind, Ted said, "They all fall for her, but she doesn't allow anyone in."

Abdel escorted Hans out to the car to be taken to the hospital. Max came over. "I didn't abandon you, Ted, though that may be what you're thinking. Trust me, I'm doing everything I can to help you."

"Could have fooled me."

"Swear to me that you're innocent before I stick my neck out for you."

"Good god," he said. "I swear."

Girard and Petit joined them, "I'll take *les Américains* to the hospital and then drive Max back to the Marceaus'," Girard said.

He calls her Max, thought Olivier.

Girard, Olivier noticed, had taken on the guise of the stereotypical American detective. Much less formal than the French. "That works. I'll finish up with Petit, and see everyone tomorrow."

Max joined them. "I can stay if you want to go over everything," she said to Olivier.

I refuse to compete, he thought, but he said, "Go and be with your friend."

"You're a jackass. *Un crétin.*" She wheeled around to follow Girard out.

Only the bartender, Olivier, and Petit remained. "Want another brandy?" the bartender asked. Without waiting for a response, he pulled a bottle of *Courvoisier* from behind him and poured one for Olivier and another for Petit.

"I've heard of you for years," Petit said. "I understand that Sarkozy has it in for you after you went after him for corruption when he was the Minister of the Interior."

Olivier smiled to acknowledge the compliment, then asked if there was a witness among the patrons. "The locals blame the

German," Petit said. "But since he spoke in English to Monsieur Clay, no one seems to know what really happened. A lot of conjecture."

"Anything else?"

"Not related to the fight. But one of the patrons said that Antoine told him he knows who killed Léa de Saint-Pern and he's going to prove it."

Olivier would pay a call on Antoine and see if there was any truth to the rumor. He thanked the police chief and told him to come to him anytime with information. They shook hands and Petit departed

"Do you live here?" Olivier asked the bartender.

"All my life. My name's Michel."

"What's the talk about Madame de Saint-Pern?" The bartender's head jerked up and Olivier added, "Whatever you say is unofficial."

Michel hesitated. "Antoine Marceau was in here the night before the wedding claiming that he was thrown out of a dinner by his sister-in-law."

So that's where he went, thought Olivier.

"He practically predicted her death. Said she was selling out. He also said she was in dangerous waters dealing with the German."

"Did he stay long?"

"He left when Monsieur Durand came in with a very thin, dark-haired woman. Antoine told me she was Durand's mother."

"What time?"

"It was late. I was getting ready to close up."

"Did they stay long?"

"Marc Durand didn't. He ordered a brandy, but ran out before he finished it, looking upset. She came to the bar and ordered champagne, and asked me how old I was. I told her twenty-one, and she said she wished she could go back in time to when her son was that age. Then she asked me something very strange. She asked me if I would want to be told the identity of my father if I didn't know. I said I didn't think so."

◇◇◇

After a few hours of sleep, Olivier arose early and by eight was briskly entering Girard's office in Epernay. "Thanks for coming in," Girard said, indicating a chair, and pouring a cup of coffee for him from the machine in the corner. "I know you have a hell of a day ahead. Max was right, by the way. Monsieur Clay's jaw is broken. You should have seen her with him. Loving like a sister."

Girard, Olivier thought, was glad to have such a major case on his hands, with interesting characters that lifted him out of the ordinary day-to-day grind.

"Aren't these 'gentlemen'"—Girard put up two fingers of each hand to indicate quotation marks—"supposed to be civilized people?"

"I've never, quite frankly, found one class of people to be more civilized than another."

"Abdel told me about finding the bottle this morning. You could call Philippe Douvier and he'd pull some strings to put Max officially on our team. I'm sure we have reciprocity with the NYPD."

Olivier thought Girard was angling toward more communication with the American cop. He became more determined than ever to keep her at arm's length. "Let's not go there yet. I much prefer her being in an unofficial capacity."

"I don't want her to be an unsung hero. I hear she was impressive the way she tackled Keller last night."

Things had gone too far. Olivier gave him a hard stare and Girard straightened his shoulders and got down to business. "There are already some problems," Girard said. "It's the German, Keller. His arm is sprained. His defense lawyer, a woman who is acting half smitten with him, says that she needs to understand why an American woman was struggling with a German citizen in a French bar, and claims that Max should be arrested for assault."

"Neither the American detective nor Monsieur Durand thought before they acted. I'm worried that an altercation between two men is being turned into a scandal. Keller is an instigator. It makes me wonder what he's up to."

Girard leaned back in his chair. "Monsieur Clay was unable to control his rage, it seems. According to Abdel's report, he was the first to physically attack. Marc Durand gave me the details."

"But he was incited to do so by Keller, and that is the part that interests me. I don't believe his claim that Monsieur Clay said something first, because there wasn't time for such an exchange. There are witnesses that can verify this. I am concerned, though, that he might have grounds for accusing Detective Maguire of assault."

Girard's lips turned up slightly, "It would be my pleasure to go and arrest her."

So arrest me, she had said the night of the wedding when they were dancing and he told her it was against the law to threaten a judge. He had playfully taken her hand…

When Girard realized that a response from Olivier wasn't forthcoming, he said, "Let me ask you. What's a NYPD detective doing hanging out with aristocrats?"

Olivier wanted Girard on his side throughout the investigation, so in order to make that happen, the civil discourse they were engaging in was unnecessary. It was the French way. But Girard was lowering it to the gossip level and Olivier didn't have time for that. He stood up. "I don't know her personally. She's a friend of Chloé Marceau's. *C'est tout.*

Olivier could see that Girard knew he had overstepped a boundary when Olivier stood up, but it was clear that he had no idea which one. "I'll have Keller in your office within the hour. I allowed Bernard and Caroline Martin to leave without questioning them. The woman was driving me crazy. I couldn't get one straight answer from her, and the husband looked so weary I thought he might have a stroke."

Olivier nodded in understanding. "I'll bring them in."

"What about Monsieur Clay?"

"The hospital released Keller and kept Clay in for the night because his jaw is broken. Might need surgery." Bad news, thought Olivier.

Girard continued, "It's strange. He left Madame de Saint-Pern for half an hour to walk the groom's mother to the Oiseau Inn. They sat in silence. "Imagine for a moment if he hadn't left her."

"I have."

"Okay. Madame Durand backed up that he was with her, but she contradicts his statement that he remained in her room and put her to bed. Do you know anything about her?"

"I only just met the two of them." Olivier saw no need in confessing to having been at the family dinner the night before the wedding, nor would he dare mention the name of Philippe Douvier in conjunction with Geneviève.

"Marc Durand. Good son, I'd say. Maybe a little too much of a mama's boy, but I see that a lot with single parenting."

"He has latched on to Monsieur Keller. I'm not sure if Keller's a father figure, or if Monsieur Durand is being opportunistic. Chief Petit talked to the owners of the inn and they claimed that Marc and his mother had a fight just before the wedding. He'll have the details for you." Olivier didn't share the bartender's story about Marc leaving the bar upset the night before the wedding.

"Tensions build before a wedding, that's for sure."

"Madame de Saint-Pern was pregnant, and was planning to have the baby."

Girard's head jerked up. "*C'est terrible!* It was Monsieur Clay's?"

"I assume so."

"How did you know about it?"

Olivier felt caught. "My ex-wife knew Madame de Saint-Pern," he lied. "Could be a rumor for all I know."

"Such an upstanding family for all this tragedy." He stopped and looked at Olivier, "And you, I understand, were busy rescuing a damsel in distress while the murder was taking place?"

I have no idea what you're talking about."

"Max explained why you were in her room so late the night of the wedding."

Here goes the muckraking, Olivier thought, only Girard's out of luck because I know what happened.

"Said she was really sick with *la grippe* and that she was about to embarrass herself by throwing up all over the table, but you got her to her room before anything embarrassing happened. That was pretty decent of you."

"It's not exactly a knight in shining armor story."

"She thinks so." Girard barely hid a knowing smile. "I've never met a woman like her. Makes me glad I practiced my English. I love her stories about her dad. He's like the American actor Clint Eastwood."

Mon dieu, thought Olivier, he's not telling the story to reassure me, but to reassure himself. He's fallen for her.

"In what way?"

"Eastwood is known to take the law into his own hands in most of his films."

"I'd like to see the article about Detective Maguire's father."

Olivier left the room. Now that he had narrowly escaped *un petit scandale,* he wasn't sure that he hadn't rather be seen as a rake.

Chapter Fifteen

Max lay in bed and thought about the night at the bar. She had come in and written four pages in her journal after leaving Girard at two. He had come on to her on their way back to the house, telling her that he found her irresistible, and please, could she come to his house the following evening and allow him to make her dinner on the grill. He pronounced it *greele*. They conversed in one-quarter French and three-quarters English and in the end she thought they were both speaking gobbledy-gook. He had insisted on walking her to her room, but she put the kibosh on that the moment it was hinted at. He was a little too full of himself, Max thought, like a guy she knew named Joe.

Maybe I've gone overboard with the charm factor in my attempt to win over Girard and Petit, she thought. Hank Maguire often compared being a detective to acting. Try to inhabit your characters, whether friend or foe, he instructed his protégés. Max had become a pro at disarming a suspect with her quick smile, or a concerned question. She had won accolades for posing as a hooker or a teenager, or a thief. She thought it came from her theater background in public school, where she became known for her character parts. She had taken hip-hop lessons, too, and modern dance, during those years. When Frédéric was killed by a drunk driver, in her grief and rage she had turned to *jiu-jitsu*.

She met Ted a few months after her brother's death at New York University. She was drunk in a bar in the village and he had taken her home and she had cried all night. She and Ted made an agreement to keep their relationship platonic, though it was never an issue for her, for she was in no state to be in a relationship with anyone, and she knew it.

Ted came from a wealthy family in the Midwest who had lost their fortune during the tech stock bubble that burst in 2002. They had gone into one hundred percent tech stocks, which put a lot of people under. Ted had gone from wealthy college playboy to broke in a day. But he had pulled himself together and worked as a waiter to pay for his tuition. They eventually became roommates. They fought bitterly after graduation when she made the decision to enter the police academy. He pleaded with her to go with him to Paris to work on his newsletter. She had her mother's blessing, but in the end she couldn't leave Hank. Her mother had wept for days over Max's decision, but she knew what she was doing. Hank took her under his wing as he never had before, and she worked hard to replace her brother. Meeting up with Ted again, under these bizarre circumstances, had brought up her past, and with it, regrets. What if she had come with Ted and focused on the French part of herself? Was she some bifurcated person whose two sides would never come together?

Realizing that this case wasn't going to solve itself as she lay in bed reminiscing, she jumped up and took a quick shower. By seven she had greeted Mimi in the kitchen and joined Jacques in the salon, where he was having coffee. She told him about the altercation in the bar, and then asked him if she could use his car to go to the hospital to visit Ted, and from there to Hans Keller's interrogation.

"Of course. Is he a strong suspect?"

"I don't know what Olivier would say. Each person on the case has his strongest suspect. Ted is number one for most officials, I think."

"And you?"

"I'll be most interested in what Hans Keller has to say today."

Jacques smiled. "I see you're practicing discretion. Even with me." He hesitated, "I am surely a suspect. As is my brother."

Max nodded.

"I decided to come clean with Marie-Christine. She said she knew all along. We have a long way to go."

Hank's other advice came to Max's mind. Learn their secrets. "I'm glad."

"I hope Olivier hasn't been too unpleasant since I insisted that you be allowed in on the investigation."

So that was how it happened, Max thought. Olivier felt coerced.

"We're managing."

"He's very private. And he's been deeply wounded."

"I finally figured that out."

The door opened and Chloé appeared. "Come join Marc and me on the terrace." Max excused herself, picked up her coffee cup and headed outside.

"So tell us what happened with Girard," Chloé said. "What a night."

"Absolutely nothing. Let's not go there."

"Have you heard from Ted?"

"I'm going to the hospital. Your dad said I could use his car."

"I wanted to let you know how the family is feeling," Chloé said, looking uncomfortable. "We—my parents, Marc, maybe me—are not interested in getting to know Ted. I know he could be innocent, but with the amount of evidence that's against him, it's too much to ask us to befriend him."

Max had already come to that conclusion. "I'll have to work twice as hard to prove his innocence, then. If your decision is based on last night's fight, isn't it fair to say that everyone was behaving irrationally?"

Chloé nodded.

Marc leaned forward. "Are the authorities allowing you to investigate?"

Max looked at him with a steady gaze. It's none of your business, she thought. Maybe it was time to enter into performance mode. She laughed. "You have to be kidding! The French police want an American detective to join them? *Jamais!*"

Marc chuckled. "I think Girard would have allowed you in last night. He appeared to be quite smitten with you."

"Aren't they all?"

Good, she thought, when Marc laughed, they're disarmed. Especially Marc, who is a little nervous about me.

"Sorry about being so sharp with you in the bar, Marc."

Marc lit a cigarette. "It was stupid and I apologize. Hans and I had a bet going. I know Ted's your friend, but we were having fun at his expense, I admit it. I told Hans that Ted was so passive that I would bet him twenty euros that he couldn't incite him to an argument."

Why do I think he's not telling the truth, Max wondered.

"Now I owe Hans twenty euros."

Chloé said, "I wouldn't pay Hans."

"He didn't expect his remark to Ted to have such an effect," Marc said. "And he certainly didn't expect a female lion to jump him."

"I was acting on instinct," Max said.

"As was I."

Max wanted to argue that she had been in control and he hadn't, but she managed to bite her tongue.

Marie-Christine called from the door, "Chloé, hurry. We have to go to the funeral home and to the lawyer."

Chloé's face crumpled. "I don't want to do either. This will make it real that Léa's gone."

"Why the lawyer?" Marc asked.

"To talk about the will, probably. Everything in Léa's office is under protection of the police, but the lawyer has copies of everything. Maman hinted that I might be the new CEO of de Saint-Pern."

Marc looked flabbergasted. "You? She must have been on something. You know nothing about business."

Chloé bristled, and for a moment looked like her mother. "Léa had no business training when she took over the company. I don't want the job, Marc, but if it saves the company, then I will do what I have to do."

Max could see that this was new territory for both of them. "Hans still wants it."

"Is that what you want, Marc?"

He jumped up, knocking his chair over, then bending down to pick it up. "There's a lot you don't know." They watched him as he walked toward the tennis courts.

"Was I beastly?" Chloé's eyes welled up. "All I need now is for Marc and me to fight. I'm shocked that he would feel opposed to me stepping into my aunt's shoes."

"Perhaps he saw himself in that role, which means this will be a huge change for both of you."

"You know it's considered vulgar to talk about money in France." Especially among those who have it, Max thought.

Max told Chloé about asking Olivier where his money came from. "You're lucky not to have the baggage that great wealth brings, Max. My parents are *bourgeois*, but they have always been conservative with their spending. My mother, I just learned, will inherit half of Léa's estate, as Léa had no children and no parents. Sad to think about, isn't it?"

"What about Antoine?"

Chloé rolled her eyes. "He has a large number of shares in de Saint-Pern that he acquired when Charles was still alive. He could tip the balance. Baptiste Dupuis has already been to see him, and it wouldn't surprise me if Hans Keller hadn't paid him a visit, too. The board and shareholders may decide to go public, in which case we would have little chance of remaining a family company."

"Didn't Léa give Marc shares to welcome him into the company?"

"Yes, but he wouldn't sell."

"Do you want to run the company?"

"I'm as shocked as you and Marc are, but I do. Léa told me the night of the wedding that she was going to reverse her decision to sell, and fight Dupuis with everything she had. I want to follow through on that."

"Any idea why Marc is so drawn to Hans Keller?"

"His mother knows him. I think Marc met him through her."

That woman knows everybody, Max thought.

"Did Marc arrange for Hans to come meet with Léa?"

"You're sounding like a detective now. And I need to sound like a wife and say, I don't know."

The door opened Marie-Christine emerged, looking stylish. Chloé ran to her, and Max heard her mother chastising her for her choice of outfit, sounding exactly like Juliette. She thought of the contrast between families. Hank's father had died an alcoholic, and Hank had paid for his mother's care until her death four years ago. Max barely knew her Irish cousins. And so far her French family existed only in her imagination. But maybe that was about to change.

◇◇◇

Ted was sitting in a chair when Max entered the hospital room. His face was bruised and swollen.

This is the result of a bet?

Max went to him and kissed him on the forehead. He spoke through clenched teeth, "So why did this happen, detective?"

"It was some kind of game Marc and Hans had going. They made a bet that no amount of taunting could get a rise out of you. Marc lost."

"And you believe that?"

She sat down. "Not really. I think it has more to do with the idea that the more attention that is focused on you, the less there will be on Hans."

"I think it was a warning."

"Why?"

"I have a pretty big following on my blog and since Léa's death it's doubled. Day before yesterday I wrote about Hans' father's company in Germany, and then like an idiot, when he baited me with the accusation, I fell for it."

"May I read the blog?"

"The police took my laptop."

"What's in it?"

"I dug around and found out why the Kellers want the de Saint-Pern Company. In a way, it's an act of revenge. Born in France, though his parents were German, Hans' grandfather Dietrich Keller, was accused of economic collaboration with the Germans during World War II. He was close friends with the *Weinführer*, a label the French gave to Germans who were sent to be in charge of wine districts. The *Weinführer*, whose name was Otto Bruckner, requisitioned the de Saint-Pern château, and used it as headquarters. Old man Keller and Bruckner were close friends. He made a fortune with his dealings, and was put on trial after the war. His property was confiscated, he would never again be allowed to do business in France, and he lost all rights as a French citizen. He had hoarded millions, though, and he went to Germany and created the Keller Company. His son, Klaus Keller, carries the flag of revenge and has sent in his son Hans to purchase de Saint-Pern. If he fails, he will be ousted from his father's company. The old man sounds like a monster."

"How do you know all this?"

"I have my sources, who prefer to remain confidential."

"The police will find out, trust me."

"Okay, then. Geneviève is a main source."

"Did Léa know this?"

"Geneviève told me. And I told Léa."

"What'd she say?"

"That she wasn't going to sell to a French traitor."

"It all went according to Geneviève's plan. She wanted Hans out of the running for some reason."

Max paused. "What if she said that to Hans Keller that night? He could have flown into a rage."

"Somebody flew into a rage. Come on, Max, you must have some idea."

Max thought about how Hans and Léa were at odds almost from the moment they met, and how daunting Hans must have thought his mission was. Maybe that was why Hans turned to Marc, the weak link, promising him an important position if he helped to persuade the other family members to accept his offer.

Ted telling Léa about the German connection could have contributed to her death, but wasn't she herself about to go to Léa and tell her about the conversation she had overheard at the bottom of the stairs between Baptiste Dupuis and Bernard Martin? Maybe Marc was right and Léa already knew of Bernard Martin's disloyalty.

"I'm flummoxed. For the first time since I've been a cop, everyone has a potential motive. There's the family angle, the business angle, and the inheritance angle. Which reminds me. Chloé said that her mother would inherit half of the personal estate."

"She is what is called a forced heir."

"And the rest?"

He shrugged. "Perhaps me. Once Léa learned she was pregnant, she told me she made a *testament olographe*, or holographic will, which is written by hand and doesn't have to be witnessed or stamped."

The perfect motive, thought Max.

"What is your personal financial situation now?"

Their eyes interlocked. "Terrible. Léa lent me fifty thousand Euros last year and I haven't paid back anything yet."

"I'm worried, Ted. I know you're hurting, but you need to take it seriously that Geneviève said that you left her room at the inn immediately. It implies that you had time to return to the Léa and kill her."

His eyes widened. "She's lying, but why?"

"No idea. You're closer to her than I thought."

"I admit that I used her. She has until recently moved in very powerful circles."

"Did you know her former lover?"

"Monsieur Douvier? I met him several times at parties. Pompous, I would say, but also charming. Exudes power. She was undone when he dumped her. I saw a different side of her with all her security ripped away."

Exactly what happened to you, Max thought.

"How so?'

"Paralyzed that she'd end up on the street. She doubled her focus on Marc. He's been under her absolute control. I used to feel sorry for him."

"Does he have any reason to resent you? He's responsible for Marceaus not wanting anything to do with you."

"I figured as much. Some of it comes from his mother who is nervous that I'll get a big chunk of the inheritance. She wields a huge influence on him. And Marc's wary of me, and what I know. Léa regretted giving him shares in the company, you know, and was trying to think how to oust him without causing a family crisis."

"Did you know that Geneviève and Hans know each other?"

"What are you implying? That Marc and Hans had a deal conjured up before Hans ever showed up? That did occur to me."

"How easy for them now that Léa's out of the way. I worry about Chloé's safety once she's running the company."

"Is that a fact?" His eyes widened. "Who knows? She might be able to turn things around. There were divided loyalties, with Marc pulling employees toward Hans and Bernard Martin trying to bring in Baptiste Dupuis. For a price, I'm sure."

"God, Ted. We're all so cynical." She told him her suspicions toward Martin, and he said he wasn't surprised.

"Léa was going to tell me something the day after the wedding," he said. "About why she was selling the company. I tried to get her to tell me, but she refused. I insisted on a hint, and she said, 'skeletons in the closet,' and ran off."

They sat quietly for a moment. "It could be the key, but it's much too vague," said Max.

Ted put his hand up to his face. "I have to get more pain medication."

"I have to go." She helped him into bed. The nurse entered, and Max leaned over and bestowed a quick kiss on Ted's forehead and ran out of the room. She didn't want to be late to Hans' interrogation. When she got back to her room she would write down Hans as her number one suspect, then create a chart and try to connect some more dots.

She worried, though, that she was getting hopelessly bogged down in emotional minutiae that had nothing to do with the case. A potential problem when inhabiting a suspect's character.

Chapter Sixteen

Olivier drove to the Palais de Justice in Reims after leaving Girard. The wall of legal books, floor to ceiling windows, the Oriental rug covering the vast floor created a formal appearance, perhaps intimidating for some. To Olivier the atmosphere was more conducive to seeking answers than the austerity of the police station. He was relieved that the police and gendarme *garde à vue*, or questioning, was over and that he could formally open the *instruction*.

Claude Reynard, to whom the police had reported every few hours, called to say that based on the evidence sent to him by Commisaire Girard, Monsieur Ted Clay was the number one suspect and should be arrested as soon as possible. It might as well be Clay as any other, Olivier thought, though for the moment he was far more interested in Hans Keller.

He glanced up and was surprised to see Max Maguire entering the room, wearing a knee-length skirt, a jacket with a Chanel cut, and cowboy boots. Her short platinum hair formed a cap on her head, and her lips were the color of his favorite rose, the *"Souvenir de la Malmaison,"* introduced in 1844 after the death of Empress Josephine as a nod to her famous château and gardens. He was glad to see her.

"Bonjour," she said. "I hope I'm not late. I stopped in on Ted, who has been diagnosed with a broken jaw, which seems to be causing a respiratory problem." She stopped and looked

around, "Wow, this room is impressive. You should see where I do my interrogations. Think oppressive gray."

He smiled. "The police stations here aren't much better. I wasn't sure if you were planning to come or not."

Olivier buzzed in an assistant who arrived with a tray of coffee and placed it on his desk. "May we have a chair for mademoiselle?" he asked. The young man nodded and left the room. The door opened again and Abdel stepped in quietly, carrying a laptop under his arm. The secretary returned with a chair for Max.

"May I give you a quick rundown on Ted?" she asked. Olivier observed that she included Abdel.

"We have five minutes, but I also want you to know that I just learned that he is going to be arrested as soon as he is released."

She leaned forward, "On what basis?"

Olivier explained that Ted's alibi was contradicted by Geneviève Durand, who said that he hadn't lingered in her room at the inn and that she had, in fact, asked him to go straight away to Léa. His explosion over a verbal taunt had shown that he was quickly aroused to anger. And a handwritten will was found in Léa's possessions that listed him as an heir to her fortune. It's being checked for forgery," he added.

"Were his fingerprints on the bottle?"

"I should get that report today. I think the arrest is premature, but Commissaire Girard and Captain Canon are caught in a whirlwind of publicity, and are feeling great pressure. It's how mistakes happen."

"I have more information that isn't in Ted's favor," Max said, "But I would still wager everything I have that he didn't do it. He borrowed fifty-thousand euros from Léa last year and hasn't paid it back."

Olivier wondered if she and Ted Clay had had a falling out for her to reveal this now.

"But I also want to let you know why I think Hans Keller lured him into a fight." She explained what Ted had learned about Hans' past and what Ted had written in his blog.

Olivier's assistant entered, followed by Keller—dressed in the suit he had worn to the wedding, and sporting a sling. Hans assessed the seating arrangement and sat in a chair across from Olivier. He looked over at Max, then back at Olivier. "Is this woman allowed to be here? After all, she assaulted me last night and I'm still trying to have her arrested."

Olivier responded, "She isn't your concern."

It was obvious that Hans was desperate to be in control. "You have the report the police gave you about my movements during the time of the wedding and after, most of which is quite boring. What else do you want?"

"To hear about the meeting you had with Madame de Saint-Pern at seven prior to the dinner at the Marceau home the night before the wedding."

"Léa picked me up at the inn and we drove to her château, where she opened a bottle of *L'Etoile*, I think a '96. We discussed the details of me purchasing her company for X amount of euros. And this brings up an important matter that is of great concern to certain of your superiors." He was looking at Olivier. "You saw me with a small leather bag when I disembarked from the plane. It contained two-hundred-thousand Euros."

"Where is it?"

"No idea. I asked Léa if I could leave it in the trunk of her car until after the wedding and she said yes, having no idea what it contained. I ran to get it from the car when I was informed of her death, and the car had been confiscated by the police. They assured me that it wasn't there."

"Did you tell anyone about it?"

"Obviously my father knew."

"It's illegal to transport such a large sum of cash across borders. What was it for?"

"It came with the approval of a French minister, Monsieur Chaumont. You might want to be careful."

Olivier flashed back to the brief and strange conversation with Philippe Douvier. He thought if there was a cache of money,

Douvier was involved, otherwise Hans would be too frightened of being arrested to bring it up. Or to transport it.

"That sounds like a threat, which will be duly noted. Anyone else?"

Hans grew pensive. "I suspect Geneviève Durand and her son of taking it. I have asked him, but he denies any knowledge."

Olivier thought Hans deserved to lose it, but he also didn't think Geneviève deserved to keep it, "I will look into it, but the death of Léa de Saint-Pern takes precedence now. You argued with her."

"I was upset the day we flew, but, trust me, it was easier for me to work with her alive than dead. She committed again the night before the wedding to signing the contract on Monday, when her lawyers would be present. She was quite emotional about it."

"You mean she was crying?"

"That's exactly what I meant. I almost felt sorry for her."

That put a different spin on Léa's decision to sell de Saint-Pern. Jacques had perhaps been prescient when he mentioned to Olivier that something was going on that Léa wasn't sharing. Had she been acting out of fear? They might never know.

"But you didn't let up. Several people said you were harassing her at the wedding reception. You took a bottle of champagne down to the bench where she sat waiting for Monsieur Clay and demanded an answer."

"That direct accusation method doesn't work with me, Monsieur Chaumont."

Olivier glanced at Max, who was listening intently. She had brought him the information that he was about to use, he realized. "What if the victim knew the story of your grandfather and grandmother who were living in Champagne in the 1940s? What if she knew that your grandfather went through a trial and was thrown out of France for economic collaboration with the enemy, and what if she threw that information in your face?"

Hans' lips were a thin line, but he didn't capitulate. "What if, what if…" he said.

"She had learned that information recently from Monsieur Clay, who had also unearthed the information that the *Weinführer* for this commune, Herr Bruckner, confiscated Charles de Saint-Pern's grandfather's château and turned it into German headquarters, all with the help of your grandfather."

"This is all fucking nonsense!"

"And what if our victim said to you that night that she would never sell to a man whose ancestor had been a traitor to France?"

Hans' face had gone white, and he simply stared.

"There was a witness to your conversation with Madame de Saint-Pern."

"Who?"

"That is private information. There were a surprising number of people wandering around the Marceau lawn that night." Olivier had never bluffed to such an extreme, but he could tell that Hans was unnerved. "We've confiscated the shoes you wore at the wedding, monsieur. And we'll get your DNA before you leave. You've been fingerprinted, correct?"

Hans nodded, numbly.

"You won't be able to leave this valley without permission. All of this will be explained by my assistant."

"But my arm." He turned and glared at Max.

"It's a simple sprain and should be fine within a couple of days. I have the doctor's report here."

The office assistant arrived to escort Hans out. Olivier explained to Max and Abdel about the secret land for sale just out of the Champagne commune, and his suspicion that if there was a bag of cash it was going toward a land deal. He wasn't sure who was involved, though. Abdel suggested that he check a few bank balances and Olivier approved. "But don't become distracted by it," he cautioned him. "We have to stay focused on the murder."

The assistant returned and told Olivier that Madame Marceau had called and said it was urgent that she speak to Olivier before her husband was interrogated. "I told her to be here in half an hour."

"*D'accord.*" Olivier spoke to Max, who had gone to the window to look out onto the gardens. "Your information about Han's past was helpful, as you can see."

"But the way you used it was brilliant. I was thinking about Léa crying when Hans was talking. Ted said something interesting yesterday. Léa told him that the sale had to do with skeletons in the closet, but refused to reveal what they were. Thanks, by the way, for not letting him get me on the assault charge."

"It was dangerous, what you and Marc did."

"I felt that I had no choice."

"But still, Hans is quite a bit taller, and strong."

"That's the point of *jiu-jitsu.* The little guy has a chance."

"Perhaps the little guy begins to *believe* he has a chance."

She looked tired. "Whatever."

"What does that mean, 'whatever'?"

"It means I'm not willing to argue. I don't think I should sit in on your conversation with Marie-Christine. I think I'll return to the house. Thanks for allowing me to be here."

She was already out of her seat and heading to the door.

"Max."

She turned, only her eyes displaying surprise at the sound of her name.

"May I pick you up this evening and go somewhere to discuss the case? We might need to start searching for those skeletons."

She seemed hesitant. Surprised, perhaps? She smiled, and it was lovely to see. "Sure."

As she was leaving, Marie-Christine appeared and spoke briefly to Max. She was today the quintessential *haute bourgeoisie* Frenchwoman—designer suit, coiffed hair, perfect earrings, erect posture, and yes, there was the Hermes scarf, the security blanket for these women. Olivier introduced Abdel, who walked over and shook hands with her and returned to his laptop. She sat across the desk from him, hands in her lap.

Olivier said, "Needless to say, you're not a suspect, but I'm hoping you can provide some information that might move the investigation forward."

"Is there anything new?"

"We think we have the murder weapon."

"The stone rabbit in the yard?"

"No, a full bottle of champagne."

She frowned. "How horrible for the industry."

Olivier knew that what she meant was "how horrible for the reputation of her beloved Champagne," but he could tell after a swift glance at Abdel that he had found the comment obnoxious.

"What I meant," she said, "is that these bottles represent gaiety and celebration, and are associated with the launching of great ships, polo, and illustrious people. They've never been associated with death. Or homicide." Her face seemed to splinter, and she reached into her Gucci handbag and brought out a handkerchief and dabbed her eyes. "Please forgive me. Let's go on."

"Where were you between the hours of midnight and two?"

"Many of the older guests were leaving and I was seeing them off. I was in and out of the kitchen with Mimi, helping with clean-up."

"Did you notice anything unusual about Léa that night?"

"No, she seemed the same, perhaps a bit more tired. As always she had men trailing behind her everywhere she went. The German, Monsieur Keller, the Anglo-Saxon, Monsieur Clay, Dupuis, all of them wanting something from her."

"I witnessed the conversation she had with you about Monsieur Clay and the baby."

"Oh, that. Don't forget the invitation she issued to Monsieur Keller on my daughter's wedding day. It was incredibly inconsiderate, and typical of Léa, to create chaos when the attention is on someone else. If she hadn't invited these two...foreigners... she might still be alive. I understand that Monsieur Clay is going to be arrested?"

Olivier nodded.

"Léa was going through a crisis about turning forty. I think she was panicked at the idea of aging, as most beautiful women do, and she thought having a baby would ward off the inevitable. In reality it does the opposite."

Olivier wanted to steer the conversation back to her relationship with Léa. "She seemed to exercise a lot of control over your family."

"She always has over Chloé. She was terribly jealous that I had a child and we quarreled occasionally over the way she treated Chloé as a best friend."

"She gave the couple an apartment in Paris?"

"I didn't object to that so much, but I hated her bringing Chloé and Marc into her company. Jacques and I had deliberately not offered them jobs with us until they had a year to really think about what they wanted. They haven't known each other very long, as you know."

"And what about Jacques?"

Her hands were clenched.

"What about my husband?"

"He borrowed money from Léa?"

"Against my wishes. "

"But it didn't cause a rift."

"No. Tension, perhaps. You know, Olivier, Jacques was always in love with Léa. He has confessed to me that he had an affair with her after Charles died. I told him I knew." She stopped this time to mop away the tears running down her cheeks. "I bring this up because I'm terrified that our family secrets will be leaked to the press, and I'm asking you to prevent that from happening."

Was she also subtly placing blame on Jacques? Olivier wondered.

"Can you imagine how it feels, to know that the man you've loved your entire life is in love with your sister?"

Olivier knew well how it felt to have a spouse stray, and empathized.

Marie-Christine cried harder. "But at this moment I would happily give up everything I have to see her again."

Abdel had stopped typing, and sat with his eyes downcast.

Olivier moved to put a hand on her shoulder, and she reached up and patted it. It's the secrets, he thought, that cause our despair.

In a few moments she had composed herself. She sat erect, again. "I'm terrified that Jacques killed my sister."

"You can't offer an alibi?"

"No, I can't. Jacques has his own room. He came into the kitchen and removed a chilled bottle of champagne from the refrigerator, and jammed it into an ice bucket a little after midnight. I can't stop thinking about the murder weapon being a bottle of champagne."

"Did you ask him about it?"

"It didn't occur to me to ask until now. Lots of people were coming in and out, and going into the refrigerator."

"It just now occurred to you that he might have killed Léa?"

"Yes. I'll ask him about the ice bucket and champagne when I return to the house."

The brutality involved in the murder of her sister was so foreign to Marie-Christine, Olivier thought, that she could blithely and ignorantly peg her husband, turning him in as though he had stolen a lawnmower. What was unsettling for him was the opposite: the suspicion that Jacques had killed his sister-in-law.

Chapter Seventeen

Chloé was waiting when Max arrived back at the house. "How was my mother during the interrogation?" she asked. "I thought she was over-the-top stressed out when she left." Max smiled at her friend's American jargon.

"I didn't want to be there," Max said. "It felt too personal."

"Which means there was something you didn't want to hear. Is it about my parents' relationship? Something you know that I don't know?" Max could see the worried expression on her face.

"You're assuming way too much. Your mother asked to speak to Olivier, and I knew it must be personal."

Chloé followed Max to her room. "Just don't tell me they're getting divorced." She picked up the book by Max's bed. "You still keep a journal?"

"Funny you'd remember that. I do, but sadly this one has turned into all the details around Léa's death."

"For example?"

"I weigh evidence against alibis against motives. I draw up charts and maps. And sometimes I come up with a genuine suspect."

"Do you think her murder will be solved?"

"I have to believe it will. It's harder when dealing with family and friends of the victim. Which reminds me, I'm surprised that Geneviève and Hans knew each other before the wedding."

"I think Hans was cozy with the Minister of Justice, and she was the minister's mistress. It has no relevance to Léa, but Marc alluded to a scheme the three of them were involved in to buy land for cash in a village called Serval that is only six miles outside the Champagne boundary. They had a tip that this land will be next to be approved by the AOC, and if it's true they will make a huge profit. But people are always speculating about that land."

So that's my connection, Max thought. "Obviously if they're paying cash, corruption is involved." Max thought Douvier was exactly the kind of crooked politician Olivier would go after. But the money's gone, and Hans is blaming Geneviève."

Max laughed. "So that's why Marc has cooled toward Hans. You're lucky to have such attentive parents."

"*Au contraire.*" She explained the trendy term, "helicopter parents."

Chloé laughed. "Then the French invented the concept."

Max changed into jeans and t-shirt. "Maybe we're lucky and just don't know it," she said. "Too bad Marc doesn't have a dad to balance out his mom."

"His mother makes my parents seem lackadaisical in their parenting," Chloé answered. "Geneviève has ruled every waking moment of his life since he was born. Once in a while he explodes at her, then he feels terrible and returns to her full of remorse."

"Do you like your mother-in-law?"

Chloé hesitated. "Let's say I don't hate her. One reason I'd like to move is to put space between Marc and her. Wait! Does that make me sound like a helicopter spouse?"

Max laughed, but then grew serious. "Geneviève needs to get over herself and leave you and Marc alone. Maybe revive her design business."

"I think we'll be supporting her. I just have to keep her out of the office. Imagine though, she had Marc when she was sixteen. He wouldn't want anyone to know this, but she promised she'd tell him the name of his real father on the day of his wedding."

"That's huge. Did she?"

"No. She talked to the local bartender and he said he wouldn't want to know and she decided that Marc shouldn't know either. She's always letting him down, and I nurture him back to health."

Max felt restless. "Hey, let's go see Antoine."

"As long as he's not a suspect in your journal."

"Everybody is." When Chloé looked shocked, Max said, "Now begins the elimination process." She tucked her hand into Chloé's arm. The air was fragrant with roses, and Max paused long enough to pass along the information she had gleaned from Olivier about the flower.

"What's happening with you and him?"

"Murder turns out to be a deterrent to romance."

"What about Girard?"

"Reminds me too much of Joe back home."

They entered Antoine's yard and called out. A response came from behind the house and the two young women increased their pace. Antoine was standing on the river bank, holding a beer. He shielded his eyes as they approached, and Chloé ran up and hugged him.

"Thank God it's you," Antoine said. "I'm expecting Captain Canon to come marching in with the cavalry any minute." He proceeded to imitate the military stance of the captain, which made them laugh. "He has a huge prejudice against rich, slovenly people like me." He leaned down to check his fishing pole that was propped up.

Max looked out onto the wide river and the leafy foliage that ran along both sides. "This is paradise," she said, enjoying the tranquility and the feel of the sun on her face. She and Chloé sat on the grass.

"How's the detecting going?" he asked Max.

"Slow, but I saw Olivier in action and was impressed. He would have the president confessing."

"That's the danger of his position," Antoine said. "Yet I still believe in what these examining magistrates do, despite the controversy. If we didn't have them, there would be no one to challenge the jackass at the top."

Chloé announced she was hungry and Antoine offered to make an omelet. The two women waited while he stopped to pick some basil from his garden. Max was glad for the opportunity to hang with this twosome. Something glinted from the leaves, and curious, she ambled over a few yards to see what it was. Chloé ran up. "What're you doing?"

"The sun must have bounced off an object here. I saw a prism, or something." They both cupped their hands around their eyes and peered into the dense foliage. "There it is," Max said. She stretched her arm inside and her hand touched an object that she pulled out and held up in the sunlight.

Chloé's hand flew up to cover her mouth and she gasped. "It's Léa's necklace. *Mon Dieu!* Antoine!" He walked over slowly, and studied the necklace as though it were a specimen of a unique species. Which it was. Léa had told Max the evening of the wedding that it was made of natural Australian pearls, each the size, and similar to the color of, a fully-ripened chardonnay grape. It was rimmed in twenty-four carat gold.

Max watched Antoine's eyes blink rapidly several times and as he reached over to touch it, Max stopped him, and asked him instead to get her a plastic bag. "It's bad enough that my fingerprints are on it. We don't want yours."

Chloé stared at her uncle. "How'd it get here? Poor Léa! Whoever killed Tante Léa…" She started sobbing uncontrollably. Antoine put his hand out, but she pulled away, and ran up the path.

"*Merde,*" he said, "If my own niece can have the fleeting thought that I killed Léa, so can others who aren't so fair." He stumbled, but caught himself. "I know I had a black-out because of that moment of becoming conscious and knowing that someone was standing over me. I don't know how a detective determines who might have done it."

"It comes down to proof, but the first step is intuition or hunch. That's my father's way anyhow, and I'm trained by him." They entered his house. "No recollection yet of who that was standing over you?"

"Let's say I have a hunch. I'll wait for a little more proof. This murderer is cold-blooded to remove Léa's necklace after killing her. If he comes to the conclusion that I recognized him, he'll come after me. He's already trying to set me up by throwing the necklace into my yard. Smart. If it was found, I'd be a stronger suspect, and if it wasn't found, he could return in the night and reclaim it. It's worth a small fortune so it must have been hard to part with it."

Max thought few people knew this side of Antoine, and was pleased and surprised that he was willing to open up to her a little, yet cautioned herself to remain objective. "Stop wondering if I'm a sociopath, roping you in," he said. "I'm a full-blown narcissist and an obnoxious drunk, but not a killer."

She laughed. "It's hard to be objective around a family I like."

"Impossible assignment, which is why they have the conflict-of-interest rule. Olivier is the best when it comes to solving crimes, but I'm glad he has you as back-up because of that. He and my brother are very good friends, and I consider him a friend, too."

"I'm in the same situation, having my friend Ted to worry about."

"He has an intelligent blog. Writes well about wine, too."

Max glanced at her watch. "I think I should call Girard and let him know about the necklace."

"I'd prefer you call Olivier. I have his cell phone number."

She hesitated, but then agreed. "I'm really starting to worry." She waited while he poured beer into a glass. "I know it sounds paranoid, but that necklace was a warning."

Max had been through this kind of paranoia with people she had arrested, some suffering from paranoid schizophrenia. "You should tell Olivier and he'll post a gendarme here."

"That would drive me crazy, but I'll think about it."

"Do you have a plastic bag I can put the necklace in?" She followed him into the messy kitchen, and watched as he dug around in drawers until he found one. "The phone's over there.

You know, Olivier has a big plan to get me sober after he closes this case. Don't tell him I told you."

"What made you say yes?"

"We had a philosophical talk, and somehow he got me to say yes. I can't think how. But once I make a commitment I rarely go back. He found a place in Belgium, I think. And no, my brother doesn't know. I've flunked out of a few, and he's given up."

Max slid the necklace into the small plastic bag he handed her, and dialed the number written on a piece of paper. Olivier answered and said that as soon as his interview with Baptiste Dupuis ended he'd drive over.

"I'm going to find Chloé," Max said.

"I'm back." They turned simultaneously.

Chloé stood with Marc, who said that Chloé had told him about the necklace. "I called Commissaire Girard."

Shit.

"Why?" Antoine asked. "We don't need any more detectives, you know."

"Because it's important evidence."

Antoine didn't take his eyes off Marc. "Max has it covered, Marc. Olivier is on his way."

Marc lit a cigarette, and Max made a mental note that these two were far from being friends.

A loud knock at the door interrupted them, and Girard asked through the screen if he could enter. Antoine motioned the officer in. "Thanks for calling the police, Monsieur Durand," Girard said pointedly. "May I have it?" He didn't smile at Max when she handed it to him. "Mind showing me where it was found?"

Max led him out to the hedge. He walked alongside her. "You should have called me."

"I was just on my way to the Marceau house to do that." He pulled a clip from the local newspaper, *L'Union*, from his pocket and tapped with his index finger on a photograph of her, which made her feel for a second that she was being attacked. Someone must have taken her picture with a phone. It was a frontal view, taken when she had stood in a pugilistic stance waiting for

Hans to come after her. Not flattering in the least. The headline read, *American takes down German entrepreneur…* The reporter mentioned her status with the NYPD, as well as her friendship with the Marceau bride.

"It looks like you took over my job," Girard said. "And the Chief Prosecutor, Monsieur Reynard, is not happy that you weren't all arrested."

"The picture makes it look a lot worse than it was. You know how that goes." She wondered how she could assuage the damage to his ego. "I'm sorry. I really don't know the protocol here."

His face relaxed a little. "Max, this necklace is serious business." He paused. "Does Monsieur Chaumont know of your discovery?"

Exactly the way Joe would behave, Max thought. Slip in a question to test your loyalty.

"Why would he?"

Girard smiled. "I'll take the necklace with me and have it fingerprinted. And if Antoine Marceau isn't too far gone from alcohol, I'll have a chat with him. He and Madame de Saint-Pern had an altercation at the dinner table the night before the wedding, I understand."

"They exchanged words, but everyone was tense that night. I have no idea what they were talking about, of course."

"Was Monsieur Chaumont there?"

Out of the corner of her eye she saw a car drive in. It had to be Olivier. "He can answer that as he's here." With that, she took long strides to the car and was upon Olivier as he opened the door, speaking rapidly, "I told Girard I didn't call you and he wants to know if you were at the pre-wedding dinner."

Girard caught up. In French he demanded of Olivier, "Did she call you to come here?"

Max didn't know if Olivier had understood her rapid-fire English.

"*Pourquoi?*" he asked. "Why? Is something wrong?"

Max remembered to breathe.

"This." Girard extracted the necklace from his pocket and gave it to Olivier who held it up in the light.

"I remember it. Extraordinary quality."

"Max found it."

Olivier looked over at her. "You like treasure hunts."

This is beginning to feel like teamwork, Max thought.

Chloé intervened. "Uncle Antoine said he thinks the necklace was planted."

Girard was curt. "They all say that. Let's go find out why he thinks that."

"Marc and I are going home," Chloé said. "I hate seeing him drunk."

Max thought Chloé made the comment about her uncle for Marc's sake, and it made her sad. She lagged behind the investigators as they walked toward the house, which gave her the chance to eavesdrop on them. Girard, she learned, was not to be trusted. He brought up Reynard's pique about her photograph in the paper, saying, "Imagine trying to go to bed with a woman who fights like that." He chuckled. Olivier shot him a sour look. "The two Americans, I take it, are a team."

"They're friends."

"Really, she shouldn't be as involved as she seems to be."

Max held her breath, waiting to see what Olivier would say. "Whatever she does is completely unofficial, and so far she's done nothing but happen onto a necklace in a hedge while visiting her friend's uncle. The fight in the bar had nothing to do with this case."

Thank you, Olivier.

Antoine was sitting slumped in the plaid easy chair. He cocked one eye open. Girard asked what he and Léa had argued about, and he said he was angry over her announcement that she was selling her company to foreigners, and yes, he had threatened to sell his shares to Dupuis Enterprises. And yes, he had gone to Le Bar after stomping out of the house.

"Someone reported that they heard you predicting Léa's death," Olivier said.

"If someone heard me do that, then yes, I probably did."

"Did you tell a patron in the bar that you knew who killed Léa de Saint-Pern?"

He blinked hard. "I said that? I probably did in that moment, but I've lost it again. It will come back."

Max could see Olivier's frustration. Yet some part of her thought Antoine knew more than he was letting on. Was he trying to protect someone? Olivier and Girard pounded him with questions about an alibi for the night of the murder. He told them about blacking out and waking up on the lawn, but didn't mention the strange presence. They sat in silence for a moment watching him as his head lopped over. He was asleep

Girard stood up, angrily, shaking his head. "He's worthless. A mass of flesh with no meaning. No purpose. He's never had to be accountable to anyone. For anything. He could have killed Madame de Saint-Pern, and have no memory of it."

Olivier said quietly, "But what would have been his motive?"

"Sometimes the motives are so weak that you can't believe it, Monsieur Chaumont. The wife puts the knife in the wrong place. Or in this case, Madame de Saint-Pern told him the truth about him, that he is a drunk and a parasite. I have a statement from his brother…"

Olivier was growing impatient. "Put it with the other statements and I'll have a look. Detective Maguire, do you need a ride to the house?"

She nodded assent.

"Detective." She turned to see what Girard wanted. "I would like to take a statement from you as soon as possible. I'll call and arrange it."

You've really pissed me off now, Girard, thought Max.

Chapter Eighteen

Olivier preferred having Max on Girard's good side. Because of the lying—about his relationship with the family and agreeing to let Max do some solo sleuthing—things could backfire. Girard was no dummy, and if he sensed the unspoken collaboration between Max and him, he might take it personally.

Max interrupted his thoughts. "I didn't call Girard."

"Obviously not."

"Marc called him. He thought it was the right thing to do."

Olivier sighed as he pulled into the Marceau driveway. "Marc likes to be in charge, wouldn't you say?"

She laughed. "That applies to a lot of us, not to name names."

He wondered if he could provoke her. "Like Girard? Who needs a statement from you? It's a ruse to spend time with you. Harmless, though."

A look of annoyance flitted across her face. "Olivier, where're you going with this? I think Girard has the perverted notion that I'm an easy target for his lust…"

"On the contrary, it's your unavailability that's making him more determined."

"I'll be clear that I'm not looking for romance, that's all."

"Shall I rescind my invitation to take you for drinks in a couple of hours then?"

"Why?"

"Because you're certain that you're not seeking romance, which means you're closing a door, and as I don't want to talk about murder the entire time we're sipping champagne, it's a *casse-tête*. A deep problem. In fact, I was going to invite you to dinner at my parents' home after we have drinks."

"I'll open the door a crack."

Her lips were turned up in a mischievous grin. She knew he was teasing.

"Just to peer out? How boring, Max."

"What to do next depends on on whether or not I like what I see."

"That's fair enough."

"Dress code for drinks?"

"Another *casse-tête*. A very major problem. *"A tout à l'heure."* He laughed as she exited his car, and she waggled her fingers mid-air.

He drove off to *la boucherie* near his parents' house and ordered two Wagyu steaks, then stopped at the market for escargots and mushrooms. His parents' house to drop the food off. The investigation had hit a wall, the first of several he was sure. In his mind that meant they weren't being creative, and the solution to that was to stop thinking so much. Thus the reason for drinks and dinner with Max. He liked it when things felt rational.

He had time for one more interview before he called it a day. He tapped in the number for Abdel and asked him to call Marc Durand in. He drove into Epernay, which was closer, and went directly to his office, where he would glance over the initial interview Abdel had conducted with Marc. Abdel jumped up, clearly upset.

"What's going on?"

"Commissaire Girard wants me to move to Bordeaux now. My transfer is complete."

"But I specifically requested you on this case."

"He said that you have a new assistant. Did you see the photograph of Detective Maguire in the paper?"

Olivier nodded. "A big indiscretion, but not her fault. Girard is wrong, Abdel."

"What? That I have to pay for her mistake?"

"I'm fast losing patience with Girard. Don't worry. You won't be going to Bordeaux."

"Monsieur Durand is on his way."

"Good. You were here with Dupuis. What did you think while listening to him boast about his many acquisitions while wearing his customary Dior suit?"

"He wants the de Saint-Pern Company as much as Hans Keller. He knows too much not to have someone feeding him information. But who that is, I have no idea."

"Dupuis would never lay a hand on anyone, don't you agree?"

"No. He'd send his bodyguard."

"Did he say why his car was in the parking lot long after everyone thought he'd left?"

"He stuck to the story about his wife's handbag. Said her migraine pills were in it. By the way, the reports are in from the shoe prints. I have all the sizes that were anywhere around the body, and am checking them out, one by one. The bridal couple's close friends, Delphine Lacroix and Yves Brun, mentioned that they had bought cocaine. Supplied by Antoine Marceau."

"I know about it. Antoine surely doesn't need money."

"Wrong. He's been cut off from the family trust." Abdel went to his table to go over interviews, and Olivier glanced at the notes from the night of the murder that Abdel had given his secretary to type up. *Marc Durand had asked Ted Clay to walk his mother back to the inn around one-thirty as she wasn't feeling well and he had wanted to be with Chloé. Later, he didn't know how much later, he had sniffed cocaine with his friend Yves. No, Yves' girlfriend Delphine wasn't with them. Nor was Chloé, who would have been furious. He had changed into jeans and t-shirt because his suit was uncomfortable. They went back into the tent and danced some more, and when someone mentioned they saw lights down below, he and Yves ran down to see what was going on. That was his first knowledge that anything had happened. He went to wake his mother up to inform her, but he didn't know what time that was.*

Marc entered the room, dressed in black pants and a white, tailored shirt. Though he appeared calm, he tapped a cigarette out of a pack, stopping to ask politely if he could smoke. Olivier thought cigarette smokers didn't know how their habit gave them away, displaying their nervousness, and putting a blueish-gray veil between themselves and the outside world. Abdel went out and returned with an ashtray, which Marc balanced on his thigh. "It's weird being here," Marc said. "I've never been in any trouble, until suddenly I'm in the middle of the murder of my bride's aunt."

Olivier told him that he understood, then got right to the point by asking about the fight he had with his mother when she had shouted, "You are nothing and you'll end up with nothing!"

"My mother and I argue a lot. I admit to being stubborn, which is sometimes necessary as she likes to direct my every move."

"Did she approve of this marriage?"

"Yes. She's very fond of Chloé."

"And the argument?"

"Oh, that. She was probably referring to Monsieur Bernard Martin who has been fighting me every inch of the way at the de Saint-Pern Company where I'm now employed. My mother has had to struggle most of her life to make ends meet and she thinks Monsieur Martin wants me ousted. I told her that Chloé and I were talking about leaving anyhow, and he could have it. I don't remember everything we said, but that's the gist of it."

His voice was even, but he didn't make eye contact. And his story of the argument didn't match his mother's.

"Were you angry at your mother on your wedding day?"

"I was tired of her."

"And so when she asked you to take her back to the inn…"

"I didn't want to leave. I thought she would start some emotional harangue and decided to ask her old friend Ted Clay to walk her home."

"He didn't resist?"

"He said sure."

"Did Léa de Saint-Pern hear him say that?"

"She complained that she was tired and wanted to go home, and Ted said he'd be back in ten minutes. Everything was okay."

"Had you sniffed cocaine when you asked Ted to walk Madame Durand home?"

"I don't remember. Maybe a little."

"And you bought it from Antoine Marceau?"

"I think so."

"There are others you buy an illegal drug from?"

"Okay. I got it from Antoine."

"I couldn't help but notice when we were at his place that you two don't like each other. I'm surprised he'd sell you cocaine, when you could turn him in. Which, in fact, you are doing."

"He doesn't like me. I don't know why."

"Let's switch to the de Saint-Pern Company. You were brought in as an intern, and then began to earn a salary. How was your relationship with the owner, Léa de Saint-Pern?"

"Good enough for her to want to introduce me to her niece. Who, of course, is now my wife." He was smiling.

"No conflicts?"

Marc frowned. "Oh, a few. I'm ambitious and impatient. She wanted me to start slowly from the bottom and work my way up and I wanted to create a new champagne, which alienated Bernard Martin. But it didn't take me long to find out that ole Bernard was skimming money off the top and I reported that to Léa."

Olivier wondered if this had to do with the skeletons in the closet. He recalled that Marc had reported the necklace to Girard, too. He glanced over at Abdel, whose eyes told him that he was writing it all down. They would definitely have to check in on Bernard Martin.

"What did she do?"

"She was angry. She also knew that Bernard was persuading de Saint-Pern shareholders to opt for allowing Baptiste Dupuis to buy their shares."

"And you conveniently chose this time to introduce Monsieur Hans Keller to Madame de Saint-Pern?"

"I helped to make that introduction."

"Did Monsieur Keller lead you to believe that if he managed to buy the company, you would be given an important position?"

"There was no contract, of course, but yes, we talked about it."

"Do you know the identity of your father?"

Marc lit a cigarette and blew out the smoke, and the only giveaway that he was nervous was that his hand shook slightly. "That is private information that has nothing to do with the case."

"You're right, monsieur."

Marc stabbed out his cigarette. Abdel had already turned on a fan and now he got up and raised a window. Marc seemed oblivious to the trouble he was causing. "Is that all?"

"That's it. Thank you for your cooperation. The three men shook hands and Marc left.

Olivier said, "He's a competent liar. We'll have to double check everything he said.

"I've already started."

"And we'll have to weigh his testimony against his mother's."

"A mother will never contradict her son."

"This one would if it meant saving her own skin."

"Then she isn't a mother."

Olivier entered the salon and Jacques came over to shake hands. Marie-Christine came in and said, "Max will be here in a moment. I gather there was quite a bit of discussion between the girls on what she was to wear since you're not revealing where you're taking her."

"And I'm not telling you either." It was good to see her smile again. "I'm doing this for myself as well as to get Max out," he said. "I'm too bogged down in details, and it hasn't been easy for me to stay as detached from my emotions as I need to be."

"We understand, Olivier," Marie-Christine said, and put her hand on Jacques' arm. Olivier wondered if they had made peace with each other, though he couldn't imagine this new-found harmony being the result of an accusation of murder.

Max entered the room and Marie-Christine said, "Well!" indicating that she was pleased. Max looked stunning in flowing white pants and a simple white tank top, a linen jacket casually slung over her shoulder, and sandals. She had tamped her hair down a bit, and wore a thin necklace that appeared to have diamonds in it.

"Chloé lent you her necklace," Marie-Christine said. "It's lovely."

"You look great," Olivier said, and they all laughed when she replied that he did, too. Once in the car, she said, "I know we aren't to talk about the case, but I did want to say that I have huge concerns about Antoine."

"Because of the drinking?"

"That, but something more. He knows more than he's letting on about Léa's killer, but he wants to be sure because he knows no one will believe him. I mean, he's lied his whole life."

"Did he confide in you again?"

"He said he's worried that the murderer thinks he recognized him and he's frightened."

"Then I'll offer protection. Don't forget, though, that paranoia goes with alcoholism."

"My father's father was an alcoholic. Thank god I've never had to live with that."

"Neither have I. But you are constantly arresting drug addicts, you said."

"Our prisons are overflowing with drug users. I have compassion for the users, but hate the dealers. They run around with suitcases full of money and have no qualms about the people they've killed with their drugs. The suitcase of money reminds me that Chloé reported that the little triad, Hans, Geneviève, and Philippe Douvier, are paying cash for land in a village called Serval."

"I wonder if the two hundred thousand that Hans claims is missing was in fact the downpayment for the land, even though he's claiming he brought it as a downpayment for the de Saint-Pern Company. When there was no contract. Max, do you know how sensitive this information is? Chloé mustn't speak of it to anyone. I'll talk to her." He put up his hand. "But for now we're off the case. *D'accord?* Do you agree?"

"Okay."

"We are entering an area called Les Faux de Verzy comprised of twisted beech trees that have only shown up in two other places, Sweden and Germany."

Max saw a sign advertising the *Parc arboxygène*, an extreme adventure park. "I'm in the wrong clothes to ride a zipline."

"Just wait." He drove slowly until they reached a sign that read The Perching Bar and parked. "Here we are." They got out and started walking to a rickety footbridge that ascended into the trees. They clutched the handrails because the bridge swayed with each step. They stepped off one walkway and started up a second until they finally reached a wooden deck ten meters above the ground.

Max stopped, and looked out onto the Plaine de Champagne and the lush treetops. "This is fabulous," she whispered. "I dreamed of living in a treehouse when I was a kid. You don't find too many in New York City!"

Olivier was pleased. He took her hand and guided her inside, where there were swings and ice buckets hanging from the ceiling. The interior was all wood and glass, and the sofa was covered with white leather. After ordering two glasses of the champagne *Zéro*, made by local winemakers Melanie and Benoit Tarlant, they strolled out to the terrace, where they clicked their glasses and sipped.

Olivier closed his eyes, "Do you smell the honey and lemon and mandarin?" Max sipped again. "That's stretching my olfactory sense a bit, but maybe the lemon. And it has a fine mousse. Ted taught me that."

Olivier smiled. "I like the citrusy freshness. It's quite lively." He felt the tension easing. It had been a perfect plan to come here. Max breathed in the sweet air. "It's funny about time. To be in places where it doesn't exist. Any chance I can sleep here tonight?"

He laughed. "You'd end up regretting missing a dinner created by a master chef."

"I like your modesty."

"Tell me about the tattoo."

It means I'll kick your ass if you don't kiss me. A line he'd never forget. She recalled the same moment, he thought, because she blushed, and sipped her champagne a tad too fast.

"I got the tattoo when I was eighteen after my brother had just been killed by a drunk driver. He was only twelve. I was crazy with guilt and anger and despair, and for a while I ran in a pretty bad crowd. It only lasted a summer, but it was intense."

"He was your only sibling?"

"The onliest, as we used to say. Though he was a lot younger, we were very close. I adored him."

"And he probably adored you."

"I think so. Hey, I didn't mean to get too maudlin. I always worry that people think I'm trying to elicit sympathy."

"Which didn't occur to me. It's an important life event."

"Good way of putting it. Everything changed. What about you? Do you have siblings?"

"I have a brother in Australia who owns a vineyard. They produce Sauvignon Blanc, It's quite good. I'm sorry to say I haven't seen him in two years. My parents left to go there after the wedding. I'm in the middle of a move to Bordeaux, as you know. I'll go soon, I hope."

A waiter came and refilled their glasses. "This wine is in my mind a scintillating combination of the grapes that are by law required to make champagne—chardonnay, pinot noir, and pinot meunier. The key is the formula, how the winemaker combines the three."

"That reminds me. The night of the wedding I had run to my room to remove my hat and stopped in the hallway when I heard two men speaking below. It was Baptiste Dupuis and Bernard Martin, who was at our table."

"Could you understand what they were saying?"

"They were discussing a formula. I thought Bernard sounded nervous. And maybe defeated."

"Bernard is on my list to interrogate, but that's business." Olivier enjoyed the desultory conversation, and the sensation of sipping wine above the treetops. "I managed to watch one of your American crime shows, I don't recall which one, two nights ago. Abdel swears by them."

"In reality, of course, cases don't get solved in an hour, and most of us are haggard from lack of sleep and we drink too much."

"I also read the article that Girard recommended about your father. Hank Maguire. He does sound a bit like Clint Eastwood. A hero in France, a country where there are very few."

"Why is Eastwood singled out?"

"The French are locked into believing you settle on your career and life, and that's the end of it. Eastwood has proved that you can keep changing and getting better."

"Many of us are brought up to believe that way. I plan to stop being a detective when I'm forty and try something different. Lots of us on the force plan to change."

"And your father?"

"He might go to sixty-five. You know, I've never been on a case without him or someone he's assigned to look out for me."

"So you don't know what you're capable of?"

"I hadn't thought about it that way. Some days it makes me feel like he doesn't have any faith in me. But when I'm rational, I know that it's about losing Frédéric."

She was soft, and open, her mysterious fragrance causing him to swoon. She had no idea how she was affecting him, and he was determined to keep it that way. He stood up, "Look how light it is at eight o'clock. June is the perfect month." He paid and led her to the footbridge, passing people on their way up. It was trickier going down. As they stepped onto the second walkway, Olivier pulled Max to him and kissed her softly, then again. She pressed up against him as they kissed, and when she pulled away and looked into his eyes, he was mesmerized. They laughed at the sensation of the bridge moving beneath them, and their clumsiness as they made their way down. In the car, he reached over and took her hand.

As he stopped in front of his parents' house, Max said, "I'm back in the fairy tale I was in before Léa was murdered. Maybe it will be like time travel, when it becomes harder to go back and forth."

"Then perhaps you'll have to stay."

"That's a simple conclusion."

She told him she thought the Chaumont two-story, stone house outside the village of Avenay-Val d'Or fabulous in its elegance and simplicity. She admired the gardens that were colorful and neat. When they entered the house, Olivier switched on John Coltrane and Max playfully whirled around.

"I know from the wedding that you like to dance."

"That was the first time I'd danced since my brother died."

"We'll have to make sure you continue." He took her in his arms and they spun into a dance around the kitchen, both of them smiling. When the music ended, he brought out a bottle of champagne and poured a glass for each of them, then removed the steaks from the refrigerator. Pulling a stool up to the center island, he ordered her to sit in the ringside seat. He put dried *cèpes*, a type of mushroom that had soaked in water, into a sauté pan, then added *champignons de Paris*, garlic, and parsley. When all the water was gone, he added the escargots.

"Snails, a universally favorite food." She was leaning in to watch, appearing to be fascinated. "I think my mother would have put more parsley."

"She cooks like this? I thought you were joking."

"I was. My mother's the exception. She's quite adventurous."

"You don't speak much about her."

"She's my best friend."

Olivier had never considered a mother and daughter being friends. He stuffed puff pastry into a dish and slid it into the oven, then turned and leaned toward Max for a kiss. When he turned back to check the pastry, she came up behind him and put her arms around his waist. He wondered if the dinner could wait. He had to make the *beurre d'ail* to pour over the mixture once it was in the cups, but he could do it later. He removed the pastry and turned off the oven. "I can't finish this now," he said. "Something much more important deserves my attention."

"What?"

"You." He grinned as he wrapped his arms around her. The telephone rang and he ignored it as he led her toward the stairs. Just as they arrived at the bottom of the stairs, Olivier's cell phone jangled. Then the house phone rang again, followed by the cell phone. "I should get that."

He walked to the counter and checked his cell. "It's Abdel." He answered. "*Oui?* When? I'll be right there."

Max was standing beside him. "What is it?"

"It's Antoine. He's missing."

Chapter Nineteen

Max, trying to ward off the notion that something bad had happened to Antoine, diverted her thoughts to dancing in the kitchen with Olivier.

"Sorry, Max. Fate keeps intervening."

"Shhh. I'm trying to make the adjustment back to the business at hand."

"Me, too. I'll drop you off at the house so you can change. And don't worry. Antoine's probably at Le Bar, though I assume they looked there." Olivier drove through the *porte cochère* and saw several police cars.

Abdel stepped out of the shadows, carrying a flashlight, though the moonlight was bright enough for them to recognize him. "The *commissaire* is already at Monsieur Marceau's cabin. The maid, Mimi, went to take Antoine dinner and found all the lights on and music blaring. She became alarmed and called the Marceaus, and they went down and looked around and didn't see any sign of him and began to worry."

"Who else is down there?"

"Captain Canon is on his way, and Chief Petit is there now."

"Why wasn't I called earlier? Obviously this happened at least an hour ago."

"It's eleven. Girard called me at 9:45. It started out with the family searching. Monsieur Durand called the police."

Again? Max thought.

"I'll meet you there." She raced into her room and peeled off her white clothes and stepped into jeans and cowboy boots, then threw on a tank top. She was at the stairs when Ted appeared. She stopped to embrace him, avoiding his bandaged jaw.

"Abdel drove me to the inn at five. He told me that you and Olivier were out. I came over here to see what's going on. I heard the sirens braying. What's happened?"

"Antoine has gone missing."

"But I was just there."

"With Antoine? Why, for god's sake?"

"Abdel picked me up at the hospital and drove me to the inn. I was bored as hell and decided to go for a drink at Le Bar, and Antoine was there."

She stopped. "Then what?"

"He invited me to his house for another drink and I said yes. Finally, I thought, someone in Léa's family is including me. I only stayed for a beer and went back to Le Bar for dinner."

"Did he say anything about leaving?"

"No. But he was afraid of being accused and locked up and also afraid that the murderer was coming for him. So much so that he told me that there was a blue vase on the mantel, and that if he was found dead and the vase was turned upside down it meant they had come for him. He told me a story about his childhood."

"Ted! I can't listen to all this right now. Do you know where he is?"

"No."

"I'm off. Go back to the inn and stay there. I'll find you.

"You don't believe me, do you? I'll put it all on my blog."

"Don't remind Girard and the other officials that you're back. Later." Once outside, she ran down the now-familiar path. Olivier, Abdel, and Girard watched her approach.

Girard said, "We've learned that Ted Clay had a drink with him at Le Bar." She could see that he wanted to impress his colleagues.

"I just saw Ted. There's nothing unusual about that, is there?"

Girard looked shocked. "Clay just got dropped off at five and he starts drinking with Antoine Marceau? *Quelle idiote.*"

Max almost burst into a series of French expletives, but thought better of it. Instead, she chose to ignore him by turning to Olivier, "What's going on?"

"We're about to go speak with *la jeune fille.*"

Mimi sat in a wicker chair, not intimidated by the officials who surrounded her. Max took a seat on the front step. Mimi explained. "This evening I walked the path down with my basket containing the sorrel soup that Antoine loves. When I arrived in his yard I thought it a little strange that all the lights were on and music was playing. I went up the stairs and the front door was open. I called out to Antoine but no one answered. I put my basket on the counter and climbed the narrow flight of stairs to his bedroom but it was empty. I went outside and walked down to the riverbank, and looked out across the Marne. Sometimes I know Antoine likes to fish at night. The sky wasn't dark yet. I saw a champagne glass on the ground, which was empty, and a bottle lay nearby. That was when I became alarmed and called Jacques, who went to Le Bar to look for him. Monsieur Durand and the German came to see if they could help find Antoine. Monsieur Durand insisted on calling the police chief, and since then I think half of the French regiment has shown up. I'm sure he's passed out somewhere, maybe with a woman. Wouldn't that be nice?"

Girard immediately started organizing a search. Abdel asked Max if she wanted check around the house with him, and she hopped up. "Do you think he's on the lam?" she asked.

"It would be completely out of character, but they're checking train stations. He's terrified of flying. We've learned that it's rare for him to leave his house, other than to walk to Le Bar. That has become his world."

Abdel went upstairs, and Max stood in the living room, her eyes darting around until they landed on a blue vase that was upside down. *What was Ted telling me about a blue vase? If it's upside down, that means someone came for him.*

She heard a shout from the river and joined Abdel on the porch. A gendarme was waving what looked like a large piece of fabric in the air. Captain Canon took it from him, and motioned Jacques to come over to identify it. Max stood watching, spell-bound. When Jacques turned to the little audience that had gathered, she knew. She and Abdel walked down to join the others.

Canon commanded his men to prepare to drag the river. Max knew the routine. If they discovered Antoine's body, they would need to find out if Antoine drowned, or if his body was thrown into the river after he was dead. It would take a long time, and there was nothing for the investigators to do but wait.

Olivier encouraged Jacques to return to the house. Marc insisted on staying, and Girard gave him a look of approval. Max couldn't get the vase off her mind, and decided to slip away and ask Ted more about it.

The lights on the river made Max think of a movie set. Ted had told her the story of the blue vase while they sipped a glass of champagne. Now she stood on the hill alone, watching the figures down below rushing around. When she walked into the lighted area at the river, Girard said, "We got him. They'll be bringing him off the boat in a few minutes." He seemed excited.

Olivier was standing in the shadow, out of the way of the confusion. "I called the medical examiner as you asked me to, Olivier." Olivier thanked Girard. "You don't suspect foul play, do you?"

"It's a precautionary action." Girard ran off to where Antoine's naked body lay in a supine position on the stretcher the gendarmes were lifting off the boat. They placed it gently on the riverbank, where several work lamps beamed artificial light onto the body.

"Grab a sheet!" someone called out, and Marc ran up to the house to fetch one. Olivier hadn't moved toward her, and she thought he might not know she was there. It was strange to think how intimate they had been, and completely carefree, a few hours ago. She recalled how it had been with Joe. When they were at a murder scene they would become brusque with each other, but later they would accept that this was the business they were in, and behave as though nothing had happened. She wondered, though, if dealing with violent deaths on an everyday basis had cut them off from their own feelings, and from each other.

"I didn't see you arrive," Olivier said. He walked over to her, and to her surprise, his hand wrapped around hers for an instant. He released his, and said, "Did you go to the house?"

"No. I went to Ted's room at the inn. He had attempted to tell me a strange story that Antoine had shared with him." She told him the story of the blue vase.

"You believe the story."

"The vase is upside down."

"This might be Antoine's idea of a joke."

"Maybe."

"We'll check it later, okay?"

He moved down to where the medical examiner was bent over the body. She thought him the same doctor who had shown up earlier for tea. Max wondered what it was like for him to be called to the property of the aristocratic family twice in a three-day period.

The doctor said, "There is froth exuding from the mouth when I press on his chest which tells me that he was alive at the time of submersion. I'd rule out suicide. He had on a robe, but most suicides remove their clothing. Often they attach heavy objects to themselves. I'm leaning toward accidental drowning."

"I want a forensic autopsy performed to make sure," Olivier said.

"Really? They're quite uncommon."

"I know."

The medical examiner shrugged. "As you wish, monsieur. We'll wrap things up here."

Girard came up and said to Max, "I'll need to speak to Monsieur Clay again tomorrow. He may have been the last to see Monsieur Marceau alive."

"That's between you and Monsieur Clay."

"Monsieur Reynard informed me today that the Minister of Justice is watching the case closely, and approves of your participation. Is this because of your father?"

"I hope not, Thomas." She knew that he was impressed by her new status, but that he couldn't comprehend how a lowly detective was under the watchful gaze of someone like Douvier and hobnobbing with the aristocracy.

She hadn't heard Olivier approach with Jacques, and hoped he hadn't overheard the remark. "Max," Jacques said, "I would like to ask you to go be with Chloé tonight. She is quite anxious over her uncle's disappearance. This will be devastating."

"Of course." A quick glance at Olivier told her that he understood. Girard looked from one to the other, puzzled. Max took Jacques' arm and they went up the path. Once at the house, she asked Jacques if she could call her father, and he offered his study.

Hank answered immediately. "I was getting ready to fly over to check on you. Your mom...."

"There's been another death."

"You got a serial guy?"

"I don't know. A panicked murderer, I think."

"Tell me about it." She did. Every detail. Even the ridiculous blue vase.

After hearing her story, Hank offered, "Antoine's death is a homicide. Hard as hell to prove that a drowning is homicide. You got a clever one." After a moment's hesitation, he said, "You okay?"

"Sad and mad."

"Antoine was another lost puppy. How many of those have you rescued?"

"A few."

"You'll feel a lot better when you nab the killer. I'm sure as a lit major you read *Crime and Punishment*, right?"

"I wrote a thesis on it."

"Remember what Raskolnikov's friends said, 'The more cunning a man is, the less he suspects he will be caught in a simple thing.'"

"I'd forgotten it. But I do remember the rejoinder, 'The more cunning a man is, the simpler the trap he must be caught in.'"

"The only reason your friend Antoine got killed was because the murderer thought Antoine could identify him. Setting it up to look like suicide or accidental drowning was a good ploy. But it still doesn't eliminate any of the suspects. Where's Oliver in all this?"

"His name's Olivier."

"Same thing."

"Impressive in all aspects. You'd approve."

"Huh. I'll put your ma on."

"*Chérie,* what did you say about Olivier?" Max smiled. Any hint of romance took precedence over murder for her mom. "There is interest, yes?"

"Sort of."

"You know I don't understand that expression."

"Parce que cela ne veut rien dire! It has no meaning. Think of it as a verbal shrug."

Hank got back on, "You can solve this case, Max. Focus on the motive. On the psychological. Write everything down in your journal. I'll run it through my personal database and see what I come up with." He had referred to his brain being a database too often for it to be funny any longer, but she smiled anyhow. "This killer's angry."

She went to the salon after she hung up, and was surprised to see Marc. "Oh, sorry," she said. "I'm looking for Chloé."

He lifted a glass of brandy, then lit a cigarette. "She went to bed a while ago. You want a glass?"

"No, thanks. Is she okay? She must have been devastated."

"She is. She knew, though, that with the drinking and all that his days were numbered. Can I get you something from the kitchen?"

"I'll be fine. The village will be buzzing with these deaths."

"No one will be surprised to learn that Antoine got drunk and fell into the river. I heard he's been drinking more since Léa's death. I hate to say it, but it wouldn't surprise me if they discover he killed her."

"Really? Why do you say that?"

"You remember the fight they had the night before the wedding. Antoine was rabid about not letting a German buy out a champagne company."

"Half of the companies were started by Germans."

"It was personal for Antoine, and fueled by alcohol. Jacques and Antoine's grandfather died in a German concentration camp. Their father never got over it and that attitude was inherited by Antoine. Jacques decided to move on."

"But, Marc, it's one thing to carry revenge in your heart and quite another to kill over it. Nothing justifies murder."

"Léa called Antoine a parasite and a nothing. A man's only going to take so much of that."

"You called the police when you learned Antoine was missing? Did you think he was dead?"

Marc sipped his brandy. "Everybody in the family was looking and no one knew what to do, so I called Girard. He's a good guy." Max didn't need to hear Girard's praises sung.

She got up to leave, but Marc stopped her with his next comment. "Hans and I were at Le Bar and saw Ted Clay having a drink with Antoine. He followed him out."

"The investigators already know all of this. What are you implying?"

"Nothing, Max." He laughed, "There's nothing to accuse him of, except getting drunk with Antoine and leaving." Max felt confused. She was the only one who thought Antoine was murdered, so why was she being so sensitive?

"Is Hans still staying at the inn?"

"Yes, and quite miserable about it, I might add. My mother is coming out for Léa's funeral tomorrow. She's concerned about Ted."

This was as chatty as Max had ever heard Marc, but everything he said felt pointed, as though there could be a double meaning. Why, for example, did his mother feel concern for Ted when she denied his alibi? And why would Marc tell her?

"I'm off to bed. *Bonne nuit,* Marc."

She went to her room and pulled out her journal and sat in the chair at the window, writing stream-of-consciousness.

Everything she had seen and heard. She smelled cigarette smoke, and looked up to find Chloé standing in the doorway. "I can't sleep, Max. He died thinking I blamed him for Léa's death. I'll never be able to live with that."

Max put down her journal and the two old friends climbed into Max's bed, just like the old days, and began to talk. Chloé admitted that she had been distraught and Marc had finally had it with her snuffling.

"I don't know what's going on with him," she said. "He's drinking too much. Maybe I'm sensitive about Antoine."

"Two of your family members have died. Give me a break!"

"Marc and I talked tonight about going to New York for at least a year. We both want to get away now. This place feels cursed."

"What about the company?"

"Who knows? For now, let's talk about something other than death and business. Like Olivier."

"I like him, Chloé. He's different from any man I've ever known."

"How so?"

"I don't know another man who goes around sniffing flowers."

Chloé giggled. Good, Max thought. They froze when they heard a tap on the door. Marc entered, and looking at his wife, asked if she was coming to bed.

"I'm staying here tonight, *chéri*. I'm already tucked in." He stood in the shadow for another moment, then abruptly turned and vanished.

"He doesn't understand how you and I are like sisters," Chloé said. "We don't have BFF's in France."

"Best friends forever. The French don't know what they're missing."

"I'm going to go to him," Chloé said, climbing out of bed. "I don't want him angry."

"Do what you need to do. *Bonne nuit!*"

Chapter Twenty

Olivier returned home to the half-prepared dinner and put it all in the refrigerator. Once again, an evening gone awry. He wondered if he shouldn't heed the message to let go of his attraction to Max; after all, it was, for both of them, an interlude. She would be returning to New York and he would move to Bordeaux and start a new life there. What was interesting was that he didn't feel that the time spent with her compromised the investigation in any way. They were both pros, and even this evening, when he wanted nothing more than to bring her back home with him, he understood Jacques' request for her to stay for Chloé.

He poured a glass of cold beer and went outside to look at the sky and inhale the fragrance of the late hour. He could imagine Antoine doing much the same. After a few drinks he had invited Ted back for more, and when Ted left, he probably walked down to the river with his bottle and glass to toast the stars, or perhaps to fish, while waiting for Mimi to show up with dinner. He thought that Mimi and Marie-Christine had been enabling Antoine for years, making sure that he ate and that his house was occasionally cleaned.

Olivier had felt the vulnerability of the human race as they brought Antoine's naked body to the shore and laid the stretcher on the ground. Had Antoine accidentally stepped into a hole? No, he knew the riverbank too well. Max was convinced that Antoine had been murdered. That was one reason he had ordered the forensic autopsy, surprising everyone. Well, why not? They had nothing to lose.

Olivier resolved not to let the story of the blue vase lead him down the wrong path. As much as he tried to fend off any speculation, he began, standing in solitude in the garden, to wonder who would want Antoine dead. He had been clear that someone had bumped into him right after the murder, and that was likely true, but he never gave a hint of who it might have been. Was Max right to think that he knew, but wasn't ready to reveal the information? How ironic that Ted Clay had been with him in his last hours. No investigator could come up with a reason for Ted to want him dead, though, unless Ted had killed Léa and thought that Antoine could identify him.

What was broken about the entire investigation, he realized, was that he knew all the suspects. He thought that if it dragged on much longer, he would surrender and allow another *juge d'instruction* to take over. It had been painful listening to Marie-Christine during her interview talking about her husband and her sister, and now he dreaded what Jacques would have to say about his brother. There would be regret, surely, and remorse. He didn't want to allow himself to think that Jacques and Léa had argued, that their old passion had flared and Jacques killed her out of jealousy and rage. Then told his brother, who had threatened him, forcing Jacques to kill him too by getting him drunker than usual and pushing him into the river.

He had to get some sleep and stop this imaginary journey to nowhere. Tomorrow was Léa's funeral, which he also dreaded. He wasn't in the least religious, and to sit through the rituals and throw holy water on the coffin felt hypocritical. Now in the kitchen, he poured more beer into his glass and put on the last twenty-three minutes of Mahler's Ninth Symphony, a favorite. He loved the comment of one critic who had said that the symphony allowed Mahler to "weep without apology." He turned the sound up and sat as though in meditation, wishing that he could weep.

◇◇◇

The church was packed for Léa's funeral, taking place in the same church where Chloé and Marc had married. Olivier saw Max standing with Chloé as he drove up and parked. Though Jacques had invited him to sit with the family, he had declined for professional reasons. He stood at a respectful distance from the crowd and watched the pallbearers remove the coffin from the hearse. Girard, looking ill at ease in a suit, joined him and they shook hands. "I suppose it's a myth that the murderer often shows up at the funeral."

"We've all heard it," Olivier said. "I find myself scanning the crowd, and hoping that he'll stand out. It's never happened."

"Me, too."

It was a long queue, and Olivier and Girard were among the last to enter the church, which resounded with the music of Bach. Olivier turned his head slightly and saw Ted Clay stop mid-aisle, wondering where to sit. A surge of compassion overtook Olivier as he realized that this man had every right to be considered innocent, and yet he had been banned from the Marceau family from the start. Ted's late arrival with Geneviève that night at the dinner had made an awful impression, and even if the murder had not occurred, Jacques and Marie-Christine would have shunned him. The autopsy should arrive today, he thought, and they would know for sure if the baby was Ted's. Ted sat near the aisle, making the sign of the cross before sitting.

But he wasn't to be alone for long as Geneviève walked dramatically down the aisle, looking quite exceptional in black and white. Her suit appeared to be linen, and he wondered if it was one of her creations. He knew she was known for sewing a rose into the hem of each of her garments, which he thought was a clever gimmick when he had learned about it from Véronique. According to Abdel's extraordinary financial sleuthing skills, Geneviève had a shrinking bank account and in fact had been asking Marc for help. These days her fashion line was not in vogue, and a year without a subsidy from her lover was probably taking a toll. She slid in beside Ted and whispered something, causing him to lean his head down in order to understand. It was an intimate gesture and would create gossip.

Max, who had turned out to be a storehouse of information gleaned from various people, claimed that Ted had had a brief fling with Geneviève a few years back when he arrived in Paris. This when she had been the mistress of Philippe Douvier? He knew that Douvier had to be following every moment of this investigation, but who besides Girard was feeding him information? His ex-mistress? Keller?

Chloé telling Max about the triad trying to invest in land had to be filed away for now, but Olivier thought he would slip out to Serval and talk to a few people. An old classmate of his lived there. Could Geneviève manage to have gotten her hands on the missing money? It would give her some financial breathing room. Now that her best-laid plans around the de Saint-Pern Company seemed to be falling apart, she might have felt desperate enough to take it all, or consider it restitution money from her ex-lover.

Girard leaned over, and Olivier got a whiff of a strong men's cologne that almost caused him to sneeze. "That woman," Girard said, staring at Geneviève. "She's the mother of the groom?"

"Exactement."

"Thin, huh?" Olivier glanced at him and saw that he was saying it with compassion, as though she had a cancer. Looking around, Olivier saw that almost everyone who was at the wedding was here, and wondered who would be around to attend Antoine's funeral.

Girard leaned over again, "Madame Durand knows the American, I understand. I wonder if she's aware we're locking him up today."

Olivier was shocked. "When was that decided?"

"The higher-ups, and the public, are demanding an arrest. Our chief prosecutor Reynard has pointed the finger at Monsieur Clay. Reynard didn't call you?"

Olivier was furious. It was up to him to decide, or at least he should have been in on the decision. It was clear to him that Reynard was enjoying the attention of his superiors and the press, and that kind of basking was bound to bring mistakes. He would explain to Max that Ted would be okay for a few days, and in fact, with him locked up they could move more judiciously. The music swelled, and Girard and Olivier returned to watching people walk down the aisle.

The priest told a couple of stories of Léa when she was a child, and brought up her rise to power in her husband's company to be among a short list of women who had made a name in the champagne world. There were readings and prayers, but Olivier barely paid attention. French funerals were rarely personal, though in some regions they were becoming more so. The hearse would take the body to the crematorium after the service and they were to meet again mid-afternoon at the burial cemetery. Close friends and family were to go back to the Marceaus for lunch now. Olivier wanted to somehow make the time to read the documents from Léa's office and home, which had been secured by the police hours after her death.

Everyone started filing out, and he had been so lost in thought that he hadn't heard the end of the service. Once outside, he caught Max's eye, and she fluttered her fingers, a funny little habit that he found charming.

"Max is coming to have a dinner with me once all this is over," Girard said. He hadn't begun to give up on seducing the blond American, Olivier thought.

"Sounds like fun."

Max approached. "I spoke with my father, and he quoted from *Crime and Punishment.*" Olivier quoted the lines that he knew she was referring to and which he had known since he was an adolescent. He was pleased to see Girard looking a bit lost in the conversation. He was also pleased to realize how easy it was to connect with Max.

"I'd like to go to Antoine's house," Max said.

Girard nodded. "Why don't we go together? Either later, or in the morning I could make some time."

Olivier thought Girard had backed off in his pursuit of Max, but something had re-ignited his flame. Olivier didn't want to bring up the private luncheon to be held at the Marceau house, so he excused himself discreetly. As he was leaving, Marc and Chloé walked up and invited Max to come with them. Marie-Christine and Mimi had organized a lunch of cold salmon and salad, and lovely meats and cheeses. Trays of champagne were brought out. Approximately forty people came for lunch, and after looking around, Olivier thought Hans Keller the only surprise. Marc and Chloé's friends, Delphine and Yves, were wandering around, so he took the opportunity to let them know that they had to come in for an interrogation and why.

He went searching for Max, and finally asked Chloé, who said she had gone to be with Ted at the inn. He rushed over. Girard was standing in the lobby with Ted and Max, who was obviously fighting back tears. "*Bien,*" Girard said, "*On y va.*"

"Yep, let's go," Ted said.

"Where're you taking him?" Max asked.

"To a *Maison d'arrêt* in *Châlons en Champ*agne," Girard said.

"Like a county jail in the U.S.," Olivier added. "He will be in a *quartier semi-liberté* which means he will have more freedom. You can visit him there." Ted turned toward Max and she held him in a long embrace.

"I've been writing my blog these past few days," Ted said. "Read it if you find yourself bored."

"I will. And I'll see you as soon as I can."

Max and Olivier stood on the street and watched the two men enter the police car, Girard in the front and Ted in the back. Olivier knew what a humiliating moment this must be for Ted.

"I only learned of the arrest a short time ago," he said by way of apology.

Max's eyes narrowed. "I'm going to prove him innocent before I leave France," she said. It wasn't what she said that made Olivier believe her, but the fierce determination in her eyes.

Chapter Twenty-one

They watched the car carrying Ted to jail until it was out of sight. Proving Ted innocent would mean stepping up the pace of the investigation, but how to convey that to the plethora of authorities who were constantly stepping on each other's toes, then backing off, Max had no idea. Even she had wavered briefly when all the facts were presented to her about Ted—his lack of an alibi, proof of his quick temper at the bar, his belief that he would inherit half of Léa s estate which would solve all of his money problems, his being the last to see both Léa and Antoine alive—but singly none of them stood up to close scrutiny. She had seen too often what happened when too many facts stacked up against a suspect, how authorities jumped to conclusions in their relief over having someone in custody. Too often the investigation stopped there, and innocent people were sent to trial. She knew Ted. His need to please and appease was something she had called him on in the past, but his overall character was stellar in her mind.

She turned to Olivier, "I'm aware that Antoine's death is presumed to be accidental drowning, but I want to go back there to look around before anyone else does. Will you accompany me?"

He gave her a skeptical look, then glanced at his watch. "I can't stand the idea of throwing more holy water on Léa's grave. Shall we go now?" She hoped she wouldn't be missed at the cemetery service. They crossed the street and walked to the hidden drive that led to Antoine's.

Marc called out to them, and they waited for him to catch up. He looked exhausted. "We are preparing to go to the cemetery to bury Léa's ashes," he said. "Are you coming?"

"No," Olivier said. "I have said *adieu* to Léa, and so has Max." Max recalled that *adieu* was used to indicate a permanent farewell.

"Tell Chloé I'll meet her back at the house," Max said.

Marc lit a cigarette. "My mother is here, Max. She likes you, and I know would like to spend a little time with you. Chloé..."

"I'll be back in an hour."

When he seemed about to follow them, Olivier said, "We'll be at Antoine's on official business."

"Anything I can do to help?"

"I'm concerned that a drug dealer came after Antoine, Marc. We need to talk, as I want the names of everyone you know who has sold drugs."

"But we have talked," Marc said, and walked in the opposite direction.

"I know these deaths are taking a toll on our newlyweds," Olivier said once Marc was out of hearing range, "but Marc's not who I would have expected Chloé to marry. Have you spent any time with him?"

"We talked last night for a few minutes. He's arrogant, and I don't know if that ever changes. He and Hans Keller were at Le Bar earlier in the evening, and he made a point of telling me that Ted went to Antoine's for drinks. He has that *je ne sais quoi,* a need to tell. We call someone like that a tattle-tale. He has called Girard twice, to report the necklace and to report Antoine missing."

"I've noticed, too, but isn't that just being responsible?"

"I'm speaking more about his character. He latched on to Hans Keller, and I don't know what happened but that's not going well, and now he seems to want to be in Girard's favor."

"I had the sense that he knew how to bend the truth when I spoke with him." Olivier paused and she knew he was deciding if he could confide in her. "I want you to know that I decided last night to recuse myself from this investigation if we don't make headway soon. I find myself floundering a bit when it comes to being objective. This conversation is a good example."

"But in interrogations you are seeking these small clues to the inner workings of the interviewees, right? My father taught me to listen to the 'words beneath the words.' What is the interviewee really saying? For example, what is Marc saying when he feels the need to tell me that Ted went off with Antoine. Is it a blame game? Or is it something else?"

They had entered Antoine's yard where a gendarme approached. "What's going on?" Olivier asked him. "This isn't officially a crime scene to my knowledge."

"Captain Canon thought it the most efficient way to keep curious people out, monsieur."

"*D'accord.*" Olivier and Max continued talking as they headed across the lawn toward Antoine's house. Olivier told her that he had requested a forensic autopsy just in case. She understood by the term that Antoine's body would be dissected because there was suspicion that his death was a criminal matter.

He explained, "I agree with Jacques that it wasn't a suicide, but for different reasons. The medical examiner told me that he saw evidence that Antoine struggled to save himself, which was one reason he ruled it an accidental drowning after a physical examination. He could have stepped into a hole or tripped in what I'm sure was an inebriated state, but with the information you gave me from Ted Clay, I want to know more."

"A thorough autopsy can guide the investigation in the right direction and a careless one can throw us off track. I've been to a few, and it's surprising how much information is in the body."

"It's macabre."

"It's the stench that almost does you in at first, but then it's like being in a lab. Where the truth often lies. I know how big you are on truth."

I have to go to that autopsy, Max thought.

Her feet hurt and she stepped out of the shoes she'd worn to the funeral, and carried them in her hand. They sat on the riverbank.

"I much prefer nature's laboratory," Olivier said, removing his jacket and putting it on the grass. They watched a boat pass. "Antoine loved the river, and he knew every curve and dip," Olivier continued in a quiet voice. "I'll never know, but I don't think he would have wandered down here in his robe. He was waiting for Mimi to bring him dinner. He was accustomed to eating quite late, as she left the big house only after everything was in order. And he surely wouldn't have stepped into the river wearing his robe." He looked out over the wide river, drinking in the beauty.

Olivier's more an aesthete than a criminologist, Max thought. She wondered what it would be like to have Olivier and Hank in the same room, for as much as Hank was pegged as a tough sonofabitch, he was also a philosopher. It was up to her to get Olivier back on track.

"I hate to distract you from your ruminations, but do you have the results of Léa's autopsy report?"

"Her cause of death was an extradural hemorrhage from a skull fracture in the back of her head with associated intracranial damage. Her cheekbone on the right side was fractured as well and the bleeding from that obstructed the breathing passages."

"And the baby?"

"Ted Clay was the father."

"It's the first time I've known the victim of a murder…"

"The same is true for me."

"Seeing her on the ground, and the smell…isn't it amazing that even after a few minutes you pick up the smell of death?"

"You know, Max, I haven't conducted many murder investigations. My specialty is corporate and political wrongdoing."

That put a different slant on the investigation. "And I deal mostly with the slimiest segment of society. People murder each other for the lamest reasons."

"I'm surprised your father would allow you in that world."

She laughed. "Allow? He insisted. I think the Irish in us likes to defy Fate. My mother hated the idea of me chasing criminals.

It was because of her that I went through university. Shall we have a look around the house?"

"But Girard…"

"We don't need him. I'm a genius at nosing around."

He laughed. They ambled up the slope, and the gendarme waved from his station on the path. The blue vase was still there. Looking impertinent. Olivier walked over to it. "Do you still find it a significant piece of the puzzle?"

Ted had offered more of the story when she went to sit with him. She told Olivier how Antoine had been afraid of UFO's coming for him when he had been a boy and his mother had devised a plan to rid him of the fear. She told him that the vase was magic. Each time the Martians came, the blue vase would suck them in and hold them until she could toss them out in the morning. She created a game with her son; if they had come he would turn the vase upside down so that they couldn't get out, and she would go to work by taking the vase to the window and shaking them out and then setting it back on the shelf. Antoine had kept the vase as a memento of her.

"So we're back in the fairy tale?"

"It seems so. A more sinister one. Where there is no happy ending."

She found his laser gaze disconcerting, feeling as though he could see into her. How can I make him understand me, she thought. "I know I sometimes talk in a cold, formal manner, Olivier, but were I to succumb to even one of my feelings right now, I would have to fly home, as I could not continue in the investigation. When you and I were standing apart and looking at Antoine's body, I felt a vast space open up, as though after sharing this we could never look at each other without that moment being there. It was the same when we came upon Léa's body."

"Those moments have to be transcended," Olivier said. "Forgive me for bringing this up, but your parents had to go through a similar process after standing over their son who had died. It was the most tragic moment of their lives…"

"It almost destroyed them. And I don't know where I am regarding his death. I keep thinking I'll go to a therapist to work through it. Much more frightening than racing to murders."

"We have to remember why we're in our respective professions. It's incumbent upon you and me to solve Léa's murder, and learn what happened to Antoine."

"That doesn't sound like a man ready to recuse himself. I agree with everything you've said. And please don't think I'm weird…but is there any way I can attend Antoine's autopsy?"

"The body was taken to a hospital in a western suburb of Paris. Why do you want to do this?"

"Because it speeds things up. It's rare for a drowning to be declared a homicide even if that's the case, because it's so difficult to prove it. I've been through two of these, where we did prove it, but only because my dad and I were there to find clues."

Hank had gone with her to her first and she'd sat on the floor the entire time while he had talked to the doctor as though nothing were unusual. But he had proven to her that if the medical examiner wasn't comfortable working with the police, problems would arise.

Olivier sighed. "Monsieur Henri Legrand is the examiner. I will speak with him, but Max, I think we're crossing boundaries that maybe shouldn't be crossed."

"He may surprise you and welcome the help."

"He is French, and the French don't welcome help." His admittance of that struck her as funny. She could see he was torn.

"You know it's hard to drown someone. There would have to be pretty significant physical disparity between the victim and the attacker. The victim would fight back."

"Not if he was intoxicated."

"We're here for a cursory look around. We didn't bring gloves."

"There are plastic gloves in the kitchen. I noticed them two days ago." They entered the kitchen and Max took them from the counter. "Look at everything carefully, with all your senses," she said, "and know that everything has relevance."

They began to move around, looking at books, at the newspapers that had accumulated. "I'll go check his bedroom," Olivier said.

"I'll continue here with papers, bank books, stuff like that." She went to the desk where a variety of papers, mainly bills, were piled up. She lifted them one by one and put them to the side. A sheaf of papers was propped up, and she picked it up and read the top page. It was dated June 23, yesterday.

"Olivier!" He emerged from the bedroom, eyebrows raised. "This document is hand-written. I think it has to do with Antoine selling his shares in de Saint-Pern to Hans Keller."

He took the paper she handed him and read it. "Antoine did what he said he was going to do at the dinner that night, which was to sell to Keller. It's sad, but not a big surprise. Everything in the bedroom is a mess, but nothing stands out. I don't see how this sale proves anything."

"What if he was forced to write that and sign it?"

"If it was Keller, he would have arrived after Ted Clay left."

"But there's no way to prove that he came here at all. Unless he admits it. And why would he tell us he came and killed Antoine?" She knew her voice was starting to sound strident from pure frustration.

"Max…"

She knew with all her being that Antoine had managed to turn the blue vase upside down before he died. But she couldn't go to others, not even the family, and declare this. "Do you believe that the blue vase might be a key, Olivier?"

Please, please, walk out on that limb with me, she thought.

The western sunlight shone into the room, and Max focused her attention on the burnished wood that she imagined Mimi kept polished. The wait was killing her. Her eyes went back to Olivier's and stayed there.

"I believe you, though not fervently."

"I don't need your fervent."

Chapter Twenty-two

The bartender Michel waved when Max and Olivier entered Le Bar at six. Several men were sitting on stools. Max and Olivier had left Antoine's and gone to his car and retrieved all of the wedding photographs taken by the professional photographer. Olivier ordered a *vin blanc* for each of them and indicated a round table in the rear that had a light over it so they could examine each proof. Abdel would later catalog every picture, but for now he wanted to see if anything jumped out. Max had already taken a handful of the pictures and was studying them. Now that they were away from Antoine's, he realized that the only reason he was considering that Antoine had been murdered was because of Max's influence.

Max was glancing through the photos as though they were a deck of cards. "Here's an interesting one."

He took the photo Max handed him and moved it into the light. Bernard and Caroline were standing with Baptiste Dupuis and his wife, looking quite cozy. He was already planning to interview them.

"Oh, wow. Hans Keller and Yves' girlfriend, Delphine. Here's another one. Good god!" Olivier took them and put them under the light. He had noticed Delphine at the wedding. She was a petite woman with an hourglass figure and a sultry smile. In the photo she looked quite enamored of Hans. In the next one Hans had his hand on her attractive derriere. And in the one following they were kissing.

"Nothing discreet about those pictures," Max proclaimed. "I can't help but think about the ice bucket and bottle of champagne. What if Keller put a bottle of champagne in a bucket and prepared to take the champagne and Delphine to a more private place, like the stone bench…"

Olivier realized that trying to follow her thoughts was like being on the tail of a kite. But he was also starting to see how she formed her theories—some of which were very good. After a few more moments of flipping through pictures, she finally looked over at him. "I know I have to be at the Marceaus for dinner at nine, but we didn't have lunch. I'm starving."

Olivier was too. He motioned Michel over and ordered the house *pâté*. Max returned to the photographs. He moved closer to her to see what she was looking at. "Here are photographs of the wedding ceremony in the church. Beautiful. And here are the newlyweds in the antique car going back to the reception. These are photographs of the afternoon reception for two hundred. There's Léa, smiling at Ted. Here she is with Chloé in a big embrace. In this one she's talking with Geneviève, but they both look unhappy. Angry, even. Wonder what's going on there."

"Put that one aside," Olivier said. "The ones of Hans Keller too."

"Chloé is the radiant bride at first, I notice, but look at this one of her in the tent with Delphine, both looking a little drunk. She looks sad. Where is Marc? Where is Yves?"

"Sniffing cocaine, I guess."

"Oh, here they are. Marc has changed into jeans and is barefoot. That's what we were all planning to do." Max sipped her wine. "Antoine is only in two photos so far."

She giggled. "Oh god. You and I got caught." She handed him the photograph of the two of them looking out over the reception crowd when they first arrived, her in the gorgeous hat, a half smile on her face, and him looking at her, appearing as smitten as a teenager.

"I'm sure I was admiring your hat."

"It looks to me like you want to kiss me."

"I did want to kiss you, and I did."

And I actually want to kiss you now.

"Look who's coming in." Olivier followed her gaze and saw Geneviève entering with Hans. They went to a table on the other side of the room without glancing around, and sat down. Hans asked for a beer and Geneviève ordered champagne. She looked out of place, wearing an outfit that might work at the Hemingway Bar at the Ritz. Others started to trickle in. Olivier's cell phone rang and he excused himself to Max, who nodded in understanding. In a moment Marc entered and went immediately to his mother's table and ordered a beer. Olivier was on the phone with Abdel who told him that the bottle indeed carried a number of fingerprints, and he proceeded to enumerate them: Hans Keller, Jacques Marceau, Antoine, and even the kids who got drunk off the champagne. "Chief Petit guessed who they were."

"Not Monsieur Clay?"

After he hung up, Max said, "Marc just came in. But not Chloé. I should probably head back to the house soon." He repeated the results of the prints found on the bottle, and she was pensive for a moment. "Do you plan to ask Keller if he handled the murder weapon?"

"Of course. The murderer was probably smart enough to wear gloves, though. I'll be back." Olivier sauntered toward the bar and ordered another *vin blanc,* then turned to Geneviève and Hans. "A stressful day."

Hans was pouting. "Try being under house arrest to know what stressful is."

"I'm afraid you'll be here a bit longer. Your fingerprints were found on the murder weapon, a full bottle of champagne." Geneviève gave a small gasp. Hans' face pinked up. "You'll need to come in for interrogation. My assistant will be in touch." Olivier picked up his wine and went back to the table where Max had continued to pour over photographs.

"From the body language I observed, you're not the most popular man in the room."

"I'll give Hans ten minutes to wander over here."

"I have set aside quite a few photographs for you to look at." She handed them to him. "Nothing more jumps out at me."

An argument coming from Hans' corner distracted them, and Geneviève marched out. Hans stood and hesitated, then walked over to their table. "I need to talk to you," he said to Olivier, barely acknowledging Max. Olivier motioned for him to sit down.

The *pâté* arrived and Hans insisted that they eat. Olivier put a portion on Max's plate and then on his. "My father has hired a private investigator to find the missing Euros. The next thing is the bottle. I put my hands on several champagne bottles that night, pouring for myself and for others. I had no motive for killing Léa de Saint-Pern, and I have a perfect alibi."

"As for the motive, we talked about this. Léa had decided not to sell to a German whose grandfather betrayed the French, remember?"

Hans clenched his hands into fists, but was smart enough to know how vulnerable he was. "So I knew I had to swallow my medicine and go on."

"But I think you were more determined than that. I found the paper where Antoine Marceau agreed to sell you his family shares of de Saint-Pern for two hundred thousand euros. A pittance, I might add. But what's fascinating is that it matches the two hundred-thousand you're claiming was stolen."

Hans pounded the table. "This is insane! I never made a deal with him. He signed nothing in front of me!"

"What about the woman, Delphine? Tell me about your assignation with her. Maybe you put a bottle of champagne on ice for a private rendezvous?"

"No! I was in the kitchen with the maid and there were others there. Jacques Marceau, came in for a bucket of ice and champagne for his daughter and her friends. And Marc asked me to hand him a bottle as he was going out to meet with his buddies who had acquired some cocaine. They invited me but I thought they were being ridiculous."

Max said calmly, "You were more interested in seducing Delphine."

"You have no right by French law to question me, *mademoiselle.*"

Olivier saw Max's eyes turn to thin slits of steel. "Then I'm asking. You were more interested in seducing Delphine?"

"She was furious with her boyfriend. So, yes."

Olivier stepped back in, "And did you see anything on your way to the inn or back?"

"I only went one way. I saw Léa standing in the garden and I approached her for the final time about selling her company. She said she wouldn't sell to me because of my grandfather's reputation. I called her whore and bitch and I don't know what else, and I'm not sorry. She'll get hers one day, I thought, as I walked up to the terrace where Delphine was waiting."

Olivier thought of the last words that entered Léa's consciousness and how her last moments, with Hans and with her killer, were fraught with men despising her. She had grabbed at a rose, which became locked in her hand at the moment of death. It was a symbol for love and purity, but even more, the rose was associated with Mary Magdalene and the Divine Feminine.

He looked around at the expectant faces and tried to think where he was when he became distracted. "With a bucket of ice and a bottle of champagne?"he asked.

"You're being redundant, Monsieur Chaumont. I already told you that I handed the bucket of ice and champagne to Marc who was taking it to his adolescent friends."

"The young woman, Delphine, returned to the house alone? You didn't walk her back?"

"She didn't want her boyfriend to see us together."

Delphine, the quiet one who hadn't made a blip on the radar screen. "I'll verify all of this. Thank you for the information. You seem to spend a lot of time with Marc and Geneviève Durand. Do they get along well?"

"They argue incessantly and I'm sick of them. Marc won't know which side of the fence to sit on until the wills are read.

Chloé might inherit, then Marc could take over. He hasn't said that outright, but I can read him. And Geneviève?" The name came out as a sneer. "She manipulated Marc's introduction to Chloé Marceau, and she pushed Ted before that to get Marc into de Saint-Pern for an internship. She will stop at nothing, that woman, and she used to have the power behind her. Now she's freaking out because none of her old lover Douvier's acquaintances will have anything to do with her. No one has invited her for a cup of coffee she told me, since he dropped her."

Hans stood up, "I haven't played my hand yet, but now I'm going to. Your Minister of Justice is a friend of mine. He has invested heavily in my father's company, and he and I are working on another investment in France. My father and I've spent many years trying to clear my grandfather's name. All of a sudden my name is bandied about your papers as though I were a criminal. On top of that I've got two hundred thousand euros missing and I will get it back!"

He stormed out.

The bartender walked over and asked to have a word, and Olivier indicated that he should sit. He looked around. "I've been really upset about Antoine. He was a friend. The night he drowned, business was slow and I was closing up and saw a large woman in a dress go by the window. It was a full moon and I went to the window to watch. She took great strides, like an athlete. I stepped out the door and asked if I could help, and she stuck up her hand as if to say 'go away!'"

"What was unusual?" Olivier asked.

"I know everybody, but there was nothing recognizable about her. I thought I should mention it to you."

"I'll make note of it. Thank you." The bartender went back to his station.

Max asked, "Where does that leave us?"

"Hitting another wall." Olivier sighed, "You're going to be late for dinner."

"The *pâté* was perfect." They said goodnight to the bartender and began walking toward the inn where Olivier had left his car.

The suggestion was out before he could reel in his thoughts. "You could come home with me for dinner."

She stood quietly for a moment before responding. "Sure."

So certain was he that she would decline that the easy acceptance caused a wave of nervousness to pass over him. He knew it was unwise to mix the professional and the personal, and there was no question now that they were in their respective, professional roles solving a crime. Maybe two. But there were things about her that continued to cause him to do things he knew were not wise.

She got into the passenger seat before he could open the door, and had her seatbelt buckled before he had made it around to the driver's side of the car. He thought about how both times they had been close to making love they were interrupted by murder. She had a point about dead bodies being a turn-off to romance. He didn't know what was wrong with him. He didn't want to be alone, but now that she had said yes, he did want to be alone. He needed to collect his thoughts, to plan for tomorrow. He had invited her for dinner. And dinner it would be. *C'est tout.*

"May I call Chloé on your cellphone?"

"*Bien.* She'll probably be upset that you aren't coming back for dinner."

"I think she'll encourage me to go with you. This way there won't be a chance of me slipping and telling the family that I'm going to the autopsy tomorrow."

Was that a given? He hadn't heard back from the medical examiner, and now he thought the good doctor would recommend therapy for a magistrate wishing to attend an autopsy. The image of Antoine's cut and bruised face popped into his mind and he couldn't seem to rid himself of it. "I'm waiting to hear, but the idea seems strange now."

"It is strange."

Chloé answered the phone and Max said she'd be at Olivier's for dinner. Then she told Chloé about Marc joining Geneviève and Hans in the bar, and Marc's mother leaving in a huff. She sounded aghast: "You can't let that happen. She'll be the one running de Saint-Pern." She listened, then said, "Okay, I'll see you later. Yep. Love you!" Max handed the phone back to him and asked, "What's for dinner?"

"Fish. I think."

She was more relaxed than he'd seen her. It was as though once she decided to solve the murder everything in her world fell into place. Whereas for him right now, he didn't know when he'd felt so fragmented.

"Have you ever played a game with yourself by trying guess who the murderer is?" she asked. "Like when you're reading a mystery, except it's real?"

"No."

"I do. I make it as far-fetched as I possibly can."

"So who would you guess murdered Léa?"

"And don't forget Antoine. We both know he was murdered. I would say Hans Keller. I would like to say Geneviève, but I think she's too much of a weakling. I'd like to be able to connect the dots between those two. There could be something there."

Olivier pulled into his parents' driveway and stopped. "I have to make a few calls before preparing dinner."

"Do whatever you need to do."

He dropped the packet of photographs as they entered the house and swore. "I'm sorry," he said. "I have a lot on my mind. The interviews are tomorrow. There are too many suspects in this investigation."

"You're not nervous about the autopsy, are you? I can walk you through it. That's what my father did for me."

"You can't be too nervous about something you know nothing about."

"That's when I'm most nervous. When I know what's going on, I'm relaxed."

Does she know what's going on now? Olivier thought. Because I don't. And she's right, it's far more nerve-wracking to not know what's going on.

"How about some champagne?" he asked.

"Sure. Thanks." He opened the refrigerator door and removed the bottle of champagne, and thought about the murder weapon they had hauled out of the woods. And the names of those who had handled the bottle flitted through his mind. That report would be released tomorrow and he knew a lot of owners and growers would be less than happy about it. Marie-Christine was right. Champagne bottles were symbols for car racing and polo games and celebrations, not murder weapons.

He took down the flute glasses and almost knocked Max over in his effort. "Sorry, I…"

"The horror of it all has just hit you, hasn't it?"

She was standing close. Her fragrance was a blend of jasmine and he couldn't determine the rest at the moment as he felt he was under a spell. Whatever it was, it was not a run-of-the-mill perfume, and later he would ask her where on earth she had discovered the fragrance that was really, he decided, the essence of her.

She had a look of great compassion on her face, as though she understood everything he was experiencing. He reached out and touched her face, and kissed her, and suddenly he wanted all of her. He took her hand and led her up the stairs to the bedroom. He couldn't wait to have his skin touching hers, to feel her soft lips against his. She slowly unbuttoned his shirt and he unzipped her dress, which fell off so easily, and there was no modesty as they stood there undressed.

Murder and all the horrible things that were threatening to overtake him disappeared. He reached for her and took her in his arms, and they fell onto the bed. He felt so alive as he kissed her over and over and moved up and down her body until their rhythms matched and their eyes interlocked and he felt he could see through to her core and he liked what he saw. He called her name, and her strong arms and thighs wrapped around him tightly, and for a long time he couldn't bear the thought of pulling away from her. They grew quiet together and their breathing became normal. After a few moments, she whispered in his ear, "Your heart beating against my heart. I like it."

They lay there for what felt like a long time. "I'll get the champagne," she said after a while, as she got up and padded across the floor in her bare feet, humming a tune. In a few minutes she was back, with the two glasses and the bottle of champagne on a tray. She had found one of his mother's aprons and that was all she was wearing. "Monsieur Chaumont, I am your waitress for the night."

He laughed as she set the tray down and poured two glasses half full, handing one to him. The crystal dinged beautifully as they touched glasses. Looking into each other's eyes, they sipped in silence. He got up eventually and offered Max one of his robes, and she followed him into the kitchen while he sautéed potatoes, then put the fish in the oven to bake. The phone calls he had needed to make were all but forgotten as they chatted easily over dinner—avoiding all talk of murders and investigations.

After dinner was over it seemed only natural that she would stay the night, neither wanting the evening to end. Later, as they were drifting off to sleep, her long leg thrown over his, he asked, "How have you managed to put all the death around us out of your mind? You seemed so unaffected tonight."

"Are you kidding? I was acting. We've been reacting so much to each other's emotions and I knew that something needed to be done to break the tension. It worked out pretty well, don't you think?"

He laughed, and turned to wrap his arms around her, noticing how well their bodies fit together.

"*Bonne nuit,*" she whispered before drifting off to sleep. He was surprised at how much he liked the sound of that as he drifted off himself.

Chapter Twenty-three

Olivier wasn't in bed when Max opened her eyes. She bolted up, slipped into the black dress, and hurried from the room to find him. He wasn't in the house, but sitting in the garden. "Oh, there you are," he said, getting up to kiss her. "Sit. I'll get you coffee."

She looked out over the expanse of vineyards that rose up behind the house. Mornings here were exquisite. She could see the bees gathering nectar from the large array of flowers that surrounded her. Olivier returned and after handing her a coffee, explained that they'd need to leave in an hour and that she was welcome to shower here. He sat in a chair across from her, and smiled. "I have a call in to Philippe Douvier. Keller might not have been lying when he said that they are in business together. At the same time Douvier is my superior, and I need to tread lightly, especially now."

Max thought now was the time to tell him about her relationship to Douvier, but when Olivier's phone rang and he picked up, she took the opportunity to go upstairs for a shower. She knew she needed to be circumspect about her feelings for Olivier, but in the shower she let herself hum a couple of tunes.

Olivier was waiting when she entered the kitchen. "Douvier cautioned me to be absolutely certain before I go after Keller. Turns out his company brings a lot of money into France. He asked questions about Marc Durand, also, and said that he knew him and thought he had great potential."

"Did he mention Geneviève?"

"Not once."

"And the land deal didn't come up?"

"It would only come up if I mentioned it. It can wait. Are you ready to go?"

Max picked up her handbag and headed for the door

Before starting the car, Olivier leaned over and kissed her. "I think last night we transcended all the darkness."

Max found it disconcerting to feel happy when there was so much sadness around, and yet, she thought, if things get awful I have these moments as a reminder. They drove along with the windows down. Olivier turned up the radio when Coltrane started playing, and reached for her hand.

When they arrived at the Marceau property, she hopped out of the car and ran up to her room to change. Chloé came from her room across the hall. "Do you have a minute?"

"For you, yes."

"Marc and I had a huge fight last night. He left."

"Keep talking while I dress." Max pulled her jeans off the chair, then changed her mind and opted for the black skinny pants, digging them out of her suitcase. "The tension has been awful for everyone. What happened?"

"Hans Keller is now accusing Marc of taking the large sum of money that Hans brought in that he at first said was a down payment for Léa's company, but later told Marc about the land deal. His mother is supposed to be a part of that, but she's convinced that she's being pushed out."

"What did you argue about?"

"I told Marc that I think Hans is using him. That was all it took to make him furious."

"I agree with you. Marc needs to stay far away from this money. Olivier isn't sure that there is a cache of money, though Hans does seem genuinely anxious."

"You're off again?"

"I'm tagging along with Olivier, as usual."

"My parents are planning a quiet graveside service tomorrow for Uncle Antoine. Maman has accepted the accidental drowning pronouncement, but papa hasn't. He said that Antoine knew that river better than anybody, every hole and every danger." She started to cry. "Marc and his mother fought again."

Max recalled Marc leaving the bar after having words with Geneviève the night before when she was there. "About what?"

"When Marc told his mother that we might spend a year in New York, she had a fit. She screamed that he has a right to de Saint-Pern. She's crazy. I don't want my parents to know any of this."

"You and Marc need to be away from all parents. But Chloé, it's more than that, isn't it?"

"Okay, our wedding night was awful. He was drunk, and then Léa was found murdered. He doesn't know why they don't let us leave for our honeymoon, and I don't either."

"God, I'm so sorry you're having to deal with all of this." Max wrapped her arms around her friend. "Olivier is waiting for me right now, but I'll be back this afternoon. You're each in the middle of your respective family dramas. Try to hang in there."

"But Marc has to come back for Antoine's funeral."

"Don't push him. Wait and see if he comes back on his own."

"Alright. I'll walk out with you." She brightened, "You stayed the night with Olivier?"

Max nodded, surprised to feel herself blushing.

"I'm a better matchmaker for others, I think."

Max and Olivier walked rapidly down a long hall in the Department of Forensic Medicine and Pathology at the Hôpital Raymond Poincaré in Garches. Olivier said, "To my surprise, Doctor Legrand seems pleased that we're interested enough to attend the autopsy. I hope this is worth the time we're taking."

"Me, too."

A young woman approached and said that Dr. Legrand was waiting for them. "He's already begun the autopsy and asked me to take you in as soon as you arrived."

A man Max thought to be in his fifties emerged from a room and shook hands with them both. He was short and muscular, wearing his hair pulled back in a ponytail. "This is a highly unusual request," he said to Olivier, "so unusual that it made me curious. Tell me the story behind this poor fellow."

They followed him into another room, where he asked Max and Olivier to put gowns over their clothes and gave them masks. Olivier filled Legrand in on the investigation.

"I got right to work after you called," Legrand said. "Detective Maguire made some salient points about the difficulty of ruling a drowning a homicide."

Max interpreted Olivier's flummoxed glance to mean he was thinking again that here was another Frenchman behaving uncharacteristically around her.

"I can say with conviction that the victim entered the water alive. He had the fine, white froth in his airways, exuding from his mouth and nostrils, which is a clear indicator." Looking at Olivier, he said, "It's a mixture of water, air, and mucus. And when I wiped it away, and pressed on his chest, it reappeared, another sure sign. This foam can appear after poisoning by morphine, cocaine, or barbituates and from epilepsy or heart failure, but the foam is finer in the case of a drowning."

Max had been listening so intently she was surprised to realize that they had arrived in a room that felt like being in the middle of a huge stainless steel refrigerator. The smell of human death, urine, feces, and blood was vaguely familiar. Legrand pulled the sheet back, completely exposing Antoine's eviscerated body. Max noticed that Olivier closed his eyes for a second, then put his hand on a shelf to steady himself. She knew he was willing himself to stay focused.

"I did a diatom test," Legrand said, "which are bacillariophyceae, or a class of algae. Their presence in liver, brain, and bone marrow indicates that the victim was alive in the water because diatoms couldn't invade these locations unless the circulation was still functioning. I consider it strong corroborative evidence of death by drowning. Also, you will notice the clenched hand.

It appears that his last action was to grab at something in his frantic efforts to save himself. That action is preserved as the muscles of the hand go into what we call cadaveric spasm. There appears to be some sort of material in his clenched fist. We will, of course, analyze the material."

Stone cold silence.

Max was sickened by the thought of Antoine grasping anything within reach, but so had Léa. Only now did she remember the rose clutched in Léa's hand. Had she grabbed it from the killer?

She didn't know how long the threesome had been standing there when Olivier broke the silence. "How long do you think he was in the water?"

"The wrinkling of the finger-pads indicates roughly six hours."

"And alcohol content? Cocaine?" Olivier asked.

"I'll let you know. I have another hour of work to do, and then will send everything to the lab. I'll put a 'rush' on it. My guess is that he was incapacitated by alcohol and maybe drugs. His liver also indicates that he was a heavy drinker."

Maybe Antoine was already at the river when his "guest" arrived, Max thought. He was expecting Mimi, but she would have known to find him there. Had he gone to look at the moon, wearing his robe, and someone had pushed him? She recalled the long-handled garden hoe protruding from the ground near the garden.

"*Docteur?*"

He turned and looked at her. "May I ask you to examine his chest and back carefully?"

"There were strange bruised indentations on his chest…here, you can look." Max did so. "But I didn't make note of injuries to his back."

"What if each time he tried to return to shore he was pushed out again with a pole or something equivalent?"

"I'll call my assistant." Legrand pushed a buzzer and a young man came in, looking cheerful. They shifted Antoine's body and the doctor picked up a magnifying glass.

"H-mm. There is bruising in the kidney region, and now that you've mentioned it, similar bruise-like indentations in the chest region. What are you thinking, detective?"

"I'm wondering if he was drunk, forced into the river by someone, and then when he tried to climb back to shore they kept pushing him back with the long handle of a garden tool. That way there would be no fingerprints."

"You have a vivid imagination, mademoiselle. The cruelty of what you are describing is disturbing."

I've seen too much, Max thought.

"*Bon.* We will meet outside in the first room. I'll join you in a moment."

Max and Olivier quietly stripped off their paper gowns and masks and put them in the trash container. Olivier sat in a chair and closed his eyes. "I hope never to do that again."

"Are you sorry you went?"

"No. How did you come up with the garden tool scenario?"

"It's like the bottle. I saw it in the yard and filed it away in my memory. Then it haunts me until I can make sense of it. When Legrand talked about Antoine grasping for anything to save himself, I thought about the rose Léa was holding in death. Did you?"

"I recall it very well. In fact, it haunts me."

Dr. Legrand entered and said that he would do his best to get results back within a couple of days. He looked at Max, "You have great courage. I hope you capture the murderer. Just make sure he doesn't find you first." They exchanged a vigorous handshake, and she and Olivier maneuvered their way through the labyrinthine halls until they finally came to the exit. They walked outside, stopping to blink in the sunlight. Both stood for a moment inhaling fresh air.

Olivier's cell phone rang and Max overheard him asking whoever was on the other end why Philippe Douvier wanted to see him in person. Olivier sounded indignant. "I'm to go there now?" He put the phone down and said to Max, "I have to go to see the Ministère de la Justice. His office is at Place Vendôme, a wonderful spot to walk around."

Max knew it well and decided it pointless to bring up the half year she spent in Paris again. The phone rang again. Olivier listened, then said, "I don't understand what's going on." He tossed the phone into his briefcase and looked at Max, "The minister wants to meet you."

Uh-oh.

It felt like the moment to tell Olivier the truth was gone before she realized it was there. No excuse: there had been other opportunities, and her uncertainty about how he would react had kept her from it. Olivier was on the phone with Abdel again, setting up an appointment to go to Léa's office and another to meet with the young woman Delphine. He drove into a parking place near Place Vendôme, and they got out. Max looked around at the grandeur of the buildings that encircled the square. It was one of her favorite areas of the city. "I have no idea why Monsieur Douvier wants to meet with you, unless Hans Keller gave him a list of complaints about you."

They walked in shoulder to shoulder, two stalwart comrades, she thought. A secretary who appeared to be dressed in a designer suit ushered them directly into Douvier's office, which was grander than any she had ever been in. He arose from his chair and rushed over and shook Olivier's hand, and then turned to her, giving her an appraising look. She proffered her hand, but he formally bestowed a kiss on each cheek. "We may not know each other but we're still family, *n'est- ce pas?* I'm trying to see if you have any resemblance to my wife or your mother, and I see a little in the smile. "

He dinged a bell and the woman appeared in the door to his office almost immediately. "*Bon*, Olivier, I know how busy you are with this investigation, but I insist that we share a simple toast." He asked the secretary to bring in champagne and glasses."

Max hadn't dared look in Olivier's direction until now, but she decided to have a quick peek and wished she hadn't. He looked worse by far than he had at the autopsy. She had heard so many awful stories about her French family, how her grandparents had disowned her mother when she married Hank, and how they looked down on the Maguires with contempt. When Frédéric was killed, they hadn't heard from any of them. Max had thought of all of them as monsters, not in the least like this man who was practically fawning over her.

"I can see if Hélène is done at the hairdresser's," he said to Max, picking up the phone. "I know she would very much like to meet you."

"No, no, please. I will try to stop on my way back to New York."

"Try! Nonsense. You must. You've never met your aunt or your grandmother."

"I tried to contact Aunt Hélène several years ago when I was in school in Paris." She had never been treated so rudely.

"I don't really know the details of what happened between your mother and her French family. Your mother was full of pride, I remember that. It was so long ago. I assume you never learned French."

Without waiting for an answer, he turned to Olivier and began speaking in French, "We can be more candid in French. My niece is not in everybody's way, I hope, with her snooping. I owe Jacques Marceau a favor, and that's why I said yes to his request for her to assist in the investigation. Unofficially, of course. My wife thought it might also help family relations."

His delight in seeing me was all show, Max thought.

The secretary arrived with the champagne and proceeded to open a bottle of *Joséphine*, made by the Joseph Perrier Company. Max recognized it as the same bottle Olivier had in his fridge. Glasses were handed around, and Douvier raised his glass, saying in English, "To solving this case."

No more mention of family.

He explained that the Minister of the Interior had given the police special permission to confiscate the records of several bank accounts. "Two hundred thousand euros isn't a pittance."

Olivier spoke through clenched teeth. "The amount is paltry for the shares Antoine Marceau signed over to Monsieur Keller." Max could tell that Douvier was surprised, and trying to hide it. "Keller is a strong suspect, and I won't compromise this investigation."

"You never have, Olivier. That's half the reason Sarkozy wants to get rid of all *juges d'instructions* and turn cases like this one over to the chief prosecutors."

"They already have too many cases, which is why we investigation magistrates are handed the exceptional ones."

"We each have our arguments, but that's for another day. I did you a favor by allowing you to take this case. I know your relationship to Jacques Marceau. That region is still a tightly knit network, Olivier, and you're part of it, whether you admit it or not. Now, back to the case. What about the Anglo-Saxon who's locked up?"

Max understood that the term Anglo-Saxon was a derogatory term, meaning all those people who were non-Catholics, though no one would ever admit that. Americans, Canadians, Australians, and others were all thrown into the category of Anglo-Saxons.

"Monsieur Clay?" Olivier said. "I happen to think he's innocent, but it may take a long trial to prove it."

"You're pretty tight-lipped as always. I'm keeping up through a colleague. Reynard is pleased with your work, but thinks you should share more with the gendarmes and the police."

"I work alone. You know that."

Max thought Douvier a whirlwind of energy and power, handsome with his shock of gray hair and penetrating eyes. He was at the top of his game, and he conveyed that with every motion. She wondered how the relationship was between him and her aunt Hélène. Obviously it wasn't great since he had kept Geneviève for nine years. Or maybe the mistress didn't upset Aunt Hélène and the marriage was just for appearances.

"How did you know my identity?" she asked Douvier.

"We know everyone who enters this country. But it was my wife who grew curious after your photograph was sent in to the Minister of the Interior's office by Commissaire Girard, who forwarded it to me."

Did Girard send in my photograph hoping to have me sent home, she wondered. Now she understood his puzzlement when the word came back that Max had been approved by the minister. And that was why he had started pursuing again. She had more status than he did. A great deal more.

Douvier hadn't stopped talking. "My wife saw your photograph on my desk and saw the resemblance. Filling your father's shoes, I see."

"He continues to fill his own, I'm happy to say."

She finished her glass of champagne and put it down. Olivier and Douvier shook hands, and she extended hers and Douvier shook it. "My wife will call," he said.

No she won't, Max thought.

She walked ahead of Olivier, striding purposefully out the door and across the vast Oriental rug and out of the building. She slowed down when they were outside, her heart pounding. "Are you terribly upset with me?"

"Your uncle is the Minister of Justice? My boss? And you didn't find it crucial information for me to know?"

"I've never met him. I had no idea that he knew who I was."

"And Jacques Marceau knows he's your uncle?"

"No. Yes. I didn't know they had talked."

"Then there was a conspiracy to keep me in the dark."

They climbed into his car, and he peeled out of his parking space.

"That's an exaggeration. There's no conspiracy for god's sake."

"I feel betrayed, and that's all I will say about it. For now."

"I had dreaded this moment all my life! And then I walk in, and he's so cool. So happy to meet me. And for a few moments I felt all of his superficial warmth and power focused on me, and I thought my parents were wrong. It was all fake. My father is right."

They drove in silence for a while. Max bit her lip to keep back the tears. She had been through two murders in a week's time, an autopsy, an investigation, family drama—and this fifteen minutes in front of the minister had succeeded in knocking her off balance. Olivier had a piano concerto playing on the radio, and was staring straight ahead. Had she betrayed Olivier by not telling him her past? Wasn't her past her business anyhow? But still, she had meant to tell him. "I'm sorry, Olivier."

"Apology received."

"But not accepted."

"Correct."

Neither spoke the rest of the way back to Champagne.

Chapter Twenty-four

Olivier drove straight to his office in Epernay. It had happened. The personal had overridden the professional. He had no idea how to bring it back around to a professional basis other than to dictate a course and stick to it. "I'm going to spend the afternoon looking at wills and papers," he said to Max. "I want you to go with Abdel to interview the woman Delphine, and we'll compare notes tomorrow."

"Go with Abdel? This feels punitive."

"Think how Abdel will feel."

A Renault Clio pulled up and Abdel hopped out and took long strides to Olivier. He spoke to him in French, "Sir, mademoiselle Véronique called to tell you that she's back in Paris and driving out for dinner this evening."

Merde! Olivier gave a surreptitious glance in Max's direction and was relieved to see that she seemed intent on watching people enter and exit the Moët & Chandon Champagne House. She obviously didn't understand Abdel's announcement. He felt a slight panic forming and decided to call Véronique and cancel the moment he entered his office. That was one of the problems with her. She thought his career a hobby.

Abdel continued, "Girard wants to talk to you about the autopsy. He didn't know you were going into Paris."

"Are we talking about a committee report? Please inform him that I'm a magistrate and not a politician waiting for a vote."

Abdel hung his head, obviously hurt. Olivier couldn't wait to be alone. "Take Detective Maguire and interview the young woman, Delphine. You have her last name."

"Why am I taking Detective Maguire, monsieur? I can do this on my own."

"Because I need her to be somewhere other than with me."

"Somewhere?"

"Va t'en! Go."

Olivier watched them get into the car, and dashed to his office and dialed Véronique. She wasn't answering. He had to stop her, but he also had to go to Léa's office. Bernard Martin was waiting. He walked the few blocks to the ornate black and gold gate of the de Saint-Pern Company and entered. Bernard was in an impressive office. Away from his wife Caroline, he seemed to have a lot more energy.

"I know how busy you are," Olivier said. "Thank you for making the time." Social discourse was the only comfortable path. Olivier had found that barking at people and demanding answers usually got him nowhere.

Bernard had several stacks of folders on a large desk. "I can leave you to the files," he said.

"Sit down," Olivier said. "Please." Bernard cast an anxious look his way. "Look, Bernard, I know some of the stresses that the company was experiencing before Lea's untimely death. I'd like to hear more from you."

Bernard hesitated. "I was once the *chef de cave,* and, as you know, created the *L'Etoile*—the same one that is appreciated by kings. In fact…"

"I know it well."

"My life here was all that I dreamed it could be when my cousin Charles was alive. He was so vibrant that it was as though he breathed creativity and power into everyone who came into contact with him. Have you ever known anyone like that?"

"One or two. Go on."

"I had been sickly as a boy, and missed a lot of school. But Charles, who was five years younger, inspired me. An only child, he was adored from the moment of his birth. I don't think he ever experienced much unhappiness in his thirty-five years. When he died, I felt that a piece of me died, too. I think the entire company collapsed in an indefinable way. Léa tried to maintain everything he had done. But curiously, I started to think each time I entered the company building that I was in a mausoleum. I had divorced my first wife by then. We had two children and it was a hardship for sure. For her and for me. I had met Caroline Rotier and fallen in love. She was so effervescent. Like a champagne!" He laughed until he began to cough, and Olivier tried to seem as amused as the storyteller, with little success.

"You and Léa ran the company together?"

"I was an equal in the beginning, and then Léa began to pull away from me. She didn't like Caroline and the feeling was mutual. And there we were, living on her property. There are approximately forty de Saint-Perns connected to the company, either owning shares or actually working there. We worked hard to uphold the tradition of keeping it all in the family. Jacques and Marie-Christine also were a part of it, and most recently, Marc Durand." He practically spit the name out.

"Who will claim this office now?"

"Marc and I are jockeying over who will inherit it. It's ridiculous for someone who has been here six months to think he should have the owner's office. His mother has come to this building twice since Léa died, acting as though she owns the place. I'd leave, but where would I go?"

Olivier could tell this was going to be his longest interview, and he wasn't comfortable in Léa's office. "I want all of this to be on record," Olivier said. "May I come later to your house, or would you prefer to meet in my office?"

"Oh, come to the house. I'll call Caroline now and set up a time." He got up and pointed to the stacks of papers on Léa's large mahogany desk. "These are business reports, earnings and that sort of thing. This is the only will that I found, written some years ago." Olivier skimmed down the will, which looked official.

"When Charles died, I had expected to be included in the will, especially after all the work I had done for the company. But Léa eventually ended up with a fortune, and Charles' father received part of it. Charles' mother was already deceased. His father only died two years ago. He adored Léa, though he was sad that there were no children. Some of the de Saint-Pern cousins had resentment toward her because Charles had left the family company to her. This is why when Monsieur Baptiste Dupuis began coming around asking questions, many were willing to sell their shares to him.

"Léa was not herself in the last weeks of her life. She felt betrayed by the de Saint-Perns, like they were ganging up on her. Her beloved Chloé was showing no interest in being a part of the company, until she became engaged to Marc Durand, and Marc became enthusiastic. Léa welcomed him into the firm, which is not the French way at all. I think underneath she was thrilled about Chloé being a part of the company, as she had no children of her own."

Olivier didn't feel it necessary to bring up Lea's pregnancy. "What's the consensus among the de Saint-Perns about Chloé?"

"We all are deeply fond of her. And to be fair to Marc, I think the problem we foresee is his mother. Marc is affable enough, and could be trained if he was willing to start at the bottom."

"Why don't we ride over to Léa's château, and then we can go to your house?"

"Good idea. I think Chloé's at Léa's house now. I saw her car when I was leaving late this morning."

"*Bon.* I'll see you there in half an hour or so."

The day had turned overcast. Olivier walked to his car in a somber frame of mind. An office employee hauled the folders from Léa's desk out to Olivier's car, and he headed for the château. His thoughts trailed back to the autopsy, and how Max had come up with her theory about the garden hoe. Was that her father's genes working, or would she attribute it to the intensive training in the field she had received? It was, after all, about using all the senses. To him, it was like looking at an oil painting and seeing it as a picture of a pond and nothing more, versus studying the three-dimensional aspects of the work, continuing to look at it until you were almost in a trance, and before you knew it you were in the artist's psyche. That was true transcendence.

He couldn't get his mind off Max. He had seen her childlike hurt when she realized that Philippe Douvier was full of guff, and meant nothing that he said. But the shock he felt when Douvier made a show over her still reverberated. He was sure that Douvier knew that Olivier had been kept in the dark, and liked having the one-upmanship over him. Olivier had been so angry at her for her subterfuge that he had almost enjoyed seeing her uncle rope her in and spit her out.

But what had made him angriest during their brief visit with Douvier was the veiled threat that he had to be careful not to step on the wrong toes, just the attitude that could jeopardize the entire investigation. Was he supposed to tiptoe around Geneviève and Hans? And Max had been put in a protective aura, too. He hated cronyism, but was Douvier right when he accused Olivier of being an insider in the Champagne network, or was he intentionally trying to create self-doubt in Olivier?

He assumed Douvier had requested an audience with his niece in order to assess her, to see if she could create trouble, and had come to the conclusion that she was just a harmless snoop. Olivier thought Douvier might be in for a surprise. He didn't think Max was vengeful, but she had integrity and would find it hard to compromise. She had been hurt by her uncle's manner and would have her guard up more than ever. She also still had to prevent her friend Ted from becoming the permanent scapegoat of the investigation.

Olivier would let her know this evening that he accepted her apology, which reminded him to call Abdel to see how the interview was going with Delphine. Abdel's cell phone was off. He left a message for them to come to the château after they were finished interviewing Delphine, then tried Véronique again, who either wasn't picking up or was out of cell phone range.

Girard called and said that Ted Clay's blog fans were demand-ing his release and that he and Reynard were beginning to think they didn't have enough evidence to keep him locked up.

"I agree."

"Where will he go if we release him?"

"Put him under house arrest in his Paris apartment."

"*D'accord*. I heard that you went to Paris to the medical examiner to talk about Antoine Marceau. Do you think it was murder?"

Olivier wondered what Girard was so nervous about. "Yes, but it's difficult to prove."

"What led you to that conclusion?"

"Imagination."

"I see. Zeroual checked in. He's interviewing a secondary suspect? She's changing her story?"

"Hans Keller is changing his, and it involves her."

"Oh, I get it. Was anybody *not* full of lust that night?"

Olivier was sure he was included in the jab. Girard had never bought one bit about Max being sick. "A bit of an exaggeration, I would say, Thomas. What you probably want to know is have we made progress and it distresses me to tell you no. I'll keep you informed of any new discoveries. By the way, it turns out that Max is the niece of Philippe Douvier. He showed her the newspaper clip of her photo. I wonder what your purpose was."

"Does she know I sent it in?"

"Her uncle told her."

The line went dead.

The magnificent gardens at the de Saint-Pern château made Olivier wish he could spend a day there to study them. Chloé rushed out and bestowed the requisite kisses on him. "I'm glad you're here," she said.

He followed her into the house, not stopping to ogle the interior as most people did. Instead, he and Chloé continued on to a closed door on the opposite side of the foyer. She took a key from her pocket and opened it. "This has always been my second home. I wonder what will happen to it."

The room they entered was more library than office. Books lined the walls, but there was also a television set in a far corner and stacks of films around it. Photographs of Léa and Charles occupied one shelf. Olivier appreciated the casual elegance, and thought that this room more than any other contained the essence of Léa. "Have you started going through her personal papers?"

"It's a good thing you called ahead. The gendarme was guarding this place as though his life depended on it. I've sorted out house bills that have to be paid, and salaries." She unlocked a file drawer. "Léa told me that most of her important papers are stashed here. Did you go by the office?"

"I have boxes of papers in my car. Some of them date back thirty years. I think Bernard saw it as an opportunity to clean house."

Chloé laughed. She pulled out an armload of files. "I think they're pretty well organized."

Olivier picked up the first one. "Here's a will dated July, 2006."

"A year after Uncle Charles was killed."

Olivier perused it. "This one is a *testament authentique*. It looks in perfect order. It has been read and signed by two notaries. The notary registered it with the central database, the FCDDV."

"Okay, I've never had reason to ask or look. Tell me."

"It's simple. Everything she has is to be divided between you and your mother."

Chloé started to sniffle. "None of this is a surprise except the fact that she's gone."

"It takes a long time to realize that it's permanent."

"What about the company? What were her wishes?"

"That's in the box in my car, which I'll start going through tonight. She will have set up a business trust, I'm sure."

"Don't be too sure. Léa was a good businesswoman, but she hated filing claims and going to notaries."

Olivier got up and walked over to the filing cabinet and pulled the drawer out. "Let's see what else is here. Ted said that she had told him she was leaving him part of her estate." He handed a stack of papers to Chloé to go through and took another for himself.

Chloé said, "We haven't been fair to Ted. He was a complete stranger to us, and a foreigner to boot. And the day after he arrives she dies, and almost immediately he's accused and locked up."

"He's being released today. There is actually very little evidence that he murdered Léa."

"I felt better knowing that someone was locked up."

"I understand. You know, I went by Lea's office and Bernard was there. It seems that he and Marc both want to move into her office."

She glanced up and he tried to analyze the emotion that flitted across her face. Anger? Shock?

"Those two have been at each other from the start. And now that I know I have some rights, or at least I think I do, I'm going to put a stop to either of them thinking they're taking that office. Everyone knows that Bernard has been helping Baptiste Dupuis purchase shares from de Saint-Pern family members who want out. He was not in favor when my aunt died. And Marc is following his mother's orders, I'm sure. What she might not understand is the concept of family that exists there. This is what I would want to reinstate."

Olivier was surprised, and pleased, to hear Chloé speaking up. "If Marc, and his mother, are determined to be at de Saint-Pern, then I won't sit at home twiddling my thumbs. My mother and I will be there as well."

"I think you'd be good at running a company. Oh, here's the will that Ted mentioned. It's called a *testament olographe*. It's written by hand, and is dated a few days before your wedding. In it, she is leaving her child one half of her estate and the other half left to you. Your mother's name isn't on it. A certain amount each year is to go to Ted for care of their child." He turned the page over. "It's signed, but I have no idea if it's valid or not. And we'll have to check to see if she registered it with the FCDDV."

"But there is no child."

"I'm not an authority on this, but then it seems that all of her estate will go to you."

"She didn't leave it to Marc and me together?"

"No."

"Then once everything is settled, I'll put his name on everything that's mine."

"There's nothing more to be done until we talk to the notaries. I'm off but will call you later. I'll take this drawer and bring it back tomorrow. I'm due for tea at Bernard's."

"Don't believe him when he tells you in a hangdog face that they're being run out of their home. They were supposed to be out five years ago, after Charles died, and they've been like squatters. Tante Léa didn't start forcing the issue until Marc and I started talking about moving back. I don't want to live there anyway. Feel free to tell them I said so."

◇◇◇

Caroline Martin was wearing a dress just a hint too small, a deep cerise red that created a violent contrast to her pink cheeks and lips. Olivier thought that this would be what he would dread most about a second wife, marrying someone who provided deep contrast to the first and finding himself with a cartoon character, someone as "effervescent as champagne." He thought Bernard looked quite miserable, and yet had to pretend to be okay with this woman. Looking around, he thought the room was a deeper reflection of Caroline. The parlor was all chintz and craft fair décor. Dolls were propped up all over and shelves were running over with bric-a-brac. Olivier said yes to a cup of tea and sat down across from Bernard who had been reading the paper.

"I spent more time than I intended at Léa's house," Olivier said.

Bernard's eyes opened wide. "I hope you found all the papers you were seeking."

"I can't answer that as I'm not exactly sure what I'm looking for. However, I do want to bring something up before your wife returns. You were overheard in conversation with Baptiste

Dupuis discussing how you could find out for him the amount of Hans Keller's offer for de Saint-Pern. That, of course, was information that was intended to stay private."

Caroline re-entered, chattering like a squirrel as she put the tray down on a table in front of the men. Bernard looked as if he had been struck, but Caroline didn't notice. "Madame Martin, will you please sit for a moment?"

She plopped down on the couch beside Bernard. If he had to, he could pull out the financial sheet that Abdel had gotten from the bank, listing all of their assets, and deposits and withdrawals. Picking up a brochure of Biarritz, he casually asked, "You're planning on purchasing property in the south?"

Caroline giggled a little too loudly, "Some day. With that upstart Marc Durand around, who knows when we'll get pushed out?"

"If Baptiste Dupuis happened to outbid Hans Keller, and finally was able to buy this company, do you think you would be secure?" He sipped his tea, and smiled. It was obvious that they were both afraid to answer, fearful of falling into a trap. "I just told your husband, madame, that he was overheard making a deal with Baptiste Dupuis. Something to do with keeping him informed of what Hans Keller was offering for the de Saint-Pern Company."

"I think somebody is making it up," Caroline said. "The stories around this murder are growing more absurd every day. People are nervous, especially now that the American man is being released. He was innocent looking enough, but no one knows what evil lurks beneath peoples' *façades*. Everybody thought he was after her money, though when he came out here he was quite pleasant…"

When Olivier finally managed to get in a word, he said, "I've done a check on your banking actions over the past year, and was surprised to find that you have a large sum of cash, some of which was sent off to a realtor in Biarritz."

Bernard sank deeper into the couch, if possible.

Caroline took over. "I had a small inheritance, but no matter, our privacy has been invaded. I don't think what we do is anyone's business, as long as we're not hurting anybody."

"But it is. Especially when your business involves a company whose owner was just murdered, leaving behind a champagne company with a stellar reputation but whose reputation might be soiled because certain people behaved with no probity."

"You don't know how badly Bernard was paid all these years. We have had to stay in this house because we couldn't afford what we wanted. Bernard was taken for granted all these years. Oh, yes, while Madame Léa's photograph was in the newspaper hosting some gala event, wearing the latest Dior, Bernard was here, making slave wages. Then this Marc Durand comes in and starts acting all high and mighty over the past few days, and his mother is worse…"

"Shut up!"

"Bernard." Her tone was reprimanding.

"Shut up before I force you to shut up." Bernard pulled himself off the couch and pointed at her. "There was never enough for you. I could never provide you with enough, and look where it's gotten us." He sat down again. "Monsieur Chaumont, arrest me. I might find more peace in prison."

"What Monsieur Dupuis gave us was a gift," Caroline said to her husband. "It wasn't a crime. You created the formula for *l'Etoile* and you can do with it as you please."

They sold him the formula for their most popular champagne?

Olivier had seen a note on a sheet of paper in Léa's handwriting that said, "Speak to Bernard about Dupuis." She surely knew. Would she have confronted him on Chloé's wedding night? Would Bernard have the rage and the strength to kill? They were there in the salon with the people who had stayed to the end.

"Where were you on Chloé's wedding night at two in the morning? Why were you still at the party?"

Caroline piped up, "I have witnesses. I was sitting in the tent watching the drunken young people dance."

Bernard sounded more lugubrious than usual, "As I told your detective, Monsieur Zeroual. I was in my car in the parking area."

"Monsieur Dupuis said that he had his driver return him to the wedding to find his wife's handbag. Was he there to meet with you? To find out what Monsieur Keller was bidding for de Saint-Pern?"

Bernard nodded. Bernard and Caroline weren't going to go anywhere, Olivier knew, and he decided to leave them to their own arguments. There would be a trial that would involve Dupuis and the Martins, he would see to that, but he couldn't deal with it now. A headache was creeping up on him, and he thought he'd go to his parents and finish going through the boxes of papers. He abruptly excused himself, and once in his car, checked for messages on his cell phone. No one had called. There was no way Véronique hadn't received his messages, and now her silence told him that she was angry. So be it.

Chapter Twenty-five

Abdel had peeled out from the parking place, and now was listening to his GPS as he drove to the home of Delphine Lecroix. Who gave a flying rip about her anyhow, Max thought. Olivier wanted us out of his hair and now has two of us interviewing someone Hans Keller claims he slept with.

Okay, okay, she thought, two men in the past twelve hours have had you riding on some celestial waves, one incredibly sensual, and the other the warm nurturing uncle—and each time the wave has dashed you to the ground.

Max had gone cold when she heard that Véronique was planning to come to Olivier's. And what made it worse was that now that she had lied for so long about understanding French, she couldn't let Olivier know that she knew that his girlfriend was about to descend, not after the uncle debacle. Plus Olivier had sent her away to work with an intense Arab who had said he didn't want her around anymore than she wanted to go with him. She put on her sunglasses and knew she looked like she was pouting. Which she was.

"Sometimes Monsieur Chaumont has to have his space. He seems pretty upset that this case doesn't seem to be progressing."

"You don't need to defend him to me. And the case is progressing but in increments. It takes patience."

"The French are short on that." He smiled, "You know, I was surprised that he went to the autopsy. That's not done here. At least I've never heard of anyone doing that."

Max sat up. This guy didn't seem upset in the least that she was with him. She explained that she had been to several in New York because it expedited things. He was interested and she explained everything that had happened in the medical examiner's office. They had the windows of the car down and all of a sudden it didn't feel like the worst move to be here going to an interview with Abdel.

"So tell me about Véronique Verize," she said. "I recognized her name in your conversation a few minutes ago."

"Oh, I can't say I know her. I mostly see her on magazine covers. My idea of beauty is different perhaps from other people."

"In what way?"

"I like to see the character of the person on the face. My grandmother taught me that. Don't look at the surface, she says. Look within."

They entered the town of Aÿ, and Abdel pulled up in front of a modest house. "I should have asked Chloé to give me the rundown on Delphine," Max said. "But I haven't had much time with her."

"You've been very busy solving this big crime."

Was there a note of sarcasm embedded in that comment, or was she just being too sensitive? "Abdel, Olivier has accused me of hustling his job, and so has Girard. Please don't tell me that you're going to follow suit."

"I don't know if I was going to say that."

"You were."

He suddenly laughed and his twinkly eyes and big white teeth made her laugh, too. "Look, we are the two banned detectives who are sent out into the hinterlands to accuse some young, unsuspecting woman of homicide. It should take us about five minutes and then we'll go have something fabulous to eat. Like something Algerian."

"Here? Get real."

Someone peered out from behind a curtain. They exited the car and walked up the sidewalk to the front door. It opened before they had a chance to knock. "Oh, Delphine, I'm Chloé's friend, Max Maguire. We met at the wedding and I'm sorry we didn't have a chance to talk…you remember Detective Abdel Zeroual?"

"*Bonjour.* Hello."

She wasn't a beauty. The features on her face were asymmetrical, but Max thought that like many French women Delphine had a certain allure. She thought some of it was attitude, how they didn't care what others thought of them the way Americans did.

"Is it okay to talk here? Is Yves around?" Max asked.

"This is okay. He's in Paris today. With Marc, I think."

They sat on a sofa in the living room, and she asked if they wanted coffee or a beer. They said no, then Max waited for Abdel to start asking questions, but he didn't say anything. It felt awkward to bring up Delphine's betrayal of Yves, but it had to be done. Maybe this is going to take longer than five minutes, Max thought. When the silence became unbearable, Max said, "Delphine, is it okay to speak in English?"

She nodded, then picked up a cigarette off the table and lit it.

"You are Hans Keller's alibi, you know," Max started. Delphine's eyes widened.

"This is no one's business."

Abdel found his voice, "I'm afraid it is. Monsieur Keller said that you both saw Madame de Saint-Pern on the way to the inn. Is that much true?"

Delphine's hand shook. "Yes. And that is all." Seeing Abdel's notebook, she asked, "Are you writing all this down?"

"I must."

Max decided to take a different tactic. "Delphine, look, no one's judging you morally."

"Wouldn't you think Hans would have let me know before he dropped this little bomb and had you rushing over here?"

I do, thought Max.

"Chloé and Marc will be furious," she said. "Marc and Yves are close friends, and Marc will judge me harshly."

"Chloé won't judge. I know her." Max stood up, "Look, the truth is I'm worried that someone else will die before the murderer is found."

"Antoine's was an accident."

"That's being questioned."

"Oh, god." Delphine lit another cigarette and began to talk. "It was impulsive on my part. Yves and Marc had been behaving like teenagers. Drinking too much and being rowdy. Antoine was part of it for a while. He…"

"Gave them cocaine. We know that."

"I had danced with Yves twice all evening. That's all. And Hans was relentless in his pursuit of me. I went to find Yves and he was passed out near the tennis court and it made me furious to see him like that. I went back and said yes to Hans. We went to the inn."

"You came back to the party alone?"

Her eyes were downcast. "It was frightening. I saw the lights where the earlier reception was held and wondered what had happened. Bernard Martin was standing on the terrace and told me that someone was injured and the police were there. I was worried that it was Yves. I ran to the tennis courts, and he wasn't there. A gendarme told me to go to the salon, and Yves came rushing in. He and Marc had run down to the lighted area, and he told me there had been an accident. We learned later that Léa was dead."

Abdel spoke in a gentle voice, "Mademoiselle, please try to think if you saw anything unusual on the way to the inn. On the way back you noticed the lights. Anything else? Did you find Chloé immediately?"

"She came into the salon, and was horribly upset, of course. I stayed away from the family."

"Anything else?"

"This is going to sound weird. I was with Hans the night Antoine drowned."

"I thought he was with Marc at Le Bar that night."

"Earlier perhaps. I'm superstitious now about ever seeing him again."

Abdel said, "Anything about the night Antoine died? Did you drive from this house to the inn? What hour?"

"It was around eleven when I left the inn. Yves was in the city and so I didn't have any need to hurry, but I also didn't want to stay the night at the inn. The moon was out. There was a woman…a large woman…almost running down the street. I thought something was wrong, but she was out of sight before I could say anything to her. She had on a hat, which I thought odd."

"What was she wearing?"

"A dark dress. That's how I knew it was a woman, but she ran like an athlete."

Max thought that like many people who were being scrutinized, Delphine was beginning to enjoy the attention. The confession hadn't been as bad as she thought. She at least had sympathetic listeners, and now she could bask a little under the attention. Max glanced at her watch. She and Abdel had their cell phones turned off. She wondered if Olivier had called, and if he'd tell her if Véronique was coming to see him.

She had become so distracted with her own thoughts that at first what Delphine was now talking about barely registered. But she could see Abdel listening intently. "That's it," Delphine said. "I cracked the door open to peer out before I stepped into the hallway and made my dash back to the Marceau house and that's when I saw him."

Who, who? Max wondered.

Abdel and Delphine had segued somehow back to Lea's murder. "He knocked lightly at the room a few doors down, and it opened and I saw it was Marc's mother standing at the door. I noticed he was carrying a plastic bag. I couldn't hear what he said but his mom opened the door and he went in. I stood there, not knowing whether to make the dash to the house or wait to see if Marc was coming back out."

"Where was Hans?" Max asked.

"I'm embarrassed to say, sleeping. I seem to have that effect on men."

"Did Marc come back?"

"Yes, after a few minutes he went sailing past Han's door again." She smiled, "This sounds so ridiculous. He probably came by to check on his mother, who hadn't been feeling well. He had complained about it to us, saying that he'd roped Ted Clay into walking her to the inn. He may have been feeling guilty."

"How long did you wait before you decided to go back?"

"Another fifteen minutes, perhaps."

Abdel thanked her, then put away his notebook, and said that he needed to go out and check for messages. Delphine and Max sat in comfortable silence for a moment. "The plastic bag," Max said. "Was it big?"

"Not so big. But not small either."

"Was he holding the bag when he passed by on his way out?"

"I don't know. I was thinking about how I was going to get back to the house unobserved."

"What do you think of Hans now?"

"I don't really know him, but I think he's okay. He's much more obstreperous in public. Almost shy and insecure in private. I like being with someone older."

"May I ask you a question between us?"

"Sure."

"Do you like Marc? I worry a little about Chloé."

"Chloé has to get him away from his mother. She has no chance as long as that woman is around."

"I know he and his mother fight, but he wouldn't be a wife beater or anything, right? I ask because I deal with that kind of shit all the time in New York."

"Yves has known Marc a long time. He doesn't like his arrogance, but thinks he'll change once he's settled in with his new life. I wonder if he will, with all the prestige he'll have now being associated with de Saint-Pern."

Abdel re-entered the room and stood waiting for Max. "Thank you again, mademoiselle."

"*Pas de quoi.* I wish you would assure me that Yves will never know."

"It's private information, but if there's a big trial then you may be called."

She sighed. "I guess I'll have time by then to figure out what I want."

"Okay," Max said. "We have to go."

They said good-bye and Max asked Abdel if Olivier had called. "He and Chloé were together at Léa's château and he has two wills and has sent them to the notary. He said that it's possible for us to come to his parents' house later this evening to go through the rest of the papers."

He must have told Véronique not to come, Max thought. She felt a quiver in her heart region.

"It was a good thing, to send us to work together," Abdel said.

She smiled at him. "I agree." They were in the car, heading back to the Marceaus. "It must be strange for you to hear women talk so freely about men and sex."

"You mean because I'm a Muslim? A little. Our cultures are so different. Mainly, I don't think women do too well in this westernized life. Our women are thought of as prisoners of their men, and many are, but women here get used. I doubt that Monsieur Keller will stay in touch with mademoiselle once he returns to Germany, for example, and that must affect her heart."

It does, Max agreed silently. It absolutely does.

"It's a lot of risk-taking. But then we have so much more freedom than women in your culture, and that seems to balance it out." They both seemed to drift into their own thoughts. After a while, she spoke, "So, the plastic bag. I asked Delphine about it when you left to go to the car. What do you make of that?"

He shrugged. "Not much. If it were me, I'd have been taking my laundry to my mother too."

Max punched his arm playfully. "*Dégueulasse!* You men are disgusting!"

◇◇◇

Max stood at her bedroom window gazing at the vineyards in the distance in the late-afternoon sunlight. For the first time since her arrival she missed the beat of New York. She found the landscape here enchanting, but wondered if she could stand the quiet nights. She could see developing a passion for growing a vineyard, but she had also observed enough to understand that the glamour happened when the champagne was being poured from the bottle. Leading up to that were a lot of people digging and plowing and baking in the hot sun. She sat down and opened her journal, and wrote: Two people saw a woman walking fast or running through the village around eleven the night of Antoine's death. Will talk to Chief Petit. Like the bottle that turned out to be the murder weapon, and the rose in Léa's hand, the plastic bag is starting to haunt me.

Chloé stuck her head in the door. "Am I interrupting?"

"Only the journal writing and that can wait."

"Ted called and we invited him to come here for dinner."

"Ted?"

"I spoke with my parents, and we realized that he has been a scapegoat for everyone. *Maman* felt badly for you, and wants to make it up to you. Can you join us?"

"There's a tentative plan to go with Abdel to Olivier's, but I can go after dinner. Pull up the other chair." Max put her feet up on the windowsill. "Is Marc back?"

"He came in a while ago and apologized. He's confessed to me that he and Yves and some others were using cocaine the night of the wedding. My parents would die, but with luck they won't find out."

"Abdel and I spoke with your friend Delphine today and she corroborated that they were using cocaine."

"Did she say anything else? I don't think she likes Marc very much. She blames him for Yves behaving like a teenager."

"She was mad that Yves only danced with her twice. I've been thinking about the ubiquitous Marc. He was everywhere the night of the wedding, it seems. He checked in on his mother after Ted left her, and he and Yves and the guys were off sniffing cocaine, and then he was in the kitchen…"

"Out with it! You're wondering why Marc wasn't with me? Is it too belittling to say he and his friends were behaving like schoolboys? If no one had been murdered, no one would have cared that Marc and his friends were running around."

Marie-Christine called for Chloé from the stairs. She jumped up and headed for the door. "Dinner's at nine. I'm off to help *maman.*"

"I'll come down to help in a minute." Max glanced down at her notes again, then out at the vineyards. She picked up her pen, and looked at her original list: Ted, Hans, Jacques, Marc, Bernard. Antoine. She scratched Antoine out. Then she wrote, "I think I know who killed Léa and Antoine, but I'm going to have a hell of a time proving it."

Chapter Twenty-six

The Peugeot in Olivier's parents' driveway didn't belong to anyone he knew. Probably a friend unaware that they were in Australia. He pulled into the circular drive behind it, and went directly to the garden to make sure that the gardener had watered the container plants. Abdel was due to come by later to discuss his notes about Delphine Lacroix. Max would join them after dinner to go through the de Saint-Pern documents and discuss the next course of action. He was starting to see the merits of having three with various levels of expertise work together. It had also been a pleasant surprise when Abdel had expressed nothing but praise for Max when he asked about her.

He hoped Max would stay over. She traveled light, with only a toothbrush, yet her presence permeated everything, even the garden, where he had watched her through the window with her face up to the morning light as though in meditation. He removed a box of papers from his car and walked to the door, balancing the box in order to open the door, when it opened and he was face to face with Véronique.

"Olivier," she said in her breathless voice, "I was beginning to wonder if you were coming home. I've already opened a bottle of bubbly." Why was a French woman using the appellation for champagne that reminded him of an American cheerleader at a football game, he wondered.

She leaned over to plant a kiss on his lips and he pulled away slightly. "What brought you here?" was all he could think to ask.

She frowned, but stepped back in order to allow him to enter. He put the box on the countertop in the kitchen and then turned to her, still not knowing what to say. She sat in the same chair that Max had occupied the night before and explained that she had called but didn't reach him and had decided to be bold and rent a car and drive out.

"I also tried to call you several times to tell you not to come," he managed to get out, "but you weren't picking up."

"I had a shoot this afternoon, *chéri,* and don't like to answer unless it's urgent."

He had been with her to a shoot and seen her answer every phone call, but he felt petty thinking it. "It's good to see you, but I'm in the middle of this case…"

"It's on the front page of every paper," she said. "I saw on television that the blogger Ted Clay was released today. I went to his blog and he's pretty good. He writes wine reviews and just did one on the 2009 Marceau *Hortense* that had people in my circle buzzing. But what's really capturing everybody's attention is his blog about this crime."

"I'm not sure what you're talking about."

"His blog is about his life, Olivier, and he puts in lots of details. In the latest one he wrote about what it's like to be in a French regional jail. Before that he wrote about the German entrepreneur Hans Keller and his background, which teems with angst and revenge and all that good stuff. Hans' grandfather was one of many Germans who came to the Champagne area to create their fortunes in the almighty grapes. But of course he was German and became the *Weinführer* of the region and was eventually sent packing back to Germany. Run out of France. Another installment followed that reads like a soap opera. His fans are numbering in the thousands, I understand."

"What's the latest installment?"

"He's not mentioning her name. Yet. But it's about someone distantly related to Hans Keller. A woman. Her grandmother was French and collaborated with the Germans during the war and was one of those women whose head got shaved and was marched out to the streets to be hissed at and scorned. She was pregnant, she claimed, by Hans Keller's grandfather. She had a baby girl. And that girl grew up and married an abusive alcoholic, and had kids. I forget how many."

"This sounds like fiction." His phone vibrated in his pocket. He snuck a look at the screen and saw that the call was from the Marceau residence.

"Clay claims it's all true and people are lapping it up. The point I'm making is that a few of Clay's fans—and I'm a big fan now—are speculating that one of the offspring of the woman who married the drunk might be Geneviève Durand. Clay drops hints, like she's a designer who sews a rose into everything she creates, or she has a weekly salon that certain politicians attend."

"This is scandalous. She could sue him."

"*Au contraire.* Madame Durand was interviewed by a newspaper reporter and my friends and I thought she was quite coy. The point is that she's a hot topic because of her son marrying into the Marceau family. It triggers the imagination: her being the granddaughter of a shamed French woman. Her mother was an illegitimate child—perhaps the child of Hans' grandfather—who grew up to marry an impoverished drunk and have a couple of daughters. And now the woman everyone knows as Geneviève Durand is related to one of the wealthiest families in Germany. The Kellers. Then to have her son marry into the Marceau family with ties to the de Saint-Pern family! What a turn of fortune."

"But people are assuming that the woman mentioned in Monsieur Clay's blog is Madame Durand. What if it isn't?"

"Then the readers made a mistake. Clay will be writing another installment in a day or two and will clarify who she is."

People were insatiable for gossip and scandal. He blurted, "Has Monsieur Clay written about the murder of Léa de Saint-Pern? The absolute tragedy of a pregnant woman killed at her niece's wedding by some deranged person who might strike again? Who happened to be his fiancée?"

Véronique grew somber. "Actually, he wrote a beautiful tribute to her. And at the end bid her *adieu.*" She got up and poured another glass of champagne for herself and took a glass from the cabinet for Olivier.

She is behaving as though she lives here, Olivier thought.

"Olivier, murder isn't that real to most of us. When I was in Africa I heard of genocide happening there, but we live in a paradise and it seems unreal. I am sensitive to what you're going through, but it's as foreign as those deaths on another continent."

His head was throbbing and he put down the glass of champagne. "I'm going to finish unloading some papers from my car. I warn you, I have a great deal of work to do. It won't wait."

"I can tell you have one of those headaches. I could help you get rid of it?" She glanced toward the stairs and a crosscurrent of thoughts left him speechless again. One was that he couldn't have Max and Véronique meeting here this evening. He decided he would cancel Max tonight, and after dinner would come clean with Véronique and tell her the truth.

He had a few hours to determine what the truth was. It was one thing to have had a night with someone, and quite another to think he had initiated a new relationship, a relationship that would never work because they lived and worked on different continents. He anticipated from Véronique a full-blown tantrum, and a threat to return to drugs, but so be it.

"We need to talk, Véronique."

"Can we talk over dinner? I'm dying to try that place in Saint-Epernay, C-Commune."

Perfect. He might even get drunk. "Okay. I need to work and then we'll go out. A couple of detectives might be coming by to go over some papers."

"I saw the photo of the blond who took down Hans Keller. She's way too sexy to be a cop."

He turned and walked out to the car and picked up a set of folders and took them into the garden where he could think. If what Véronique had said about the blog was true, it explained how Geneviève and Hans Keller knew each other before the murder. They had the same grandfather. It was hard to wrap his head around that. He knew he was engaging in speculation, but he couldn't help but think that perhaps it was Geneviève who brought Keller into the rarified atmosphere of the French administration. It could also explain why Hans latched onto Marc so quickly. Geneviève must have fed Ted the information that he put on his blog. She was in the business of reinventing herself, and perhaps this was her new method. She was already becoming a sympathetic character to Ted's readers, and it would be easy to enter the fracas of the murder as a *tragédienne*. It was no secret to many that she coveted a significant role at de Saint-Pern.

Olivier wished that Max was here, sitting across from him and discussing what he was thinking. He couldn't put her off another second. He dialed the Marceau house and couldn't help but smile when she said hello. "I hear the interview went well."

"I think so. Delphine and Hans definitely hooked up, as we say. I can tell you all about it when I come over. The Marceaus invited Ted to dinner, so it will be after that."

"Max, I have to cancel tonight. I have an unexpected visitor…an old friend…"

The silence lasted too long. He wondered how she knew. "I see."

"We'll talk tomorrow." He went inside. Véronique was watching a film. She waved and turned back to her story. He dialed Abdel's number and when he answered, said, "I've had a change of plans…I have an unexpected visitor…"

"I'm almost there," Abdel said.

This time Olivier hesitated, unsure if he wanted to expose his duplicity to the upright Arab whose opinion he valued. But what excuse would he give for cancelling? "In that case, come ahead. Véronique is here. We can spend some time working on the case and then I will take her to dinner."

Abdel didn't say anything, even if he thought it. Olivier poured another glass of champagne and observed Véronique from across the room. He studied her thin, child-like arm that rested on the top of the sofa, and her hair that was a raging mess, which on her looked quite divine. With no make-up, her face was almost plain, and far more beautiful than when she was peering out from magazines with so much makeup he could hardly recognize her. She had told him that he was the only honest man she'd ever met, and that troubled him now.

Abdel came to the door and Olivier met him in the driveway before he could be distracted by a conversation with Véronique. "The papers are in the car. I've already taken a box to the garden and we can work there," he said. "Let's go through these quickly if possible. They're mostly old documents from Charles de Saint-Pern, which I think are quite irrelevant to the current business and the murder. Then we can move into more recent documents." They began the process, with only the sound of birds flying around, settling into their nests before dark, as accompaniment.

They had been at it for at least an hour when Abdel called out, "Monsieur! Here's a paper dated almost thirty-one years ago. A document signed by a Tristan de Saint-Pern."

"Charles' father. Let me see." He opened the page wider and scanned it quickly. A woman named Louise Abel was a signatory. How odd. He went back to the top. Tristan de Saint-Pern was giving Louise Abel the sum of five hundred thousand francs. The document went on to list conditions: she must move out of Champagne forever, she agrees to release Charles de Saint-Pern from all paternal duty of the child, and agrees to not list him as the father on the birth certificate, and she must forfeit all rights to any part of the de Saint-Pern Company. The terms continued on to the next page. Olivier sat, stunned. He wondered if Léa had ever gone into these files. Did she know that her husband had a child somewhere?

Just then he saw Véronique ambling toward them, ravishing in tight jeans, stilettos and a red silk top, smoking a cigarette and smiling. She tossed her hair back and put her hand out to Abdel, who stood quickly to shake it. "I remember you," she crooned to him and Abdel returned her greeting, and her smile.

"It's nine o'clock, Olivier," she said. "I'm hungry."

"The hour of *entre chien et loup,*" he said. Between the dog and the wolf. When Abdel and Véronique gave him inquisitive glances he explained that it was the hour when dark descended, a melancholy time for many. He thought he was describing himself in the moment. "We'll wrap up here in five minutes," he said to Véronique, and took his vibrating cell phone out of his pocket and answered.

"It's Legrand."

"Ah, monsieur. You have news?"

"I'm ruling Antoine Marceaus' death a homicide. The indentations and bruises from a blunt object helped a great deal in making my decision. It seems pretty clear to me that he entered the river drunk and each time he tried to return to shore he was pushed back with the handle of the blunt object. Rather brilliant detecting on your assistant's part."

"Thank you for allowing us to observe."

"It was a good partnership. I'd like to propose that we work together more often."

"Let's have a meeting. I'll make sure this request goes to *le ministère. Merci.*"

He told Abdel that Antoine's death was a homicide, then poured out the story on Ted Clay's blog that Véronique had told him about. They looked again at the document signed by Tristan de Saint-Pern and Louise Abel to see if there was any connection forming.

"I can find the blog in an instant on my laptop," Abdel said. "But we'll have to go inside."

"Did anything jump out at the interview with Delphine Lecroix other than her dalliance with Monsieur Keller?"

Abdel said that nothing seemed too odd, except that Monsieur Durand had a plastic bag with him when he went to his mother's room, and that Detective Maguire had been very thoughtful about that on the ride home. Olivier smiled, imagining her creating an entire scenario, as though she were writing a screenplay.

"Anything else?"

"I think she'll be surprised to learn that you have company."

"Véronique will be leaving in the morning and I've already told Max that I had an unexpected guest arrive. It really shouldn't be any great concern."

"At the risk of jumping in where I do not belong, I hope you do the right thing where Detective Maguire is concerned."

Olivier was already entering the house, and was embarrassed when Véronique bounced over and bestowed a playful kiss on his cheek in front of Abdel. As he turned away from her he said to Abdel, "Let's meet at eight tomorrow.

Chapter Twenty-seven

Max had excused herself when Olivier called and quietly gone to her room and closed the door before a maelstrom of thoughts threatened to overtake her. She scrawled her raw emotions in her journal, filling it with expletives, then adding, *Véronique is there with him at this very moment, dancing around the kitchen, rolling around in the sheets with him, drinking champagne.*

The room couldn't contain her. She stepped into her sneakers and ran down the stairs; pausing for a moment, she decided to run to the river, and took off at a slow trot. The trees became a blur, and she ran faster along the trail that went through the forest, until she couldn't feel her body. The endorphins had kicked in as she arrived at the river, and she stopped, panting. A blue heron flew up, startling her. She didn't know she was crying until the panting had become loud gasps. The emotions that had engulfed her were surprising. She had had flings before and had moved on without emotion when they ended.

It took some time, she had no idea how long, before the gentle flow of the river lulled her into a state of quiet. The bliss she had experienced with Olivier the night before was self-contained, already a memory. It had nothing to do with commitment, or with the future in any way. She understood that when her mother had met Hank they had fallen in love, and she was the result of that union. Her mother had given up her inheritance and her family in order to be with a man who had little understanding of her culture, and could only offer her an unconditional love.

Max realized that she quite possibly had fallen in love with Olivier, though her girlfriends would laugh at her if they heard her speak that way. Even if he felt the same way, she had to be practical about the fact that they lived on two separate continents. Hank had guided her through the labyrinthine trails of detective work, but Juliette was her heart's guide, and she knew what she would say: the moments they had shared was all there was, and it had to be enough. And on a more practical level, she would remind her daughter that Olivier had a girlfriend when Max arrived on the scene, and that that was part of the equation, even as they felt the intense attraction to each other.

Hank would tell her to put all of her energy into the investigation. She thought back to when Ted had arrived earlier in the evening and showed her his most recent blog entries. He confessed to her that the mystery woman he referenced was indeed Marc's mother. Geneviève Durand had to have some underlying purpose in revealing all of this to Ted, and having it publicized. Max was nervous for Ted, knowing that Geneviève could be leading him into a trap. What was she after? If she could prove her lineage, would she expect some sort of compensation from Hans' family?

"Max?" Chloé came and sat beside her. "I saw you run out the door, and figured you'd headed this way. *Ça va?* Are you okay?"

"I am now. Olivier doesn't know that I know, but Véronique is with him. He called and canceled our plans to meet tonight…"

"*Merde alors!* If you want to run away I'll go with you. Marc and Hans aren't speaking because Hans accused Marc of taking his money. Marc is mad about the information Ted has put on his blog about the 'mysterious woman' who everyone thinks is Marc's mom. And my mother just accused me of taking the dress that she plans to wear to Antoine's service, forgetting that I'm quite a bit smaller. And if we don't make it in time for dinner I anticipate a catastrophe!"

Max jumped up. "Let's go. I needed to sort out my feelings. But I need to focus on the investigation."

"Later tonight we'll go to c-Commune, a great little champagne bar in Epernay. Marc will join us."

"I'm not opposed to drowning my sorrows in champagne."

Jacques and Marie-Christine could not have been more gracious, Max thought, as the five of them gathered around the table. Max had noticed that tension rarely showed up at the table here, other than the night when Geneviève and Ted arrived late. Mimi had made roast pork which was served with a chilled pinot noir, the red grapes used to create champagne.

Jacques opened a bottle of the Marceau's *Hortense* when Mimi brought in the requisite plate of cheeses. Ted explained to Marie-Christine and Jacques that his blog was receiving a lot of attention lately because of the story about Hans Keller and his family. There's another story, he told them, that I uncovered about a woman who had an affair with Hans' grandfather. Marie-Christine was fascinated and wanted to know more, but Ted said that they would have to go to his blog site and read about it. It was much too long of a story to tell over dinner.

"You will also see from reading my blogs that your *Hortense* is my favorite champagne," he added. Max had willed herself not to allow her thoughts to go to Olivier, though she wanted desperately to share with him what was going on with Ted's blog. Abdel was a computer whiz, though, and would fill him in on the details.

Ted's role in Léa's life wasn't mentioned at the table, nor was either family death, or even Ted's brief time spent in jail. These were topics that were subconsciously banned from civil discourse. Max had no intention of bringing up her attendance at Antoine's autopsy, nor did she mention the visit to see Delphine, and she certainly had no desire to bring up Olivier's name.

Max thought Ted and Chloé were amusing as they discussed various places they liked in Paris and the latest films. Marie-Christine turned to Chloé during a lull in conversation and said, "*Chérie,* that dress I was asking you about was in your room. Thrown into the corner."

"*Maman!* This is absurd. Your dress is much too big for me." She lowered her voice, "Mimi may have made a mistake and put it there when she was organizing clothes for the cleaners. She is getting older, you know." Marie-Christine pursed her lips, but seemed to accept the explanation.

Chloé rushed off to call Marc, and Jacques lifted a glass to Max and said, "It means a lot to us to have you here. I don't know how to appraise your detective work because you share nothing with us, but you are a good support for our daughter."

Jacques said to Ted, "Why don't we adjourn to the billiard room and I'll challenge you to a game before you leave?"

They all followed Jacques into the vast room upstairs that not only contained a billiard table but a reading area. A table was set up with a large, uncompleted puzzle on it. Marie-Christine came also, which was a surprise, and sat with Max on the sofa. On the table in front of them was a stack of photograph albums.

"May I look?" Max asked.

"Of course."

Max smiled at seeing pictures of Chloé as a child, and exclaimed over one of Léa as she remembered her. A gorgeous woman admired by all. Recent articles and photographs of Léa had been chunked into one of the albums. "I haven't had time to sort them out," Marie-Christine said. Max glanced at the recent article that in its headline referred to Léa as "the grape goddess" and wondered if the vast public would ever get enough of scandals of the wealthy and famous.

She stopped at seeing a photograph of Charles in front of his plane. There were photos of him with dignitaries, at a wine tasting in Bordeaux and one of him labeled "Le Petit Prince," the same one that hung in Marc's room, and probably in hundreds of other little boys' rooms. Max was about to close the album when a photograph of Charles surrounded by a crowd caught her eye. "He seems quite special," she said to Marie-Christine, who leaned over to examine the picture.

"Special in our language doesn't imply something good," Marie-Christine said. "In fact, it is the opposite."

"He was *magnifique,* then?"

She laughed. "We would say simply *pas mal.* Not bad."

Max studied the woman in the photograph gazing up at him. "Did he know Geneviève Durand?"

"No, no. Certainly not. Let me see." Marie-Christine slid the album onto her lap. "These are old photographs that were Charles' before he ever married Léa." Mimi entered with coffee on a tray and set it down. "Mimi, come look at this photograph." Then to Max, "Half of Paris was at that event where ten people received awards from the administration for their contributions to France. Oh, there's Charles' father, Tristan, in the background. I recognize him."

"He was a baron?"

"Yes, and really of the old school. Tradition above everything else. He adored Léa, thank God. He had a heart attack two years ago and that was when Léa really had to start running the company, though she was doing most of the work before that."

Mimi had been studying the photograph. "The woman is Louise Abel." Ted and Jacques had put down their cue sticks to listen to Mimi. "I used to go to Aube to see my sister Josette and I remember the family. This photo is of Louise."

"She bears a strange resemblance to Marc's mother, it's true," Marie-Christine said.

"It was the photo that shows her profile that caught my eye," said Max.

"Louise was from a very bad family," Mimi said, pulling the album closer to her. "One of the worst. Her sister was murdered and everybody thought her father killed her but they couldn't prove anything. This one, Louise, had a lot of boyfriends according to Josette, who was a little obsessed with the family after the murder. Then Louise got lucky. The de Saint-Pern boy, Charles, became attached to her." She looked up from the album, "I'm talking about a long time ago, thirty years ago. Louise was slightly older than Charles. Of course he was very sheltered and probably had never had a date. They were still kids."

Ted then related the story about Geneviève that he put on his blog. He said that he had been seeking the next part of her biography, but Geneviève had told him that Marc was angry that the person in the story was so obviously her. "I think she wanted her story told," Ted said. "She was using me to reveal something. I think she wanted the Charles de Saint-Pern story out."

Marie-Christine asked, "Because her son is now married to Charles de Saint-Pern's niece?"

They sat in mutual awe of what seemed to be in front of them. "The only difference is the name. Do you think Louise is Geneviève Durand?" Jacques said.

"What happened to the young Louise?" Marie-Christine asked.

"We heard that she got pregnant and left," Mimi said. "But that is rumor. No proof, whatsoever."

"But what you're saying is that Marc could possibly be the son of Charles de Saint-Pern. I wonder if Léa had any idea of this."

Skeletons in the closet, Max thought. She said quietly, "We don't know if Marc knows."

"But what if he *does* know?" Marie-Christine asked.

Jacques cautioned his wife about jumping ahead. "He had no reason to sneak around about that," he said. "Don't tell Chloé until we know more."

Chloé entered the room and they all pretended to be busy. When Max said she had to make a phone call, Chloé reminded her that they'd be leaving soon for the bar.

Max went to Jacques' study and tried to call Hank at his office, to no avail. Ted stuck his head in the door and said that Chloé told them to go ahead to the bar and she and Marc would meet them there. Max raced to her room and dabbed on lip gloss and gelled up her hair. She slipped into her cowboy boots and put on a black blouse that she thought might be too revealing, and thought to hell with it, and ran to meet Ted at the car.

"I haven't had a chance to thank you. Really thank you," Ted said. "The champagne's on me tonight."

"I don't think either of us is in a position to be treating the other."

"The blog is actually starting to pay off."

"The information on it is provocative. I'm obsessed with this story of Geneviève now, but worried, too. I hope there won't be any retaliation from Marc or her."

"I started the story about Hans Keller because I was furious with him and I was being vindictive. Geneviève had told me about it when she was drunk. I was also mad at her for not being honest and giving me an alibi. I still don't know why she did that."

He pulled in front of the wine bar in Epernay. "They're supposed to have a great supply of local champagnes. Many you've never heard of."

The interior of the bar reminded Max of a Valentine's Day card with the red and white décor. Large bright red chairs and sofas provided stark contrast to the white ceiling and columns interspersed throughout. They went to a table in the corner. A waiter came at once and Ted ordered the tasting, comprised of five champagnes from different vineyards. "How am I going to get rid of this champagne habit when I'm back in New York chasing perps?" Max said.

The front door swung open and Max heard a woman laugh, followed by the familiar loud voice of Girard. She turned to see who he was with, and swung quickly back around. "Ted!" she hissed.

"What?"

"It's Girard and Olivier, and Olivier's girlfriend."

"So? Stop slumping down like that." The waiter arrived with a tray and placed the wine in front of them. "She's fucking gorgeous. They're looking around and will eventually see me at which time I will be forced to raise my hand and wave."

"I want to leave."

"Go ahead if you want to call attention to yourself. Drink your champagne, and try to tell me what just happened to your self-esteem."

"I slept with him."

"Oh, god. What a jerk, then, for him to bring her here."

Max had downed more than half her glass, and Ted put his hand up to request the next round. "You know that the finer the bubbles the better the quality of the champagne, right?"

"Then this is very good champagne. What're they doing?"

"They just ordered a glass each, and it looks as if Olivier is ordering dinner. I hear the *rillettes deporc et morilles* is excellent. And yes, Girard is staring over here. He just got up. Sit up straight. He's handsomer than Olivier, actually."

"Max," Girard said from behind her. "I thought that was you. And Monsieur Clay, we meet again." Ted stood and they shook hands.

"Come join our table if you like," Girard said.

"Chloé and Marc are coming," Ted said.

"Then perhaps I can join you for a little bit?" He pronounced the words "leetle beet." Ted nodded, and he took the seat next to Max. "You haven't forgotten our dinner, right?"

"I've had some other stuff on my mind."

"Monsieur Chaumont invited me here tonight to catch me up a little. Perhaps later I can fill you in. Sorry, Monsieur Clay, but it's official business and Max has been sort of an adjunct. You were naughty not to tell me about your uncle," he added, turning back to her. She knew she was glaring at him, but she couldn't control it. "You must know that you are receiving a lot of credit for insisting that Antoine Marceau's death was a homicide. The medical examiner agreed with you."

"What I've noticed is that the French are extremely reticent about offering praise."

"I just praised you, and you rejected me."

Chloé and Marc entered and waved. They stopped at Olivier's table and after a few minutes wandered over to the threesome. Girard stood up and shook hands with Marc. Max thought Girard seemed to be fawning over him, or him over Girard, she couldn't tell which. She had downed her second tasting glass. Ted offered Girard a glass and he refused, saying he'd go home and have a beer. "I grew up here and so never knew what all the fuss was about with the champagne." Max determined that he was sitting too close to her, and slid her chair back a bit.

Marc sat down, and ordered for Chloé and himself. "Any luck with the investigation?" he asked Girard.

Girard smiled, "It's rarely about luck. But the investigation is certainly moving along. Which reminds me, your friend Yves Brun is the one we don't have on record. He was too drunk the night of the wedding to answer any questions."

"He's still in Paris. Here's his cell phone number." Marc took out his phone and found the number and Girard put it into his cell. Max had felt exhausted ever since Olivier entered the room with the willowy model. For the umpteenth time, she thought about leaving, but knew her cowboy boots would make a big racket if she crossed the tile floor now. She'd just have to wait. Scanning the entrance way from her slightly hidden place behind a column, she saw Hans enter with Delphine Lacroix. She wore stilettos, which were indeed making quite a racket as she walked. Marc sat up straight and stared at them, "What's he doing with *her*?" Delphine glanced over and looked almost as shocked to see them as they were to see her.

One big surprise party.

Chloé jumped up. "I'm going to say hello."

Marc stood up, "I'll come, too."

"No fighting, though," Chloé warned him. "This is Yves' issue."

Max was left sitting with Ted and Girard again, not only feeling sorry for herself but for Chloé as well, who now had to be on guard that her new husband wasn't going to hit someone. Her third glass of champagne, she could see, was wending its way to her via the waiter. A few of her cells had gone into relax mode. Chloé returned in a few moments and sat down, looking heavy-hearted. "We can't believe our friend has taken up with Hans. I don't mean to gossip, but this is going to break Yves' heart."

Marc had on his surly face. He shrugged. "I say, good riddance." He raised his hand for another glass, and turned his attention to Ted, "I hate this blog business. My mother is being ridiculous. I hope you won't let her go any further with this. It will start involving me, and I won't be happy. I know you don't want to cause a rift."

Ted sipped his champagne, "That's not my intention, Marc. The one to speak to is your mother."

"I already have. I think your source has dried up." Tension ran high. They all turned when a woman's voice trilled. Véronique was laughing up at the waiter. Max didn't dare look. Girard stood to leave, and offered to drive Max home, but she wasn't going to abandon Ted again. Or take the chance of Girard groping her. She declined his offer, and went back to her champagne. When she next looked up Olivier was standing by their table, with Véronique at his side.

"Oh, sit down," Ted said. Max avoided eye contact with Olivier and dutifully said hello to Véronique when introduced. Véronique leaned in as if they were old friends and said, "I told Olivier that you're too sexy to be a detective when I saw your picture in the paper. And I was right."

"You arrived today?"

Véronique's response was playful. "Yes, and I've never seen Olivier so busy. He's been ignoring me, but not much longer, right?" She pooched up her red lips, and said, "*Je suis fatiguée. I am tired,*" as she translated to Max.

She's letting me know she has leverage, Max thought.

Olivier said, "I must speak in private with Detective Maguire for a minute. Please join me outside," he said to her. She nodded and stood up to follow him, and realized she was on her way to being drunk. Hans motioned Olivier over and introduced him to Delphine, who smiled up at him.

Hans leaned in to whisper to Olivier and said, "I'm not as worried about the money."

"Oh. A miraculous recovery?"

"I think it will all turn up. No sense in getting the police involved."

"I agree, but understand that I'm already involved." Max accompanied him outdoors. "Look, Max," he said, "I'm sorry about this mix-up."

"Your personal life is not my business. I was aware that you had a girlfriend…"

"I committed too early in the relationship with Véronique. It's not working."

"But it's still a relationship." She looked up at him, "I really want to continue with the case and I hope we both have the grace to do that, Olivier."

She shifted into detective mode, and hoped he couldn't tell that she was slurring her words. "I was going to call you. We went through photograph albums tonight at the Marceaus and realized, with Mimi's assistance, that Geneviève had an affair with Charles de Saint-Pern when she was fifteen."

"I tried to call *you*. Among Charles de Saint-Pern's papers is a document signed by Tristan, Charles' father, and a woman named Louise Abel. Are you telling me…"

"Louise changed her name to Geneviève Durand when she moved to Paris."

"Will you go with me to Paris tomorrow? I want to meet with Marc's friend Yves, and I will make an appointment with Geneviève. I also think we ought to meet with Léa's therapist, a woman named Adèle Lausanne."

"It doesn't sound like you need me for any of that."

"I *want* you to come."

"Girard told me that Dr. Legrand is calling Antoine's death a homicide."

Olivier smiled. "Thanks to you for that. I'll pick you up at eight tomorrow morning."

The door swung open and Véronique stalked out to the parking lot, and began speaking in rapid-fire French, "You *putain!* You could have told me you're fucking her. She left her *sillage* in your bed. I should have known when I saw her photo. And the cowboy boots. It's the worst fashion statement I've ever seen. I'm leaving tonight. Drive me home so I can get my car."

"We'll discuss this in the car. I'm coming." He turned to Max, looking mortified, "What she said has nothing to do with you."

I understand French and it has everything to do with me, Max thought.

"What is *sillage*?" she asked.

He answered in an impatient voice, "It's a scent that wafts by after one has walked past."

He turned and walked briskly to his car, and Max thought she must look like a lovesick cat.

Chapter Twenty-eight

"I'm sorry," Olivier said for the second time in an hour to two different women.

"Forget being sorry." Véronique pulled a cigarette out of her designer bag and lit it with the gold Cartier lighter Olivier had given her, which he now regretted, as he wished she would quit smoking.

"I don't consider us in a monogamous relationship. At least we've never discussed it."

"You're right, we haven't. But I'm ready to be."

"And I'm not. There is a guest room at my parents'."

"You've got to be kidding. I won't stay there if you're rejecting me."

Olivier noticed she was slurring her words, and thought Max had been as well. Véronique had barely touched her dinner. They had fought before and made up within hours, and he sensed that was her expectation now. But this time he felt emotionally detached and knew he had been thinking for some time that it wasn't working. At the moment he resented the relationship wedging into the investigation. He simply wanted the time to think about all that had transpired over the past twelve hours. "I have to work tonight when I get home, Véronique. Tomorrow is a very crucial day in the investigation. "

She sulked the rest of the way home and when they arrived she immediately poured more champagne. Olivier decided to have a glass of *Calvados,* and took it from the cupboard, furious at Véronique for her jealous tantrum and mad at himself for finding himself in such a predicament. "Look," he said. "Let's call a truce."

"How do we call a truce when war hasn't been declared?"

"That wasn't a declaration of war back there?"

"I'm jealous."

"I can't do anything about that."

"Olivier," she said, downing her champagne, "You're the one man I had faith in."

"I'm sorry to disappoint you."

"Are you in love with the detective?"

"No. Of course not."

"So you had a little fling. What's the problem? Come to bed." She's changed her tactic, he thought.

"I can't. I will be up most of the night working. I told you that."

"I'm not going to stay here under these circumstances." She marched out to her car. Olivier followed her, and she put her window down. "You've had too much to drink, Véronique. Stay here and drive in tomorrow."

"You're offering me the couch? *Va te faire foutre!*" The car sped off. It wasn't the first time she had told him to go to hell. He quickly dialed Abdel and asked him to pull her over and give her the choice of staying in a small inn, which he would arrange, or being returned to his house. He pulled out his briefcase and began to go over his notes. He yawned, and was about to call Abdel again when his phone rang and Abdel said that she was at the inn and the proprietor would expect to hear from Olivier. He added that she had been quite belligerent. Olivier called the inn immediately to offer his credit card, and then felt badly about how he had treated Véronique, but he didn't know what else he could have done. He did not have the emotional wherewithal to cope with someone of her temperament, especially tonight.

He tried to put her out of his mind and rehash the day. The story with Geneviève was almost too fantastic to absorb, as was the synchronicity of what he and Abdel had discovered in Tristan de Saint-Pern's documents at the same time that Max was finding the picture of Geneviève in the old photograph album at the Marceaus'. There was a convergence occurring that reminded him of why he was in this line of work. Until this evening, he had had some doubts that they would be able to solve the murders. He thought about Léa again, and how bravely she had been creating a whole new life for herself, taking a risk with a man from a different culture who was financially insecure, and deciding to have a child with him at age thirty-nine. He recalled her commenting that he needed someone to loosen him up, and then spontaneously calling Max over to ride with them to the airport. He slipped into bed and felt the fragrance of Max wafting over him, the *sillage* as it were, and wished that his arms were around her.

A few hours later, with very little sleep, Olivier strode into the Marceau salon and shook hands with Jacques, who was having his coffee alone. He began to tell Olivier about their discovery in the photo album the evening before and Olivier told him that he already knew. He then confided in Jacques about the document signed by Tristan de Saint-Pern. "I'm deeply concerned about my daughter," Jacques said. "If Marc is the son of Charles de Saint-Pern, I would never forgive his mother for not telling Léa or us."

"Perhaps she did tell Léa."

"Then we needed to know also. Maybe this is why Léa decided to quickly sell her company and move to America. I told you there was more to my story."

"One problem, though, is that Geneviève signed a document which forbade her from ever revealing her son's identity."

Jacques sat, pensive.

"Max and I are going into Paris today to meet with Marc's mother, and I want to speak with Marc's friend, Yves Brun."

"Chloé told me about the young men sniffing cocaine. You know I have no tolerance for that. I find Marc to be quite immature. I really have grave worries about the marriage, and have from the beginning."

"I know."

"Marie-Christine told me in detail about her interview with you a few days ago. I think we're going to be okay. We need closure on Léa's murder and Antoine's death, though."

Olivier paused, wondering if he should reveal that Jacques' brother was murdered, too. He was afraid that if he didn't Jacques would find out from Girard, or worse, Philippe Douvier. "We heard from the forensic autopsy and Antoine's death was not an accident."

Jacques' eyes widened and he clutched his chest and doubled over. Olivier got up, alarmed, as Marie-Christine entered with Mimi behind her. Marie-Christine went to Jacques, who held her hand until he was able to compose himself. Then Olivier told them about the circumstances and how they had proven it. Max walked in, and gave Olivier an inquisitive look, then sat down.

"There's an element of cruelty here that is unimaginable," Jacques said.

Max told them the story of the blue vase, how Ted had learned it from the evening spent with Antoine, and then told her about it. They seemed spellbound, and Olivier thought of the healing power of story. "I remember that vase," Jacques said. "We've listened to him so little over the years. Once my mother was gone, which was devastating to him, I realize, he simply couldn't manage."

Mimi spoke, "He came to my house once a week on my day off and we talked, and often we fished." They stared at her, obviously unaware that this had happened. "He was really brave to have managed to turn that vase knowing that he wasn't going to survive but wanting to leave a clue behind. He was afraid of the killer but knew he had to try to prevent more deaths. He knew all along who it was, I'm sure."

"I want Hans Keller arrested," Jacques said, "even if I have to call Philippe Douvier and the Minister of the Interior. Hans

Keller held my brother hostage, forcing him to sign his shares in de Saint-Pern over to him. It's all so obvious."

"Jacques, please don't call the ministers yet. Wait until Max and I are back from Paris."

"Then guarantee me that we're safe. And that you'll be here for Antoine's service tomorrow morning."

"We'll be back as quickly as possible. As for your safety, I want us to continue as though today is just another day of a boring investigation. As long as everything seems calm, there won't be anything for the murderer to react to."

He and Max exchanged glances, understanding that it was time to leave. Once in the car, he began to outline the day ahead. He picked up his cell and called a number and within minutes he had agreed with Yves to meet in a café near the Pompidou Museum, where Yves worked as a junior curator. Olivier had already established a time to meet with Geneviève at her apartment, and Léa's therapist would give them time in the afternoon.

Max reached into her bag and uttered an expletive. "I left my journal in my room," she said. "I've been writing notes non-stop. Last night when I got home I drew up a map with the crime scene in the center, and had everything radiating from there— the tent, the house, the terrace, the inn, the kitchen, and then I tried to place everyone somewhere at the hour of death. Jacques in his room with the shutter open, Mimi stumbling across Léa and walking back up to find Marie-Christine, Chloé in the tent, Marc all over the place…"

"And what about Yves."

Max had her eyes closed, visualizing. "I saw him with Marc when he came down to inquire about what was going on. Antoine blacked out, then awoke and went home."

"Hans' alibi, for now, seems pretty solid."

"I wonder, though, if he bought that alibi. He could offer a lot of money to Delphine. I recall now that she told me that she passed Bernard Martin on the terrace when she was rushing back to the tent from the inn.

"Dupuis was in the parking lot waiting for Martin to tell him what Hans Keller was offering for de Saint-Pern."

"Oh, I didn't know about that."

"Those two are in collusion, and there's a good chance I can have one of my colleagues go after them for bribery and other corruption. I also think Bernard is full of resentment and anger, even though he tries to keep it from showing, It's possible that he could have killed Léa."

"But who forced Antoine to sign over his shares of de Saint-Pern to Hans? I think I should call Chloé and have her hide my journal."

"Your door is closed? Who knows about it?"

"Only Chloé."

"I wouldn't worry." They were entering the city, and Olivier began to pay more attention to traffic. He swerved to miss a car and swore, forgetting to ask Max why she looked so worried. He had debated about bringing up last night, decided that they were in professional mode and to do so would interfere with their focus. He was impressed with Max's easy manner after last night's scene, and had the fleeting thought that she was now unavailable. He pulled into a parking garage and they both exited the car and headed for the street.

"I hope that Abdel won't think I'm taking his place today," Max said.

"He's busy with forensics. The shoe prints are driving him crazy. There is a pair that can't be matched. Dress shoes like all the groomsmen wore. But it could be a guest, too."

Yves waved from the café where he sat drinking a *café au lait*. He had sandy-colored hair and wore Rayban sunglasses. They shook hands and Max ordered what Yves was having and Olivier ordered an espresso. "God, this has been a nightmare," he said. "Marc has been keeping me informed."

Olivier dove in. "I would imagine that you don't recall much, as my detective said you were too drunk to answer a few questions the night of the murder."

"It's true that I passed out near the tennis courts, but I remember everything before. And some after, though Delphine would say otherwise. She would probably even go so far as to say I didn't know she had taken off with the tall German. I saw them dancing and I thought it better to get drunk than start a fight. She'll be back once she realizes he has no intention of taking her on that exotic cruise he's been promising her."

"Would she take money from him for providing an alibi?"

He paused. "Probably."

This is a betrayed man talking, Olivier thought.

Olivier said, "I saw you with Marc when you came down to the crime scene immediately after the police arrived. Where were you coming from?"

"We'd been dancing like crazy. You probably saw us spinning Marc around earlier in the night." He laughed. "It was a wild night. Marc went to check on his mom, he said, and after a bit returned with news that the police were arriving. I jumped up and we went to find out what was going on."

Olivier interjected, "Marc changed into jeans. Why?"

"A group of us had brought casual clothes as we had some notion of having breakfast at sunrise. Marc had already changed when he came to find me, and I decided to change too."

"Where did you go to change?"

"In the woods."

"Why not in the house?"

"We were avoiding his father-in-law. You know, everything had felt a little out of control all day. Marc and his mother were snapping at each other, then they had an argument at the inn, and Marc was furious when he left there. He also knew his new bride was upset with him for getting drunk."

"Did he want to marry?"

Yves looked caught in a trap. He shifted his position in the chair, and waved his hand for another coffee. Olivier glanced over at Max, who hadn't taken her eyes off Yves. He wondered how much she had understood. "No."

"Was he in love with someone else?"

Yves' eyes dropped. *"Oui."*

"Can you tell me who?"

"I don't know. He never told me her name. I think it's irrelevant, for he also said that it could never be. He was doing what his mother and Léa wanted."

"Léa?"

"That's what he told me, but he was bitter about it. I didn't get it. I thought Chloé was great. I've been friends with Marc since elementary school, but he's unpredictable. Very hard to read."

Olivier pushed his cup away. "Is there anything else that you can say that would help me, Yves?" When he didn't reply, Olivier said, "You know that Antoine was also murdered."

Yves gasped. "No! Marc didn't tell me that!"

"He doesn't know. We just learned yesterday."

"I liked Antoine very much. He was so friendly that night. And drunker than we were, I think."

"He and Marc got along well?"

"Okay, I guess. Antoine said whatever he thought, and he told Marc that he thought he was faking it with Chloé and that made Marc really mad. But he got over it."

Olivier paid, and they walked together through the big square behind the museum. Olivier gave him his card in case anything else came to mind. He and Max went back to the car and drove to the narrow street in front of Geneviève's apartment. Olivier filled Max in on the conversation with Yves.

"Something has been bugging me since Chloé told me about the wedding," she said. "Her emails didn't have the *joie de vivre* that I would have expected. We talked a couple of nights ago, though, and even when she is upset with Marc, she defends him."

Olivier sighed, "People marry for all kinds of reasons. Certainly not always for love."

"I think Chloé's in love with Marc, but she has felt some disappointment and doesn't know what to do with that. She's been protected and isn't used to things going awry."

Olivier tapped in the code on Geneviève's apartment building as before and they walked through the courtyard and on to the small elevator. Geneviève was in trousers and a man's shirt and her hair was whipped up into a careless chignon. She gave them a warm smile, and said that she had coffee ready. Or champagne if they preferred. They said they preferred coffee, and went to the salon.

"You always have a fresh rose blooming," Olivier said. "It's a wonderful touch."

Geneviève had the tray of coffee ready and began to pour as they arranged themselves on the sofas. There wasn't a hint of anything unusual except that her hand shook when she poured the coffee. Oliver got up and handed a cup to Max and took one for himself.

"Max," she said, "What a vacation this has been for you. I'm sorry that I haven't had the opportunity to entertain you properly. I hope you'll stay long enough for that to happen."

Olivier said, "You won't be surprised that I'm curious about how Ted Clay came to blog about his story of Hans' background and then the story of a woman who some presume to be you."

"I had told him my story a couple of years ago, never thinking he would write about it. Marc thinks he was being vindictive, but I'm not so sure."

"People see it as a rags-to-riches story."

"They still have no idea what it's like to be poor, and to have a child out of wedlock and try to raise him. It's more common today, but I struggled."

"But you had money from Tristan de Saint-Pern."

She couldn't hide her shock. "How do you know that?"

"Your contract was among a stack of documents handed over to the police."

"The bastard hangs on to me from the grave. It was enough money for me to go to seamstress school and helped for a few years. I went back to him to ask for more when Marc was two and he threatened to have me jailed. He had the influence to do that, and to have my son taken away."

"Did Marc ever meet his father?"

"Once. At a big airshow. Charles was receiving a big award. Marc was four. Charles was shocked, and furious. He told me I must never show up again."

"Does Marc know who his father is?"

"I had always said I'd tell him before he married. And I did."

"How did he react?"

"I know now it was too much of a shock. He had idolized Charles, as did so many of his friends. I took him to many air shows as he was growing up and he wanted to become a pilot. I thought he'd be happy with the news, but it was the opposite. We fought at the inn. He told me that he was calling the wedding off, that he didn't love Chloé. I thought it was wedding jitters."

"That's when you told him he was nothing and would have nothing. It would been the decent thing to do to let Chloé and her family know about Charles being Marc's father."

"I owed them nothing, Olivier. I know these people. Marie-Christine would have assumed Marc was after her sister's fortune. He and Chloé will be fine, and I think Marc will come to be a great asset to the company."

Max asked, "How would you say Marc got along with Léa?"

"They had a hard time establishing boundaries at first, but once they did, he came to adore her."

"Ted said that you were upset when he told you he and Léa were going to have a baby."

"Ted lies. He also said that he stayed with me for a half hour or so when he walked me to the inn that night. He was using me for an alibi."

Olivier said, "Curiously, we don't have an alibi for Marc either."

"He was with Chloé when I left the reception."

"There's a gap. A wedding guest saw him run through the hall of the inn and knock on your door. That was at two-thirty a.m. You answered and he handed you a plastic bag. What was in it?"

"I never saw a bag. Nor did he come to my door."

"Sorry," Max interrupted. "May I use *les toilettes*?"

Geneviève didn't hide her annoyance. "You know where it is."

Max left the room, and Geneviève said, obviously irritated, "Hasn't she learned that it's impolite to do that?"

Olivier shrugged. "You are content here, now, Geneviève?"

"Content? I have never been content. When you are an orphan, and I was essentially, you can never feel that everything is okay. Before all this, I was close to being content, though. I was glad for Marc, that he would have a good family, and a good wife, and that he would have a place to shine, for he's very smart."

"Hans claims that quite a large sum of cash is missing that he brought into the country, and he mentioned that you knew about it."

Her lips turned up ever so slightly. "Did he? I have a terrible memory."

Olivier knew it would be fruitless to pursue that now. "And did you hope to find a place for yourself at the de Saint-Pern Company?"

She broke into a smile, but it wasn't pleasant to see.

Chapter Twenty-nine

They were in the courtyard when Max said, "All the photos of Charles de Saint-Pern were ripped off the walls and taken off the shelves in Marc's bedroom. And the model planes were gone." She pulled a piece of paper out of her pocket, "But this was still there." Olivier took it and looked at it. "It's a receipt for the wedding clothes that were rented. I should have remembered. There was a problem with Marc's shoes. The company sent two pair. Here's the receipt for two pair of shoes."

Their eyes interlocked.

"One pair might match the mystery shoe print?"

Max nodded. "Think about it. He went down there in his wedding attire, including the shoes. He carried a rose to her. His mother's trademark. They argued and he killed her. He had the presence of mind to rush to his room and change into jeans, and shove his clothes into a plastic bag. He waited to see Ted returning to Léa, then ran to his mother's with the bag of clothes. Geneviève knew in that moment what her son had done, and she decided to try to protect him. He ran back to the table and threw the full bottle of champagne into the woods. I'm torn between excitement at having solved the puzzle and resistance over accepting who the murderer likely is. And, this is crazy, but his was the last name I wrote in my journal."

"You make it sound like a *fait accompli* when all you have is an extra pair of shoes. Earlier you told me that you thought

Delphine Lacroix would take money from Hans Keller for giving an alibi for him and Yves."

"I'm just thinking out loud. Nothing is *fait accompli,* so don't put words in my mouth."

"What would Marc's motive be? You know, Max, you get lucky and sometimes I think you're really quite clever with what you turn up, but other times your quick assessments border on the irresponsible."

"I agree with everything you're saying, except I'm only saying these things to you. Let's say Marc went to tell Léa about his father. Who knows if she knew or didn't know about her husband's child. About the skeletons in the closet. Though I think if she knew she would have prevented Chloé from marrying him."

"Or pushed him into it."

"What if she blew up at him? Geneviève said he adored her. Yves said he was in love with someone else. Even Léa thought he was in love with her."

"It's another scenario. Most of it made up."

"Okay. We'll stick to the shoes. I think we'll find a match."

"We don't have the shoes. There are two pair somewhere, according to this receipt. His fingerprints weren't on the bottle, nor have they turned up anywhere else."

"He wore gloves at the wedding."

"Now we have the shoes and wedding gloves, all missing. No doubt in the plastic bag as witnessed by a woman who admitted to being drunk, and who might be lying to protect the man she was sleeping with."

"Marc's groomsman's clothes are in there, too. The clothes he was wearing when he killed her. I don't think Geneviève would tell you the whereabouts of that bag if you put her in a torture chamber."

"We haven't found her place of vulnerability yet. Nor Marc's."

"I don't think he has one."

They were in front the therapist's office. Adèle Lausanne rose when they entered her office and greeted them warmly. A stack of newspapers were on her desk, and she said, "I'm trying to catch up on the case. This is a great tragedy, and I can only imagine how you must be feeling. Both of you."

She turned to Max. "How is your French? I'm happy to convert to English if you are having trouble." Max glanced over at Olivier, who still looked a bit surly, but he acquiesced. "Please, ask me whatever you'd like, and if there is a question of patient confidentiality, I'll be clear about it."

Max thought she'd like to spend a week asking this woman questions. She was imposing, but not in the least intimidating. Around sixty, her hair was a deep auburn color most often seen on French women with dyed hair. Her eyebrows were arched perfectly over deep-set brown eyes with flecks of gold, and her lipstick was earth-toned. She was slightly overweight, but she carried it well. She exuded self-confidence.

"That's a lovely Buffet painting on the wall behind you," Olivier said.

"It was a gift from my husband. I cherish it for that reason. Now, ask away."

"When did you see Léa last?" Olivier asked.

"Four days before the wedding. She talked quite a lot about her former husband's company, and how there was dissension among the de Saint-Pern members. She was thinking about selling because of some potential conflicts. But she was happy about the baby due in six months."

"Did she talk about her relationship to Marc Durand?" Max asked.

"That's an interesting question. Why do you ask?"

Olivier said, "We've had conflicting accounts. His mother said that Marc adored Léa, and others noticed conflict. Léa was worried when I spoke with her before the wedding that Marc had moved up too fast in the company. She called him ambitious, but perhaps there was opportunism in there as well."

Adèle gave a subtle nod, and said, "I'm concerned about doctor/patient confidentiality here."

Olivier explained that if she didn't answer he could subpoena her, as another life might be at stake.

"Okay. Léa had been told by her husband months before he died about the son born to Louise Abel. This topic had arisen because Léa couldn't get pregnant and she had accused Charles of being sterile and he told her his secret. Léa became more determined than ever to have a baby with Charles, but it wasn't meant to be. She decided to try to find her husband's son, and hired a private investigator to locate the woman and her child. But when Charles learned about it he begged her to drop it. His father was still alive, and he knew it would cause a rift. However, after Charles died, Léa started the process again and this time she was successful. She already knew that Marc was Charles' son when Ted approached her about Marc working for de Saint-Pern. She thought it was meant to be. She was intrigued by the idea of getting to know him, and agreed to hire him. To Léa, Marc was the son of her beloved husband, and her thrill of having what she considered to be a piece of Charles still on earth superseded any thoughts of caution that might have arisen. She welcomed him into the company."

She paused for a moment and asked, "Do you mind if I smoke?" Max and Olivier, mesmerized, shook their heads. She picked up a pack of *Gauloise brunes* and removed a cigarette with her elegant fingers. Max flashed back to Sorbonne days when she and Chloé went through a phase of smoking the raw unfiltered cigarettes, the dark and bitter taste of them akin to drinking a cup of espresso. Here it was incongruous, the elegant woman and the coarse cigarette.

"I used to find smoking those extremely pleasant," Max said.

"They've taken the *brunes* off the market, but I have a great source. And when it's gone, I'll stop."

Olivier brought them back to the topic of Léa and Marc by asking when Léa began to regret her decision.

"When she realized that Marc was falling for her. At first she was very touched, but then she grew worried. By this time she was with Ted, and besides, she thought of Marc as a son.

"Léa then introduced him to Chloé?" Max asked.

"He complied, and went out with Chloé, but he finally told Léa that he was in love with her and she told him it could never be. But she didn't tell him why."

"And Marc's mother, Geneviève?" Olivier asked.

Adèle grew thoughtful "I have never met the woman, but my guess is that her reaction to Marc's 'adoration' of Léa was jealousy and resentment. After all, Geneviève had been paid to leave Champagne and never return, which was humiliating. She may have dreamed of revenge for years and devised a plan for her son to work his way into the de Saint-Pern company and reclaim what was rightfully his as Charles' heir. She, I learned through Léa, had pushed Ted Clay into talking Léa into hiring Marc. She must have been shocked when Marc came home raving about Léa. I would suspect that Geneviève's resentment toward Léa grew. She no doubt expressed a lot of resentment toward her, and as she is Marc's only family, I'm sure she wields a great deal of influence over him. He must hate her for her control."

"He probably began to hate Léa, too," Olivier said.

"That's likely. *Bon.*" Madame Lausanne closed her eyes as though she were trying to picture something in her mind. "I want you to understand that I warned Léa that Marc's reaction may be harsh if he ever found out about his biological father."

"Learning from his mother the night before the wedding that Léa was pregnant must have been horribly upsetting," Max said. "And his mother revealed his father's name that same night."

"She's even crueler than I imagined," Madame Lausanne said.

"Poor Chloé," Max said.

"Could his rage have led to murder?" Olivier asked.

"Yes."

"We think Geneviève may have hidden evidence," Max said.

"She isn't protecting him as much as she is herself. She has a lot to lose if he's found guilty." The sunlight that had been shining through the transparent curtains had faded and the room had taken on a gloomy cast. "This is a tragic story," Madame

Lausanne said "It was good to meet you and I'm sorry. I shall miss Léa."

Olivier shook hands with her, "You're one of France's quiet heroes, Monsieur Chaumont. If we didn't have our *juges d'instruction*, I'm afraid of what we'd turn into."

Olivier and Max walked briskly to the car. "I don't want to start and end my day with an apology, though I know I owe you one," Olivier said.

"My father would say 'It's the thought counts.' You know, Olivier, I think the shit's about to hit the fan."

"Whatever that means, it doesn't sound good."

"Trust me, it isn't."

Chapter Thirty

Olivier and Max were quiet on the drive back to Sourières, lost in their own thoughts and processing everything they had just heard. "*Tu es dans la lune,*" Olivier said finally. "It's an expression we use when someone is lost in thought, meaning you are on the moon."

"I was thinking of Geneviève and Marc's story. How she went into survival mode at sixteen, or maybe younger. Think of the contrast to Chloé who has never had to think about survival. You and I work for justice, but that strikes me as universal injustice."

"Everyone is dealt a different hand in life and we all must choose how to handle it. In Geneviève's case, there was the possibility that the next generation, meaning Marc, could transcend the unfortunate circumstances he was born into. It's clear he didn't have anyone in his life to balance out his mother's fanatical determination to use him to set her life right. She purposely established his biological father as a heroic figure for him without telling him the truth about their relationship. Then decided to blast him with that truth at the worst time."

"Geneviève wanted to make Léa pay for all the ways she felt she had been wronged, but instead Marc loved her. She should be held accountable for these murders in my mind. That makes her an accessory. Too bad she won't be an accomplice."

"Keep in mind that even though we both believe that Marc committed these murders, we still have no physical evidence.

It was a rewarding intellectual exercise in Madame Lausanne's office, but proving all of this is a different story."

"We have to find that plastic bag that Geneviève denies Marc brought to her room," Max said.

"We're also still looking for the money that Hans is convinced Geneviève absconded with."

"It was cash. If I were a thief, I'd hold onto it. Bury it."

"I have a feeling Hans was told by Douvier to stop screaming about the money." He turned off the highway. "I'm much more worried about someone getting hurt. When you were out of the room I warned Geneviève that she wasn't to speak to Marc or anyone else about our interview. I wish now that I had put her under house arrest. I still could."

"I can't imagine her obeying your dictum."

"Abdel is tapping her phone line. I received permission to do that."

The late afternoon light was splendid, bathing the vine-yards in a golden glow. Olivier felt wired, and thought again that he would like to be able to arrest Marc Durand and be done with it. But of course there was the matter of finding the evidence.

"What about the woman running through the village?" Max asked. "Delphine mentioned a large woman in a dress walking rapidly past the inn, and you said that the bartender looked out his window and saw her too."

Olivier shrugged. "Sounds like an apparition. I'm going to speak to Chief Petit and see if the description conjures up some-one in the village. What made you think of that?"

"We just passed a large woman in a dark dress."

"I'll feel better if I'm around Marc. You know, I think for the first time in my life I'm going to call Marie-Christine and invite myself for dinner." He dialed and spoke for only a moment. "I've lucked out. Mimi is preparing *la potée champenoise,* a dish made of *gammon,* leeks, carrots, potatoes, and turnips."

"What's *gammon*?"

"The raw cured hind leg of a pig. My mother includes Monteau sausages, *petit salé*, which is salted pork loin, and smoked bacon."

"Sounds enticing. It just occurred to me that we haven't eaten since morning."

They were in Sourières. The sunset, with multiple shades of pink, reminded him again why he loved this place. "I know this may not be the most appropriate time to discuss it," he said, "and it may not matter to you, but Véronique and I are *finis*. Over."

Max smiled sweetly. "I'm no expert, but a fight doesn't mean the end of a relationship. I'm just glad that we're able to finish this investigation together."

That's your response to me sending my girlfriend away? he thought.

"You are your father's daughter, I think."

"You mean I'm obsessed and vengeful and have a take-no-prisoners mentality?"

"I didn't know about the vengeful part."

"Hell, yeah! I'm seeking revenge for Léa's and Antoine's deaths."

"What happened to justice?"

"That's when I'm in an idealistic mood. At the moment I'm not."

Chloé and Marc were sitting at a table on the terrace when Olivier drove in, looking content and peaceful.

"How was Paris?" Chloé asked when they walked up to them. "*Maman* said you had to get things from your apartment, Olivier."

"It was an errand day. Picking up clothes from the cleaners and paying some bills."

"Poor Max. I hope Olivier didn't hold you hostage all day."

"It was fine. I walked around, and browsed in a couple of shops. An easy day."

"Good. I'll run in for glasses and you can join us."

"I can do that." Marc jumped up and went into the house.

"He's been the old Marc today," Chloé said. "We've been going through so much, but today we walked to the river and talked. A no-pressure day."

Olivier realized that the sensation he was feeling that was causing dizziness was doubt. He and Max had been almost cocky about an arrest when they left Madame Lausanne's office, quickly taking the onus off Hans Keller, who remained the most logical suspect. But he and Max weren't alone. He had conferred over the phone with Girard, Abdel, and Claude Reynard, who had decided it was time to arrest Marc before something happened. This would be a second arrest in the case, and there was still plenty of room for error.

Max excused herself, saying that she didn't feel well. Olivier wondered if she was having similar thoughts.

Max opened her door and turned on the light and began looking for the journal. She was sure she had left it on her bed, but it wasn't there. She calmly rifled through her suitcase, then searched the closet. As her nervousness grew, she began throwing clothes and looking under everything. Writing Marc's name down last and underlining it would tell him what he wanted to know. That he was a key suspect.

She opened her door and peered out into shadowy hall, then pressed the button on the wall and the hallway was flooded with light. She started toward the stairs, then paused. Maybe she should take a quick peer into Chloé and Marc's room to see if her journal was there. She went quickly across the hall, stopping to listen to the voices down below on the terrace. The aroma of the *potée champenoise* wafted up and she was almost overcome with hunger. She turned the knob of Chloé's door and quickly stepped into the room in her bare feet. She reached over and flicked the switch of the lamp. If Marc took my journal he wouldn't leave it in the open, she thought. She opened a drawer, and looked, then another. Her nerves were on edge. The doorknob turned and Marc entered, quickly closing the door behind him.

"Looking for something?" He took a cigarette out of his pocket and stuck it between his lips, making him look like a gangster from the 1930s.

"No. Well, yes. I'm missing my journal."

"And you think Chloé or I took it?"

"I thought maybe I had left it in here." They were speaking in whispers.

"When were you in here?"

"Yesterday. Only for a minute. But I had my journal with me."

He flicked an ash into the ashtray. "What's in it? I've never understood journal writing."

"Oh, thoughts about this and that."

"Kind of like your friend Ted's thoughts about my mother's life that he felt compelled to write on his blog?"

"My writings aren't public."

"You weren't taught that the minute you write something down it's no longer yours? I was."

"I think we should join the others, Marc."

"I wish you liked me."

"I do. I mean, we don't know each other very well yet, but I have no reason to dislike you."

"I think you're disappointed in Chloé for choosing me."

She found her voice returning. "That's not true." She reached over and turned on the ceiling light. "Sorry. But I can't see in that dim light." The bright light surprised him and emboldened her. She thought she could take him down if she had to, thanks to the years of *jiu-jitsu* training, but she hoped she wouldn't need to. "I'm going downstairs."

"Okay." His cell phone rang and he turned his back to her to answer. Max scanned the room and her eyes alighted on a dress draped over an easy chair. Black. She grabbed it quickly, then ran to her room, threw it under her bed and made a loud noise bounding down the stairs.

Marie-Christine had joined Chloé and Olivier. "Where's Marc?"

"He's making a call. I just saw him."

"Dinner will be in five minutes. I wonder where Monsieur Clay is."

He came around the corner as she spoke. "Madame Marceau, *pardon,* I was writing my blog and the time flew away. I could smell the *potée champenoise* all the way from the inn. Everyone, including the owners, wanted to follow me here." Marie-Christine laughed, and Max could see that Chloé and Olivier were as surprised as she was to see her response to the man she had resented until recently. Max noticed that his jaw was almost healed. Marc arrived and put his arm around Chloé, managing to avoid shaking Ted's hand. They entered the dining room together. As they were all settling into their chairs for dinner, Jacques brought out a 1996 *Hortense* champagne. Mimi came from the kitchen and began serving. Max wasn't hungry, and looking over at Olivier she noticed that he wasn't eating either.

Marc was unusually animated, telling a story about a trip he took to Los Angeles once, but Max was barely listening. When the conversation hit a lull, Ted asked what time the service was for Antoine and Marie-Christine said ten. "We shall keep the attendance limited to mostly family but of course you are welcome to attend, Ted," she said. "According to Antoine's wishes, there won't be a church service. It will be brief."

Marc said, "My mother is coming for the service. She's family now."

Max thought she could have sliced through the sudden tension with a knife.

"There's no need," Marie-Christine said. "It's a long way for a fifteen-minute service."

Before Marie-Christine could reply, Chloé said, "I think it's lovely of Geneviève to make the effort. She's coming." Marie-Christine's lips pursed, but she didn't say anything else. Mimi arrived with the *gâteau au champagne,* and Max commented on how wonderful it was. Marie-Christine, glad for the chance to change the topic, explained that it was a sponge cake made with champagne that had gone flat. She then reminded Chloé that she had promised to lead a tour through the chalk *caves* the following afternoon."

"Marc and I wanted to go into Paris. What will you do, *chéri?*" she asked, turning to her husband.

He shrugged. "You can join me in the evening." Max sensed that Marie-Christine was finding reasons to keep her daughter close. When dinner was over Ted excused himself and went back to the inn. Half an hour later Olivier said his good-byes and Max offered to walk him to his car. She took the opportunity to fill him in on what had happened upstairs with Marc.

"Are you sure it isn't in your room? Everyone seemed so pleasant and harmonious tonight. I started to think that we're rushing this arrest business."

"I had the same doubt until I went upstairs. I think Marc is acting, and it makes me nervous. The hairs on my arm stood up when I was in their room." She took a deep breath, "I saw a dress on the chair and impulsively grabbed it as I was leaving." She explained about Marie-Christine's dress, how she had accused Chloé of taking it, and then it ended up in Chloé's room.

"What are you saying?"

"I think the large woman running through the village was Marc wearing Marie-Christine's dress."

"Okay, can you get it and bring it down to me?"

"Yes." She sprinted back to the house and retrieved the dress, returning to Olivier in just a few minutes.

"It could be dangerous for you here tonight. Come home with me."

"That's not a good idea, Olivier. It would be hard to not let things get personal again and I can't let my emotions distract me from this case right now. And besides, I feel like I need to be here."

He surprised her by smiling. "I understand. Go back to the house and make sure you lock your door when you retire."

"I will. Don't forget I'm a *jiu-jitsu* competitor."

"If I hadn't seen you in action I wouldn't let you stay. I can have a gendarme come for the night."

"It's okay."

They stood together, both hesitant. Olivier walked away. This time Max watched his back until he was out of sight.

Chloé and Marc were playing checkers and Jacques was reading a biography of Napoleon when she entered the salon. Marie-Christine and Mimi were in the kitchen, and Max walked in to ask if she could help. Marie-Christine closed the door quickly behind her, and grabbed Max's arm.

"What's going on?"

"Jacques and I are worried. Chloé seems to be completely enamored of Marc again. It makes me wonder if we've jumped to conclusions."

"I second-guess all the time. We'll know more tomorrow."

"It's okay for her to lead a tour, right?"

"It's perfect."

Max went back into the living room and told Chloé she was retiring to her room. Marc said in a genial voice, "I told Chloé that you were looking for your journal and thought it was in our room, but she said she didn't think you'd been in there."

Jacques looked up from his book which Max was sure he hadn't been reading.

Max said, "Oh, I went in looking for you yesterday, Chloé, and thought I may have put it down."

"We can look together," Chloé said. "I'll come up with you." She walked beside Max in the hallway. Once no one could hear them, she said, "Marc was upset about the journal. He thought you were accusing him, Max."

"Of what?"

"What do you mean, of what?"

Theft or murder.

"I wasn't. He doesn't know I keep a journal, and if he did, why would he care?"

"I told him that it's your detective diary." She laughed. "Maybe he's nosey like you."

They had arrived at Chloé's door. "Come in and look anywhere you want." Max wanted to sit down and tell her friend of all of her suspicions, but couldn't trust her not to run to Marc. Chloé turned on the ceiling light.

"Let it go," Max said. "Really. It's not that big a deal. It has all my personal junk in it."

Chloé glanced over at the chair and said, "Now, where's my mother's black dress? She asked me about it before dinner and I told her I'd bring it down to her."

Max shrugged. Marc came up behind her and she stepped aside. "What's going on, *chérie*?"

"*Maman's* funeral dress is gone again. I think Mimi must have come looking for it."

Marc's face grew angry. "I can't believe how much you and your mother have focused on that goddamn dress."

"You don't have to get upset about it. I'll go ask Mimi…"

He mimicked her, "I'll go ask Mimi. I'll go ask Mimi. This house full of women is driving me crazy. I'll tell you what, *I'll* go ask Mimi. Maybe I'll tell her she should retire while I'm at it." He gave Max a scathing look as he wheeled around and marched down the hall.

"Well," Chloé said wistfully. "We did have a good day. But this is what I was telling you about Marc's temper."

"Do you want to sleep with me tonight, Chloé?"

"That will only make him madder."

Max decided she should be gone when Marc returned, and headed toward her room. Not very long after that, she heard their raised voices. She tiptoed out of her room and stood outside their door making sure Chloé wasn't in any danger. Their voices grew softer and soon she heard Chloé saying to Marc that she forgave him. He needed Chloé still. But it wouldn't surprise her if he didn't try to bolt tomorrow. That was Olivier's problem, not hers. Twice more she got up and listened at Chloé's door, but all was silent.

At two she walked down to the stone bench and sat down. The night air fragrance lulled her into a peaceful state. When she returned to her room, she was able to fall into a deep and restful sleep.

Chapter Thirty-one

Olivier scanned the small group gathered at the Columbarium, the pyramid built to hold ashes, in Epernay. Marie-Christine had brought bouquets of irises and mock orange blossoms, their citrusy fragrance permeating the air. The priest was preparing to start *les obsèques*. Somehow Hans had worked his way into the crowd, and Olivier was sure that Jacques and Marie-Christine were too polite to refuse to allow him to pay his respects. Delphine, he noticed, stood apart from Hans and everyone else, yet kept casting glances in Hans' direction. Olivier thought it obvious that Hans had already cast her off now that he was certain to be leaving within the next day or two. Her ex-boyfriend, Yves, stood with Marc and his mother. Ted had joined Marie-Christine and Jacques. That had been a surprise, learning that this little trio was on its way to becoming friends.

Marie-Christine had confided to Max, and she had told Olivier, that she and Jacques understood that Ted's blog about Hans and Geneviève had played a role in guiding the investigation. But it was Chloé who had explained Léa's genuine feelings for Ted, and who had brought him into the fold.

Abdel had called last night to tell Olivier that the rental company had indeed sent two pairs of shoes to Marc and had only received one back. They still needed to find the missing shoes. After Olivier telephoned Canon and Girard, they had unanimously made the decision to arrest Marc. Douvier had called

Olivier, and when told of the pending arrest, asked if Geneviève was aware. To Olivier's astonishment, Douvier had asked him to drive into Paris and meet him at Geneviève's apartment. He went, and now, standing in the sun, he relived every moment.

Geneviève had come to the door, looking disheveled and wild-eyed. Douvier came right to the point, "It's horrifying," he said to her, "the control you've had over Marc. This is your fault."

Geneviève had opened a bottle of l'Etoile, and now she asked if they would like a glass. Both men declined. "Marc will be arrested for two murders tomorrow," Douvier said, "but something is missing. A plastic bag containing his bloody clothes. And god knows what else."

Geneviève flushed, and reached over and poured champagne into a glass. "I never saw a bag."

"A witness saw you take the bag. As things stand now, my dear, you might be considered an accessory to murder, in which case you drove him to it, but, if you don't tell me where that fucking bag is, you will be brought before the judges as an accomplice. Trust me, you will go to jail."

Olivier turned his head as the two former lovers stared each other down. "I despise you," she said to Philippe. "You deserve to be blamed, too."

"One more thing. My name is never to be uttered by you. Any mention of my name in association with this case will put you in jail for the rest of your life. You have one minute."

Geneviève poured a glass of champagne and downed it. "Madame Léa de Saint-Pern is hiding it." Then she giggled. Both men stared. "The fabulous Léa adored Marc, her husband's son, and he adored her. Until he didn't."

Olivier wondered if there was such a thing as a psychological accomplice. Those people who poison the air with their specific hatreds.

"Explain," Douvier said.

"It's beneath her casket."

"And the money?"

"Fuck you, Philippe. You left me with nothing. This two hundred thousand is nothing to you. I'm going to tell Olivier now about our

little scheme to buy land that you know will soon be designated as Champagne. You should be dragged through the courts."

"The money. Five seconds."

"It's in the plastic bag with the clothes."

"You're never to contact me again," Philippe said. "You will remain under house arrest until I say you're not. Let's go, Monsieur Chaumont."

Olivier followed Douvier, and as soon as the door closed they heard glass shattering. Douvier was the first to speak as he stood waiting for his driver, "We will talk when this madness is over."

Olivier could have stayed in Paris, but wanted to be in the country. He had been shaken by the scene between Geneviève and Douvier. When he got home, he poured a glass of brandy and went to the garden where he rehashed what had happened. Their exchange had been vitriolic and he saw clearly the disadvantage of being completely dependent on someone. Geneviève had exposed Douvier's plan to purchase land, and Olivier knew that every word was true. He tried not to think about the ramifications of what that would involve in the future, but didn't succeed. When a gendarme came to pick up Marie-Christine's dress the following morning, Olivier had not closed his eyes.

The sound of someone crying brought Olivier back into the moment. Some mourners had stepped forward to pour holy water over the urn. Chloé stood with her new husband, the man who he now believed murdered her aunt and uncle. Olivier felt despair for the young woman who had fallen for the wrong man.

Max was beside Chloé, her head bowed. They had spoken before the service and she had conveyed to him Chloé's state of denial about Marc. She explained that she had been up most of the night, worrying about Chloé and listening outside her bedroom door for any signs of trouble.

He wondered if Captain Canon and his soldiers had dug up Léa's grave yet. Olivier remained in the background as the last people stepped forward. He would grieve for Antoine later. The group broke apart. Most would be going from here to the Marceau home where Mimi had prepared platters of food. Olivier watched Marc take Chloé's hand, and winced when he saw the grateful smile she bestowed on him.

This time Jacques invited Girard to come to the house, but he and Olivier decided that he would stand out too much. Girard would wait for Olivier to call. Chloé, they decided, should be allowed to lead the tour, which would keep her out of the way. And Girard had been adamant that Max accompany her, especially when Olivier suggested that she stay.

◇◇◇

Chloé had a lilt in her step as they entered the reception area of Marceau Champagne in Epernay on Avenue de Champagne, which was in stark contrast to the way Max was feeling. She couldn't believe she was going to miss the arrest, but had worked to accept that she was back-up, if that, on this case. Still, the idea of listening to Chloé prattle on to a group of Brits about champagne was anathema to her. Chloé went to the desk to receive her instructions and returned to say that they would start in ten minutes with a dozen people.

Max soon learned the reason for her friend's insouciance. "Marc thinks Hans Keller will be arrested today," she said. "And then we can go on our honeymoon."

"Did someone tell him that?"

"Girard did."

Girard was trying to throw Marc off-track, Max thought. She also thought it possible that Marc had believed him, pleased that his scheme to set Hans up as the prime suspect had worked. While sitting on the stone bench in the middle of the night, Max had reasoned that Marc had forced Antoine to agree in writing to sell his shares in the de Saint-Pern Company to Hans Keller for the same amount of money that Hans had started accusing Marc of stealing. It was a brilliant ploy. And quite vindictive.

Max, feeling duplicitous, said that Hans was probably being arrested at this moment. She expected that Olivier, Jacques, and

Marie-Christine would be walking in before the tour was over to tell Chloé the sad news that her husband was the main suspect.

Chloé said, "This will be a good opportunity for you to see the famous *crayères*, or cellars. The French word is *craie*, which is chalk." Max knew Chloé was rehearsing, and wondered how she could be so unsuspecting.

Chloé said, "The white chalk gives the champagne its acidity and its character. Marceau is small, producing only two and a half million bottles a year."

"No wonder Mimi can make cakes out of it."

Chloé laughed, "I hope the Brits appreciate your humor. I know you won't be able to keep quiet. Speaking of which, here they come."

Max turned and smiled at the group of tourists, most of them middle-aged and on the dowdy side. Chloé introduced herself and led them into the office where she told them the stages of making champagne, then told them to follow as she led them down a hall and opened a door to a steep staircase, cautioning them to be careful. "Ours is a smaller house," she reminded them, "and our cellars are not as ornate or elegant as some of those belonging to the bigger houses."

"But more authentic," one of the English visitors said.

"I hope you brought your sweaters," Chloé said. "The temperature here is perfect for storing the champagne. Eleven degrees centigrade." Max calculated quickly that that was fifty degrees Farenheit. She shivered involuntarily. She hadn't brought a sweater. "These caves were first excavated two thousand years ago by the Gallic slaves to provide building materials for the city," Chloé intoned. They continued down another flight of stairs and Max asked how far they had descended.

"One hundred feet." Air shafts tapered upward to the ground above.

They stopped at the bottom of the stairs and Max gave an involuntary gasp. The *caves* were bathed in a soft light, and the sense of mystery and reverence caused the guests to go silent. No wonder France had proclaimed the caves national historic monuments. "There are thirty-five tunnels extending out from here," Chloé said.

A tourist asked, "How do you keep from getting lost?"

"Sometimes I do," Chloé said. "But I won't today." She waved to some workers down the *allée* who waved back. Max made note of the small tractors used for hauling the champagne racks around. As they followed Chloé, they passed stacks of stored champagne. "These champagnes are blends, some comprised of one hundred different wines. This is why the cellar master plays such an important role. They are the ones who decide what the champagne will taste like in the end."

Max wondered how the arrest was going. The sound of a small tractor used to move the crates cracked the silence. Max put her hand up to touch the warty looking walls and drew it back instinctively after feeling the cold, slimy surface. Mushrooms grew on the surface. Light was now provided by dim light bulbs. There were *bas reliefs* along the walls, with the prominent theme being either angels or wine.

Chloé had started to describe the process called *remuage* where the bottles stored on a slanted rack were gently shaken and turned by hand. The tractor came closer and Chloé had to raise her voice. "I apologize," she said finally, "Let me check to see what's going on."

Chloé walked toward the tractor and the driver, wearing a casquette, or black cap, pulled down over his forehead, a royal blue uniform, and gray rubber gloves, turned the vehicle sharply at her approach and drove out of sight.

Chloé returned to her group, "He might be new on the job," she said. "They're not supposed to come close to the tourists. Now if you'll follow me, I'll show you how the corking is done." The tourists followed like lemmings.

Max, impatient, motioned to Chloé that she was going to the office to make a phone call. Chloé nodded her head and moved ahead with the group. After a few minutes Max realized she had gone the wrong way and began retracing her steps. She could hear the tractor speeding toward her again and Max decided to ask the driver directions to the office.

She heard a loud crash, and ran to see what was happening. The tractor had hit a rack of champagne bottles. Whoever was driving had no idea what he was doing. And it occurred to Max that no other workers were around. Something was horribly wrong. She wished she had stuck with Chloé.

She spotted the tractor up ahead and started running toward it. She would give him a piece of her mind in French. The driver waved, but she couldn't see his face because of the hat he wore. She waved back, though, and put up her hand for him to stop.

It took her a couple of seconds to realize he was making a beeline for her.

What the hell?

She started running in the other direction. The surface of the dirt floor was uneven, which slowed her down. The tractor was gaining on her. She stopped and, using all her weight, pushed over one of the racks holding fifty bottles of champagne, hoping it would provide a barrier. Several of the bottles broke and champagne began forming a rivulet. She heard the tractor running over the bottles and the sound of its motor getting closer. She rounded a curve and recognized that it was a cul de sac. There was nowhere to go but up the stacks. She turned before hoisting herself up, and was horrified to see the face beneath the *casquette*.

Chapter Thirty-two

Olivier stood at the tennis courts watching Marc and Yves in a fierce contest, and figured that the game would consume them for at least another forty-five minutes. The last of the guests would have departed by then. He wished now that he had insisted on keeping Max here, but Girard and the others had been persuasive in their argument that the arrest was practically a done deal and she wasn't needed. He suspected Girard was nervous about her receiving public attention that belonged to him. Max had resisted leaving, but when Jacques implored her to stay with Chloé, she had acquiesced.

Girard had been shocked when Olivier had presented all the data to him about Marc that had made him the number one suspect. "He's been so helpful," he said. "I don't know how I misjudged him the way I did."

Olivier thought he understood how that had happened. Max had told him on the ride back to Paris that she had been required to take a psychology course that focused on personality disorders because the majority of the criminals she arrested had some form of psychopathy. She said she would label Marc an alienated sociopath, and more specifically, a cheated type. When Olivier had asked her to explain, she had said that because of real or perceived inadequacies, these people felt rejected by society. He had argued that Marc had not seemed to behave like one who was rejected by society, but Max had convinced him otherwise.

Marc had come to believe that he had been wronged by others, and this had led him to the stance that rules didn't apply to him. A slippery slope indeed, Olivier thought.

Max had placed a lot of blame on Genevieve because of all the verbal abuse and manipulation. In the moment he faced Léa, Max had said, Léa could easily have become his mother in his mind. The mother who had screamed at him his entire life for being inadequate. Léa may have mocked him the night he had murdered her, or been condescending, or become enraged. No one would ever know. Nor would they know unless they got Marc to confess that Léa's murder had been premeditated. There would be no question, though, about Antoine's murder. Olivier had been stunned by how calculating the murderer would have to be to pull it off.

Olivier entered the house and told Jacques it was time to call Girard. Jacques went to his study, and Olivier punched in Abdel's number. Olivier knew he was just on the other side of the wall, waiting for the call. "Go directly to the tennis courts where you can keep your eye on Marc, while I wait for Girard."

Olivier went to the terrace. In ten minutes it would all be over. Jacques came up to him, "This is a nightmare. I can't imagine what this arrest will do to Chloé."

"We will all care for her, Jacques. She's strong."

"We should have given her more freedom at a younger age. She might not have fallen so hard for this handsome stranger. She didn't know how to judge his character."

"Nor did we."

Girard approached. "There aren't any escape routes. Are we ready?"

"All set."

The two of them, followed by two policemen, started to the tennis courts. Abdel came running up. "Monsieur, they're gone!"

Olivier swore and ordered Girard and his men to scour the premises. He could think of only one place that the police didn't know about. Antoine's. "Come with me, Abdel!" Jacques followed at a lope, and when they arrived, out of breath, Jacques noticed immediately that Antoine's pleasure boat was missing.

Olivier sent Jacques back to inform Girard about the boat, then looked at Abdel. "They could have gone to Paris, where it would be easy for Marc to get on an airplane, or…"

"To Epernay. To find his wife."

Olivier dialed Girard's cell phone and told him to send his men to Paris to check airports and trains. He and Abdel got into Abdel's car. Olivier said, "There's a lock northwest of the town. Drop me at the Marceau Company and continue on to the lock."

"Do you think Mademoiselle Marceau is waiting for him?"

"She's deeply loyal. And naïve," Olivier said.

"And our American detective has no idea what's going on. Which means she'll try to stop them."

"Let's hope Marc and Yves are on their way to Paris. Drive faster."

◇◇◇

Max was perched atop the six-foot high rack of champagne, thinking she would give anything for a gun. The tractor was out of sight again, and it was eerily quiet. So they botched the arrest, she thought. Marc must have known all along what Olivier was up to. She waited a few minutes and decided that he wasn't coming back. She climbed down and started running down the corridor the tractor had taken. She had to get to Chloé.

When she rounded the corner she saw Marc and Chloé moving toward an exit sign. He was holding her hand. "Chloé!" Max called. They stopped.

"Max. I thought you had gone to the office."

"Where's your group?"

"I took them to the office, and then came to meet Marc."

Marc was smiling. "We have to get going."

"Where to?"

"We're going on our honeymoon," Chloé said.

Didn't Marc just try to kill me, she thought.

"Marc, I saw you back there."

"I don't know what you're talking about."

"You just tried to run me down."

She noticed that he had removed the worker's uniform, and wondered where he had stashed it.

Chloé stepped forward, "Max, you're being ridiculous. Why would he do that?"

"Because he knows I'm going to try to stop you."

"Come on, Chloé," Marc said, taking her arm. When she hesitated, he said simply, "Max." Their eyes interlocked. "You stay here. I'm warning you."

"Marc!" Chloé said. "What are you warning her about?"

"Come on!" He pulled her harder and she almost fell.

"I'm not going until I know what Max is upset about."

They were almost at the workers' elevator. "Ask her."

"Max?" Chloé said.

Max stopped and looked at Chloé. Marc was holding a pistol over her head. He's got me, Max thought. "I'm upset because I think you should tell your parents you're taking off," Max said. "They'll be hurt." She saw Marc's jaw relax, and the gun was already out of sight.

"Oh, Max. I'll call them once we're in Paris."

They were at the elevator. "May I come up with you?" Max asked. "I can take your car back to the house, Chloé."

Marc acquiesced. Max figured that Yves must be waiting for him. They boarded the elevator, and it lumbered up. Max knew that by now Olivier and the police were searching for Marc. She would stay close to Chloé no matter what, and try to protect her. She exited the elevator first. They were behind the office building, and there was Yves in his car, just as she had thought. She saw a figure duck, and realized that the police were on task. A beautiful sight.

"*Au revoir*, Max," Chloé said. When she leaned in to hug Max, Max put her hand on Chloé's back, and shoved her as hard as she could. Chloé sprawled, and Max took the opportunity to seize Marc's jacket. He jerked his arm back and hit her squarely on the cheekbone, causing her to step back because of the pain.

He leaped into the front seat and Yves drove off. Max knew they wouldn't get far.

Olivier and Abdel stepped out from behind a car. "Your face," Olivier said to Max, pulling a handkerchief from his pocket and tapping it gently on her cheekbone.

Abdel lifted Chloé up. To Max's surprise, she looked stoic. "Are you okay?" Max asked.

Chloé nodded. "I knew from the moment Marc showed up here," she said. "I'm not as stupid as everyone thinks."

"You're a great actress, then," Max said. "I was convinced that you had planned this getaway with Marc."

"I knew to play along with him. I was terrified that he'd do something to you," Chloé said. "And he did."

Jacques walked out of the building and embraced his daughter. "I've been sick with worry," he said. "All of you, come back to the house. The police will take care of Marc. And Marie-Christine will put something on your face," he said to Max. "She's in the office."

"Abdel and I are going to the police station," Olivier said. "Max, you can come if you want."

"I'm staying out of the limelight," she said. "Let Girard bask in his glory."

The instant she turned, a photographer took her picture. She heard Olivier laugh.

◇◇◇

Chloé spoke first in the car on the way back to the house. "It will take a long time for it to sink in that I married a murderer." When she saw her parents stiffen, she said, "The only way I can heal from this...mistake...is to talk about it. Marc is quite sick, I know, but one day I will try to figure out why I needed him in my life." Her mother turned around and took her hand and squeezed it. It made Max miss her own mother. She would call Hank to let him know the way the story had unfolded before she went to bed.

Once they were back at *chez Marceau*, she ran upstairs to shower, all the while assuring herself that she didn't need Olivier.

She was leaving in a few days anyway, she thought. She repeated Chloé's words, applying them to herself, "I need to ask why I feel I need him in my life."

This is the major question for my future therapist, she thought.

She contemplated the question for a while as the warm water flowed over her, and heard herself say out loud, "I want him in my life because I've never felt this way about anyone before." She emerged from the shower with new resolve. She would let Olivier know how she felt.

She picked up the bottle of Casta Diva perfume her mother had probably saved for months to buy her. Juliette had explained that perfume used to have an essential mystique that had gotten lost in the mainstream perfumes. "Casta Diva" was the name of an aria from Bellini's opera, *Norma.*

Dressed in fresh clothes, Max opened the door and heard Ted's voice wafting up from the entrance hall. She passed the upstairs billiard room and skipped down the stairs on the other side of the house where Olivier stood talking with Ted.

Both men paused. "My god, what is that fragrance?" Ted asked.

Max smiled. She was about to tell him when Olivier said, "Let me guess. Come closer." He inhaled and closed his eyes. "I know it. Casta Diva. Frangipani, white musk, and perhaps jasmine, though I'm not sure which kind."

Ted stepped back in mock amazement. "How the hell did you know that?" Then, to Max, "I smell your mother in all this." He turned to Olivier before Max could stop him and said, "You know, her mother is from the old French aristocracy. She was a de Laval. I idolize that woman."

"I second that, " Chloé said.

Max turned to follow them, but Olivier took her arm. "A de Laval?"

"They disowned my mother, so she's a Maguire."

"She is French, Max. And so are you. Or at least half of you is."

"I'm ready now to own that."

He took her hand and led her to the kitchen. "You said that maybe things might be different between us after this case was solved. And I said they will be. And they are. I'd like to prepare dinner for you tonight after our little celebration here. I promise, there will be no interruptions!"

"Sure!" She said it with the same certainty that she had pretended to feel when she first went home with him. Only this time she meant it.

A sound made them turn. Mimi was smiling broadly. "Me no speak English," Mimi said, putting her hands up in he air. They laughed and went back to join the family.

Girard was at the door. "I can't stay. I have an interview in an hour," he said. "We were swarmed by the police and photographers. Strangely, Marc doesn't seem upset by the attention."

"Part of the personality disorder," Max said. "These people are sensation-seeking. He'll think he's being admired, or feared."

Girard said, "Madame Durand is under house arrest in Paris. My men went to the cemetery and the bag was there. The shoes that match the footprints, the wedding jacket with blood on it. The works. Also a small leather bag belonging to Monsieur Keller, who is leaving now for Germany."

Max looked over at Olivier, and his eyes relayed the message that he'd tell her everything when they were alone.

"And Yves Brun?" Olivier asked Girard.

"He said Marc was going to blackmail him if he didn't help him escape. I think it's about drugs. We have plenty of time to find out. "

They entered the salon where Chloé sat on a divan, her head on her mother's shoulder. Ted was at the table with Jacques. He said, "I've been offered a contract to write a book about wine tasting. Someone read my blog and liked it. But I want all of you to know that I intend to pay back to Léa's estate every penny I borrowed from her."

Jacques said quietly, "I would have expected you to say that. Now it's time to bid farewell to Léa and Antoine." He waited for them to pick up their glasses. "*Adieu.*"

"*Adieu*," they all said in unison, as though the word was a benediction.

Max noted that the bubbles in her glass were miniscule, the color a deep gold. Jacques made a toast to the investigative team, and to Max, "Who," he said, "is like another daughter to us."

Jazz was playing in the background and Jacques turned it up when Etta James came on singing, "I Just Want to Make Love to You." Olivier put down his glass, then took Max's and placed it beside his on the table. "Let's dance," he said.

All eyes were on them. Max couldn't believe how self-conscious she felt.

"Olivier."

He led her onto the terrace and slid his arm around her waist. The sun would be setting in an hour and she could already visualize the riotous colors that would fill the sky, matching the vivid colors in Marie-Christine's garden. Deep pinks and violets, with enough blue mixed in for effect.

"Music transcends everything dark, Max. You should never have given up dancing."

Olivier swung her around, and she saw Jacques leading Marie-Christine out to the terrace to join them. Ted followed with Chloé. Girard stood sipping his champagne, with Abdel beside him, grinning.

"As much as this has been one of the worst two weeks of my life, I don't want to leave," Max said to Olivier.

"You'll be back. This region is like a magnet."

You're the magnet, Olivier Chaumont, Max thought, but that's a discussion for another time.

To receive a free catalog of Poisoned Pen Press titles, please contact us in one of the following ways:

Phone: 1-800-421-3976
Facsimile: 1-480-949-1707
Email: info@poisonedpenpress.com
Website: www.poisonedpenpress.com

Poisoned Pen Press
6962 E. First Ave. Ste 103
Scottsdale, AZ 85251